The Stolen Child

"Where the wave of moonlight glosses
The dim gray sands with light,
Far off by furthest Rosses
We foot it all the night,
Weaving olden dances
Mingling hands and mingling glances
Till the moon has taken flight;
To and fro we leap
And chase the frothy bubbles
While the world is full of troubles
And anxious in its sleep.
Come away, O human child!
To the waters, and the wild
With a faery, hand in hand,
For the world's more full of weeping
than you can understand."

From The Stolen Child – *William Butler Yeats*

The Stolen Child

Book 1 of the Exiles series

By Peter Brunton

Brain Dead Publications

2015

Copyright © 2016 by Peter Brunton

First Printing: 2016

ISBN 978-0-9949679-1-6

Brain Dead Publications
220 Steeles Ave West
Brampton, ON, L6Y 2K4

www.bdpub.com

Cover art created by Ameshin
http://ameshin.deviantart.com

To Mum and Dad.

For everything.

Acknowledgements

This book was a long time in the making. It took a lot of work, not only to find the story I wanted to tell, but also to become the kind of person who was capable of telling it.

I will never be able to recount every single person who has helped in some way to make this a reality. Just know that I am grateful to every one of you; to my incredible family and friends, to every person who has ever offered a suggestion or a word of advice, to everyone who read a draft or let me bounce ideas off of them, to everyone who followed my blog, to everyone who in some small way encouraged me... Thank you. From the bottom of my heart, thank you.

With that being said, three people deserve special mention, for being with me every step of this journey, pushing me to do more, to do better, and never letting me give up.

Frankie, Amanda, and Katie, the three of you have been a constant source of encouragement and strength, and it was because of you that I pushed myself to tell the very best version of this story that I could. Thank you for everything.

Book 2 is coming, I promise.

Chapter 1 - Rain

The city was empty. She wandered through silent streets, strangely lonely without the press of bodies, the sound of engines and the smell of exhaust fumes hanging over every intersection. She passed by shops and cafés, their doors open, their signs lit, but with no one inside. As she walked her fingertips traced a pattern on the walls and railings that she followed at each turning; a thin line of rust, like a trail laid out for her. She wondered who could have left it there, seeming so natural, yet so purposeful. The trail passed over iron, stone and wood alike, not seeming to care for its own impossibility. It simply was, almost as if it had sprung into being for her alone to find.

She followed the trail as the sky above turned ashen grey with clouds and the wind picked up. She heard a lone bird's distant cries, but apart from the wind they were the only sound. One tiny voice in the empty city.

She walked on, following the trail of rust. Somewhere in the back of her head she felt sure that the streets she followed weren't quite connected up right. One moment she was on a road in Tottenham, then she turned a corner into Elephant & Castle, then another side-street that lead her out onto Tuffnell Park Road. The London in her dream was not the London she knew, but it was familiar all the same, and she became increasingly sure that her path was leading her ever closer to the heart of the city.

At last she turned a corner and found herself faced with an ancient red-brick archway, stained black with a century of smoke and covered by a pair of heavy wrought-iron gates. The trail lead past the gates and into the deep shadow of the tunnel.

Again she heard a bird's cry, this time quite close. She looked up and saw a raven perched atop a low wall. It cawed again and cocked its head to peer at her with one glossy black bead of an eye. She saw herself reflected there; a tiny figure, lost in her tattered white hooded jacket and patchwork jeans. A slim face, with the skin pale and pulled tight to the bones, peered out at her from under a nest of tangled blonde hair that spilled out over her shoulders.

The raven danced back a step and turned to look at the gate. She looked as well, reaching out to feel the rough texture of the iron. As her fingers brushed the metal she saw tiny patches of rust form. They began to grow, eating into the metal, spreading like frost on a window-pane. The heavy iron began to shrivel, staining red and crumbling away into tiny flakes, with a sound like dry paper, or dead leaves crunching underfoot. Instead of falling, the flakes of rust wafted gently upwards as if on a warm breeze, though the air was cold and still. The gate continued to dissolve, flaking away a few inches at a time, the cloud of rusted metal drifting upward into the grey sky.

With a loud cry the raven abandoned its wall and landed heavily on her shoulder. Talons dug into her jacket, but to her surprise she felt no pain. She had the curious impression that it had come to protect her, though from what, she wasn't sure.

The last fragments of the gateway dissolved and she descended into the darkness of the tunnel, only the touch of her fingers against the wall to guide her through the gloom. She seemed to walk for a long time without any sound other than the slight ruffling of the bird's feathers against her hair.

She emerged onto a street she did not know, but a glance upwards told her exactly where she was. The gleaming sharpness of the Shard Building rose above her. It was like a perfect blade of glass thrusting into the sky, as if it had somehow pierced the heart of the city and pushed out through the other side.

As she stared up at the tower of glass and steel, she saw lines of rust begin to crawl up the edges of the angular shape, dark red streaks that rose to the very tip of the blade. Against the shining mirror of the glass, the rust looked like dried blood. All around her the buildings that lined the streets began to dissolve into flakes of rust. Clouds of rusted metal drifted upwards into the sky as brick and concrete crumbled. Cracks lined the pavement, and twisting oak roots began to push up between the slabs. Only the Shard remained, the panes of glass crumbling away to reveal bright shining steel underneath, a knife blade poised to carve open the grey clouds overhead.

A steady drum roll brought Rachael to her senses. Rain hammered against the roof of the cardboard box which had sheltered her, as the chill of the morning air worked its way into her bones. She pulled her jacket tighter around herself and tucked her knees to her chin. Breathing hard into the small space that she had made between her legs and her belly, she tried to curl herself around the pocket of warm air that formed there. Her thoughts were a jumble, the fading ghosts of the dream still dancing through her head like scraps of paper caught on a breeze. Hammered down to nothing by the rain, the sides of the box gave way and her shelter collapsed around her. She pushed aside the sodden cardboard and shook off the rainwater. Digging into the trash pile by her bed, she pulled out a threadbare old backpack and slung it across her shoulders. She brought her hood up, pulled the drawstrings tight and hunched up against the sharp chill in the wind as she stepped out of the alleyway.

A flock of umbrellas drifted through the streets. Rain hammered at the fabric in a constant rhythm, adding another layer to the swelling sound of the city awakening. Her fingers itched and her muscles ached with the night's sleep and the cold air. Glancing up at the buildings around her, keen eyes began to pick out a line. Then she tightened the straps on her backpack, set her head down and started to run.

She wove between the crowd, vaulted the railing that bordered the road and darted out through the traffic as horns blared and brakes squealed. The far railing vanished beneath her feet, and then she was leaping up to catch the lip of a windowsill. Toes dug into cracks in the brickwork, pushed her up to swing across to a drainpipe, and then she was scrambling upwards, ignoring the upturned faces below, ignoring the shouted complaints and muttered curses. She pulled herself up onto an open rooftop and fell into a sprint. Rain hammered down, but on the tar paper roofs her grip was sure. The air always seemed clearer up above the streets as she moved from rooftop to rooftop, dropping down into narrow roads, mantling low walls, and scrambling up buildings to reach the hidden routes that kept her free of the crush and the press of London.

She didn't know where she was going to. It didn't matter. All that mattered was running, the thrill of every jump nearly missed, the terror in every slippery step. The feel of the wind, as if she might take flight. When she ran, nothing mattered. When she ran, she was free.

When the coldness had finally left her body and her legs began to tire, she settled down on a low wall over-looking the entrance to a subway station. Her stomach was a knot of pain, twisted tight around nothing. She hadn't eaten since yesterday morning.

Barely ten yards away a ragged man with a filthy beard, dressed in the remains of a blue puffer-jacket, had rolled out a mat of damp cardboard and laid a hat down for loose change. For a moment she thought of joining him. She'd heard from some of the vagrants that you could make good money in the right places. But then the police would come, as they always did. For men like him it meant little enough. They made their carefully prepared excuses as they hid their carefully prepared signs. Then they packed up, moved on, and found another spot to beg. Outsmarting the law began to look like an elaborate game, raw desperation hidden away beneath a kind of ragged pride.

She could never do that. A fourteen year old girl wasn't the same thing as a wretched old alcoholic hoping for his next fix. For her, the police would pay attention. For her, there would be forms and procedures, and people in suits sitting in glass offices.

She couldn't beg, any more than she could risk the shelters or the soup kitchens. She felt sure that the moment a teenage girl walked in, thin as a rail and shivering with the cold, there would be phone calls and policies to follow. There would be social services, and foster homes. Better the open sky and a rooftop where she could hear the pigeons fighting for roosting space. Even the hunger wasn't so bad when she thought about the alternatives.

She dropped down from the wall, pulling her hood down to conceal her face. Another wave of passengers emerged from the tunnels and she slipped between the press of bodies. She began to move faster, holding tight to the straps of her backpack with one hand, racing towards the platform below. A middle-aged man with a sharp haircut and a sharp suit was too busy looking at his phone to notice her. The man was solidly built, and when they collided she was thrown against the wall, slipping down three steps before she was able to steady herself. As the man staggered his phone tumbled from his hands, bouncing down the steps. Rachael saw a spiderweb of cracks fill the tiny screen.

Swearing at her, the man dashed back through the crowd, elbowing a young woman aside as he scrambled to pick up his shattered phone. Rachael didn't wait for him to turn and look up.

Leaping to her feet, she dashed back up the steps and out onto the street again. At the next underpass she took the steps down and sprinted through the narrow tunnel to the far side of the road.

Secluded in a side-street, she leaned back against the wall and struggled to breathe. With shaking hands she reached into her pocket and pulled out the fat leather wallet that she had lifted from the man's jacket. The trembling in her fingers was so bad that the first time she tried to open the wallet it fell on the ground, scattering credit cards. She scooped it up quickly and sifted through the contents. Accusing eyes stared up at her from a driver's license; a hard, scowling face. The man couldn't even manage to smile for a photo booth. She flipped through the debit and credit cards, discarding them all until she found one in bright blue, with the word 'Oyster' emblazoned across the front. That one she pocketed. Prepaid rail cards were always a good find. At the back of the wallet she found a crisp twenty pound note, and a fiver that had been folded up behind the driver's license. Tucking the money into her sock, she wiped the wallet on her sleeves and dropped it into a sewer grating. Her heart was still pounding in her chest as she walked away.

The MacDonald's by Kings Cross Station was a narrow, L-shaped space, wrapped around the corner of a building. It was a little past one by the time she got there, and the place was packed with tourists, teens, clean cut suits and yellow jacketed workmen. She slipped into the crowd and stayed quiet.

As the queue moved forward she was jostled and elbowed, squeezed between the taller men and women around her. She caught glimpses of wrinkled noses and disgusted or pitying glances. She mumbled her order to the boy behind the counter, trying not to meet his eyes, and a minute later she was squeezing through the crowded doorway with a greasy paper bag clutched to her chest.

It was hard to keep herself from cramming whole handfuls of food into her mouth right there and then. She forced herself to be patient, tucking the paper bag away in her backpack. Better to find somewhere quiet, somewhere safe. From across the street she caught a heavyset man staring at her. He was leaning against the wall with his hands thrust deep into the pockets of a brown leather jacket. By his heels sat a large brown mastiff, rippling with muscle under mangy fur. Just like his dog, the man had an ugly look about him, his shaved scalp revealing a long and jagged scar. She shivered, and chose a different way.

She kept moving, following weaving paths across the streets and buildings, moving up high when she could. The rain was still coming down heavily, soaking through her jacket and into her backpack. The craving for food was made worse by having it so close, growing damp in the pouring rain as she ran. Finally she arrived at a familiar back-street between an office building and a hair salon, with a wooden fence across one end. Some empty rubbish bins made an easy step up to the top of the fence, and from there she could swing across to the sill of a bricked up window at the back of the salon. Holes in the crumbling brickwork formed hand and foot holds, until she could grip the edge of the sloped roof and pull herself up. Then it was just a matter of bracing herself on the sharply angled black slates and kicking off across the gap to land on the roof of the office building.

She almost missed the jump. The worn down soles of her trainers, all the grip long since gone from the rubber, skidded on the soaking wet slates. She tumbled, flailing, and her fingers barely snagged the edge of the office roof. Gripping tight, she tucked her legs up in front of herself and only just managed to soak up the impact with the wall. For a moment she just held on, the stone parapet tearing at her fingers. She felt paralysed, unable to make any movement for fear of falling, but sure that any moment now her grip would fail. At the last moment she kicked out with all the strength her legs had, hauling herself upwards, oblivious to the pain in her hands. Muscles burning, she dragged her body over the edge of the rooftop and collapsed onto the other side.

She stared at the sky, drawing ragged breaths, feeling every muscle burn with the strain. The cold air tore at her lungs as the rain washed over her face. She flexed her fingers experimentally and tried to move her arms a little. Blinking, she shook the water from her eyes. The rain was finally easing off.

She rolled over onto her knees and stood up. It had been a while since she'd missed that jump. She'd been so distracted by the hunger that she hadn't even considered the wet slates. Feeling like kicking herself, she trudged across the rooftop to a familiar hidey-hole beneath a ventilation duct. The duct was warm, and tucked away beneath it she felt her clothes begin to dry a little. She undid the hood of her jacket and let her hair spill out.

Unzipping her backpack, she pulled out the now sodden paper bag. Her burger was damp, the bread all mushy on one side, but she hardly cared. She forced down mouthful after mouthful, any other thought obliterated by the simple ecstasy of food. She devoured a box of fries just as quickly, washing it all down with sips of water from a plastic bottle. Finally she eyed the second burger she'd bought. Fighting temptation, she tucked it away for later.

Delving into her pack once more, she produced a bundle of plastic bags which she carefully unwrapped. Inside was a large pad of stiff white paper, somewhat wrinkled with damp despite the plastic, and a small bundle of pencils. Resting the pad on one knee, she picked out a soft pencil and began to sketch. Bold lines swept across the page, picking out the rough shape of the river, bulbous and grey, the North Bank skyline rising like crooked teeth above it.

Hours passed as she lost herself in the movements of the pencil on the paper. When the sun finally showed itself from behind the thick blanket of cloud it was long past noon. Her legs were numb, pins and needles sparking as she moved them for the first time in hours.

She looked down at the page again, seeing the whole drawing for the first time. She had half a mind just to scrap it, but instead she closed the sketchbook and carefully wrapped it up again. The battered pages were filled with abandoned pieces, never quite as good as she wished they could be. In the plastic bag lay another four sketchbooks, their pages all filled with the results of an endless succession of empty days. They were warped by the damp and mostly falling apart, but she kept them all the same.

She crawled out from the space under the vent and stood up to stretch her sore muscles. As she stood, her eyes took in the rooftop and she stopped dead, clutching her bag to her chest in alarm.

The boy was perched on the far edge of the roof, crouched low, his feet balanced on the parapet. There were holes in his jeans and he wore boots that must have come from an army surplus store. The tails of a long black coat were bunched around his heels. The way he perched, he looked a little like a bird.

His look of astonishment mirrored her own. For a moment they both stared at each other, not moving, not breathing. Then, unable to help herself, she glanced away. It was only for an instant, her eyes searching for a way down, wanting to be sure of an escape. When she looked back to the boy, her breath caught in her throat. He had vanished. It had only been an instant that she had looked away, but already he was gone. She heard a flutter of wings. Startled pigeons taking flight.

She ran to the edge of the roof and looked down, sure he must have jumped off. It was three stories, a hard drop even with a hang from the edge; she'd done it herself, once or twice, but it had frightened the life out of her every time.

The street was empty. There was no sign of him at all.

Chapter 2 - Sky

The clouds gathered beneath the city like foam on the waves of a stormy sea. Arsha stood at the railing, the cold air running over her thickly gloved hands as bright sunlight warmed her face. Her goggles were pushed up over her forehead, the leather strap pulling her hair back. She closed her eyes and listened to the sounds of the city. The creak of the wires, the hollow booming of the wind against the canvas balloons, the soft humming of the lightning crackling through the floatstones.

Sunlight scattered off the myriad windows, off the brass and steel of the railings and support struts. Wind hammered at the wood-panelled walls of the many structures that had been lashed, bolted, and welded together over the years, to form a single vast and labyrinthine mass, suspended high above the clouds.

Ships dotted the skyline around her, fat bellied galleons and trade cogs drifting on the breeze as they waited for permission to dock. Here on the upper levels it was still quiet, the university only barely creaking to life as students slouched towards the first lectures of the day, but down at the docks she knew it would be a riot of activity as ship after ship was unloaded, their cargoes whisked away to the storehouses before filtering up to the shops and cafés of the merchant districts.

She heard the sound of a door closing. Her father's footsteps were slow and solid as he crossed the observation deck towards her.

"I thought I might find you out here."

His hands settled on her shoulders, and he leaned down to plant a kiss on the top of her head. She smiled up at him. He was clean shaven, his hair neatly combed and waxed. That meant he had a meeting today, probably with the dean and the bursars.

"Morning, Daddy. Are they making you sign things?"

"A final review of procedures, for the arch-dean. Just formalities. We'll still be setting off early tomorrow."

"They'd better not try to change anything now. You've been planning this for months."

"They all take months of planning sweetheart, and a lot of paperwork. But it's mostly just saying the same thing in a dozen different ways, so that everyone will agree that you meant it when you said it. Even if you didn't."

"Like, 'I, Professor Rishi Chandra, promise not to do anything incredibly silly or dangerous whilst running around the middle of an uncharted jungle exploring ancient Ur ruins that no one's seen for a thousand years'?"

He laughed.

"Yeah, I've been telling them that one for years."

"But you still make me stay at the camp," she added, scowling.

"Taking stupid risks is my prerogative. Keeping you safe is my job. At least until you're sixteen."

"That's not even a year. What difference is a year going to make?"

A look of uncertainty flashed across his face.

"You forgot again, didn't you?" she said, grinning.

Creases lined his face as he squeezed his eyes shut.

"You can't be fifteen already."

"And three months." She stuck her tongue out, laughing at his pained expression. "You got me a holographer, remember?"

"No... That was your fourteenth, surely..."

She shook her head.

"Fourteenth was the new sending stone. You had it engraved."

He nodded.

"So," he sighed, "apart from embarrassing your old man, what are your plans for the morning, young lady?"

"I'm supposed to meet Shani after her first lecture, so we can go down and wait for Milima and Abasi at the docks."

"How long before they pull in?"

"About an hour, I think. Look."

She pointed at one of the ships drifting low over the clouds. It was a slender little thing, dwarfed by the trade-ships that surrounded it. A sleek body with wide canvas wings, two float-stones mounted on outriggers just above the twin propellers. It was an explorer's vessel, and it was the only place she'd ever really thought of as home. The Triskelion.

"It'll be good to see them again. You remember we've got dinner planned tonight?" he said.

"Meet at the department, six thirty. I remember."

"OK, well, I'll see you there. Now I really should get going. You've had breakfast, right?"

She rolled her eyes.

"Go sign your papers, Daddy. Or whatever they want you to do. I bet it's all really boring."

"Crushingly dull." He gave her shoulder a squeeze. Then he was gone, long strides carrying him across the observation deck.

She took one last look at the open sky, and then she followed him inside.

On her way down to the café, Arsha stopped in at the apartment to collect a few things. Their lodgings were on loan from the university, whilst her father and his assistants were staying in Skytower, and in the three months they'd been living there she still hadn't managed to make it feel like any kind of a home. She snatched up her bag from the back of a chair, and was turning to leave when she heard a soft trilling sound from atop the dresser, as Penelope lifted her head from under her wing and shook her feathers out. Mother-of-pearl eyes gleamed under shining silver eyelids as the tiny mechanical bird cocked her head from one side to the other.

"Well come on then," Arsha said, standing impatiently in the doorway. With an almost musical sound of metal wings fluttering, Penelope crossed the short distance to land on Arsha's shoulder, tucking herself up just under the wave of her hair. She reached up to stroke the back of Penelope's head, the little bird twisting to nuzzle her fingertips. Though her metal body gave no heat, Arsha always felt sure there was a spark of warmth when the little autom pressed up against her.

By the time she reached the café where they'd agreed to meet, Shani was already sitting at a table overlooking the concourse. Her long plaits were pulled back in a loose braid today, and she wore a bright green tunic with silver embroidery. Like her mother, Shani had skin the colour of polished ebony, and a smile like sunlight.

"Hey you," she said, as Arsha slipped into the chair across from her. "Ordered you a coffee."

"How was your lecture?" Arsha said, depositing her satchel. As she settled herself, she felt Penelope poking her nose out from under her hair. With a friendly chirp, the little bird dropped down onto the table.

"Ugh. Boring. Markus goes on and on," Shani said, tickling Penny under the chin with the tip of her finger. "Hey, want to see something neat?"

Arsha nodded, and Shani produced a small object from her bag; her sending stone, the crystal a deep amethyst with squared off corners, set in a brass frame.

"This is a new weave I've been working on. You link it to your harmonic, right, and it listens to all of the waves that are playing in your area... And then, you just, you know, whistle or hum a little at it, like, any song you have in your head, and it finds you the wave that's got the closest thing to that. So, you know, whatever kind of music you feel like listening to, it'll find it for you. Come on, grab your stone and I'll swipe it over to you."

"That's really cool," Arsha said, smiling. "But, I don't think I'll be able to use it much. Most of the time we can barely even get the Guild station. I don't think they'll even have that where we're going now."

"Yeah, Tyren's really the middle of nowhere huh? Hey, don't worry, you'll find ways to entertain yourself. Maybe you'll meet some nice Tyren boys, eh?" Shani smiled and gave her a friendly slap on the arm.

For a moment, Arsha tried to return the smile. Then her face fell, and she felt a twisting knot tighten in her stomach.

"It's not going to be the same," she said, miserably. "Not without you. First Elim left, and now you're here studying, and it's just me..."

With a solemn look, Shani gave her hand a gentle squeeze.

"Maybe it's time to think about what your father said. Going to the Guildhall to study. Boarding school could be a lot of fun. I bet there's a bunch of kids there whose parents are explorers or archaeologists just like your dad," Shani said. With a shrug she added "Or captains, like mine. It's not like we're the only ones that have, like, weird parents and stuff."

"Yeah, I know. It's just... What if I hate it there? What if no one likes me? Or what if I don't make any friends, or I'm no good at my classes, or..."

"None of those things are going to happen. Arsh, you're like one of the nicest people in the world, and you're smart, and you're fun, and I love hanging out with you. My friends all think you're awesome. Do you have any idea how crazy that is? University students are not normally impressed by fifteen year old girls."

Arsha felt her cheeks tingle, and for a moment she had to pretend to scan the concourse as a smile crept across her lips. At that moment a waitress arrived with their order. Arsha was blowing the steam off her coffee when Shani's sending stone chimed. She waved a hand over the crystal, and the message flickered into view, suspended over the surface in faintly glowing letters of light.

"Oh, hey, that's Mum and Dad. Someone missed a slot, so now they're pulling in to dock already. Come on, we gotta go."

They drank their coffees quickly and snatched up their bags.

"Come on," Arsha waved at Penny as they set off. The little bird swept into the air, gliding over their heads as they walked.

Once they left the brightly lit concourse, the corridors of Skytower grew tighter and darker, ceilings low and crowded. Arsha had to coax Penny back down onto her shoulder for fear that she wouldn't have room to fly. They made their way down a creaking old stairwell, and emerged into the bustling chaos of the docks. Arsha breathed in the familiar scent of canvas wax, smoke and engine oil. Keeping to the upper catwalks, they watched as the dockers worked the level below, carts laden with crates and barrels being hauled by broad shouldered men and women in grease stained overalls.

Eventually the girls found their way to the dock where the Triskelion was pulling in. Through the tall windows that ringed the catwalk she could easily see the ship ahead of them, floatstones still dancing with energy even as the propellers were slowly coming to rest. She could almost hear the the canvas snapping in the wind.

"Hey, hold up," Arsha said, pausing to reach into her bag. She pulled out her holographer and raised the viewfinder to her eye. Gently squeezing the capture, she froze a few stills of the Triskelion in the dock.

"Are you done playing with that that thing yet?" Shani laughed, as Arsha tucked the holo away in her bag again.

They made their way down a small stairwell, and through a

heavy door that lead them out onto the pier. As they stepped outside, the wind struck them both like a hammer. Arsha pulled her goggles down as Shani produced a scarf from her bag.

The Triskelion's deck was long and flat, save for the vast form of the conning tower that rose up over the aft. The bridge had a curved window across its entire front, giving a clear view over the deck. Just below, at the base of the tower, was the heavy iron hatchway that lead inside. As they crossed the deck, Arsha saw the hatch swing wide as two figures emerged. With a sudden thought, she pulled out the holo from her bag again and caught a quick still of Abasi and Milima as they were stepping out onto the deck.

"Seven Names Arsha, did you really have to?" Milima called out to her, laughing as the wind whipped around her. Abasi heaved the door to and turned just in time, as Shani flung her arms around the both of them. Arsha caught a few more quick stills, as the couple embraced their daughter. Then the three of them were strolling towards her, Shani clinging to her parents arms as she walked between them.

"Hey you," Abasi said, his voice booming like thunder as he threw an arm around her. She squeezed her arms around his rotund waist, and pressed her face to his chest as the man towered over her.

"Uncle Abasi. How was your trip?"

"Long," Milima said, peeling Arsha away from her husband, and pulling her into a fierce embrace. Milima smelled of cinnamon and nutmeg, a sure sign that there was a fresh load of pastries and cakes waiting aboard the ship.

"So, listen, we've got dinner at seven," Shani said, "Arsha's dad booked some super fancy place in Upper East. What do you guys want to do to kill time until then?"

"Oh I don't know dear. Whatever you like," Milima replied.

"Is Liam going to be joining us at all?" Abasi added, with a curiously hopeful look.

"Ugh, no." Shani made a face. "Liam and I, uh... We kind of split. Look, it's a really long story."

"Oh sweetheart," Milima said, putting an arm around her daughter. "If you want to talk about it we could find somewhere quiet..."

"Maybe later." Shani smiled, and patted her mother's arm. "Come on, let's head up."

Arsha trailed behind a little as they walked, listening to the conversation as Penelope chirped happily in her ear.

The day passed in a gentle haze of shops and cafés, as Abasi and Milima caught up on Shani's life at the university, and filled the girls in on what they'd been doing. In the three months since dropping off Arsha and her father at Skytower, Abasi and Milima had been travelling all across the Guildlands and beyond, gathering items that her father had needed from various far flung outposts. It wasn't especially exciting, but after months cooped up in one place, Arsha envied them. She missed the Triskelion, and her cosy little cabin.

As six o'clock rolled around, Abasi and Milima made their way back to the ship to change into something suitable. Shani made her excuses likewise, and Arsha found herself walking alone back to the apartments. She was trying on a matching deep blue salwar and kameez when her father knocked and poked his head in through the door.

"Hey Daddy," she said, "is this OK for tonight?"

"You look perfect, love," he said.

She pulled a face.

"You always say that. It doesn't help if you always say it."

He laughed.

"Listen, I've got one more errand to run. Can you wait down at the department for me? Micah and Ilona will be there already."

She nodded.

"And you do look perfect. Just like always."

She felt a tingling in her cheeks, even as she rolled her eyes at him.

"Alright, I'm going," he said.

After picking out a gold shawl from her wardrobe, Arsha settled Penelope on her shoulder again, and set off down the avenue. At a doorway with a brass plate that read 'Department of Exploration and Archaeology' she knocked politely, and a grey haired porter let her in with a smile.

She made her way through the twisting maze of corridors, finally stepping through a set of double doors that lead into the lab. Long worktables lined the room, nearly every inch of them now covered in neat stacks and rows of equipment. Tools were laid out and labelled by size, stacks of supplies had neat little tags indicating type and quantity, and more still were already being packed away into crates filled with straw. Piles of loose equipment, as yet unsorted, dotted the floor throughout the room.

Ilona sat to one side on a wooden stool, with a notepad resting in her lap. The woman was wearing a black dress with silver trim, cut in the Novarsi style that she preferred. Her pale blonde hair was pulled up into a tight bun, revealing the delicate sharpness of her features, the paleness of her skin standing sharp against the black satin. The woman was staring at her notes intently, and didn't seem to even notice when Arsha entered the room.

Sat between two benches, crossed legged on the floor, Micah was slowly untangling a small mountain of climbing rope. His dark hair was tied back in a pony-tail and his shirt sleeves were rolled up. One braided forelock had been woven with a handful of coloured beads. He turned at the sound of the door, and whistled when he set eyes on her.

"Hey there little bear," Micah said with a broad grin. "You look exceptionally pretty today."

She smiled, and propped herself up on one of the benches.

"Dad got you working late?"

Micah shrugged, broad shoulders moving expressively.

"Gotta get done. We're still pitching to set off early tomorrow if we can."

"You're not going to change?"

"We'll catch up and meet you guys at the restaurant. Or something. Honestly I'm just glad we're finally going to be out there doing something again. I gotta tell you, girl, I am literally losing my mind cooped up here behind all these books."

"Goodness, it's almost like assisting a Professor of Archaeology involves more than just knowing how to fold a rope. How terrible for you," Ilona said. Her tone was sharp, but Arsha had seen the two of them argue often enough to expect that. She'd never really quite understood the way Micah and Ilona were with each other, but the fact remained that no amount of bickering and sniping had ever seemed to keep the two from remaining friends. Or, something like friends. She wasn't really sure if she knew exactly what to call it.

Hefting a coil of rope, Micah just shook his head, sadly.

"I swear you and Rishi live behind those books of yours. You're like a fated match, the two of you. When you going to admit it and just tie the knot already?"

Ilona's eyes narrowed, just a little, but the woman said nothing.

"What do you say Arsha?" Micah continued, ruffling her hair as he walked past, "How'd you like to have Ilona for your new mum?"

"Fates, you are such an ass," Ilona snarled. "Talking about her mother like that..."

"Hey, hey, OK. I'm sorry," Micah said, throwing up his hands in a gesture of surrender as Ilona scowled at him.

"It's OK. It really doesn't bother me," Arsha said. "I mean, I never knew her, so it's not really like I can miss her or anything."

She did her best to sound unconcerned, but an uneasy silence still fell over the room. It was always awkward, the way people were so wary of discussing a woman she'd never even met. She supposed it must have been different for people who'd had a mother and a father, but all she'd ever known was growing up with her dad. She'd spent so much of her life aboard the Triskelion that she'd never really been lonely. There had always been Micah to give her piggy-back rides around the deck, or Milima to read her a bed-time story and stroke her hair as she drifted off to sleep. She'd explored every inch of their floating home playing hide and seek with Elim and Shani, crawling through hatchways and hidden nooks until their parents went mad trying to find them. All of the crew had become her family in their own ways.

The silence ticked on. Ilona's eyes were fixed on her notes again, as Micah went back to counting off carabiners. Arsha was still wondering if she should say something when the door swung open and Shani swept in. Arsha found herself momentarily dazed by the sight of the older girl, looking gorgeous in a flowing gown of green and gold, with a brooch at her neck.

"Hey sweetie." Shani smiled at her. "You look stunning."

Arsha looked away, feeling her cheeks tingling again.

"Our parents are waiting outside, if you're ready to go," Shani added. "Oh, hey, Micah, I have got to show you this."

As Shani danced across to where Micah was sitting, Arsha got up and began to make her way outside. At the entrance to the lobby, she paused. Milima and Abasi were standing alone together in the empty lobby. Milima's face was upturned, Abasi's hand resting lightly on the back of her neck as her husband's lips met hers.

Arsha coughed. Giggling, Milima took a step back, nodding in her direction.

"Hello again, trouble," Abasi growled, smiling.

Arsha just smirked at him, and stuck her tongue out.

"Your father's outside, love," Milima said. "Had to take an urgent sending all of a sudden. I don't suppose you know where Shani got to?"

"Showing off one of her new toys to Micah, so, I don't know, they'll probably only be all night," Arsha replied.

Abasi sighed, and rolled his eyes.

"Why did I ever let that girl near one of those stones in the first place?"

"Oh I don't know dear," Milima replied, patting his arm, "perhaps because your daughter is doing something she's incredibly passionate about, and can probably make a very successful career out of?"

Abasi just rolled his eyes again. Moments later, Shani glided into the lobby, Micah and Ilona following close behind her. Micah was talking whilst Ilona listened with pursed lips, in what Arsha recognised as their version of an animated conversation.

Shani glanced around the room at everyone.

"So, are we just waiting for the esteemed professor?" she said. Almost on cue, the outside door opened, and Arsha's father walked in.

She sensed the change in him as soon as he stepped through the door. It was in his eyes, in the way he walked, in the way his hands moved at his sides, as if he wasn't entirely sure what to do with them. The others sensed it too, and for a moment no one spoke.

"Rishi, what's wrong?" Abasi said, breaking the silence.

"Nothing's wrong, Abasi, it's just..." He pushed a hand through his hair, seemingly not for the first time. "Something's come up." He paused. "How quickly can you plot us a new course?"

"Well," Abasi said, speaking with an almost exaggerated caution, "that depends on where we'd be sailing to."

"It's..." He paused again, as if unsure how much he could say. "It's beyond the Veil. A city called 'London'. We have to set sail as soon as possible."

"Rishi, come on now, what's wrong?" Milima stepped forward to lay a hand on his arm. "All these plans we've been making..."

"Yes, I know. I'll explain things to the dean tonight. As best I can, anyway."

"But why? What in the world could be so important that you need to abandon everything you've been working for this last year? What is this about?"

"Milima, you know I wouldn't ask, not unless it was absolutely necessary."

"So we just have to trust you?" Milima scowled.

"Can you?"

For a moment, Milima said nothing, her eyes fixed on his. Then she gave a nod.

"I'll have the ship ready by daybreak," Abasi said.

The argument apparently settled, her father turned to look at Micah and Ilona, both of whom had been watching everything keenly, but without saying a word.

"I'm so sorry about this. I'll have arrangements made for both of you to stay here at Skytower. Or, I can pay for passage if there's somewhere else you'd like to be."

Ilona's sharp features pulled back into an angry sneer.

"You absolutely must be joking," she snarled. Her father's eyes creased with sadness.

"I really am so sorry. This situation..."

"Professor, I think what 'Lona's trying to say," Micah interjected, "is that we really don't give a rat's arse what the situation is. We're not sitting this one out just because the plans have changed. I know how much this expedition meant to you. Whatever this thing is that's come up, it's obviously pretty damn important."

"You feel the same, I take it?" her father said, looking at Ilona. The woman inclined her head, ever so slightly.

"Well, thank you, both of you," he said. Micah raised his hands in an easy-going gesture.

"You did promise me we'd get to travel. I've never been past the Veil before."

Despite his outward calm, Arsha had known Micah long enough to recognise the nervousness in the man's eyes. That same nervousness was lurking behind every face in the room, a tension crackling in the air, as her father excused himself and stalked away, his shoulders hunched over as his coat flapped around his heels. Arsha felt Shani's hand enclosing hers, a gentle, reassuring pressure as the woman smiled at her, a little sadly. Neither of them seemed to have any idea what to say.

Chapter 3 - Tracks

A door stood in front of her, the blue paint long since peeled and faded to an awful grey. Plastic numbers barely visible, the gold painted finish all worn off. The last door in a line of grey doors on the third floor, overlooking a concrete courtyard. The grey doorways faced onto a grey balcony, with a metal handrail painted white, but chipped and rusted with age and disrepair. Below, broken swings and a creaking see-saw. Bottles, cans and mouldy paper bags. The smell of piss and vomit.

A grey door, just like all the others, yet every detail had been seared into her mind. Every fleck of paint, every scratch and stain. The precise way that it stood, not quite shut. A crack, showing a last glimpse of the apartment beyond. She could hear the muted sounds of shouting. An argument. A television turned up too loud. The dull thump of a bass-line pounding through the concrete walls.

She should go back. Not walk away like this. Go back and do something. Do something, but she didn't know what. She couldn't remember what she was doing here. Couldn't remember what was beyond that door... What could be so important. What she was running away from.

The thought lurked in the back of her mind, like a space where a tooth had been. She felt the flaking paint of the railing, the rusted metal rough against her fingers.

What was she doing here?

The ugly space in the back of her mind. Something trapped in shadow. An emptiness, sucking her in.

White paint, flaking on her fingers as she rubbed them together. The door, slightly ajar. Bass-line pulsing in her skull. Thudding, like a heartbeat. Like the feeling you get as the headache first begins to settle in.

The door creeping open. The gap widening. The emptiness sucking her in.

What was she doing here?

The last door in a line of grey doors, creeping open. She knew. She knew what was behind that door. She should have closed it then. Should not have let herself look back and see that door, half-open.

She should have closed it. Her feet were like lead. Her heart pounding in her throat. The bass-line, thudding in her head. One foot, then the other. Closer to the opening, the darkness, the emptiness. She held out a shaking hand towards the handle, but it continued to swing wider, moving just beyond her grasp. She reached out, a desperate whimper escaping from her lips as she leaned in closer.

And then the door frame was not a frame, but a vast archway, growing higher, wider. The darkness came rushing forwards. Her feet could not hold her, and the whimper became a scream. She was falling, falling down through that vast opening, falling into the darkness that rushed up to swallow her.

Rachael woke to find herself surrounded. Bodies pressed in all around as a thunderous sound bellowed in her ears. The carriage swayed violently as it swept around a bend in the tunnel. The clamour of voices could barely be heard over the constant rumble reverberating from the tunnel walls. They rode through total darkness, buried deep within the earth.

Slowly, her breathing calmed. Rachael checked her bag, the contents apparently untouched. She had little enough to steal, but the thought still nagged at her. The woman in the next seat glowered at her from the corner of one eye, before returning to her sudoku puzzle.

For the price of a single ticket, you could ride the Circle line until midnight. The underground was warm and dry, the trains rattling on through the same dark tunnels as they had for a hundred years, smelling of oil and grime. After the encounter on the rooftop the day before, she had retreated down into the tunnels, somewhere safe, hidden away. Curled up in a corner seat on the train, she kept her bag hugged to her chest and her hood down low, doing her best to simply shut out the sound of the other travellers.

The hours ticked by as the train pulled into one station after another, the crowd in the carriage shifting, changing shape, but never really seeming all that different. Sometimes she sketched, picking a face at random and letting it flow out onto the page. She liked drawing people on the underground. They tried so hard to block out everything around themselves, to become completely disengaged, and yet they allowed so much of themselves to flow to the surface.

She drew, and sometimes she dozed, head tucked against the corner of the window frame. Days on end of huddling in doorways and alleys had left her exhausted, and it was easy to nod off in the warmth, rocked to sleep by the gentle but insistent swaying of the carriage.

Somewhere half-way between dreaming and waking, she noticed that a man was watching her from across the carriage. He had steel grey eyes, tanned skin and a buzz-cut. He wore a patched black leather jacket. There was a tension in him that unsettled her. Still groggy, she clutched her bag tighter, ready to slip out at the next station. The train slowed, coming to a stop with a hiss as the doors opened. For a moment she couldn't move, trapped by the press of bodies squeezing past. She was ready to slip into the crowd when she glimpsed the empty seat where the man had been sitting. As the carriage began to fill again, like a tide coming back in, she searched the crowd but saw no sign of him. Uneasily, she stayed where she was. Most likely, she'd only imagined the man was looking at her.

The train moved on. Time blurred, and she felt sleep pulling her back in. When she awoke again, she wasn't sure how long she had been sleeping for. She was alone. She supposed it was late; likely the trains would be stopping soon. In spite of the noise booming from the walls of the tunnel, it felt strangely quiet in the empty carriage. Small gusts of wind pushed the litter around the floor, as lights flickered past in the darkness.

Then she saw that it wasn't litter, but tiny clouds of golden brown leaves that danced across the floor of the carriage. The more she looked, the more she saw, covering the ground like a field in autumn. Some unfelt breeze lifted them in tiny clouds and flurries, to weave through the air and scurry over the seats and around the hand-rails. She reached out to catch one. Paper-thin, it crumbled between her fingers.

The voice was barely a whisper. How she had even heard it over the sound of the train, she could not guess. She couldn't even say where it came from. She only knew that she had heard one word, whispered close, almost to her ear.

"Rachael."

The train rolled on. The leaves continued to dance and play at the air, though she could not feel the slightest breeze, and the word repeated itself, almost an echo.

"Rachael."

She clutched her bag to her chest and tucked her knees up close, becoming as small as she could be. Glancing about the empty carriage, she summoned up the courage to cry out.

"Who's there?"

The only answer was the whisper of her name once more, as if close by. She looked about wildly, unsure of what she could possibly have missed, but there was not a single person, not one thing out of place, save for the swirling clouds of autumn leaves.

Then the patterns of the leaves began to change. It was slow, at first. It took her a while to realise that they were gathering, spiralling gently inward towards a spot at the centre of the carriage. The cloud of leaves began to rise up like a pillar, still swirling in tight spirals.

Rachael watched in fascination as the pillar of swirling leaves grew taller and broader. Distinct shapes formed at either side, branching away. Then she saw that the shapes were not branches but arms. The form of a human figure began to emerge, taking slow steps towards her, one hand outstretched. The movements of the leaves grew ever tighter, until they were gathered together into a solid mass. A woman's body with the shape of a simple dress about it, and a face emerging from the pattern of leaves. Empty spaces formed eyes and a mouth. Then, in a voice that was a thousand rustling leaves on a cold autumn day, a single word.

"Rachael."

Rachael closed her eyes and screamed.

When she finally drew a breath, the thundering of the train seemed to crash in on her. She heard the sound of voices, and opened her eyes to see a carriage full of passengers, crowded in around her.

As the train pulled in at the station she fled the carriage, and collapsed against the tiled wall of the platform. She pulled her knees up and hid her face, as tears stung her cheeks.

The woman's face was still clear in her mind. With trembling fingers she struggled to undo the zip on her bag, fumbling in the depths until she retrieved a small container made of clear orange plastic. Barely a half dozen tablets remained at the bottom of the pill bottle. She fumbled the cap loose and swallowed one. Then, pressing her thumbs to her temples, she closed her eyes and tried to slow her breathing. Eventually the sound of her heartbeat quietened to a dull thunder. She could feel white hot marks where her nails had dug into her palms. Her hands were still shaking.

When she opened her eyes, she saw a man watching her from further down the platform. It took her only a moment to realise that it was the same man she had seen on the train. Still unsteady, she got to her feet and waited just long enough for a large crowd to block her from his sight. Then she slipped out of the entrance to the station, weaving her way through the crowds. Before long her pace began to slow, her footsteps feeling lighter and lighter. She had the strange sensation that her body was starting to melt, bleeding out into the air around her as she walked. At each turning she reminded herself to check if she was being followed, but if the man was still tailing her then she could see no sign of him. She knew it was the drugs making her feel light headed, making her forget which street she was on, or to check for signs of pursuit. It was hard to keep it all in her head anymore.

She kept moving, pulling her hood low to cover her face as she ducked down into a narrow passageway. The alley wound it's way between two crumbling old Victorian buildings, shutting out most of the chaotic buzz of the streets. As she passed another bend in the path, she saw a shape detach itself from the darkness up ahead. The figure's face was hidden in the shadows, but Rachael could make out a voice, low and soft.

"You're being followed. He was waiting back at the entrance to the alley."

A cold shiver ran through her as she caught a glimpse of his face. The boy from the rooftop. He was wearing the same clothes she had seen in him the day before. His long black coat made him look oddly shapeless in the gloom.

"There's another one waiting in the courtyard ahead. They think they've got you trapped in here."

Barely seeming to notice her confused expression, he turned to nod at the wall to her left.

"No... Wait. You... You weren't real," she mumbled, mostly to herself. It took her another moment to realise he was looking at a rusted old iron drainpipe that was bolted to the brickwork.

She glanced back over her shoulder. Her fear was a dull, muted roar, clawing it's way up through her gut, struggling against the lightness that clouded her thoughts. She wondered if she really was hearing the sound of footsteps approaching from beyond the last turn in the alley, or if it was just her imagination.

"I saw you on the rooftop. But you weren't really there."

A look of irritation flashed across his face.

"We don't have time, come on," he said.

"Why are you following me?"

"To keep you safe. From them," he said, glancing nervously back down the alleyway.

The sound of approaching footsteps grew louder. With no time left to think, she grabbed the drainpipe and started to climb. Shifting her weight over the parapet, she rolled clear as the boy vaulted over just behind her. Before she could speak, he turned to her with a finger pressed to his lips. With his other hand he pointed down at the street below.

Rachael slowly peered out, just enough to glimpse what was happening below. She saw a tall, heavily built man in a tan coat walking past. From the other direction, another man approached him. Rachael shuddered as she recognised the dark skinned man in the black leather jacket.

As both men looked about the vacant alleyway, Rachael ducked back into the cover of the rooftop. When she dared to risk another peek, the taller man was holding something in his hand. It might have been a phone, or a walkie-talkie.

"Sorry boss, we lost her," he said. Then he tucked the device away in his pocket, and the two men walked on.

Rachael pulled herself back from the edge a little. The boy kept watching with keen eyes, until the men were out of sight. Then he sat back against the low wall around the rooftop with a look of relief.

Slowly, Rachael got to her feet, and took a step back.

"OK, what the hell was that all about?"

Scarcely seeming to pay her any attention, the boy started rooting around in his satchel.

"I'm serious, what's going on here? Why were you following me before?"

"I told you, because of those guys. They're some sort of gang or something, I guess. They've been snatching kids. You know, young girls, like you. There's this big Greek looking guy with a scarred head. I think he's their boss. I caught some of them tailing you, a few days back, figured you where their next mark, right? Didn't want to see you get hurt."

The boy finally stopped sifting through his bag, and pulled out a pair of bright purple crisp packets. He held one out to her.

"Monster Munch?"

For a moment she just stared at him, as his outstretched hand hovered before her. Finally she snatched the packet from his hand, and sat down.

"So you didn't think of just telling me all that? Like, 'hey, there's this gang of bad dudes planning to kidnap you'?"

He looked away, almost as if he was embarrassed.

"Yeah, I did. But... I dunno. I mean, you're not exactly approachable."

Rachael frowned.

"Gee, wonder why?" she said.

"And I guess... I kind of liked just watching you," he added, still staring out across the rooftops. "You know, when you're out running, or when you're drawing and stuff.

Rachael felt herself blush. She looked down at the crisp packet in her hands. The purple plastic split with a loud pop.

"They're pickled onion," he said. "Hope that's OK."

She shrugged.

"Food's food, man," she said, digging in. She pulled a half empty water bottle from her bag and took a mouthful. She held the bottle out to the boy. He tipped it back, taking a long gulp. A little spilled down his chin.

"Thanks," he said, passing the bottle back. Then he smiled, and held out his hand.

"I'm Justin," he said.

"Rachael," she said, though she made no move to take his hand.

For a moment they ate in silence. When the bag was empty she licked the foil clean. Finally she crumpled up the empty packet and let it fly away on the breeze. Leaning back on her elbows, she stared up at the overcast sky. Her head was starting to clear a little.

"I should go," she said.

"Why?" he said.

"I dunno. Because."

"They're probably still looking for you," Justin said.

"Yeah, well, I can look after myself," she said, begin to feel a little irritable. "Now I know what I'm dealing with and all."

She turned to pick up her bag.

"Why do you want to leave?" he said. She stared at him as he got to his feet and checked the buckles on his satchel. She honestly couldn't say if it was anger or curiosity she was feeling, as she found herself reaching for words that she couldn't find.

"Come on," he said, "There's a baker's nearby, gets really busy about now. You do it right, you can lean over the counter and snatch up some pasties while no one's looking."

He looked so at ease, so relaxed as he stood there smiling at her, brown eyes warm and friendly. It was only when she looked at his hands that she saw they were shaking, just a little.

She smiled. It was a strange feeling.

"OK," she said.

In the end they struck out at the bakers after Justin tried to slip a whole loaf of bread under his coat. They barely escaped, pilfered sandwiches scattering across the tiled floor as they ran. After that they bought hot-dogs from a street cart, and when the balding old man wasn't looking Rachael helped herself to the contents of his change jar. They ate in a park, drinking water from a guttering old fountain that had a coppery tang, and they pissed behind an overgrown laurel bush in the shrubbery, taking turns to keep watch.

Eventually, they found themselves sitting on a rooftop, overlooking the railway tracks, where nearly two dozen lines gathered together into the chaotic tangle of King's Cross Station. They sat with their legs over the edge of the roof, heels knocking against the wall. The rumble of the trains mingled with the constant buzz of noise that filled every part of London's streets. She ran her fingertips over the brickwork, feeling the rough texture as a prickling sensation against her skin. The world was beginning to feel brighter and sharper, every sound a little clearer.

"Do you ever wish it was you?" Justin said, nodding at a passenger coach. "Y'know, sitting on one of them trains. Going home?"

She shook her head.

"Not really. Home is here, you know? Lived in London my whole life."

"Where abouts?"

"Tottenham. Estates. It's not really somewhere you'd want to go back to, you know?"

"So you left?"

Instinctively, she glanced away.

"Yeah. Something like that," she said. "What about you? Where'd you come from?"

He leaned back, and looked up at the darkening grey sky.

"That's, uh... A really complicated question," he said.

She turned to look at him. The rumble of a passing train reverberated up from the building.

"Man, you are trying really hard to be all mysterious and stuff, ain't you?"

A look of irritation flashed across his face.

"What, and you're not?"

She scowled, and looked away.

"Listen," she said, after a moment, "thanks for helping me out back there. That was real good of you man."

She pulled herself back from the edge of the roof and stood up, shouldering her pack. He looked up at her, surprised and confused.

"I'll see round, OK?" she said, turning to leave.

He was on his feet before she'd gone three steps, grabbing her by the elbow.

"Hey, where you going?" he said.

She shook his hand off.

"Don't get personal, dude," she snapped.

"Those guys could still be after you. You know that right? You should let me stay with you."

She glanced back at him, and for a moment there was something unsettling in his eyes. A strange mixture of fear and determination.

She forced a shrug.

"Fine, whatever man."

As she started to walk again, he fell in stride beside her. At the far end of the roof, she dropped down. She heard the thump as he landed just behind her, but already she was picking up speed, cutting back on herself. Another drop, and she was darting down a narrow street, towards the embankment over the train yard. She heard him scramble down the embankment behind her, heard him shout something, but she wasn't paying attention to the words. There was a wall of parked carriages up ahead, and she hit the ground rolling, right between the wheels. Coming up on the other side, she turned and jumped, catching a handrail to haul herself up onto the carriage roof. Looking down, she glimpsed the tail of his coat disappearing as he rolled under the carriage, now heading in the wrong direction. Quietly, she dropped down, and sprinted away, back towards the embankment. The sound of her footsteps against the gravel was buried in the thunder of another train passing.

Back on the streets, she kept running, cutting back on herself a couple of times, until she was sure she had lost him. Feeling strained and exhausted, she slipped around the back of a supermarket, arriving in a narrow side-street with a loading dock. Cigarette stubs littered the ground, and towards one end of the alley a pile of disused metal shelving had formed. She settled down against the wall, opposite a mound of broken boxes. She pulled out her water bottle and took a long swig. The bottle was still pressed to her lips when she heard the sound of footsteps, and looked up just as a shadow fell over her.

She recognised the man from the train instantly, steel grey eyes regarding her with a compassionless gaze. His companion was the man from the alleyway, fair haired, broad shouldered, and seeming even taller now that he was looming over her. His eyes were blue, and cold.

They didn't even speak. Both men just reached down to grab her by the arms. She tried to scream, but ended up choking on the mouthful of water. As fingers like iron wrapped around her arms she kicked away, but they were far too strong. She continued to struggle in their grip as one of the men clapped a hand over her mouth. She lashed out, catching the grey-eyed man in the leg, but his grip did not falter.

Then, as they hauled her to her feet, she saw a movement above. A dark shape, descending. Briefly, she had the impression of outstretched wings. The figure crashed down onto the taller of the men, knocking him to the ground. Rachael was thrown backwards by the impact, landing hard against the wall. For a moment she could only register the pain that exploded across her body.

Dazed, vision blurred and struggling to breath, she could still hear the anger and confusion in the men's voices. She looked up in time to see the taller man go flying backwards, as Justin landed a hard kick to his jaw that seemed to leave him stunned. Then the steel eyed man lunged at the boy from behind. Justin wheeled around, a flicker of bright silver in his hand quickly resolving itself into the shape of a knife. The blade plunged through the man's hand, blood flowing over bright steel and dark skin. Justin wrenched the knife free, and wheeled around to plant a knee into the man's guts. He doubled over.

Then Justin was kneeling at her side, pulling her up with strong hands. She found herself looking into his brown eyes, and saw that they were flecked with tiny spots of gold.

"You're OK?" he said.

She nodded. Already, both of the men were struggling to their feet, hands reaching for weapons.

"Good," Justin said. "Let's go."

She didn't have to think about it. Together, they ran.

Chapter 4 - Secrets

Arsha's cabin aboard the Triskelion was tiny but cosy. A scattering of wooden statuettes littered the top of her dresser, the tools she'd used to carve them now buried in one of the drawers. A half finished dress was draped over the back of a chair, the needle tucked into the middle of a seam, and books lay scattered across the floor around an unmade bed. On the desk in one corner sat the pieces of a harmonic she'd been trying to build, with Shani's help.

Arsha was sitting cross-legged on the bed, with her sending stone cradled in her hands. She concentrated and felt the stone respond. She held the image of Shani's sigil in her mind and let the connection come to life. Moments later a ghostly image of Shani's room appeared before her. The girl was sitting on her bed, surrounded by the pieces of whatever project she was working on. Her hair had been pulled up into a winding mass of braids that spilled down one shoulder.

"Hey sister. I miss you already. How are you holding up?"

"Missing you too. I really wish you were here right now," Arsha said.

"I know. I'm sorry sweetheart. But your Dad insisted you had to stay with him, and I couldn't just go skipping out on school right now... Believe me, I thought about it. I really did."

"No, it's OK. Its not your fault."

"So, did you find out what all the noise is about yet?" Shani said. Arsha shook her head sadly.

"Dad's been... Weird. He's just in his cabin all the time. He's been going through all his old journals, looking up stuff for whatever he's doing now. Everyone else is just..." She shrugged, helplessly. "Like, Micah's acting like it's all no big deal like he always does, and Ilona's just..."

"Just being 'Lona. Yeah, I know. The more worried she gets, the more stone-faced she gets, as if that was possible. I think I nearly died the last time I saw her smile."

"She smiles plenty. She's just... Quiet," Arsha said.

"Babe, you don't have to defend her. I love 'Lona to bits, but she's not exactly sociable, you know?"

"Yeah, I know," Arsha said, with a sigh of resignation.

"How are my parents doing?"

"They're fine, I think. I sort of get that they both know a little, but they can't talk about it. So everyone's just, you know, not saying anything. Milima's spending all her time working on stuff. Like, whenever she's not in the engine room she's cleaning something or fixing something."

"Yeah, that sounds like Mum alright."

"And Uncle Abasi's just, you know, quiet."

Shani nodded.

"Hang in there kid. It'll all pan out. Your dad's an odd guy sometimes, but he's not, you know, crazy. What people say about him, it's all rubbish. He's one of the smartest guys I've ever met. And he always knows what he's doing, you know? Even it when it looks like he doesn't."

"Yeah. I know. I just... I know there's stuff that he doesn't talk about. Things he keeps to himself. But this is different. He's different. You can see it, the way he's been acting. Whatever this thing is, I think it's really messing him up," Arsha said, staring down at the floor as she spoke.

"He'll sort it out, Arsh."

"I just wish I knew why. Why he's acting like this all of a sudden. Like, if I could just know what that sending was about. Even if I just knew who it was, maybe it would make some sense."

Shani nodded, and seemed about to say something. But instead, her lips pressed into a thin line, as Arsha looked up at her, expectantly.

"What?"

"It's just..." Shani paused again, and then her shoulders fell a little. "You could find out. If you really mean it. About knowing what the sending was. There's a way you could find out."

Arsha felt her stomach twist.

"How... How would I do it?" she said.

Her father's study had changed little over the years. She could still remember how his old mahogany desk, scratched and scarred by years of use, had once towered over her. The leather chair, a bed that was never made, and shelf upon shelf of books. Every wall was covered with them, carefully bound with hide straps to keep them from shifting with the movements of the ship.

Her father's library had always fascinated her. As she grew older she had begun to borrow heavily from his collection, diving into one book after another. The unfinished volumes would pile up in her room until she came staggering back with armful after armful, and the cycle began again. She couldn't say why she never seemed to finish any of the books she started. It just seemed like whatever she found behind those well worn covers was not what she was looking for there.

That would be her excuse, if her father woke; that she had crept into his room late at night in search of the book that kept eluding her. It was a poor excuse. She hoped desperately that she wouldn't have to use it.

She had waited in the hallway for hours until at last, one ear pressed to the door, she had begun to hear faint snoring from the other side. Her father often stayed up long past when anyone else in the ship had gone to sleep. Already a greyness was showing on the far horizon, glimpsed through the porthole in the corridor, and she was afraid that soon Abasi would be up and about. A lifetime aboard ships had made the captain a tenaciously early riser. With how late her father worked, she often wondered how the two had ever found enough time together to become such close friends.

She slipped into the room, easing the door closed behind herself. Her father had never even made it to the bed. He was sprawled in his leather chair, head to one side, a fountain pen dangling between his fingers. She looked around for her father's coat. Her hands were trembling as she checked each of the pockets in turn. His sending stone was not there.

Then she saw it, propped up beneath the lantern on his desk, gilded frame gleaming under the flickering ghostlight. A lump formed in her throat and she fought to swallow it down. She felt as if her heart might shatter her ribcage as she inched across the few scant yards to his desk. He was close enough to touch, faintly snoring. A little trail of drool had formed at the corner of his mouth. For one terrifying moment, she had to suppress an overwhelming urge to laugh. She reached out to lift the sending stone from the desk. Her hands were shaking so hard that the smooth stone nearly fell out of her grasp, and she barely caught it before it struck the desk. She heard a sudden intake of breath, as her father shifted a little in his seat and then settled again. Heart still pounding, she slipped out the door.

Out in the corridor, she leaned back against the wall and let out the breath she'd been holding. She pressed the sending stone deep into her pocket and stole away back to her bedroom, cursing her own curiosity.

As she was passing the main stairwell, a sudden sound froze her in place. One of the doors lining the corridor swung open and a tall figure stepped out. In the darkness, it took her a moment to realise it was Micah. He was mostly undressed, just a pair of loose pyjama trousers on.

"Mmm? Hey kid," he mumbled, rubbing his eyes.

"Hh... Hey," she did her best to smile.

"Up early?"

"Couldn't sleep. I, uh, went up to the kitchen to get a drink," she said, trying to sound as natural as she could.

He nodded.

"You?" she added.

He gestured at the door to the bathroom, just behind her.

"Oh."

He smiled.

"I'd best get back to bed," she said.

As she stepped past him, he laid a gentle hand on her shoulder.

"Arsh... Are you doing OK?"

"How do you mean?" she said.

"With all this, I mean. Your dad dropping everything, all of us suddenly running off to a city past the veil. I know it must all seem... Rough."

"I'm OK."

She shrugged.

"You sure?"

Trying not to fiddle with her hands too much, she gave him a reassuring smile.

"I'll deal with it. I mean, Dad's gotta have a plan, right?"

"He always does," Micah said. He sounded so confident, like he always did. It was enough to make her wish she believed him.

"Anyway. I should get back to bed."

She smiled, and stepped away.

"Yeah. Nature calls."

Micah nodded and slouched off towards the bathroom, as she ducked through the door to her cabin and pressed it closed behind herself.

Breathing hard, she threw herself down on her bed and buried her face in her pillow until her heart finally stopped beating so fast. It would have been so easy to just fall asleep, there and then. Instead, she had to force herself to sit up and rub the tiredness from her eyes. She removed the purloined sending stone from her pocket. For a moment it lay in her open palms, gleaming in the dull light. There was a sick feeling in her stomach as she thought about what she was doing. She almost wished she could just throw the stone in the bottom of a drawer and forget about it.

Instead she carefully laid the stone down on her bedside table, next to her own. Touching one hand to each, she focussed on her sending stone, and the weave that Shani had left there. She felt the thread uncoiling, like a rising note at the beginning of a symphony. Shani's weaves always felt like music. As she focused, she could feel the weave sliding into her father's stone, wrapping around the subtle locks that prevented her from seeing what lay inside. There was a feeling of tension, and then release. The contents of the stone opened up before her, choices flashing into her thoughts. She directed her attention to the recent calls. The past few days had been a flurry of activity. She skimmed through the most recent, mostly outgoing calls to names she did not recognise. Delving deeper, she came to a single sending, received a few days past, at just after six thirty in the evening.

Strangely, the sender was unnamed. She pulled up the memory of the sending from within the stone. Immediately, two ghosts joined her in the room. The first was her father, no surprise. The second was someone she didn't know. A woman. Arsha was immediately struck by her beauty. Her age was hard to guess, but she had a slim, perfectly shaped face framed by long black hair that fell straight down her shoulders, and large, gentle eyes.

"Maya?" her father gasped.

"Hello Rishi. I'm sorry, I know it's been a long time."

"No, of course. I understand. Maya, isn't it dangerous for you to be calling me like this?"

"It is. But this is important."

"Maya, please... You shouldn't be putting yourself in any danger for my sake."

Maya covered her mouth, as she made a sound like something between a laugh and a sob.

"Fates, Rishi, do you have any idea how much I've missed seeing your face?"

"I've missed you too, Maya. You're keeping well?"

"The Chamber keeps me safe and sound, as always. They even let me take walks in the gardens these days. I have a bodyguard now. I'm one of the elect."

"That's good," her father said, his tone suggesting that he was having to bite back something else he might have said.

"Rishi, my sweet, you don't have to pretend to be happy for me. I know it kills you, seeing me trapped here."

"It's like chewing on glass, every time I think of you being stuck in that place. But it's good, that they let you take walks. You always loved the gardens."

"You're thinking of the estate, aren't you? Fates, how did you put up with me? Always chasing at your heels."

"You were never a bother, Maya."

She lowered her eyes a little, smiling demurely. Her father seemed to gather himself in the momentary silence.

"Maya, why did you risk this? Calling me?"

"A dream I had."

"A dream? You mean..."

"Yes. A vision."

"Maya, you can't. You know what it means, sharing a vision without..."

"Rishi, please don't. I know what it means, but I have to. You'll understand."

"I can't let you do this, Maya. Not for me."

"Yes, you can. You have to. I can't explain it, Rishi, but I feel it. I was meant to share this vision with you. I think... I think it was only meant for you..."

"You haven't told them, have you? Fates, Maya, faking dream records..."

"I told you, I can't explain it. I just know."

She saw her father press one hand to his forehead. He seemed to be trying to steady his breathing. Finally he looked up at her again.

"OK. If you've risked this much to tell me..."

"Thank you," she said.

Her father just nodded, swallowing.

"In the dream... There was a city. A city beyond the veil. A clock tower with four faces, old and much loved. A great wheel in the sky, by the edge of a river. Towers of glass. A bridge with two gatehouses. A palace."

"London," her father said, in obvious surprise.

"London? Really? I didn't know."

"It has to be London. It's one of the great cities in the Hearth."

Maya nodded, calmly.

"There's a girl, Rishi. Young. She's running away from something. She's scared and in pain. I saw a boy with her, but I couldn't see his face. He seemed to be made of shadows and smoke. Fates Rishi, he frightened me. Just looking at him made me feel sick. They were running through the streets, and there was an animal, some kind of animal hunting them. They were surrounded by broken glass and clouds of falling leaves, like autumn. She's connected to you, Rishi. I don't know how, but I could feel you hanging over her. Like a ghost. Like, you've been haunting her, or she's been haunting you."

Her father looked ashen as Maya related this.

"But there's more," the woman continued, as if just speaking the words was painful. "I saw this girl, standing in an open space in the middle of the city... And Arsha was standing with her."

Arsha felt a coldness in her gut, a feeling like someone's hand clenching around her stomach. In the memory of the sending, her father's eyes widened.

"You're sure? You're sure it was her?"

Maya nodded, with a sadness in her eyes. It almost seemed like an apology.

"They were standing together, Arsha and this girl. Their hands were bound together with red string, wound all around them, spilling over the ground. The girl, her other hand was covered in a gauntlet of iron, rusted and old. The boy was with them, watching them. I could see his shadow, surrounding them both. And Arsha... I don't know Rishi. She seemed like she was trying to make a choice. The kind of choice that changes everything about you. I remember she had wings, Rishi. Wings of iron, rusted, like the gauntlet the girl wore. I'm sorry, I don't suppose any of this makes any sense to you?"

"A little," he said, his voice hollow.

"Good. Because there's one more thing. There's been... Talk. Rumours, around the Chamber. You know how it is. We're not supposed to discuss dreams, but when something big happens... You can feel it in the air. A Seed, Rishi. A Seed is going to open."

"Maya, are you... Are you sure?"

The woman shrugged.

"Is anything sure? From what I've heard, just about every one of the elect has had the same dream."

"Except you?"

"It was the last part of the dream. The girl... She looked at me. Right at me, with eyes full of so much anger and sadness. And then she held out her hand, the hand covered by the iron gauntlet. It was there, in her palm. The Seed. Oh Fates, Rishi, I could feel it. I could feel its power."

"Maya, I..."

Her father seemed unsure of what to say.

"Thank you. For telling me," he managed, at last.

"What are you going to do?"

"I don't know. I have to..." he floundered. Arsha saw that his hands were shaking. He seemed to be resting his weight against a wall. "Your father and I, we have a lot of debts to pay, Maya. I think... I think this might be the worst of them."

For a moment, Maya was silent. She seemed to be studying his face, with an expression of sad longing.

"Rachael," the woman said, softly. "Her name is Rachael. She whispered it to me, just as the dream ended. Do what you can for her, Rishi. Do what's right. I know you will."

"Thank you," her father said. It was almost a whisper. Then the sending ended.

Arsha sat on her bed, the stone cupped in her hands, staring into the distance as she wondered what to make of it all.

Chapter 5 - Scaffolds

"This looks good," Justin said.

A fence had been erected around the construction site, metal bars slotted into concrete feet, but there was space enough between a pair of un-braced sections for the both of them to squeeze through. Past the fence they dashed across a short stretch of open ground and into the cover of the scaffolds, draped with heavy tarpaulins. The wind ran through the tarps, making them snap and ripple incessantly, a constant and uneven percussion in the cold air. Rain splashed her face, driven through the gaps in the sheeting by the sudden gusts of wind.

At first she thought they might climb one of the scaffolds to find a spot to sleep, but she was nervous of the way the platforms swayed, and it didn't seem as though there would very much protection from the rain. They kept looking, moving quickly, careful to stay away from any light as they explored the skeletal structure. Eventually Justin found a ladder that lead up to the second floor. The flooring itself was still only partially laid, but there were enough plank walkways thrown down for them to move around on. They found a stack of spare planks with a tarp tied over them. She undid a corner, cold fingers fumbling with the knot, and secured it to a nearby pillar to create a small covered space. The shape reminded her of the tents she used to make in her grandmother's garden, with bedsheets and string tied to an apple tree that never grew any fruit.

It was late and she was tired. Her hands felt clumsy, and her legs ached from running. They crawled into the space beneath the tarp and wrapped Justin's coat about themselves. He put an arm around her, and she slid easily into the crook of his shoulder.

Her thoughts drifted back over the last few days. After the attack behind the supermarket she had been mostly incoherent, too scared to really think. She'd followed him without thinking, not sure of what else she could do. That night she had slept in a church doorway whilst Justin kept watch. When dawn broke, she'd found him tucked against the edge of the church steps, dozing with his coat pulled up over his knees. The night after that, they'd sheltered beneath a disused railway bridge that did nothing to keep out the sharp autumn winds. When Justin had offered to bundle up together under his coat, she couldn't find any reason to refuse. Curled up together, comforted by the warmth of his body, she'd slept more soundly than she could remember in a long time.

The days had also passed more easily. Though Justin was a stranger to London, his keen eyes could easily follow her lines as they danced across the rooftops, and his light fingers were always ready to snatch up food, money, or anything else he could steal away with. At times she had actually begun to enjoy herself. It was only in the quiet moments that she found herself thinking of the men from the alleyway, or the way the blood had glistened as it ran down the blade of Justin's knife.

Rachael woke with a start. Eyelids flickered open as she remembered where she was. Justin was sitting bolt upright, his body forming a black silhouette against the light from the street. At first she couldn't tell what might have woken him. Then, through the faint sounds of the city, she heard something much closer to. It was the soft crescendo of a falling length of chain. He crept to the nearby window frame and she followed, leaning over his shoulder to get a look. She saw the clustered silhouettes of a group of men entering the site. One of them had a pair of bolt-cutters in his hand.

"It's those guys from before," she whispered. "How'd they find us here?"

"I don't know. Wait," Justin said.

Down below, one of the men at the back of the group addressed the others in a voice like pouring gravel. He spoke with the calm assurance of someone used to giving orders.

"Search in pairs. Signal and detain."

The speaker was a short, broadly built man with a squat and ugly shape crouched at his heels, sniffing the air. Something about him seemed familiar. Then the light caught his face, and she recognised the ragged scar that ran across his bare scalp, and the shape of the mangy dog at his heels. To either side of him she could make out two figures in long coats of gleaming red and gold. They were dark skinned, with wavy black hair and sharp features. The older of them had a thick beard, but there was little else to tell them apart. The rest of the group were comprised of tough looking men in jackets and jeans.

At the scarred man's command, the four toughs broke away, moving slowly through the site, sweeping the light of their torches through the empty rooms. It wouldn't be long before they reached the upper floors, and only a little longer before their hiding place was discovered.

A snarling sound caught her attention. She stole another glance at the dog on the leash, and a chill ran through her. What she saw wasn't a dog at all. The leader of the strange group had an old man collared and leashed at his side, dressed in tattered rags. There was foam on his lips, and his hair was a mane of tangles.

Pulling back from the window frame, Rachael closed her eyes, and tried to shake off the image in her mind. It couldn't have been real. She was sure of that.

She felt a hand on her shoulder. Opening her eyes, she saw Justin's expression, calm and focused.

"We've gotta get outta here," she whispered, though she hadn't the slightest idea how. The scarred man and the tall brothers in their long coats were still waiting at the gate. The only other way through the fence was at the back of the site, where they had slipped in. That meant going down the ladder, and through the men searching below.

"I'll jump the one nearest the ladder," Justin whispered. "You run while he's distracted."

She saw a coldness in his eyes, like the edge of a knife.

"Justin, wait..."

She grabbed his shoulder, as he began to move.

"What?" he hissed.

"I don't know, just... Wait, OK?"

She looked around again, hoping for any other way. Then her eyes settled on the back wall of the building, where a garbage chute had been hooked up to the scaffolds.

She nodded, and Justin followed her gaze.

"OK," he mouthed.

The second floor was mostly a patchwork, pieces of finished flooring connected by planks that bridged the openings. One long plank was all that connected them to the back wall, where the garbage chute began.

Justin gestured for her to go first. While he sat back in the shadows, watching the torch-lights flicker below, she crept out onto the plank. She felt it rocking slightly under her weight. She crawled, inch by inch along the length of the beam, as the men on the floor below swept through the building. She could hear them talking, calling out areas cleared in hushed tones.

She was about halfway across when she saw the movement at the front of the building. The man with the voice like gravel, and the ragged mutt that shuffled at his heels. He strode into the building like he owned it, casting his gaze about imperiously. She forced herself to breathe and continued sliding along the wooden board, one inch at a time. She was almost there. She could have reached out and touched the lip of the half-finished concrete floor when she heard a howl, somewhere between the cry of an animal and a wail of deep anguish. The sound seemed to move through her body like an electric shock, and she very nearly slipped off the beam. It rattled beneath her, rocking perilously back and forth. As the movement subsided she glanced down, and once again she saw not a mangy hound but a ragged man with wild and frantic eyes, too much white showing as he stared into her with an awful hunger.

The man with the scar looked up and gestured, one hand pointing, almost lazily, as all eyes turned to her.

"Run!" Justin yelled, and she scrambled onto the hard floor. Rolling to her feet she glanced back to see him dashing across the narrow beam, as the men below made for the ladders. Justin grabbed her hand and together they ran towards the chute.

"Just like a water slide," she told herself.

The plastic tubing thundered like a drum as she slid down. Metal ribs scratched at her hands and face, everything flashing past in a few seconds until she tumbled head first into a jagged mound of rubble. Dazed and battered, she barely had time to crawl clear as Justin came crashing down after her.

They sprinted across the open ground, torchlight lapping at their heels. She glanced back as Justin searched for the gap in the fence, to see the four men closing in. Over the shouting she heard a single barked command.

"Take them!"

"Quickly," Justin hissed, standing with one leg through the gap in the fencing. She followed him through, her heart in her throat.

As soon as they were through, Justin set off at a dead sprint. She followed him into the dark streets. As they ran she heard a wretched howl that seemed to split the air and made her insides writhe with fear.

They carried on running for a long time, until her lungs burned so hard that she felt she would collapse. At last they made their way up to a rooftop high above the streets. She lay on her back, gulping like a beached fish, feeling every part of her body burning and freezing at the same time.

As her head began to clear she looked up to see Justin leaning against a vent, looking nearly as worn down as she felt. Slowly, aching in every joint, she pulled herself to her feet. They would need a new place to bed down for the night. The thought of putting her head down anywhere seemed almost impossible. Her body was buzzing with nervous energy, she was freezing cold and she hurt all over.

She still hadn't the slightest idea what had just happened. In Justin's expression she saw only a hardness, as if he was still ready for a fight.

"Justin," she began, softly, but the words wouldn't come to her. It was all too confused, too impossible.

"It's OK. I think we lost them. I hope," he said. His expression remained unreadable. In a way, she was glad of that. At least one of them seemed to be in control of themselves.

"What just... No. This is too crazy. Those weren't just a load of gangers. They sounded like they was army or something, and there was those two weird looking blokes in the red coats and all... And that... That dog he had with him. What the hell?"

Justin gave her a curious look.

"You didn't really see a dog, did you?"

Rachael felt the hairs rising all down the back of her neck.

"How... How'd you know that?"

"It wasn't a dog. It was a hollow man," Justin said, turning away.

"A what?"

The words barely had time to leave her mouth. He pressed a finger to his lips and hissed a "Shhh."

In the sudden stillness the sound of voices in the street below sent a chill down her spine. Justin glanced over the edge of the rooftop and gestured for her to do the same. She moved to the parapet and peered over. There were men moving through the street, their outlines familiar. At the back of the group she could already make out the shape of long coats flashing red under the street-lamps. Caught momentarily in a pool of light, she saw the wild eyes and tangled hair of the leashed man. He was sniffing the air like a bloodhound. Then his eyes fixed on hers and he let out a howl. She shot back from the edge, but it was already too late. She heard the voices in the street below and she knew they had seen her.

She could see the fear in Justin's eyes, though he tried his best to hide it. Her mind raced, hoping for any idea that might see them to safety, but only one thought came to her, repeating over and over.

"Run."

Numb hands fumbled on slick black slates. Plastic drainpipes rattled as she scrambled hand over hand. Loose tiles slipped under errant steps, cascading down onto empty pavements. Tires screeched and horns blared as she bolted across streets and intersections. Justin was with her, but he slipped in and out of her sight. She told herself that he could keep up, that he could look after himself. It was better than admitting that at that moment she just didn't care. The only thing that mattered was getting away from that wild-haired man, away from those animal eyes.

She ran as fast and as hard as she dared, but the icy air tore at her lungs and the harder she ran, the more often she had to pause to draw breath, muscles screaming their protests. Every time they stopped, it was barely a few minutes before she caught sight of familiar silhouettes moving purposefully in her direction. The harder she pushed herself, the weaker her legs grew. On the rooftops tiredness was deadly. A misplaced footstep, a poor grip on a handhold and the pavement was the last thing she would see.

Still they ran, staying low now, keeping to the streets, cutting across walls and fences where they could. She was approaching a T-junction when Justin tackled her out of nowhere, strong hands gripping her arms as he slammed her into a wall.

"The hell?" she gasped, barely able to squeeze the words out, she was so short of breath.

"Hold still," he said in a voice like a whip-crack. There was a metallic clicking sound as the knife appeared in his hand, the blade gleaming in the dim light.

She froze, pressing herself back into the wall as he held the knife up. Breathing shallow and fast, she looked at his face, watching his eyes for some sign of his intention. Everything about him was focused and sharp. The knife hovered at the very lowest edge of her field of vision. She saw him press the point of the blade to his own thumb, blood welling up around the tip as it sank into the skin. She couldn't help but shrink back as he moved his bleeding thumb towards her face, and with a snarl of frustration he grabbed her by the chin.

"Hold still," he repeated, his voice a low hiss.

She felt his thumb press against her forehead, moving slowly and deliberately across the skin, tracing some kind of pattern. Moving his hands away at last, he closed the blade and tucked it back into his pocket. She let out the breath she had been holding.

She could feel the anger flaring inside of her as the shock subsided. She was about to push him away when she heard the sound of footsteps from the street up ahead. Justin shifted forward, forcing her back into the shadows. They were pressed up close to the wall of a building, in the darkness between two street-lamps. His body was tight against hers, their faces touching as she watched the far end of the street out of the corner of her eye.

The scarred man stepped out into the intersection, his 'hound' sniffing the air in front of them. The tall brothers in the long coats were with him, and she saw the rest of his men spread out behind, searching the street. Then the thing on the leash paused, one hand raking at his tangled hair as he looked about frantically. He seemed lost. She heard grumbled curses, and then a loud thump as a boot caught the wild haired man in his side, rolling him over with the force of the kick. He yelped in pain, more like a dog than a man, and sprang to his feet again in the same hunched crouch.

She wasn't sure if it was her heart or Justin's that she felt pounding at her chest, as the wild haired creature took another look around, sniffing the air. Then he fell to the ground, curled up into a ball and began to whimper.

"Lost it," the gravel voiced commander said.

"Commander Korban," one of the tall men began. The younger and leaner of the two, she suspected, by the tenor of his voice. "This had better not be all that our money is worth."

"He's lost the trail. Don't know how, but it happens. We'll try again tomorrow, Mi'lord. That's all we can do. He'll be useless like this."

"A hunting dog that can't hunt should be put down," the older brother growled, his voice deep and fierce.

"Good hollow men are a tricky catch. This one's done well so far. It's just a hiccup."

"Korban, my brother and I do not expect 'hiccups' from a man of your reputation," the younger man said, smoothly. Rachael desperately wished they would just move on. All it would take was for one of the group to look a little too closely into the darkness where she and Justin were hidden.

"Mi'Lord Bhandari, I have my reputation because I know exactly how things work out here in the field. If you can find a man who'll promise you a job will never go awry, then I'll show you a man who's never been near a real job in his life. Get used to it. Sir."

"Yes, I see it certainly wasn't for your courtly manners that you were recommended," the younger man sneered.

"You don't pay me for courtesy," Korban growled.

The argument seemed settled. With another swift kick, Korban got their 'hunting dog' moving and the group turned away, disappearing into the night.

Slowly exhaling, Justin took a step away, glancing to either side.

At first she didn't even feel as if she could move. She still seemed to be pinned to the wall by the ghost of him.

"Justin... What just...?"

He nodded to their left. It took her a moment to realise he was looking at a low windowsill that would make a good foothold.

"Rooftop. Come on."

"Justin, wait," she hissed. "What the hell just happened back there. What was that... What was wrong with that man? And the thing you drew..."

She reached up to touch the mark on her forehead, but before her hand was even close, he caught her by the wrist. She'd forgotten how fast he was.

"Don't touch it. Not yet."

He let go and she snatched her hand away. She stared at him, furious.

"You know, any time you'd like to start making sense, be fine with me. How did they even find us? It was like that old guy was... Sniffing us out or something."

"That's what a hollow man does," Justin said with a sigh. "You... You take a person and you clear out what's inside. It leaves a space where you can put the thing you want. And then they search for that thing. They follow it anywhere, because it's the only thing they have left. They're used for tracking. It works best on people who are already a little... Gone. Closer to the Dream. But it makes them dangerous. By the time the change sets in, they're more like animals than people."

She stared at him, her mouth open in astonishment.

"Justin, what the hell does any of that mean?"

"It doesn't matter."

"What do you mean, it don't matter?"

"I mean you won't even believe me if I tell you, so what's the point? Come on, we should get off the street."

He turned away, testing the windowsill to make sure it would hold his weight.

"Come on. They can't track you any more, but they'll still catch us out here if they double back."

He began to climb, and Rachael had no choice but to follow him up. At the top he turned to give her a hand over the parapet. Exhausted, she dropped down against the nearest chimney, drawing deep breaths.

"Will they come back?" she gasped.

"They can't track you now. That ward will hold for a while."

"That what? What are you even on about?" she said, as he slumped against the parapet. "None of this makes any sense man. It's just..."

"Crazy, right?" he said, glumly.

"You're not funny."

"I wasn't trying to be."

"So just tell me what's going on already?"

Justin just gave her an exhausted shrug.

"What do you want me to tell you? I tried telling you the truth, and you told me I was nuts."

"Telling me a bunch of stories ain't the truth."

He held out his hands, palms open and empty.

"Then I've got nothing left."

"How do I even know you're not with them?" she said, starting to get to her feet.

"Because I had a knife at your throat down there, and I didn't give you up to them. Seems like that would have been the easy thing. Rachael, I'm on your side here. If you believe nothing else, believe that."

Eyes narrowing, she regarded him carefully, but it was hard to argue.

"Fine. You're with me. So what do we do now?"

"Now? We get some sleep, I suppose. We'll have to get moving in the morning. I can keep refreshing the ward, but they'll find other ways to track us."

She said nothing. She felt as if she had used up all the words.

Justin was right. For now, sleep was all she had left. On the cold rooftop, torn by the wind, she pulled her knees up to her chest and closed her eyes.

Chapter 6 - Circle

With her father's sending stone held loosely in one hand, Arsha paused at the foot of the stairs and took a breath. Once again she repeated the lie that she'd been carefully rehearsing; that she'd found her father's stone where he'd left it on the bathroom sink. Just an absent minded mistake. It wasn't her fault. She had to keep telling herself that, but the thought just wouldn't seem to stick. She could feel her hands trembling.

She looked up the stairwell, towards the bridge, and reached out one hand to grip the railing. Then she heard a door opening, and the sound of voices from above. She froze, one foot on the bottom step. Her father and the others must have just stepped out of the Captain's ready room and onto the bridge.

"You can look for your damn stone in a minute Rishi, this is important," Milima said, her voice clear and sharp.

"Yes, Milima, I'm sure you think it is, but right now, I really don't..."

"Rishi, we'll be in London in a little over a day. Don't you think it's about time you told us just what in the Seven Names we're doing out here?"

"Rishi, she's right." Abasi's voice, deep and gentle. "When you told me where we were going, I didn't ask any questions, because I trusted that it was important, and that you'd tell me everything in good time. But you can't ask me to take my ship into a situation like this without you at least telling me what we're doing."

There was a long pause in the conversation. She wondered what could be happening. Then she heard her father's voice again, quieter this time. He sounded tired, worn down.

"There's... There's a girl. She's in danger. And I have to protect her."

"Why?" Milima replied. "Rishi, I don't mean to be cold, but there are millions of young girls out there that need protecting. Are you going to go chasing after every single one of them? Why is it so important that you save this one child?"

There was another long silence. Arsha held her breath and pressed herself up against the wall, as she counted off the seconds.

"Because if we don't," her father said, heavily, "a Seed is going to open in London."

"Seven..." Milima gasped.

"Rishi, you can't be serious," Abasi said.

"It'll tear the Veil apart. The damage will be unimaginable," her father continued.

"And this girl, she's going to open it?" Abasi said.

"That's right. Unless we can get to her first."

"Fates, Rishi, you should have told us sooner. We could have brought help, we could have warned the Guild, alerted the Wardens..."

"Abasi, what makes you think they would listen? If I, of all people, told them a Seed was going to awaken, and that somehow no one else, not even the Chamber of Foresight, knew a damn thing about it? Why would they believe me?"

"So how did you find out?" Milima said, her tone taking on a razor fine edge. "If even the Guild doesn't know yet..."

"Or haven't admitted that they know," Abasi interjected. "If a Seed really is going to awaken, the Chamber would predict it. They couldn't miss something like this."

"Which means someone in the Chamber..." Milima continued for him. "Seven Names. Rishi, if they find out. Gaining access to a prediction. Spying on the Chamber. If they ever learn what you've done..."

"Rishi, she's right. You know the rules about the Chamber of Foresight. This is incredibly dangerous."

"If they can prove it," her father replied, curtly. "Which they never will."

"Rishi, you can't know that," Milima said.

"Maybe not, but I trust my source. And if I'm wrong, it's on my head."

"Seven Names it is. Rishi, if they even suspect, they'll come after all of us with everything they have. Even if they can't prove it, they'll find something. We could be charged with trespassing the Veil, breach of the Accords..." Milima said, her voice rising like thunder.

"Milima, love," Abasi said, his voice soft, "it's done now. And Rishi is right. If we let this happen..."

"The damage this thing could cause, if it awakens," her father added.

"You really want to talk to me about damage?" Milima replied, her voice a sharp hiss.

"Fine. So we turn around. We walk away and do nothing. Is that what you want?" her father said, sharply.

"You know damn well I don't. You're right, we're committed now. But I don't like this one bit, and you had no right to lead us into this in the first place. That's the thing about trust, Rishi. You're supposed to earn it."

When Arsha heard the sound of Milima's footsteps on the stairs, she barely had time to react. Without even thinking about it she slipped her father's sending stone back into her pocket, just before Milima rounded the corner and saw her standing there.

"Arsha? What are you doing love?" Milima said, looking almost as shocked as Arsha felt.

"I... Ummm... I was just coming up to ask if... If we'd be putting in any time soon," she stammered.

"Uh, yes, I imagine we'll need to stop to recharge soon. We're coming up on an outpost in a few hours."

"Oh, OK," Arsha said.

"Listen, love, why don't you go down and check on the washing for me?"

Arsha nodded, feeling a wave of relief wash over her. She turned and slipped back down below decks, taking the stairs two at a time, her heart still pounding.

The outpost was little more than a slender spear of rock thrusting up out of the water, surrounded by crashing foam. At its peak a tower had been built, scaffolds branching out to form piers and lookouts. Balconies and walkways surrounded tall windows that splashed bright sunlight back at them in reflected sprays.

She was glad of the chance to get off the ship and away from the tension that seemed to be hanging in the air, like a gathering storm. They had an hour before the lightning cages would be charged again, and she wanted some time to herself. She wandered through the silent galleria, past shops that were shuttered and empty. The place would be busy enough when real trade came through, but right now they were the only ship around. Hardly worth turning up the lights for. It didn't matter. She was glad to be alone.

Her thoughts tumbled over and over in her head, as she replayed the conversation she'd overheard on the bridge and the dream that the woman had described to her father. As she tried to fit the pieces together. It all seemed to come back to something called a seed, and to the girl. A girl that she was connected to, somehow, though her father hadn't seemed eager to let Abasi or Milima know about that detail.

As she stepped out onto the docks the wind began to pick up, turning the warm air chill, and she suddenly wished she had worn more than just a thin blouse. She rubbed her arms and considered slipping back inside when she saw a lone figure standing out on an empty dock, leaning across the railing. Even in the glare of the sunlight she recognised her father's thin frame. He wore his old greatcoat which whipped around him, snapping in the breeze. As she watched, he leaned forward to rest his forehead against clenched knuckles. He seemed tired, worn thin, like a shirt so badly frayed that it was holding together by its last few stitches.

Forgetting the cold, she began to walk towards him. He didn't even seem to notice her approach until she leaned against the railing beside him. His head turned slightly, and he blinked in surprise.

"Arsha," he said, surprised.

"Hey Daddy," she said as she leaned out over the railing. Seeing the goosebumps on her arms, he pulled his coat around her shoulders, covering them both. Neither of them seemed to know what else to say. They stood together, staring out at the endless ocean, the wind whipping at their hair. Eventually the breeze died down and the sun began to warm the air again.

Tucked away in the pocket of her blouse, Penny stirred. The little bird wriggled out of her hidey hole and hopped down onto Arsha's arm, chirping lightly. With her typical curiosity, Penny began hop from spot to spot, moving down Arsha's sleeve before jumping across onto her father's arm.

"Hello," he said, a little surprised. "Shouldn't you be inside?"

"She likes the breeze," Arsha said, stroking Penny's head lightly.

"Does she now?"

He shook his head, with a distant look.

"You've had her a while now... Back in Avanen, that was where you bought her, right? That ridiculous vendor with all his automs. I swear you fell in love with that bird the moment he put her in your hands."

Arsha smiled at the memory.

"Yeah. I couldn't bear to give her back. She's too beautiful."

"Yes, I remember you handed over every coin you had. I had to argue the salesman down just so you could afford her."

"Liar. I saw you slip him the rest of the money after I was walking away."

"You really saw that? Arsha, you're too sharp for me, I swear."

She saw him smile. It was only a moment, something fleeting that seemed to pass through him, vanishing as quickly as it came. Already she could see that he was looking past her, past the ocean and the horizon, to something only he could see. She could almost feel the weight that seemed to be pressing down on him.

"Daddy... Are you OK?"

It took so long for him to say anything that she wondered if he simply hadn't heard her.

"No. I'm not OK, love," he said, at last. He moved his hand to cover hers, and squeezed it tight. "There are some things I have to put right, some things that I've been running from for a very long time."

"Is that... Is that why you have to find her? The girl, in London?"

For a moment he was taken aback, his eyes widening as he turned to look at her. Then his shoulders fell.

"You heard us arguing, up on the bridge."

She nodded.

"Arsha, love, I'm sorry. I didn't mean for..."

For a moment he seemed to be looking past her again, his thoughts turning inward. Then he shook his head sadly as his eyes fixed on hers, his expression earnest.

"Arsha, I didn't mean for you to be caught up in any of this. Believe me, I wouldn't even have brought you along if not for... I'd just rather keep you close right now. For your safety. I know you must have a lot of questions, and I'll try to answer them all eventually, but now isn't the time. I can't keep you away from this, but I don't want you to be a part of it. I'm sorry."

She couldn't hold his gaze. Turning away, nervousness twisting in her stomach, she bit her lip and held her breath. Her body felt tight, like a wire stretched to breaking point.

"But I am a part of it... Aren't I?"

"Arsha, what do you mean?"

Hardly able to breathe, she reached into her pocket with one trembling hand, and produced his sending stone. She could barely look at him. Still, she caught the way his expression shifted from surprise to a cold, dark fury.

"Arsha, what have you done?"

"I'm sorry," she whispered, holding out the stone. He made no move to take it.

"Arsha, I have to know... Just how much did you see? Just what exactly did you..."

He seemed scarcely able to draw a breath, he was so angry. She could see the way his shoulders trembled.

"Arsha, what did you see?"

She tightened her grip on the railing, sure that it was the only thing keeping her standing. For a moment her mouth moved silently, as she tried to find the words, any words at all.

"That woman... The dream that she told you about. About the seed, and me, and that girl."

He squeezed his eyes shut, his head tilting back a little.

"Fates, Arsha... Of all the stupid things you could have done..."

"I'm so sorry, Daddy. I didn't mean to make you mad..."

He opened his eyes again, looking at her with a horrified expression.

"Arsha... Fates, Arsha... I'm not angry, I'm terrified. What you've done... Knowing this... Do you have any idea how much danger you've put yourself in? Why do you think I didn't even want to tell Abasi and Milima about this? Why do you think they still don't know just how I got access to that prediction? Do you have any idea how dangerous that information could be?"

He took her by the shoulders, leaning in close.

"Arsha you must never tell anyone about what you saw. Not a single soul. Not our friends, not the others on the ship... Do you understand me? Forget about this, forget you ever saw it."

For a moment she felt as if she couldn't breathe. Her throat seemed to have closed up.

"Daddy, stop it," she whispered. "You're scaring me."

"I know, sweetheart, I know, but this is for your own safety," he said, still holding her by the shoulders, not letting her move or turn away.

"But I'm not safe, am I? Even if I hadn't found out about any of this, I'd still be connected to this girl, to this thing with the seed, and I don't understand why you won't tell me why. How can I be safe, when I don't even know what to be safe from?"

"It's better that you don't know. Fates, Arsha, what even possessed you to go prying into all of this?"

Feeling a sudden rush of anger, she pushed his hands away and took a step back.

"Because no one will tell me anything. Because everyone has all these secrets and I can't stand it. You're supposed to be my dad. You're supposed to dig up rocks and get excited about flood plains and erosion. You're not supposed to do stuff like this, and I can't understand why everyone is just OK with it."

With a heavy sigh he let his arms fall to his sides, everything about him seeming exhausted, helpless.

"I don't know," he said.

"That's it. You don't know?"

He turned to look out over the endless grey ocean, leaning his weight against the railing.

"I suppose it's because they trust me. Honestly, I don't know if I deserve that trust. I've been a very poor friend to Abasi and Milima lately. And not much of a father to you. I have to try to make up for that."

He turned to look at her again, with a solemn expression.

"Do you trust me, Arsha?"

For a moment the wind picked up, flicking a few loose strands of her hair into her eyes. She angrily pulled them aside.

"Of course I trust you," she said, feeling the words catching at her throat. "You're my dad."

She saw the way his hands tightened around the railing. Saw the sadness in his eyes.

"That's all I can ask," he said. "And when the time is right, I will explain everything. I promise."

Her throat felt dry. She nodded.

"OK. But..." she paused, her stomach twisting. "I want to talk to her."

"Who?"

He looked puzzled.

"Rachael. That was her name. That's what that lady said. I want to talk to her."

He pushed a hand through his hair.

"Arsha, love, she's a world away from us, and the other side of the Veil. You can't."

Fixing him with her stare, Arsha kept her mouth pressed into a hard, thin line.

"You'll know a way. You always do."

For a moment, he was silent. She could feel him turning something over in his mind. His eyes closed and he let out a breath.

"OK," he said.

They chose the cargo hold for the task. Arsha sat on the floor, surrounded by as wide an empty space as they had been able to clear. Above her the ship's launch rested in its cradle, waiting to emerge onto the deck when it was required. Crates and barrels had been pulled aside, stacked against the walls with ropes and netting. Micah and Abasi were securing the last few loads as the preparations for the ritual began. Both men were quiet, their expressions uneasy. Her father had told them all a little of what they were doing. Just enough to fend off any further questions.

Milima walked around her in a slow circle, pouring out finely crushed salt from her hand. It formed a series of broken rings, each contained inside the next, joined by strange symbols. Arsha could hear the woman whispering under her breath, but could not make out the words.

Her father stood at a distance, watching with an uneasy expression. Beside him Ilona stood with her hands folded in front of her, her stiff formality giving away just how nervous the woman was.

In the dim light of the hold she found herself studying the details of Milima's tattoos as if seeing them anew, though she knew them all by heart. She wondered if there was some connection between the swirling patterns of the tattoos and the sigil on which she was sat, painted on the floor of the hold in some kind of dye. It was still slightly damp.

Finished with the crates he had been securing, Abasi walked to where her father was standing and laid a gentle hand on the man's shoulder.

"Rishi, you are sure about this?" he said.

Her father nodded.

"I know, Abasi, I know. But it's what Arsha wanted... And there's no danger. If we're going to find this girl, talking to her really is the best place to start. I imagine all of this will be very shocking to her, and we have to gain her trust somehow. I wouldn't have suggested it if Arsha hadn't, but..."

Abasi said nothing, but in his eyes Arsha could see that he was holding back a good many questions. Questions he didn't want to ask in front of her.

Milima finished pouring and nodded at Ilona, who stepped forward and set herself down, across the circle from Arsha. The woman was wearing a black dress, trimmed in silver lace, and Arsha found herself suddenly worried that it would be damaged by all the salt.

Ilona looked into her eyes, her gaze calm and steady, but the woman didn't say a word. Then Milima knelt beside them.

"OK, Arsha, are you ready?" Milima said.

She nodded.

"Good. I'm going to lead you both. Ilona will create the link for you. What you have to do is enter into a place of sharing. You're going to share your mind with Rachael's, and it's going to be difficult, because she isn't prepared for this. Normally, you would be sharing with someone who was ready to receive your thoughts. This is different. And it won't be anything like a normal sending."

"How do you know all this?" she asked. She couldn't help it. Milima smiled, and ran her fingers across the lines of her tattoo.

"I'm a Herdlander, remember? There are many things we know that the Guild would rather we didn't. I first learned the linking ritual when I was a little younger than you are. Of course, it was a lot longer before I lead one."

"Why don't people talk about Herdlanders knowing magic?"

"Mostly because we don't call it that. These were the ways taught to us by the Man of Many Faces. The Guild wants to call it magic, because the Guild is afraid of anything it can't understand. For our part, we keep our practices to ourselves, and try to avoid antagonising them. We have enough trouble in our lands, without giving the Guild any more reasons to distrust us."

Arsha turned to look at Ilona.

"Then, where did you learn?"

Ilona gave her a quiet smile.

"I'm just as new to this as you are, Arsha," she said, "but the ritual needs three parts; the leader, the speaker, and the power. That's me."

"Why you?"

Ilona did not answer, though her quiet smile seemed to waver, just for a moment.

"Well, if we're ready..." Milima said.

Arsha turned to look up at the woman and nodded. Ilona simply tilted her head very slightly and closed her eyes.

"Now, I want you to start by breathing very slowly," Milima instructed in calm, even tones. As she spoke, she placed two small bowls on either side of the circle, their contents smoking slightly. The smoke had a sweet, spicy aroma, and it filled her nose and her lungs as she took deep breaths.

"Now reach out and take Ilona's hands. Feel her power, flowing into you, through you, and back into her."

Arsha reached out, felt Ilona's slim fingers interweaving with hers, their hands clenching tightly together. There was a reassuring solidity to Ilona's grip.

"Clear your mind. There is only an empty sky before you. A mask hangs in the sky. See the mask."

Milima's voice was steady, her tone gentle, leading her forward step by step.

"The mask is the colour of the sky. It settles on your face. You become the mask."

Her eyes closed, she pictured the mask settling on her face.

"The mask is around you, in you. You are the mask. Your eyes are closed now, but soon you will open them. Your new eyes will open and you will see differently."

Her whole body felt light, as if she was floating in that open blue sky.

"There is a thread, stretching all the way out to another world. That thread begins in your heart, and stretches out into the sky. Feel the thread. Feel it tremble with every heart-beat. Another heart beats at the other end of that thread. Can you feel that heart-beat?"

"I can feel it," Arsha said, her voice catching in her throat. It was astonishing how real it felt, the sound of that other heartbeat intertwining with her own.

"When you open your eyes, your hearts will beat as one, and you will be a part of one another. You will speak to her thoughts, and she will speak to yours. When you open your eyes, all this will be gone. You are a vapour now, but when you open your eyes you will become real. Open your eyes."

Arsha did as she was instructed. She caught a brief flicker of the dark wooden walls of the cargo hold and the ghostlamps hanging overhead, but already it was fading as her new surroundings seemed to fall into place.

A rooftop, one of many amongst the tall buildings that surrounded her. Grey streets filled with strange vehicles. Red bricks, stained black by smoke. Sounds of people and the thunder of engines.

The girl was sat across from her, resting against some kind of silver-grey metal container. Her clothes were worn and stained, the designs strange. She had a pretty face under the tangle of blonde hair that shaded her eyes, skin pale like Ilona's. The girl's legs were out in front of her, and her eyes were closed. She looked desperately tired.

Arsha realised that she had no idea what to do now.

"Um... Hi?" she said, with a nervous smile.

Chapter 7 - Shadow

Rachael sat on the rooftop, huddled in her jacket, staring out over the city with dead eyes. Barely visible through the wall of cloud, the sun was just beginning to descend towards the horizon.

After their narrow escape from the construction site they had been constantly on the move. Rachael had slept little, and she had a feeling that Justin was sleeping even less. Food had been scarce, with both of them unable to risk returning to their usual haunts. Every time the sun set, Justin had repeated his strange ritual, drawing the mark in blood on her forehead. To keep them from following her, he claimed. Each time she watched him pierce his thumb with that knife blade she felt a chill run through her body, but arguing had been pointless.

Even running was beginning to seem pointless. She was tired. Tired of everything. Tired of being cold and hungry. Tired of being frightened. Tired of watching the few remaining pieces of her life fall apart. She felt like an insect with its legs being pulled off one by one.

She let her head fall back against the ventilator duct. It was cold outside and the air felt damp, like it would rain again soon. She wondered when Justin would be back from whatever he was doing. Scouting, he had called it. Finding out more about the people who were after them. She wondered if it would really do any good. If anything would. She just wanted him to be back. She just wanted to sleep. Her eyes began to drift closed.

The sound of a voice woke her. Rachael's eyes flicked open and she looked up. Sitting across from her was a girl of about her own age. Her skin was dark, and her black hair was tied up in a ponytail.

"Sorry, sorry, I didn't mean to scare you," the girl exclaimed, holding up her hands.

"Who the hell are you?" Rachael snapped in surprise. As the shock passed, she gave the girl another look over. She was curiously dressed, in baggy green trousers and high topped leather boots, with a loosely fitted white tunic.

"I'm Arsha. You're Rachael, right?"

The girl turned her head to look around, with an awe-struck expression.

"Wow... So this is London? I mean I'd heard about it, but... I've never seen a Hearth city before. It's so different."

"Who the hell are you?" Rachael snapped, "How'd you know who I am? You following me too?"

"No, no, I just... Someone was following you?" the girl said.

"That's cute," Rachael said, halfway to her feet. "Act like you don't know."

"Don't know what? What happened?"

Rachael shook her head in astonishment. She got to her feet, striding forwards to stand over the girl, her fists clenched at her sides. Arsha looked up at her with a trace of nervousness in her eyes.

"What the hell is this? What's your deal, Arsha? Why are you here talking to me, if you're not one of them what was trying to run us down the other night?"

"It's OK, it's OK," the girl said, holding up her hands. "I'm here to help."

"Right. And I should believe you because...?"

The girl looked completely at a loss. After a moment she just shrugged, helplessly, her eyes downcast.

"Yeah, you're not convincing anyone here," Rachael said.

"I'm sorry. I've never done this sort of thing before. My dad could explain better, but he can't talk to you like this, so it kind of had to be me. Sorry."

"And what's your dad got to do with this?" Rachael said. She had to admit that curiosity was overcoming her now. Arsha seemed so pathetically helpless that Rachael couldn't imagine the girl was any threat. But at the same time, there was something about the way that she sat there, with her legs folded under herself, totally defenceless, that suggested she was either very cool headed or entirely sure that she was in no danger.

"Well he's an archaeologist. We live on a ship, called the Triskelion. It's small, but it's nice. We're on our way to London right now. That's why I'm talking to you like this. My dad wanted to let you know that we're coming to find you. We're going to keep you safe from those guys who were chasing you, and anyone else."

"Yeah, that's great. So I need you to keep me safe now, do I?"

"Sorry, I didn't mean it like that. I just mean..." Arsha paused for a moment, as if trying to collect herself. "We're coming to help. That's why my dad wanted me to talk to you, to let you know that... That we're coming to help," she finished, limply.

"Sure. How's it I have a hard time believing that? And if your dad's out there on this ship, how's it you're here talking to me?"

Arsha looked puzzled for a moment.

"Well, I'm not really here, obviously. I mean, this is just... Well it's sort of like a sending, I guess."

When the girl stretched a hand out towards her leg, Rachael

stepped back instinctively, Arsha's hand passing through the space where she had just been. In that same moment, moving on instinct, Rachael reached down to snatch at Arsha's collar, meaning to haul the girl to her feet.

But when her hand met the girl's tunic, it passed straight through. Straight through her whole body, as if there was nothing there at all.

"I'm sorry," Arsha squeaked. "I just meant to show you it was a sending, was all."

Rachael heard the words as a kind of distant buzzing. The girl was still sitting in front of her, seeming in every possible way to be real. Or almost every way. Already she could see how the breeze didn't quite seem to touch the girl's hair. How she had felt nothing when the girl's hand passed so close to her.

"No. No, no, no, don't be this, don't be this," she mumbled, feeling the words collapsing into each other. Rachael staggered back a step, and fell down against the ventilator duct. The metal thundered with the impact. She felt her knees curling up to her chest, felt herself collapsing down into a place deep inside, like a seed in the darkness. Distantly, she heard the girl's voice, shrill with concern, but already she knew that it was just her imagination. Her eyes were closed tight as she repeated the words over and over, until they became a buzzing noise, blocking out everything else. Her heart thundered in her chest as she drew rapid breaths. Her desperate prayer echoed through her thoughts, trying to wish the world away.

Arsha felt the link break, like a glass shattering in her hands. The rooftop became a jumbled blur, a whirlwind of flickering images that spiralled apart to leave her floating in darkness. Arsha tried to call out, to tell the girl it was OK, but Rachael was already gone. The comforting darkness suddenly felt strange and frightening. She seemed to be tumbling, falling, though there was no sense of an up or down. She called out again and heard a voice answer. Milima's voice, calm and steady.

"Let it go, Arsha. Let it go. Close your eyes, take a breath and slowly remove the mask."

She forced herself to breathe. She imagined her eyes closing. Felt her fingertips brush her face, brush the edges of the imaginary mask.

"Feel yourself returning. The mask floats away. The thread is gone."

Her body seemed as light as a feather.

"Open your eyes."

There was a sensation like a sudden movement, as the ship fell into place around her. For a moment she was surprised to feel the floor underneath herself. Dizzy, she nearly toppled over.

"Careful sweetheart," Milima said, her calm tones breaking into bemused laughter. Her hand gently supported Arsha's shoulder.

Arsha sat up, her head spinning. Everything was exactly as it had been. Milima was looking into her eyes with concern as Arsha shook off the headrush. Sat across from her, Ilona's eyes were still closed, her breathing deep and slow.

"Are you all there?" Milima said, leaning in close to study her eyes.

"Yeah. I'm OK," she said, casting a worried glance over at Ilona. Their hands were still entwined, though Ilona's grip had slackened.

"Give her a moment," Milima said. "It's different, being the power."

Ilona's eyes slowly fluttered open, as if she was awakening from a very deep sleep.

"Are you OK?" Arsha said, unable to keep the worry from her voice.

Ilona nodded, releasing Arsha's hands.

"What about you," her father said, stepping closer to the circle. "Are you OK, love?"

"Yeah, I'm fine, it's just.. I think I messed up. I talked to her but..."

He held up a hand to silence her.

"Tell me in a moment. You're sure you're OK?"

Arsha nodded.

"So, when do we get to find out who this mystery girl is?" Milima said, pointedly.

"In time," her father said. "Thank you all for your help, but I really should talk to Arsha alone now."

Milima stood and gave her shoulder a squeeze. Then she held out a hand to Ilona. Ignoring it, the woman tried to stand, but her legs wouldn't seem to take her weight. Milima caught her just in time, and gently lifted her upright. Abasi and Micah followed the women out, without a word spoken between them. The door closed and Arsha was alone with her father.

She realised that she was still sitting cross legged on the floor. Her legs felt numb.

With deliberate care, her father extinguished the smoking bowls with handfuls of sand. Then he stopped just in front of her and held out his hand. She took it, unsure of what his silence meant. Carefully he lead her out of the circle. Only when she had crossed the outer ring did he let go.

She looked up at him, not quite sure what to say as he leaned back against a nearby crate.

"You did well," he said, at last.

"Thanks," she said. It felt a little awkward, just standing there, so she hopped up onto a barrel, her heels making a knocking sound.

"What did you make of her?"

"Rachael?"

He nodded.

"I don't know. She was angry and scared and... I don't know. Confused? Like she didn't really know what was happening. She said that people had been chasing her."

She saw him frown, saw the concern in his eyes, but he said nothing.

"And there was... It was weird, it looked like she had something drawn on her forehead. It was mostly covered by her hair, but it was some kind of symbol. It might have been done with blood."

"I don't know if I should be worried or happy about that. It sounds like someone is trying to hide her. It certainly explains a lot."

"Hide her? How?"

"Well, it could be a ward. A kind of small spell that conceals someone's Fate, for a little while. I had been trying to trace her with a number of, uh, old tricks that I know. This is the first time we've had been able to make any kind of contact though."

"What does that mean?"

He gave a heavy sigh, and looked at her sadly.

"It means I may need your help again before all of this is done. Whatever connection you have to this girl, it might be the only thing that can get through that ward."

Arsha swallowed, and nodded.

"We have to help her. She's all alone."

"We will," he said. "You did well, sweetheart. I'm proud of you."

He slipped one arm around her shoulders and placed a gentle kiss against her forehead.

"Go rest, pet. You'll be tired after the ritual."

She was, desperately tired. The nervous tension of the last few days seemed to be crashing in on her like a tidal wave. Her legs had gone to jelly, and she wasn't even sure she could walk back to her room.

Her father seemed to sense what she was feeling. In a single motion he scooped her up, and she pulled herself tightly to him as he carried her back to her room. She felt as if years had fallen away from her and she was a small child again, bundled up in her Daddy's arms.

Rachael heard the way his footsteps smacked across the tar-paper roof as he ran to her side. She felt Justin's hands around her shoulders, heard the trembling in his voice.

"Rachael, what happened? Are you OK? What happened?"

Angrily, she pushed him aside, jumping to her feet.

"Get away from me!"

"Rachael, what's wrong?"

"Just get away," she repeated, her voice raw.

"What happened?"

He was on his feet again, eyes wide with concern. She turned away.

"It don't matter. It wasn't real."

She started to walk away, not wanting to see his face any more. Unable to bear that look of pity.

"What? Rachael, what wasn't real? What did you see?"

Anger flared inside her as she wheeled about to face him, eyes full of fury.

"Would you just stop? Stop acting like this is normal. Like it's OK for me to be seeing things that aren't here, like it's normal for all of this to be happening. I don't know what your deal is, playing along like all of this makes sense, but I know what I am."

At last, she saw his sympathetic mask crack, if only a little. Saw the way his fists clenched at his sides, the way his lip curled into a sneer.

"What? What are you?" he shot back. "Why don't you tell me?"

"You want me say it?" she shouted, taking a step toward him. "I'm crazy. Messed up in the head. A total nutjob. You hear me? Drugs, doctors, the whole deal. You think this is new? I've known about this all my life, and you trying to act like it's not all in my head is the opposite of helping."

She expected him to get angry, shout back at her, lose what was left of his cool. She wanted to see that mask shatter. But in his eyes she saw only sadness. He reached out to rest a hand on her shoulder.

"Rachael, I don't believe that for a minute."

"Yeah, well maybe you're crazy too," she said, pushing his hand away.

"You actually think that? You think that all of this is just in our heads?"

As he reached for her again she took a step back, eyes narrowing.

"Just who the hell are you, anyway? You keep acting like you want to look out for me, but I don't know nothing about you. Who are you really, Justin?"

She took another step back, her weight settling on the balls of her feet. Ready to fight, or to run. He didn't come any closer. He just stood there and watched her with those sad eyes.

"I'm here to protect you, Rachael. That's the truth. I was sent to keep you safe, by someone who cares about you very much," he said.

"Right. Because there's anyone out there that cares about me."

"Your mother does."

The words felt like a shard of ice stabbing into her gut. Eyes narrowed, she looked at him with a cold rage.

"That's not funny," she said.

"It's the truth," he said, with an unearthly calm.

Her laughter was a sick and bitter thing, rising up like bile in her throat.

"My mum's dead, you asshole."

"No, she's not. The woman who sent me here, she's your real mother, and she's been searching for you for a long time," he said. "Rachael, your whole life, you've been lied to. Whatever family you knew was just an illusion. A trick. You never belonged in this world. It was just a cage they put you in."

"This world? What are you even talking about?"

"Everything. Everything you've ever known, this whole world, this whole universe is just a speck in the Dreaming. There are thousands of worlds out there, worlds where anything is possible. That's where your mother is waiting for you. Far out into the Deep Wild, where your father imprisoned her after he stole you away. That's why she sent me, to keep you safe, to bring you home."

"Justin, what the hell is this?"

"It's magic, Rachael," he said, with a resigned sigh. "That's what this is. Magic and gods and monsters, and all the other things I didn't want to talk to you about, because I knew you'd look at me just like you're looking at me now."

She could feel her breath growing short as she looked into his eyes and saw the conviction there, the unbending, unyielding force of his absolute belief.

"Jesus," she said, her voice barely more than a whisper, "you really are crazy. You actually believe all this. That I'm some kinda magic princess, and it's all up to you to save me? Do you even know how insane this sounds?"

He took a step forwards, reaching out towards her.

"Of course I do. Rachael, I know this isn't easy for you to believe, but you have to trust me," he said.

Her eyes narrowed, as she studied his.

"No. I really don't," she said. She could feel her hands shaking as she turned and walked away.

"Rachael, stop," he called out, but she ignored him. She expected him to come running after her, but the only thing she heard was a flutter of wings. Then something flashed in front of her face. A dark streak, blurred with motion. She thought it looked like a raven.

She glanced back for a second, but saw no sign of him. Then she looked up to see the bird wheel around in front of her. With a sudden turn it swooped down. She skidded to a halt as the bird spread its wings to hang, suspended, in the air before her. In her alarm she stumbled and fell backwards onto the ground, as the raven flew over her. Then, seeming to play out in one long and flowing movement, though it couldn't have been more than a heartbeat, the bird disintegrated. Its body became a cloud of oily black smoke, bursting outwards in a liquid motion. The smoke moved like it was alive, roiling and shifting to take on a larger form, a body framed with cape-like wings. Then it condensed down, the wings becoming the tails of his long coat as Justin's body formed from the smoke.

He fell with catlike grace to land on the balls of his feet, splayed fingers of one hand catching the ground. He was poised above her with a predatory look in his eyes.

Her heart thundered in her chest, and her breath caught in her throat. She was transfixed by his glare as her brain scrambled to comprehend what she had just seen.

She laughed. It seemed like the only sensible thing to do. It was so impossible, so ludicrous. Like the entire universe had decided to play a cruel joke. For a moment he seemed taken aback, unsure of how to react. It didn't take long for her bitter laughter to turn to screaming, as she felt a wave of cold terror seize her. Hands clawed at him as she squirmed away. A foot lashed out and he reeled backwards. Halfway to her feet, she stumbled towards the edge of the rooftop. Laughing, sobbing, she gasped for air, feeling as if she was trying to breathe underwater. Hands fumbled in the depths of her bag, finally closing around the plastic pill bottle. Justin stood and crossed the roof to her in three long strides. Her fingers shook as she tried to prise the cap loose. Then he snatched the bottle from her hands.

"Did they tell you this would help?" he snarled, gesturing with the clear orange container. "That if you took the pills and closed your eyes, all the scary things would go away?"

Feebly, she tried to pull it from his grasp, but he turned and hurled it from the rooftop. Heart pounding, she rolled away from him, stumbling to her feet.

"What... What the hell are you?" she said, struggling to breathe. She could feel her pulse pounding, feel the world shaking, as if someone had turned up the volume on everything. The sound of the city, the wind, the car engines, it all seemed to thunder in her ears, a cacophony of noise.

Slowly, he turned to face her again. She saw his features soften, saw the anger fading from him, but all she could think of was the blood glistening bright red on the blade of his knife.

"I'm someone who cares about you. Shouldn't that be enough? I'm asking you to trust me, Rachael. Haven't I earned that?"

"Get away from me," she said. She almost felt as if she was

choking on her own words. "Just... Get away."

She stumbled back a step.

"Rachael, wait," he called out to her, a fading note of command in his voice. She stared at him, horrified. "I'm sorry that I scared you. I just needed to show you it was real. It's all real. You've been telling yourself a lie, all this time."

She saw the pleading look in his eyes, but she felt only disgust. She turned and ran, dropping down from the rooftop into the alleyway below. Just once she glanced across her shoulder to see him watching from above, but he did not follow. Down in the street she found the plastic bottle, lying in a puddle. The cap had shattered. The last few tablets were dissolving in the rainwater.

Chapter 8 - Lights

Rachael walked with her head held low, as the lights from the cars washed over her in the darkness. Far below her feet the trains thundered on, a low rumble reverberating upwards through her body. Empty cans and crisp packets crunched beneath her heels, and she heard shouted laughter in the distance.

London never slept. She had spent countless nights walking the city streets alone like this, and always there was the light, the movement and the thunderous sound. The heat of bodies pressed together, the sudden turn of laughter to violence, the smell of vomit, piss and beer. At night the pulse of the city seemed louder, more palpable. It was an animal thing that grunted and howled in the dark.

Her feet ached. It had been two days since the rooftop. Two days since she'd left Justin. She'd been wandering aimlessly, not really caring where she went, or where she ended up. Just the shape of the pavement beneath her heels and the sounds of the city enclosing her from every side. Even as night fell she kept moving, trying to outpace her thoughts as the sky blackened with heavy clouds.

When the park gates loomed out of the darkness, she was barely surprised at where her wandering feet had taken her. Though the streets and apartments of her old neighbourhood looked altogether the same, the park seemed worse for wear. Perhaps she simply imagined that it had not been so thoroughly strewn with glass and dog-leavings when she had been here last. Perhaps it was only her memory of the place that seemed brighter and cleaner than where she now stood. How much could it have changed, in a little more than a year?

She wandered across to the swings and sat down, hearing the familiar creak of the rubber, the groan of the metal frame as it shifted under her weight. She tilted her head back and looked up into a starless sky.

No, not starless. Not entirely. A single point of light hung suspended above her. For a moment it seemed as if her vision was swimming, until she realised that it was drifting from side to side, coming closer, growing brighter. She leaned forward as it fell, like a dandelion puff, but glowing like a firefly. It was a tiny thing with no discernible form. Just a ball of light. It came to rest in her cupped palms. She felt only a very slight warmth. It seemed to hover just over the skin. She looked up, and saw more lights begin to appear. Hundreds, thousands, all drifting down across the sky.

The memory came to her so suddenly that she felt an overwhelming sense of vertigo. Maybe five or six years old, she had come out into the very same park at night, only to see a thousand of the tiny drifting lights, like the one she held in her hands. When she'd caught one to bring home, her mother had told her how nice it was. It was only later that she'd really heard the way her mum had said the words; an adult playing along with a child's game. She had never seen the little light.

That had been a long time ago. Before the drugs and the doctors. Before the nights spent curled inside a blanket, screaming into the darkness.

She stared at the little glowing light, feeling wave after wave of memory wash over her. It was like a river, deep and dark, and beneath that surface she knew there was something else lurking. Something she didn't want to contemplate.

"It's a ghostlight. They slip through, sometimes. From the other side."

Startled, she pulled her hands away, letting the tiny light fall. She looked up, and saw him standing by the gate to the park. The hem of his coat brushed the grass. Her shoulders tensed.

"I'm sorry. I know you told me to stay away. It's just... That's not a choice I get to make," Justin said.

"The hell do you mean?" she said, her voice coming out as little more than a hiss.

"Just what I said. Whether you want me here or not, this is where I have to be. I'm sorry."

"You think... What... That if you just keep following me, I'll give up and pretend nothing happened? You think you're going to show me how much you care, just by not listening when I tell you to get lost?"

He shook his head.

"No. That's not it at all. If you don't want me around, I'll respect that. If you tell me, right now, that you never want to see me again... You won't. Not ever. But I'll be watching. I'll be there to keep you safe. Always."

"Are you sick in the head? Why would anyone do that? What do you think you're gonna prove?"

He shrugged, helplessly.

"I made a promise. To keep you safe, no matter what. Even if you hate me, even if you don't want me."

"Well, take your promise and stuff it. You don't owe me nothing."

He shook his head.

"It wasn't a promise I made to you."

Curious, she studied his eyes, trying to see some sign that he was leading her on. He seemed, as always, completely and entirely sincere.

"This is crazy," she said, shaking her head. Then she looked up at the soft little lights, drifting down all around them. "I'm crazy."

She heard his footsteps on the grass as he walked towards her, slowly, giving her time. Time to run. He held out a hand to catch one of the tiny lights, letting it rest in his palm. A ghostlight, he'd called it. When he was standing a few paces from the swings, he held out the ghostlight towards her.

"Rachael... I know what you're dealing with. Believe me, I do. Because I took the pills, and I went to the sessions, and I learned how to pretend I was normal. Just like you did. Because for years I let them tell me that the world is dull, ugly and grey. That everything mad and impossible and beautiful could only be something I'd imagined. That I could only be crazy, to see a world that was more than just... Ordinary. It's a lie, Rachael. It's all a lie. There truly is magic in this world."

He stepped closer and reached out to take her hand. Gently, he pressed the ghostlight into her open palm.

"I came here to take you away from this. To show you where ghostlights grow."

She lowered her eyes, looking into the soft little light in her palm. Then she raised her hand, pressed her lips together and blew out a sharp puff of air. The tiny ball of light shot out of her hands, dancing off into the sky like a dandelion seed. Watching it go, she couldn't help but smile, if only for a moment.

She turned away, unable to meet his eyes. The rusted metal frame of the swing groaned in protest as she sat down again. A moment later, he took a seat beside her. Together they listened to the sounds of the city, and the jumbled melody of chains and springs moving gently in the wind.

"I used to pretend I was flying," she said, speaking to the open air. "There's that moment, when you get to the top of the swing, just before you come down, when it feels like it. Like you're flying."

She looked over at Justin.

"But I suppose you don't have to pretend."

She swallowed.

"Why didn't you... You know... Show me that, before?"

"Because I was afraid you'd react..."

"Like I did?"

"Yeah."

"So, what, you were waiting for me to be ready? I mean, as if I'd ever be ready for that."

"It's more than that. The things I can do... They can be followed, by people who know how. Like the men who are after you."

"Who were those guys anyhow? And what do they want with me?"

"There's a power in you, Rachael. In your mother's blood. Those men want to control that power. Make you a prisoner. They've come from another world, from beyond the Veil, just to find you."

"Beyond the veil? What's that supposed to mean then?"

"It means... It means other worlds. Endless, impossible worlds that you couldn't even imagine."

"So these guys are, like, aliens or something?"

"No, they're human, just like us. They're people who left this world a very long time ago."

"How's that even possible? I mean, we've barely got, like, rocket ships and stuff now."

"It's not like that. I'm not talking about, y'know, other planets and stuff. I mean worlds, like... Worlds. Everything. Whole universes. Like, have you ever had a dream where you were someplace else, and everything was different? Even simple things like gravity?"

"I guess."

"Well, what if that was a real place? What if you could go there, just by stepping through a door? That's the kind of place they come from."

"Just by stepping through a door?"

"Sort of. It's a bit more complicated than that."

"Are they the only ones? These guys that are following us?"

"Maybe?" He shrugged. "I don't know. There could be more."

"So with the changing, you didn't want to be too... Loud. I guess?"

"Right. And it's difficult. Beyond the Veil, changing is easier. But here, in this world... It takes so much strength to reshape yourself like that, and all of that strength has to come from somewhere. This world is so dead to magic. It takes everything just to turn into a tiny little bird."

"You can turn into other things? Bigger things?"

He nodded.

"If there's power to draw on..." He turned his eyes upwards. "Much bigger."

"Oh."

She looked out over the park, feeling the surreal emptiness of the place. Her eyes settled on an old merry-go-round, the paint peeling from the rusted metal.

"Come on," she said, as she dropped down from the swing.

She grabbed the handle and began to push. For a moment he just stared at her with a vague look of bewilderment. Then, with a half-hearted shrug, he grabbed the other handle and they pushed together. The dry axle resisted at first, but soon they were moving, chasing each other around the circle as the merry-go-round emitted a metallic squeal. They went faster and faster, until the movement of the wheel was pulling her along. Barely able to keep up, she ran a few more steps and then pulled herself aboard. Justin ran with it for a little longer before jumping aboard. Huddled in the centre, they both held tight to the bars as the world spun around them. She leaned her head back and grinned at him. He smiled back, something utterly joyful bursting through from inside. For a moment it seemed as if the whole world just fell away and there was only that smile. Just for her.

The merry-go-round began to slow, and she loosened her grip.

They sat back to back, resting their heads against the post at the centre of the wheel, feet spread out in front of them. The wind was picking up, rattling the chains on the swings and climbing frames. Dead leaves skated across the grass, making little pirouettes as they danced. Every now and then the merry-go-round creaked beneath them.

"Did you really come to protect me?"

"To protect you. To bring you home."

"And if I don't want to go wherever this home is?"

"Then I'll be by your side, wherever you do want to go."

Through the bars, her hand found his. His grip was firm and sure.

"Justin... Who are you, really?" she whispered.

"I told you who I am," he said.

"My knight in shining armour. Right. Except you forgot your horse and all."

For a while, he didn't say a word. She could hear the sound of his breathing, feel the slight movement of his shoulder against hers.

She turned away, and pulled her hand back from his.

"Justin, I can't do it. I can't believe in all this like you want me to. This is crazy, and it don't matter how much I try to tell myself it isn't, because I know, I just know..."

She felt the platform wobble as he stepped off. His feet crunched against the wood chips as he walked around to stand in front of her. Slowly, almost solemnly, he knelt in front of her and reached out to take her hand again, pressing it between his own. He leaned in close, his wide brown eyes locked on hers, and she found herself becoming all too aware of the sound of her heartbeat, thundering against her chest.

"Everyone believes in something, Rachael. This is what they taught you to believe in; this ugly, grey world that they called 'Normal.' Tell me, is it better there?"

A grey door filled her mind, still part-way open. A glimpse of a beige carpet, streaked with cigarette burns. The world they had made her live in.

She shook her head.

"No. No, it's not."

"Then come live in mine. If we're wrong, at least we're happy. And if we're right, we'll fly above them all."

For a moment, all she could see was his eyes. He was close enough that she could feel his breath in the air, and she barely even noticed herself resting one hand, lightly, on his arm. Her lips were dry. Without really thinking about it, she stroked his hair back.

Then she heard the sound of footsteps on the grass.

They sat up together and looked around to see the men closing in from every side, a loose circle forming around them. Shapes in the darkness, beginning to take on definition as they emerged into the pools of light around the playground. Rough faces, rough clothes. She recognised the stocky, gravel voiced man. Korban, the others had called him. In one hand he still held the leash, stretched taut as the wild haired man pulled towards them, clawing at the grass with his gnarled hands. A little back from the group, the brothers in their red and gold coats. The older of them, hard faced and serious, a scowling mouth mostly hidden by his thick beard. The thin one wearing a satisfied smirk, his hand resting on the jewelled hilt of the sword at his waist.

"Well," the younger brother said, obviously amused, "it's a good thing we got here when we did. I do believe something rather unchivalrous might have been about to occur."

Justin sprang to his feet. She took his hand, stepping off the merry-go-round to stand beside him. The four men closed in cautiously. She heard the clicking sound, as the blade appeared in Justin's hand again.

"You'll know when to run," he whispered.

She gave the slightest of nods, just enough to show that she'd heard him. They stood together, as the circle closed in. She looked around for a weapon, but there was nothing to hand.

Justin turned and locked eyes with the nearest of the four, a looming figure with a scarred face and long, dark hair. Muscled rippled under her shirt as the woman stepped forward. Rachael saw Justin flex, moving on the balls of his feet. Glancing around she saw how the other three were hanging back just a little, ready to move in as soon as the fighting started.

"Now, now. If you'll just put that knife down young man, there's no need for this to get bloody," the younger brother announced. "My name is Rakesh Bhandari. My brother Naveen and I are men of honour, sworn Knights of the Guild. I'm sure we can resolve all this without... Unpleasantness."

Looking at the cold eyes of the four thugs surrounding them, Rachael could already see the violence lurking there. There was no question how this was going to end, no matter what anyone said.

The towering brute of a woman took another step forward. Her mouth slowly twisted into a smile.

"Listen, kid, Jocasta here's got about twenty years experience and another hundred pounds of muscle on you," Korban said, gesturing at the woman. "I admire your spirit, but you gotta know when to quit."

Justin said nothing, but Rachael saw the smile that crept onto his lips. He held out his hand and let the knife fall, landing point down in the soft ground.

"Smart move kid," Korban said, nodding to his men. The four goons began closing in, still cautious. As Jocasta loomed over the both of them, Justin looked up at the woman, still smiling. For a moment no one moved. The two of them seemed to be waiting to see what would happen next.

It was almost too fast for Rachael to follow. Jocasta lunged, reaching down to catch the younger man in a hold. In that same moment Justin slipped to one side, and somehow caught the woman's arm, twisting it around behind her back. In the same motion, Justin kicked his fallen knife up into the air. He caught the knife in his free hand, flipped the blade point down, and stabbed it into the back of Jocasta's neck. The woman roared in pain, staggering forward with her hands clamped over her neck, as blood poured down her shirt. Before the woman had even hit the ground, Justin was moving again. One hand flicked out towards the nearest of Korban's goons as he danced past her. There was a flicker of silver in the air, and then the knife landed in the man's shoulder. His other hand caught Rachael's arm as he turned and pushed her towards the space where Jocasta had been standing.

She heard a cry behind her and glanced back just for a moment. Where Justin had been there was only a blur in the air, a feathered shape that lashed out with steely claws.

Korban reached into his jacket pocket and produced a heavy looking revolver. Before she could even shout a warning, Justin cut back on himself, turning over in the air to rake the man's face with his claws. He was a hawk, she realised, sleek, fast and deadly. Korban staggered backwards, blood pouring into his eyes. As the gun fell from his hands, so too did the end of the leash. The wild man rolled to one side and came up on his haunches with a terrible howl.

Without another thought she turned and ran. Dimly, she saw the lights of the road approaching. The sound of her breathing was so loud in her ears that it blocked out everything else. She vaulted the fence and hit the pavement running. Glancing back, she saw a brief flash of light and heard the crack of a gunshot. Silhouetted, she saw a man reeling backwards, the outline of a large bird against his face. The flare of light faded, and the darkness flooded back in a hundred times deeper. In the moment of silence that followed she heard a sound like an animal panting heavily, growing louder and closer. As her eyes readjusted she made out the shape of the man, running with a lopsided, loping stride. Any thought of going back for Justin left her that instant.

She ran on through the narrow streets, lines of cars parked nose to tail on either side of her. She came to a junction and picked a direction at random. Too late, she saw that she had chosen wrong. Before her lay a small cul-de-sac, vehicles lining the street in front of towering grey apartment blocks. She doubled back but it was too late. The old man came shambling out into the middle of the junction, moving on all fours. His eyes were fixed on her.

He was only a man, she told herself. She did not have to run from one man, though everything inside her was screaming to do exactly that. He was only one man. She could fight him, beat him. Escape. But she knew that were many terrible things that one man could do to her. He was old, but he was taller and stronger, and the wildness in him terrified her. She could see it in his eyes, dark holes into nothingness. She could see that he was broken inside.

"Little girl? No. Not a little girl."

She could smell the stink of him as he approached.

"Not a little girl at all. Not anything."

He advanced another step, and his stench preceded him like a wave.

"You're not here," the man screamed, his mouth forming around a torrent of spittle as the words howled out. "Empty! Empty!" He lurched forward, with a sudden and violent energy. She darted back, his grubby nails barely missing her as she turned and ran deeper into the cul-de-sac, hoping against hope to find a some way through. The sound of his footsteps followed her, as he continued to howl and roar.

"Can't find you. Smelled you out. Did what I was told. Good boy gets a treat. The little girl's not here. She's just an empty hole. I did what I was told."

His ravings were nothing but noise in the air as she ran. For a moment she thought the distance was growing, her surer strides outpacing his drunken lurching. Then a ridge in the pavement caught at her toes and it seemed as though one leg was simply kicked out from under her. She crashed into the hard ground. Palms, elbows, chin, all exploded with fire. The breath was ripped from her lungs. Through the pain and the dizziness she could still hear him coming.

A van was parked by the side of the road. She rolled sideways, slipping underneath. She squirmed her way into the narrow space as quickly as she could, but a gnarled hand wrapped itself around her ankle, and she could move no further. Her body scraped across the pavement as he dragged her loose. Desperately, she grabbed at the underside of the van with bloodied hands, tears stinging her eyes, but he was too strong. Cold metal dug into her hands and her grip weakened. She was being pulled into his grasp, inch by inch.

The hand on her ankle jerked hard and her grip gave way entirely. Then he was on her, a mass of hair and bone and muscle and the overpowering stink of him. She felt the sweat of his palms as bony hands caught her wrists.

"Can feel you. Feel the little girl, but she isn't real, can't be real. Nothing inside there, nothing inside."

Ravings spilled from his mouth, and she tasted his saliva as it splattered her face. A hand against her shoulder, pushing her down, pressing her into the unyielding tarmac. She kicked, felt something recoil, but he was oblivious to whatever pain she might have inflicted. He leaned in closer, his eyes locked on hers.

There was a sound, like paper rustling in a breeze, and then a grey blur streaked across her vision. The impact hurled him across the street, the sheer force rolling her to one side. Something dark splattered the ground beneath her hands, and Rachael felt a wet spray against her face. She heard a crunch, then a noise like damp cloth tearing and a gurgled scream that died almost as soon as it began.

Her hands were pressed to the tarmac, her face inches away from a slowly spreading pool of dark red liquid. She wondered if maybe it was hers. Arms shaking, she tried to stand, but her trembling legs would not take her weight. She moved until her knees were folded under herself, sat up, and forced herself to look around.

The old man lay unmoving, the pavement wet with blood around his body. The wolf stood over him, drawing great lungfuls of air, its flanks heaving, blood dripping from lips that curled back from yellow teeth. There was a constant sound in its throat, the low rattle of a growl. It turned to look at her, and she felt her heart seize in her chest. Her hands twitched, and sweat dripped from her brow, but she could not move. Her body felt cold.

Then, as the creature looked into her eyes, the growl softened, then ceased. A large pink tongue swiped across blood-splattered jowls. The wolf padded forward, eyes widening in an expression of sadness. Head close to hers, a soft snout rubbed gently against her cheek. Almost without thinking, she reached up to stroke the smooth fur behind one ear.

"Justin?"

He sat down and pressed his head against the side of her neck, eyes closed. Her legs were damp, the denim of her jeans soaked through with blood. As much as the thought of it should have made her sick, it simply didn't seem to matter. She was floating in a hollow space. The cold, the hurt, the damp, the smell and the feel of it all seemed distant and faint. The soft fur beneath her hand, the warmth of him, was the only thing she seemed truly aware of.

Chapter 9 - Shelter

Arsha pressed her hands against the bulkhead and waited for the world to stop spinning. When she seemed to be standing on her own two feet again she opened her eyes and straightened up. Her stomach still felt strange, but she grudgingly decided that she'd be all right, for now.

Her father had warned her that crossing the Veil would be different, but the reality had been even more unpleasant than she had expected. Even her cycles weren't quite as bad. It was a little over twelve hours since they had cleared the ways, and the dizzy spells had grown less frequent, but only slightly less intense.

Steadier, she braved the stairs up to the bridge. In spite of her queasiness, this was something she had to see. She came up to find her father and Abasi already there. Abasi was at the helm and her father was examining the lumen-displays over one of the consoles. Traceries of light played out on the glass windows, projecting information; velocity, distance, angle of motion. One sweeping line for the horizon.

Past the displays all she could see was a darkening sky and an endless spiral of heavy grey storm clouds below. Her heart sank a little as she saw that there wasn't even a glimpse of the city.

Abasi turned and caught her expression.

"Storm rolled in about an hour before we did," he said. "I'm keeping us over her, for now."

"The storm's not what worries me," her father added.

Following his gaze, at first she couldn't make out anything but the wall of grey cloud. Straining her eyes, she finally saw the sleek white ship nestled in the clouds. It lay on the far side of the storm's eye, made tiny by the distance, though she guessed it was nearly a match for the Triskelion in size. It's hull was brightly painted in designs of brilliant red and gold.

"They were also here when we arrived," Abasi said, with a heavy sigh.

"Who are they?" she said.

"It's the Jyoti. She's registered to House Bhandari," Abasi said.

Her father examined another display, his lips pressed into a thin line.

"They're staying veil-warped?" he said, glancing past Abasi, towards the distant vessel.

"As tightly as they can, by the looks of it," Abasi replied.

"What does that mean?" Arsha interjected. "Veil-warped?"

"We try to be, uh, discreet, when we're this side of the Veil," her father said, considering his words carefully.

"Because they don't remember the Exile," she prompted. Sometimes, he seemed to forget just how much of this he'd already taught her.

"Right. The Veil keeps them separate from the other worlds. But it does more than that... It keeps everything about the Exile locked away. The Hearth is like the calm eye in the centre of a storm. So when we travel here, through the Veil, we sort of bring a part of it with us. By keeping that Veil around our ship, we make it..." He faltered. "... Hard to find, I suppose."

"They don't see us?"

"No. They just don't realise it," Abasi said.

"Oh," she said, not sure that she really understood. "So... Why did those other guys come here? What does House Bhandari have to do with this?"

Abasi turned to look at her father, and for a moment neither of the men spoke.

"It's a little complicated," her father said. "I've worked with Manindra... With Lord Bhandari, in the past, and I know the man is obsessed with Ur artifacts. The Seeds in particular. If he's learned about what's going to happen here, that a Seed is awakening, you can be sure that he'll try to get his hands on it."

"But how would he know?" Arsha said. "You said maybe even the Guild doesn't know yet."

"Yes," her father sighed. "I suspect Manindra is the cause of that. He has many allies within the Chamber of Foresight. It wouldn't be easy to suppress a prediction of this scale, but for Manindra, I think it would be possible. He could certainly pull enough strings, if he wanted this badly enough. And I know that he does."

"If you're right, Rishi," Abasi added, "then it means we're alone out here. Just us and the Bhandaris. No Guild backup."

"I know. I'm not planning to start a fight, Abasi. Trust me on that."

"Fates, I wish I could," Abasi said, shaking his head.

"If you know this Manindra guy... Lord Bhandari... Why can't you talk to him? Tell him how dangerous this is?" Arsha said.

"Because Lord Bhandari doesn't exactly think very kindly of me, sweetheart," he said, smiling in a way that suggested there was something else he was holding back. "Besides, Manindra won't be here on the Jyoti. He'll have sent his sons to do his dirty work. Rakesh and Naveen, probably."

"And just what do you plan to do about this, Rishi?" Abasi said, without looking up from the controls.

"Get down there and find the girl. Before they do," her father replied.

"And do you have any idea how you're going to find one girl in a city of millions?" Abasi said, still not looking up from the console he was studying.

"Some," her father said. "Arsha, you've been practising with Ilona like I asked you to?"

Arsha nodded.

"I'm... I'm getting the hang of it, I think. But, I still haven't managed to find anything."

"No, I wouldn't expect so. A seeker only really works over a short distance. That's why we'll be taking the Zephyr down. Once we're flying low over the city, you should be able to make a connection more easily."

Abasi looked over at the two of them, incredulous.

"Rishi, you can't be serious. You're taking Arsha down there with you?"

"Out of necessity, yes," her father replied. "I'd hoped to use some other method to find the girl, but she's being warded. With Arsha's connection, we should be able to track her down with a seeker, if we get close enough. It's the best option we have, and I don't like it any more than you do."

"It's OK Uncle Abasi," Arsha added, giving the man a brave smile. "I wanted to help. Really."

Abasi gave them both a strange look, as if there was something he was struggling to contain. With a forlorn shake of his head he turned away.

"Alright, I'll start getting the Zephyr ready," he said, heavily.

"Thank you." Her father nodded. "Arsha, you should go find Ilona, get some more practice in. I'll call you when it's time to go."

"OK," she said, wondering if it was the lingering effects of the Veil that was making her feel nauseous, or something else entirely.

Rachael didn't really remember him changing back. Just the sight of his face, an outstretched hand pulling her up from the cold ground. She remembered walking, his coat around her shoulders. Streets passed by in a haze, as she heard the rumbling of thunder overhead.

They came to an alleyway behind a burned out shell of a building. Another relic of the riots a summer past. She sank to the floor, huddled against the cold brickwork. Justin knelt beside her, his face heavy with concern. She felt his hands on her shoulders, saw his mouth moving, but she couldn't make out the words. Her body seemed to contract in on itself, everything collapsing in toward some silent core where she could be safe and alone.

Rachael felt his arms around her, as he urged her to stand. His hand went to brush the hair out of her eyes, but she batted it away. His mouth kept on moving, making sounds that she could not understand. The legs of her jeans were soaked black with blood. She held up her fingers to inspect them, sticky and glistening red. She doubled over, felt the acid tang of vomit splash the back of her throat. For a moment everything swam.

She shivered in the cold, as Justin wiped a rag across her mouth. Footsteps blurred together. Boxes, bare floor, garbage piles and a metal bin that was blackened with smoke. A couch that had been scrapped and salvaged many times over. She laid her head down and sleep took her.

Her dreams lead her through darkened streets, chased by something that she only glimpsed. Something wild and savage. A wolf, howling towards a moonless sky. A man with blood and foam around his lips. Sometimes she caught the flicker of a long coat. The streets kept leading her round in circles, and all the while the creature was closing. Finally she stumbled and fell. She looked up to see the creature charging at her, long hair wild and matted, lips dripping with blood. But it had Justin's face.

When she woke there was a fire burning in the blackened oil drum. Her thoughts were foggy, her eyes dimmed with the faint traces of sleep. It took her a while to focus past the flickering light playing at the edges of the steel drum, to where Justin sat on an upturned milk-crate. His head was hung low, his whole body curved over, elbows resting on his knees. His shoulders rose and fell with each breath. The fire cracked and popped, the sound mingling with the downpour outside. The couch smelled damp and the air was smoky.

Her wrists hurt. As she rubbed at them, she saw that her hands were clean. She noticed a bucket of water on the floor, its contents stained dark.

She saw that Justin was watching her with a guilty expression. She realised that he was looking at her cheek, where the man had clawed at her. Touching her fingers to the skin she could feel the ragged, stinging lines his nails had left.

"Don't," she whispered, her voice hoarse. "Don't look like that."

He turned his eyes away.

"I'm sorry," he said. The words didn't really seem to convey whatever he was trying to express.

"Don't want to hear it. You ain't my knight, or my bodyguard, or whatever. I never asked you to be looking after me."

"I was supposed to be."

"Be what?"

"Your knight."

"Right. On your quest to bring me home."

"You still don't believe any of this is real, do you?"

She stared at her hands, remembering the way the old man's blood had glistened under the street lights.

"I believe it. I have to. Nothing else makes sense."

"I'm sorry."

A pause.

"Did you kill him?" she said, still unsure of her own jumbled memories of the attack.

"Yes," he said, his voice faint.

"Good," she said.

Justin nodded, his eyes fixed on the embers of the fire.

"I'm coming with you," she said, at last. "I mean none of this is gonna start making sense any other way, right? So, this place you're supposed to take me to, wherever that is... I'm coming with you."

"It wasn't supposed to go like this," he said.

"What?"

"In my head... I imagined it would be different," he looked up and met her eyes. "Sorry. That probably sounds really stupid."

"A bit, yeah," she said. He winced.

Silence stretched out between them, as she struggled to find something to say. Anything to take her thoughts away from the swirling storm inside her head. She could feel it all thundering away inside of her. The fear, the sickness, the screaming vertigo of the whole world collapsing underneath her. She could feel it all, even as she forced it back down, deep inside.

"Tell me about her," she said. "The lady who sent you. My... My mother."

"She's... I don't even know where to start." He pushed a hand through his hair. "She's gentle. And beautiful. But she can be scary, sometimes. Not in a way that makes you want to run, but more like... Like she could be dangerous, if she wanted to be. But you know that she'll never turn it on you. That she'd never hurt someone she loves. You know she'll protect you, with all that power. And she's graceful, and delicate. She moves like water, or... Like leaves when they're caught on the air. Like she's always dancing."

"This place, where she lives..."

"It's somewhere called the Deep Wild. Past the Borderlands, so far out that no one has gone there in... In a really long time."

"Wild? Borderlands?"

Rachael scrunched up her forehead.

"It's how they talk about it. The worlds they come from out there. Each one is part of this endless space called the Dreaming. They're connected by these pathways that you can only see if you know how to look for them. Like, roads that aren't on any map.

Here, where we are now, it's right at the centre of it all. It's like a safe space. A world where none of this stuff can get in. They call it the Hearth. But the further out you go, the more the rules start changing. The Guild controls the lands around this world, what they call the Borderlands. Or at least they try to. But out in the Deep Wild... That's where the Guild doesn't go. No one goes there. No one except for people like her."

"Why?"

"Because she's not like us. She's powerful, in a way that they can never understand."

"Like, a... A sorceress or something?"

"Or something like that," he nodded. "The part of the Wild where she lives, she created it herself. She didn't have to find a world, she just imagined one and it came into existence."

"You're saying people can just create new worlds?"

"She can. I suppose that means maybe you could too."

Rachael considered this for a moment. It seemed like too much to even think about.

"Can you tell me about it? The world she made?"

He nodded.

"It's always autumn. But, just before the leaves fall, when the grass is wet from the rain and there's that smell in the air, like the world is holding its breath. There are forests where you can walk for days, and there are wild horses..."

"Horses? Did you learn to ride?" she said.

"Yeah. And dance, and recite poetry and fight with a sword. All the things a knight should know."

"Knights should know dancing and poetry?" She laughed. He shrugged, but she saw the faint hint of a smile.

"Well, that's what I was told," he said.

"Tell me more."

"She has a castle. An actual castle. You can see it from any part of the land. It's called the Bower Castle. It's built right into the arms of a tree... But, I mean, a tree that's taller than anything you've ever seen. Taller than any of the towers here in London. The arms spread out like an old oak, and the castle sits right there."

"I'm going to live in a castle?"

"You're going to live where-ever you want. Rachael, all of this... It's just a tiny little bubble in the Dreaming. It's just... Like a passing thought. You're going to see whole worlds. Anything you want."

"I think... I think I'd like that."

She saw a flicker of a smile play around his lips.

"So what happens now?" she said.

The smile faded.

"That's the tricky part," he said.

"Tricky how?"

He hesitated, drawing a slow breath.

"Because I don't know how to get there."

"You what?"

"It takes a lot of power, to reach her lands. To go out into the Deep Wild. Even the Guild don't know how."

"So what was the plan, genius?"

"She told me about something called a Seed. There are several of them, scattered across this world, hidden. They're ancient, and very powerful. Something that her people created a long time ago. And there's one right here in this city."

"And this helps us get out of here?"

"That's the idea. But first we have to find it. Even with all that she taught me, there's no way that I could ever find it. It's more than hidden, it's... Buried... Under the skin of the world. It can only be found if it wants to be. But you can find it. You're her daughter, and that means you have her power in you. It knows you. It was made for you."

"So that's it? I'm supposed to find some magic seed, and take us both out of here, because, what? Dumb luck? Did you at least bring me a flipping instruction manual or something?"

She jumped to her feet and stalked past him. He whirled to face her, leaping up from where he sat.

"Rachael, please. This was the only way. This thing... It belongs to you. It'll call out to you. It has to."

"Yeah, great plan you got there," she said.

"Where are you going?" he called after her.

"Outside. Get some fresh air. Try to listen for this seed calling," she snarled.

She stepped out into the narrow street behind the building and sat herself down against one side of the doorway. The sky above was thick with clouds, and the air felt heavy and damp, the pressure of the storm swelling invisibly around the whole city. It couldn't be long now before it broke.

She couldn't really say how long she'd been sat there when she heard the sound of footsteps. He sat down on the step beside her, pulling his coat around himself. She couldn't help but notice how he left a space between them. She turned to glance back into the building behind them, walls blackened with scorch marks and smoke.

"I suppose we can't stick around here for too long," she said, knowing full well that she was avoiding his eyes. "Whoever dragged that couch in there and all that... They'll be coming back soon, right?"

"They already did," he said.

She gave him a sharp look.

"And you..."

"Told them to leave. That's all. They didn't argue."

His expression was calm, sincere.

"That's all?" she said, not quite sure that she believed him. He just nodded. The silence hung between them, like a prickling sensation on her skin.

"You know it's funny," she said. "I... I hid out in a place like this. Just after I left home. It was just after the riots. I was so scared. I just kept thinking it'd all start up again, and there'd be police, and people setting stuff on fire and all, and I'd just be there in the middle of it. But nothing happened. I stayed there for three days. Then the people what owned the shop came back, and I had to move off."

Justin said nothing. She could tell he was watching her, quiet discomfort radiating from where he sat. She could feel him holding back whatever else it was that he wanted to say.

"I don't get it," she said. "Why'd you do all this? Why'd you want to find me, protect me... What makes you think I'm worth all this?"

There was a sadness in his eyes, as he reached out to squeeze her hand.

"You are worth it, Rachael. Trust me."

She looked away, swallowing nervously.

"But even... Even if you think that now... You spent years training... And you came so far..."

"When you meet her, you'll understand. Your mother, I mean. Rachael, she's incredible. She saved me. Saved my life. Or saved me from it, I suppose."

She turned to look at him, searching his eyes for some sign of his meaning. He seemed nervous.

"What do you mean?"

"It's..." he faltered. She said nothing, gave him time to find the words.

"I got moved around a lot," he said. "Lots of different families. Foster homes."

She nodded.

"It'd be maybe six months, or a year, that I'd be in any one place, you know? And I tried to fit in, I really did. But it just never seemed to work out. After a while, I didn't even bother unpacking my stuff. It's like... It's always good at first, you know? When you arrive, they're always nice. They give you a good meal, and they hug you, and buy you presents, and tell you everything's going to be better now. But it's not, because sooner or later you see the look. The disappointment. Because you're not what they wanted. You're not right. And eventually they get tired of waiting, you know?

Waiting for you to get better. To turn into the person they were wanting. And that's when it starts falling apart. And you don't know how to stop it, because even if you wanted to be the person they were looking for, it's like... Like you're staring at something on the other side of this big ravine. And you can see it, but you don't know how to get there. So you just let it go... You know what's coming, and you can't do nothing to stop it, so you just wait. And then it starts all over."

He looked up at her, and just for a moment she glimpsed the pain in his eyes.

"Does that... Does that make sense?" he said.

"No, it does," she said, nodding. "Like, you keep trying to be different, but... It's like gravity, isn't it? It don't matter how high you jump, cause you always fall down."

He nodded.

"But you see, then she found me. At night, I started dreaming. Dreaming of her forest, her castle. And she told me that she'd been searching for someone like me... Someone who needed a place to belong. She told me about her daughter... About how you'd been stolen away from her. She told me that it was up to me to find you, to bring you home. That she would teach me all the things I needed to know. That no matter what happened, no matter how many families gave up on me, that I would always have a home in her castle. That she would always be there for me."

He looked at her with a burning intensity.

"That's why. Because she's the one person who never gave up on me. She's the only real family I've ever had. I'd do anything for her, Rachael. Anything for you. I've been preparing my whole life for this, to find you, to bring you safely home. I know everything about this seems crazy, but it's what we have, and I know she wouldn't have sent me out to find you if she didn't believe it would work. She knows what you're capable of, Rachael, more than anyone else possibly could. She believes in you. And so do I."

Rachael turned away from him, unable to hold that earnest gaze any longer. She could feel her heart pounding in her chest, cold sweat prickling her skin. The word 'mother' seemed to echo through her thoughts, over and over.

"You don't think she'll be disappointed? In me? After all this time she spent... After everything she's done..."

"It's not like that, Rachael," he said, reaching out to touch her shoulder. "You're her daughter. It doesn't matter what it takes, what it costs... She just wants you back. You're the only thing that matters to her."

She looked away again, letting her eyes roam the skyline. Eventually she settled on one building in particular, dominating all of the others. A strange thought occurred to her.

"Why do they call it the Dreaming, Justin? This place that's outside our world?" she said.

"Because it's where our dreams come from," he replied. "These worlds, they're like bubbles, but the bubbles are all a part of this endless place called the Dreaming. It's... Everything. Anything. It's like... Possibility. Pure possibility. That's what we see when we dream. Glimpses of all those impossible worlds. Even the things she taught me to do... That's what magic is really. Dreams, that you make real."

"Could that be how this thing is calling to me? In my dreams?"

He nodded, his eyes nervous, but sharp.

"Then I think... I think maybe I know where it is," she said. "This seed... I think I know where to find it."

Chapter 10 - Exiles

A pair of wooden covers had been lifted open on huge steam driven arms in the middle of the Triskelion's deck, to allow the skiff to be raised up from the hold below. It was a slender little ship, resting on iron runners that looked like insect legs. From prow to aft it was maybe thirty foot long, and the twin propellers, mounted on long outriggers, accounted for most of its width. At some point Arsha had taken to calling the little boat 'The Zephyr', thinking it sad that it didn't merit a name of its own, and it had quickly caught on with the rest of the crew. Eventually Abasi had paid for the name to be painted across the ship's prow in letters of bright gold.

As she stepped out onto the deck, Arsha saw that Micah was already waiting, shielding a crumpled roll-up from the wind. He had his tan greatcoat on, and the sleek silver shape of a lightning ballista hung across his shoulder. He turned as she approached and dropped the cigarette, grinding it under his heel.

"Hey there little bear. How you feeling?" he said.

She shrugged, and pushed her hands deeper into her pockets.

"OK, I guess. What about you?" she said.

"Kinda nervous," he said, rubbing his hands together.

"Really?"

"A little, yeah." He smiled. "But it's gonna be OK. Your dad always gets us through."

He paused for a moment, fingers still clearly itching for the discarded cigarette, before he continued.

"Did I ever tell you there was this one time in Ruija when your dad and I were working around some old caves, and this whole cliff face nearly came down on top of me, like..."

Micah's story was cut short by the clattering sound of the door opening behind them. They both turned to see her father and Ilona step out onto the deck. For a moment, no one said a word. She saw the way her father pulled his coat tighter around himself, the shape of the revolver on his hip still visible beneath the heavy tanglecloth. Around Ilona's right hand she could make out the fine silver tracery of her arc-gauntlet. She didn't know whether to feel nervous or comforted by the sight of so many weapons.

"Well are we going to stop pissing about and do this thing or what?" Micah said, visibly shivering in the cold.

Her father gave a solemn nod, before turning to look at her, his expression seeming to have been carved in stone.

"Whatever happens down there, you stay close to Micah, you hear me? He'll be looking after you."

She nodded, too nervous to speak. From the corner of her eye she saw Micah's reassuring smile.

They crossed the deck together, the shape of the Zephyr looming over them. Her hands felt clumsy in her leather gloves as Arsha took hold of the rope ladder and climbed up.

She felt a hand on her shoulder, as Micah joined her at the railing. Micah put a hand to either side of hers, his long arms easily surrounding her, leaving her no place to fall. Turning to look up at him, she smiled, and he gave her shoulder a reassuring squeeze.

The sound of the propellers grew to a thunderous roar. Her father pulled back on the wheel, and the ship lurched and swayed as it lifted clear of the deck. For a few minutes, Arsha didn't move a muscle, her hands wrapped tightly around the iron railing as they swung away from the larger vessel.

The violent swaying settled down after a while, as her father set the boat on a slow downward spiral. She watched the Triskelion growing smaller in the distance. Then the clouds swallowed them up, and she could barely see anything at all.

There was a sudden flash, followed by a deafening roar as lightning arced across the ship, dancing across outriggers and down into the belly of the Zephyr, where she knew it would end up in the lightning cages, safely stored away. Half the cages had been left empty, giving them room to soak a good few bolts before they had to bleed any. Arsha knew all of this, but she still felt nervous, glad of Micah's reassuring presence.

A second bolt of lightning flared across the propellers, and in the brief moment of illumination she caught sight of her father's face through the clouds. Even behind the googles she could see the calm focus in his eyes, his steady hands guiding the wheel. Another burst of lightning flashed around them, and then the tiny ship broke through the clouds and she saw the vast expanse of the English landscape open up beneath her.

Under the lights of Tower Bridge Station, two security guards stood beneath the overhanging roof, hunched over their cigarettes as they tried to stay clear of the wind. They wore long black woollen coats with suits and ties underneath. Young men with neat haircuts and smart faces, meant to look modern and sleek like the building they stood watch over. Emblems of the new city growing up out of the old.

The nearer of the two men looked up sharply, as Rachael came running out of the darkness of the underpass. The lights of the nearby railway station picked out her face, hair tangled, blood smeared across her lip. Her jacket hung open, torn halfway loose from one shoulder. As she ran towards the men, a wave of relief showed on her face.

"Jesus, you gotta help," she called out. "He... He attacked me."

"Hey," one of the men said, catching her by the shoulders. "What happened kid?"

"It was... He..." She fumbled for the words. "He was holding me down. I bit him. I just got away." She pawed at the blood smeared across her mouth.

"Who was it? Who done this?"

"It was this guy... We were together, and..." She faltered, unable to go on.

"Took it too far, right?" the man growled. "Rick, get the police on the line will ya? Let's get her inside."

His partner nodded and produced a mobile phone. She was lead up to the revolving glass doors of the building, as the guard fished a key out from inside of his coat and turned it in the lock by the door. As she waited, shivering in the cold, she glanced upwards at the sheer immensity of the building that towered over her.

The Shard had seemed vast from a distance, but up close it was impossible. Even lit by floodlights, the angled glass walls vanished into the darkness overhead. She hoped, desperately, that she was right. That this was really where her dreams had been leading her.

The lock clicked and the man pushed at the revolving door with one gloved hand. At the desk inside a third guard was scowling at them both.

"Matt, what's going on here?"

"I'm just bringing her in for a bit, until the police get here. Some lad got pretty rough with her, sounds like. She's in a right state."

"Ah, Jesus," the guard at the desk muttered, his eyes going to her tangled hair and her blood smeared face. "Yeah, get her in, we'll sit her down in the security office."

"Thanks Charlie," Matt nodded. She was lead past the desk, and through a door with a sign that read 'SECURITY' in bold type. She imagined rows of televisions showing grainy CCTV feeds, but what she found was a couple of desks with computer monitors, a couch, a coffee table, and a small kitchenette just off to one side.

"Here you go," Matt said, as he settled her down on the couch. "Get you a cup of tea, love?"

"Please," she whispered. "Milk. No sugar."

"Sure thing." He nodded and patted her hand. He had a reassuring smile.

As Matt busied himself at the kitchenette, the door opened, and the guard from the desk leaned in.

"Station says they'll have an officer down as soon as they can, but, well, Saturday nights eh?"

"Well, she can stay here for now, yeah?"

"Yeah, they said to keep her here, so no sense worrying about it now, mate. If those twats from the site office want to make a fuss then we were just complying with police instructions, right?"

The door closed, and Matt came over with a steaming mug of tea, which he pressed into her shivering hands.

"Listen love, I gotta get back outside, but Charlie's at the desk on the other side of that door. If you need anything, just holler, alright? Police officer'll be here soon enough, and you can just stay here until then. Pop the telly on if you want."

"Thanks," she whispered.

"It's alright love," he said, giving her an awkward pat on the shoulder, as he stood to go. She sipped her tea, as the door swung closed behind him.

It took everything she had to just sit there, waiting, slowly counting off the seconds in her head. To not run and hide. She counted a full five minutes before she went to door and gently pulled it open.

The man at the desk looked around as she peered out.

"Hey... Uh, it's Charlie, right?" she said.

"Yeah, what's up?"

"I... Um... I was just wondering where the um... The loo..."

Charlie held up his hands, gesturing for her to calm down.

"Alright darling, I hear ya. It's just round the corner and then a little on." He gestured, and she nodded, gratefully.

Past the corner, she could easily make out the signs for the toilets. Deciding to make a good show of it, she went into the ladies, and counted off another two full minutes before slipping back out into the corridor.

Instead of heading back to the front desk, she ducked across the hall to a door with a sign that read 'STAIRWAY FOR USE IN EMERGENCY ONLY'. She paused, just for a moment, wondering if there would be an alarm. Then she pushed the door open and started running. By the time she reached what must have been the thirtieth floor she was feeling the strain. She set herself down on the stairs for a moment to rest. As her breathing slowed, the silence of the empty building crashed in. She listened for the sound of alarms or angry security guards racing up the stairs. She seemed to be safe, for now.

Rachael closed her eyes and tried to feel whatever it was she was supposed to be feeling. The 'seed' they were searching for, this thing that was supposed to belong to her. She tried to empty her mind, to reach out for the power that Justin had talked about. There was nothing.

She got to her feet and carried on up the stairway, until she came to a doorway. On the other side a ladder lead up to the roof above. She scaled the rungs and emerged into the freezing cold air. Above her, a narrow protrusion extended another thirty feet, with a single ladder leading to the very top.

She heard the flutter of wings, and looked up to see a dark shape above her. The black cloud reformed, leaving Justin kneeling on the rooftop beside her, the wind whipping his long black coat around him.

"Coast is clear, I think," he said, having to speak up to be heard over the wind. "Did you... Did you find it?"

She shook her head.

"I don't even know what I'm supposed to be looking for here. Does this thing just appear when I get to it, or what?"

Justin shrugged.

"I don't know. I've never done this before."

She turned away, and walked to the edge of the rooftop. As the shape of the streets snapped into place, she felt a dizzying wave of vertigo. She had never imagined the view from so far up. From where she stood, the whole city seemed to be frozen in place. It was just a sea of lights, scattered over an uneven pattern of rooftops, all strangely flattened by the distance. Even the tallest towers of South Bank seemed small from where they stood.

"God... This is the highest I've been. Like, I've never seen the city like this before."

Justin nodded.

"It's all different from up here," she said.

She felt a hand on her shoulder. When she turned to see Justin's face, he was staring into the evening sky with a nervous expression. Rachael looked up to see a dark shape detach itself from the clouds. At first she thought it must have been a plane or a helicopter, though she couldn't imagine why anyone would be flying through a storm like the one that was brewing over them. Then as it circled lower she saw that it wasn't any kind of flying vehicle that she had seen before. She could just make out the shape of the wooden hull, and the hazy circle of the twin propellers that extended from the ship's flanks. There seemed to be people moving about on the deck.

"A ship? An actual flying ship?" she said.

Justin nodded.

"That'll be them," he said. "The Guild. We need to hurry."

"Easier said," Rachael growled. "I've still got no idea what I'm flipping well looking for up here."

"Focus. Shut out everything else. Try to hear it. It's not a sound exactly, but it's like... Like the feeling you get, when you hear a song you know."

She pulled her hood up and closed her eyes, trying to listen, but she heard only the sound of the wind. No matter how hard she tried nothing seemed to change.

"Maybe we need to be higher," Rachael said, glumly. She looked at Justin, hoping for some sign of the easy confidence she'd seen in him before, but he looked as unsure as she felt.

"I don't have any better ideas," he said.

She nodded, and looked upwards.

"I guess that was the easy part," she said, eyeing the series of ladders that surmounted the sheer sided core of the building. It was flanked by half finished panels of glass that barely concealed the bare grey structure within. For one horrible moment it made her think of a broken bone. She put her hand on the first rung and began to climb.

Chapter 11 - Thunder

As they broke through the cloud layer, her father set the Zephyr on an even keel, slowly circling above the city. Arsha stared down at the view in amazement. London was a sea of lights, as if the earth been set on fire. The thick black line of a river snaked through the ethereal glow, sharply dividing the two sides of the city. She saw smaller pinpricks moving through the streets like brightly coloured ants, and hazy points of light drifted on the surface of the water. Spotlights picked out gleaming towers of glass and steel, clustered around the riverbanks. She saw the shape of a giant wheel standing over the water, it's purpose unclear.

"Abasi just waved us from the Triskelion," Micah announced. "Says the Jyoti just launched two skiffs. They're following us down. Looks like armed men aboard."

He paused for a moment, then added "What do we do, Professor?"

Her father turned to look up at the dark clouds above them.

"We find the girl," he said, as if it was the simplest thing in the world.

"And if the decide to start shooting at us?" Ilona said.

"They're trying to intimidate us, not start a fight," her father replied.

"You're sure of that?" Ilona said. Rishi scowled, and said nothing.

Micah turned to look at her, forcing a smile.

"I guess the next part's on you, kid," he said to Arsha. Ilona reached into a pocket in her skirt and produced a small object on a fine silver chain. The seeker looked like a series of silver rings, nested one inside the last, each one able to spin freely. At its centre was a deep blue crystal that glowed with a faint light. Arsha sat herself down in the centre of the deck as Ilona knelt across from her. Arsha closed her eyes for a moment and tried to shut out the roaring of the wind and the thundering of the propellers. She told herself that she was back in the hold of the Triskelion, where she had been practising with Ilona for the last few days.

Ilona held up the seeker on its chain, hanging between them like a gleaming silver eye.

"OK Arsha, focus. Look into the eye of the seeker and focus on Rachael's face," Ilona said, her voice a soft but insistent monotone. "Let everything else fall away. You are alone, floating in an ocean of darkness. There is only her face."

Taking slow and even breaths, Arsha let herself fall into the darkness. This part came easily, almost naturally. She began to conjure up the image of the girl's face, but even in the stillness behind her closed eyes, she could not seem to hold the shape of it. No matter how she tried, the details kept slipping from her grasp. It was like fumbling for something underwater. She screwed her face up in concentration as she tried to reach for the image that kept eluding her.

"Professor, cloudbreak, 2 o' clock."

She opened her eyes to see Micah gesturing towards the overcast sky. Against the dark clouds she saw two slim white shapes moving across the sky. The skiffs were narrow and slender, smaller even than the Zephyr. Open topped boats with maybe half a dozen men aboard each of them, sitting on low benches right up against the hull. If she squinted she could just make out the shape of the rifles the men carried on their shoulders.

"Hey 'Lona, whatever you guys are doing there, you might want to make it happen just a little bit faster," Micah said, looking nervous. Arsha saw him glancing down at the spark chamber of his lightning ballista. Then Ilona placed a gentle hand on her shoulder.

"Keep your eyes on me, Arsha. Focus on my voice, focus on the seeker. Try to picture her face."

Arsha nodded, took another deep breath. She could feel her heart thundering in her chest, no matter how hard she tried to calm her breathing. Pushing it aside, she let herself sink into the darkness once more, and remembered the feeling of a mask settling onto her face. The way her features had become stone. She thought of Rachael, and remembered the girl's eyes. Hard, sharp eyes, fierce and unyielding.

Then, around those eyes, she began to see details fill in. Dark clouds above. The city spread out below. She was somewhere high up. Very high. She caught glimpses of glass and steel. Then another figure. A boy, dark haired, eyes keen and watchful.

She looked again at the girl's surroundings, and the city far below. Then she looked up at the clouds above, and saw something glowing softly against the dark sky.

Arsha opened her eyes, and ran to the edge of the deck. Leaning out over the railing, she scanned the endless sprawl, until her gaze settled on a single gleaming spire. For a brief moment she felt the thread stretching tight, pulling at her insides.

"There," she cried out, pointing. "That's where she is."

Following her to the railing, Micah produced a slim brass telescope and raised it to his eye.

"Fates, you're right," he said. "I can see a girl and a boy, right up there on top of that tower. What are they even doing, trying to get themselves killed?"

"I don't know," her father said, "but it won't be long before one of those skiffs spots them up there. Everyone hold on."

Arsha clung tight to the railing as her father spun the wheel and pitched the Zephyr's nose down hard.

Standing at the very top of the Shard, buffeted by the wind, Rachael watched the ships descend towards them. The largest vessel was already getting close to the tower, close enough that she could make out the figures standing on the deck.

She turned to look at Justin. His mouth was set in a thin line, eyes cold, as he watched the approaching vessel. He said nothing, but she could see the way his fingers flexed, as if aching to reach for his knife. What good it would do them now, she had no idea. They were completely exposed. Even if they tried to run, it was a long way down.

The ship slowed as it approached the tower. The sound of the propellers descended to a dull roar. She could see a man in a long coat standing at the railing, and a woman in a black dress with a cloak around her shoulders. Between them was a smaller figure mostly concealed by a heavy coat and a pair of goggles. As she watched, the figure pushed the goggles back, revealing a familiar face. The girl from the rooftop. Arsha.

The girl smiled and waved. Rachael felt her stomach turn.

"Rachael. Rachael," Arsha called out to them. "We're going to get you out of here. It's going to be OK."

Rachael stared at the girl in disbelief. Justin leaned in close.

"Does she know you?"

"It's the girl that saw. On the rooftop. Only... She wasn't real. I mean, she wasn't really there. God, how can this be real?"

"What did she say?"

"That they were coming to find me. Her and her dad, or something."

"Cute trick," Justin said. "They couldn't catch you, so they tried to get you to come to them instead."

"What are we going to do?"

"Stop them. They can try to take you, if they want. It won't go well for them."

She saw the steel in his eyes, as he watched the vessel approaching.

"Justin you can't do this. You can't fight all of them."

She saw a cruel smile twist at the corner of his mouth.

"A promise is a promise, Rachael. Just focus on the Seed. That's what matters now. That's our way out."

"God, as if. I just want this to be over, Justin. I just want to stop running."

"Soon. We're nearly there."

His hand settled on her shoulder, his grip firm, strong. Still, she shivered as she looked past the approaching vessel and saw the other two ships coming closer. They were smaller, sleek and vicious looking things, red and white paintwork gleaming in the light from the Shard. One of the small ships began to circle the tower, as the other swooped down into the streets below.

"Just find the Seed. That's all you have to do now," Justin said.

Nodding, she closed her eyes and tried to focus, but all she could hear was the pounding of her heart.

Arsha watched as one of the skiffs touched down in the street below, disgorging men into the plaza beneath the tower. The other was orbiting the tower, closing in on them. She saw the look of grim determination on Micah's face, as his eyes followed the approaching vessel.

Turning towards the tower again, she waved at Rachael and the boy who stood with her.

"Rachael, come on. Please. We have to go, now. We have to get you out of here."

She yelled as loud as she could, her voice growing hoarse, but the girl wasn't listening. Rachael's eyes were closed. Only the boy was watching them, with a look of pure resentment. As his eyes met hers, Arsha felt a shiver run through her body.

Then Micah's hand was on her shoulder, pulling her back from the railing. In his other hand he held the lightning ballista. She looked up and saw the skiff pulling up alongside them, the crewmen levelling rifles in their direction. Micah went to raise the ballista, but Ilona slapped his hands down before he could even bring the weapon up.

"Fates, do you want to get killed?" the woman hissed.

"You there," a man called to them from the deck of the skiff, "pull away from the tower. This airspace is restricted, and you are in violation of Guild Accords."

"By whose authority?" Micah called back, still keeping his weapon pointed down, for now.

"By our authority," the man said. "Stand down and remove your vessel from this area.

Though her father hadn't said a word, Arsha could see the grim look on his face, his hands gripping a little too tight on the wheel as he watched what was happening.

"What do we do, Professor?" Micah said, giving her father a helpless look.

Still not saying a word, her father raised the throttle and span the wheel. The roar of the propellers grew as they pulled away from the building. As the distance grew, Arsha watched Rachael and the boy growing smaller, barely visible against the vastness of the glass and steel tower.

Rachael watched the ship peel away, as the men on the smaller vessel kept their weapons trained. She could feel panic seizing her now, the world seeming to blur as her heart thundered in her chest. She turned to Justin, catching him by the collar.

"Just get out of here. You can... You can turn into a bird or something, fly down, you'll be safe. Just get out of here."

He put a hand to her shoulder.

"I'm not doing that. I'm not leaving you."

"But we're trapped here. This is all... It's all gone wrong. Justin, I can't get out of this, but you can."

He pulled her close, his eyes locked on hers.

"Rachael, don't you get it? I'm never leaving you. Never."

"Because of your stupid promise," she said.

"Because of you," he said. "Come on, we can do this. Your mother had a plan. We can still... We just have to figure this thing out."

"It's not working, Justin. None of this is happening the way you planned."

The small ship continued to circle the rooftop. She could hear the men aboard shouting at them, but the words didn't seem to matter any more.

"God, what are they even waiting for? Why don't they just do it already?"

Her voice shuddered as she spoke the words into the freezing air. She could feel his strong arms around her, but it wasn't enough. They were alone, and powerless.

"They're waiting because they know how dangerous I am," Justin said, his voice strangely calm. "They know what I can do."

He let her go, and turned towards the small ship. Even in the face of the rifles levelled at them, he stood firm, stalking calmly towards the edge of the rooftop. She could see the defiance radiating from every part of him, but she knew it was an act. There was nothing they could do.

She turned away, the lights of the city filling her eyes. It was strange how beautiful everything could be, seen from up high, burning bright in the darkness. She gazed out over the rooftops below them, and for a moment she glimpsed a movement atop one of the nearest towers. A figure, captured for an instant in the glare of a floodlight. A shaved scalp, a brown leather jacket, and a familiar silhouette. Korban's hands cradled something long and slender, raised in her direction. She heard herself shout a warning just as a flash of light illuminated the man on the rooftop and the rifle he was aiming.

When the shot hit him, Justin's body didn't even seem to move. There was hardly any sound. Part of his coat simply burst open, a small hole glistening dark red inside. Then a thunderous crack shook the sky, and his body went limp.

Someone shouted his name. She supposed it must have been her. Her hands clutched at his, and she no longer saw the sky above or the streets below. There was only his face, skin pale, eyes distant and unfocused. She shook him by the shoulders, screaming his name over and over, screaming at him to wake up, get up, do anything at all. A dark stain was spreading across his shirt. She fumbled at the wound, but she couldn't remember what she was supposed to do. There was something about bandages, or pressure, but the thoughts seemed to crowd into one another, and she couldn't make sense of them all.

"Get up. Please get up," she begged, her throat hoarse from screaming. Justin gave no answer. His eyes were fixed on something in the far distance.

Her head was spinning. She seemed to be the only person left who remembered a world where nothing worked like this; as if all the rules of the game had changed, and everyone was just carrying on as if it was normal. And yet, in some way it seemed as though everything finally made sense. As if the rules were at last becoming clear. All the chaos around them seemed to fall away, and beneath the sound of the wind and the rain there was something else. Like the feeling you got when you heard a familiar song. His knife had fallen from his pocket. She picked it up and unfolded the shining steel blade.

She lifted the knife over her head, clasping the handle tightly in both hands, and with every ounce of her strength she slammed the point down into the rooftop. The knife sank deep into surface, deeper than she would have thought possible. She released the handle and sat back.

At first, nothing happened. She could hear the sound of engines, slower now, as one of the slim white ships pulled up alongside the tower. The men on board were getting ready to leap down onto the rooftop. It didn't seem to matter any more. Around Justin's body, the dark crimson pool was slowly spreading.

The change began with a grinding sound. Where the knife had pierced the rooftop a crack began to form, spreading, widening. She felt the building shake beneath her, and saw the looks on the faces of the men with the guns. Somewhere below her, she heard the sound of iron girders groaning, and something shattering.

She was tired. So tired. Her body shivered in the cold air as she crawled to Justin's side. Gently, she pulled his head into her lap and leaned forward, trying to shield his face from the wind. She saw his lips moving, as he tried to whisper something. She lowered her face towards his, until she could just about hear him over the thunder of the propellers.

"You did it. I can feel it, Rachael." He coughed, violently. She saw blood on his lips. "Everything's going to change."

Chapter 12 - Lightning

For a moment, nothing happened. Then she felt Justin's body begin to dissolve. One moment he was there with her, the faint beat of his heart through his ribcage, the rise and fall of his chest under her trembling hands. Then there was a feeling like waving your hand through a cloud of steam. Black smoke flowed out around her. The men on the boat were shouting. They looked nervous. The smoke grew, rolling outwards until it filled the whole of the rooftop. The dark cloud expanded as it rose into the sky, gathering like a storm overhead. Details began to form, each gleaming feather larger than a kite. The raven's body was so vast that it could have been an aircraft. Its glistening black eyes were the size of beach balls. Talons dug deep into the rooftop, ugly yellow and large enough to lift a car. Black wings shook out, the back draft rocking the tiny ship as it pulled away from the rooftop. For a moment the curve of the raven's beak seemed like a cruel smile.

She felt the tower tremble beneath her feet as he took to the air.

The tiny boat turned to flee, but Justin took off after it, wings cutting the air in motions that seemed slow, almost gentle, until she realised just how fast he was moving.

She could hear the gunshots ring out like rain on a pavement as the crew opened up with everything they had. Tufts of feathers burst loose as blood poured from a dozen wounds, but they were nothing more than pin-pricks. Talons lashed out, raking huge gouges into the hull, until one drew a ragged line across the back end of the deck and pure white light burst out from inside.

The ship was bathed in a crackling haze as bolts of lightning arced across the hull. Justin reeled back, wing feathers smoking. She saw the men on the deck collapse, writhing in agony. One fell over the side, a small dark shape plunging towards the city below. The ship fell after him, tumbling out of the sky.

Looking around, she saw that the raven was gone; that vast black form had disappeared into the darkness. She couldn't even hear the sound of his wings now. The ship was still falling towards the streets far below. The second of the small white boats was also gone. Perhaps, she decided, Justin was off chasing it. In the distance she saw the larger airship swinging around towards them again. The building trembled.

Hearing a sound, she turned and saw a man's face emerge over the side of the rooftop, dark skin crowned with dark hair. Rakesh straightened up, his red coat blowing in the wind. One hand rested on the hilt of his sword. Rachael got to her feet, standing to face the man as he advanced on her with an icy stare.

"You stupid little girl. Do you have the slightest idea what you've just unleashed?"

"Screw you. None of this woulda happened if you all had just left us alone."

"None of this would have happened if we'd been willing to do this right the first time," Rakesh said.

The sword gleamed as it slid from the scabbard. She heard a sound on the wind, like rustling leaves. Then Justin appeared, cresting the side of the roof, his slipstream blowing her hair wildly. For a moment he simply hung suspended in the air over the rooftop, before swooping down, long sharp claws raking at the ground. Rachael looked around in time to see Rakesh roll aside, the talons barely missing him.

As Justin wheeled around to swoop in again a bright flash filled the air and she breathed in a hard, metallic scent. There was a loud 'crack' as the lightning bolt missed Justin by inches. She turned to see the larger vessel flying straight towards them at full speed. Standing at the prow, feet firmly planted and a long barrelled weapon of some sort nestled firmly in the crook of his shoulder, a man in a tan coat sighted and snapped off another shot. Again, the burning smell, as the lightning bolt creased Justin's flank, charred black feathers falling away as the raven peeled off, diving below the edge of the tower. She called his name, her ragged voice coming out as a sound like metal scraping on metal.

Below the body of the ship she saw a rope ladder dangling. A blonde haired woman in dark clothes was hanging by one hand, her foot resting on the very last run, black cloak rippling in the wind as they neared. Glass panes rattled and broken shards fell loose in a glittering rain as the ship roared overhead. At the last second the woman let go, plunging towards the rooftop. Her cloak billowed out like wings.

Rachael watched the woman fall. She was astonished that anyone would even try to drop from that height. A flash of blonde hair showed amidst the tangle of dark clothes as the woman rolled and came to her feet, breathing hard, eyes alert.

Then Rakesh was on her, snatching hold of Rachael's arm with a grip like iron. As she was hauled to her feet, Rachael saw the second of the small white ships had returned. She could hear the buzz of the propellers as it drew close to the tower. Looking up, Rakesh gestured at the ship to come closer. As it neared the rooftop he moved towards the edge, dragging her with him. She twisted in his grasp, but she couldn't break free.

"Hands off the girl," Rachael heard the strange woman say, her voice sharp like a knife. Rakesh threw a glance back across his shoulder and his expression turned to one of faint amusement.

"Ilona? Fates, I'd heard the rumours, but... You know I just couldn't believe it really. That the little Karvonen girl was shacking up with a crew of explorers. With Chandra, of all people. Amazing."

"Tell me, Rakesh, did your father teach you to be an obnoxious little shit, or is it just breeding?" the woman growled.

Sneering, he turned to face her.

"You know, I think I still don't believe it. I don't think you ever had it in you to run away. I think your parents finally kicked you out. It wasn't like they ever had a hope of finding a respectable man to take you. A little too much wear on the goods, don't you think?"

Eyes flashing with rage, Ilona took a step forward. Then they all heard the rippling in the air, the sound coming from somewhere below the edge of the rooftop. Rachael looked down and saw the dark shape skimming the surface of the tower, rushing up towards them, and towards the approaching ship.

Justin struck the small white boat at its centre, the spine of the ship breaking across his shoulder as splinters of the shattered wooden hull rained around him. The ship fell, two broken halves continuing to disintegrate as they spiralled down towards the city below.

Barely slowed by the impact, Justin rolled into a dive, plunging towards the rooftop. Talons flashed out as Rachael dropped to the ground and Rakesh threw himself clear. Ilona rolled aside, bringing up one hand in a clenched fist. The woman's sleeve had fallen back to reveal a fine tracery of silver wrapped around her hand and arm, surmounted by a blue crystal. Sparks crackled around the silver filigree and a bolt of lightning arced out, striking Justin as he passed. His cry of pain was deafening, but Rachael felt a strange surge of joy as she saw one wing-tip catch the woman in the side, hurling her backwards. Ilona tumbled head over heels, nearly tipping over the edge of the rooftop as her limp form skidded to a halt. For a moment it seemed as if the blow had knocked her out, but to Rachael's astonishment the woman's eyes fluttered open again. With gritted teeth Ilona pulled herself to her feet.

Dipping a wing, Justin wheeled across the sky, coming around for another pass. Then she heard the sound of propellers growing louder, and in the darkness she made out the shape of the larger ship approaching, the last one still left flying. Rakesh was on his feet again and making his way towards her, the sword held loosely at his side. Then she heard another sound, and turned see Ilona charging headlong at them from across the rooftop. Rakesh turned and readied his blade, but Ilona wasn't coming for him. The impact made Rachael's head spin, as one arm caught around her midriff. She felt the rushing wind and a sickening lurch in her stomach as Ilona carried her clear off the edge of the roof. For a moment they plunged through open air, nothing below them but the city streets. A dark shape tore across the sky just above them, a blue light moving in the darkness. She caught a glimpse of the trailing rope ladder, as Ilona reached out a hand.

The woman's fingers closed around the ladder, and her other arm tightened suddenly around Rachael's waist, crushing the wind out of her. Her vision swam as the city pin-wheeled below them. Ilona's face was creased with pain, eyes squeezed shut.

"I strongly suggest you grab ahold," the woman grunted, eyes closed and teeth still gritted against the pain. "It's a very long fall."

Rachael grabbed onto the nearest rung and held on tight. She felt a momentary urge to try to kick the woman off, but even the thought of it seemed like suicide.

Her hands shook, her fingers numbed by the cold.

"Climb," Ilona roared, and she did so without thinking. Above them the engines screamed as the ship gained altitude, going flat out. On either side of the hull two massive blue crystals crackled with electricity. Her hands were numb with the cold, and as she caught each rung she felt sure it would slip free of her hands again at any moment. As the ladder twisted to and fro, she caught sight of a dark shape beneath them. Justin was closing on them, his wings cutting the air in long, sweeping arcs.

She reached the top and a pair of strong hands caught her by the shoulders and lifted her aboard. A tall man with a tanned skin and dark hair that was pulled back into a pony-tail. His duster coat rippled around them both as she collapsed onto the deck. The man smiled, as if he had done her some kind of favour. Rachael felt her stomach twist.

Arsha could feel the relief washing over her as Micah pulled Rachael and Ilona up onto the deck. Already they were flying away from the glass spire at full speed. She could hear the wretched sound of the engines as the vast black shape of the raven came after them.

"Everyone hold onto something," her father said, shouting to be heard over the engines.

Arsha grabbed onto the railing and saw Ilona do the same. Micah threw an arm around Rachael, who seemed too stunned to even struggle as he grabbed at the opposite railing. Then her father threw a lever and the crackling of the lightning in the floatstones ceased.

For a moment, nothing happened. Then her stomach felt as if it was going to lift up into her throat as the Zephyr went into free-fall. Suddenly the sprawl of endless grey was rushing up to meet them.

"Micah, get this thing off my tail."

"I can't get a clear shot from here," Micah shouted back. Halfway down the deck he was holding tight to the railing. Rachael was now holding on as well, seeming more worried about not falling off the ship than anything else.

They were still pitching forward, nose down, heading for the buildings below and the dark shape of the river beyond. Micah began to climb the railing, hand over hand like a ladder. Arsha looked around herself and caught sight of two coils of rope, stashed at the back of the deck. Grabbing the nearest one, she looped one end over the railing and threw the other end to Micah.

He grabbed the rope in both hands and nodded to her as he got to his feet. Using the rope to brace, he walked up the sloping deck. When he got to the back railing, he pulled the rope around himself in a loop and slung the other end across the hand rail, wrapping it around a few times before handing it to Arsha.

"Hold tight," he said, and then leaned back into the sling he'd made. He levelled the lightning ballista and fired shot after shot. The bird ducked and weaved, but several shots came close, and after a bolt carved a scorched black line across the feathers of one wing it seemed to lose some distance on them.

Then she felt the crackle in the air as her father slammed another lever home, re-engaging the lightning cages and bringing the floatstones to life. The propellers screamed as they skimmed the tops of the nearest buildings, plunging towards the river. Her father spun the wheel and brought the Zephyr around in a tight arc. She felt the spray as one propeller skimmed the water. They levelled out, flying just a few feet above the river, weaving between the strange looking ships that dotted the surface. Up ahead Arsha saw a bridge looming over the water, two towers facing each other across the span, their tops connected by a walkway.

When she realised what her dad was about to do, Arsha's heart caught in her throat. He brought the Zephyr even lower, white spray surrounding them as the hull rode the water. The raven was still chasing them, vast wings tearing the air apart with every stroke.

Rachael screamed in terror as Tower Bridge whipped over their heads, barely missing the tops of the propellers. As the ship began to climb again, she glanced back just in time to see Justin plough through the top of the bridge, pieces raining down in a cascade around him. White plumes dotted the river as the debris crashed into the water with a thunderous sound. The force of the impact whipped his body around, and for a moment she watched as he spiralled down towards the surface of the Thames. At the last moment Justin levelled out, claws raking the surface of the river. The ship continued to climb higher as he gave chase.

Above them the clouds loomed, reaching down to envelope them. The air grew colder and she shivered furiously, barely able to hold her grip on the railing. Heavy grey mist filled the air around them, until she couldn't even see the deck in front of her. Then the clouds vanished and she was staring at a sky turned from black to silver by the light of a full moon.

A moment later the clouds beneath them burst apart, as Justin tore through into the open air. Rachael stared in awe. Caught in the silver moonlight, he was beautiful. His feathers shone, and the light gleamed from his beak and talons. She saw clearly the smouldering lines scored across his plumage by the lightning bolts.

"Faster," the young man shouted from the back railing.

"We can't go any faster, Micah. The engines are about to explode," the older man at the wheel replied.

Micah shook his head and hefted the long silver rifle that he carried. Seeing him move to take up a firing position again, Rachael didn't even think before throwing herself across the deck at him. She slammed into his back, and the impact knocked him off balance, the weapon nearly slipping from his grasp. He fell against the railing, tipping halfway over. Then a hand grabbed her by the shoulder and hauled her back. Ilona threw her across the deck and she slammed into the far railing. She lay there, gasping for breath, with the icy air burning her lungs.

She rolled over and crawled to the nose of the ship, using the railing to stand. She looked back and saw Justin closing even faster. The man raised his weapon and turned to fire, but already Justin was almost upon them.

She heard a crack of thunder that seemed to split the sky open. An arc of lightning as thick as a tree trunk seared the air above their heads, missing Justin by a little more than a few feet. It took her a moment to realise that the lightning had come from above the clouds. Then a shadow fell over them, as another ship soared overhead. It was the size of a battleship, shaped like a Roman trireme, with a nose that sloped back as it rose up to the deck. From the rear of the ship curved wings extended outwards on either side, forming a cross with the fins that protruded both above and below. Below the ship's nose, a turret like protrusion wheeled about, angling a massive brass spike that appeared to be some kind of weapon, taking aim for a second shot. Lightning jumped from the tip of the spike again, ripping across the sky as Justin peeled away. Swooping down, trailing smoke from his scorched wing feathers, he vanished into the clouds.

As Justin disappeared, the young man raised the rifle to fire off a few parting shots. Screaming with rage, Rachael threw herself across the deck at him, lashing out wildly. Micah turned, startled, holding the rifle across his chest as a shield even as Arsha tried to step between them. Then Ilona grabbed at her, but this time she spun and kicked at the woman's shins. Ilona dodged back and the kick caught in her cloak, throwing Rachael's balance off. As she recovered, the woman slapped the silver gauntlet against her chest. There was a tiny blue flash, and every muscle in her body seemed to light on fire, convulsing with pain. She never even felt herself hit the deck.

The Zephyr levelled out and Rishi eased off the throttle, slowing to docking speed. He pulled the tiny ship around so that they were flying level with the Triskelion and set them on the deck.

Pulling herself up from the floor at the back of the boat, Arsha walked across to the where Rachael lay.

Breathing a heavy sigh, her father ran a hand through his hair.

"Ilona..." he said, disapprovingly.

"Don't start." Ilona said, a hand clutched to her bruised side.

"You should get Milima to see to that," he said at last, turning away. With a strained expression, Ilona turned and began to climb down the ladder. Micah and her father set about lowering Rachael down to the deck below, and then Micah carried her inside. Arsha watched it all in a kind of daze. As the adrenaline faded, she found her head swimming as she struggled to take in everything that had just happened. Then her father turned towards her. It was just the two of them left out on the deck, moonlight casting everything with an unearthly glow.

His hands were strong as he pulled her close.

"Thank you, Arsha. Thank you. I'm so proud of you. You were incredibly brave out there."

She felt the warmth of him, as she let her face fall against his chest. His arms enclosing her, his long coat shielding her from the wind. She knew she should feel safe and protected in her daddy's arms, but she couldn't seem to block out the way his voice trembled, the way his body seemed so frail, so small. In all her life, she couldn't remember a time she had ever heard her father sound so scared.

Chapter 13 - Clouds

The room smelled faintly of lavender and old timber. The air was heavy and stifling. Her body was all tangled up in thick layers of blankets. She could hear, or at least feel, a muted humming in the distance. Then she heard the sound of a door opening. Light footsteps on a wooden floor moved closer, and Rachael felt herself tensing up beneath the covers. She kept her eyes closed and forced herself to breathe slowly.

The footsteps came to a stop beside the bed, and she heard the rough scraping sound of someone pulling up a chair. Then the room was quiet again, except for the soft rustle of pages being turned.

She desperately wanted to open her eyes, even just a crack, to see who was in the room with her. Perhaps see where she was. She told herself to wait; they'd leave eventually, and she'd be free to explore.

Memories began to piece themselves together as she pretended to sleep. The fight on the rooftop. The people in the strange clothes, with their strange weapons and their flying ships. She wanted to tell herself they were just fragments of a dream, but nothing could be as real as the acrid smell of burning feathers as Justin was forced to flee. She remembered his rage, the way his screams had split the sky. She remembered the terror pounding in her skull and pulsing through her veins. The way each frozen breath tore at her lungs. She remembered that dizzying moment as the whole of the city was spread out below her, with nothing to save her from falling except the hand of her captor. She supposed that she must be on their ship now. The humming sound she heard was the engines rumbling away somewhere in the distance.

Justin would come back for her. She was sure of that. The thought lay at the back of her mind, something constant and unquestionable. Like a stone. She had never trusted anyone in the quite the same way.

There was a shuffling sound from beside the bed, and a quiet cough.

"You're not really asleep, are you?" said a voice that it took a moment to recognise. She pictured the girl's face. 'Arsha', that was her name.

"Sorry, it's just kind of obvious. Your face keeps moving. And you're breathing too fast," Arsha continued. "I mean, it's OK, if you don't want to talk or whatever. I've got a book to read. I just thought... you know... you might want to talk."

Carefully, Rachael opened her eyes. Arsha did indeed have a book open on one knee. The girl was dressed in loose silks, brightly embroidered in blues and greens. An old fashioned brass lantern sat on a small table beside her, giving off a hazy white light, though Rachael saw no sign of a flame.

"Hey," Arsha said, smiling as she closed her book.

Rachael sat up, and as the covers fell back she realised that she was in her underwear. She snatched up a blanket, and Arsha tried to conceal a smile.

"It's OK, I've got them too," the girl said, giggling.

Rachael scowled at Arsha, not saying a word.

"Sorry. Your clothes kind of... ummm... reeked," Arsha said. The girl paused for a moment, then extended her hand.

"So, we sort of met. I'm Arsha," she added.

"Yeah. I know," Rachael muttered, without making any move to take the girl's hand. "So, what... You're keeping an eye on me now? Make sure I don't escape?"

Arsha scowled.

"You were out cold. We wanted someone to stay with you, make sure you were OK."

"How long?"

The girl looked confused.

"How long have I been here."

"Oh. Since last night. It's evening now. Milima will have dinner on soon, if you're hungry."

"Great. Kidapping and room service. You guys are the best," Rachael said, her voice dripping sarcasm.

"Kidnapping?" Arsha's eyes narrowed indignantly. "We rescued you, from that monster."

"Yeah, good going," Rachael snarled. "That 'monster' was my friend. He was..." She couldn't even shape the words around the lump that formed in her throat when she thought about Justin. Again she remembered the smell of scorched feathers in the air. "He was the only person that's ever done right by me, and you tried to kill him. Nice rescue."

"He was trying to kill us."

For a moment it seemed that Arsha's indignant expression was masking something else. Rachael saw a glimmer of fear in the girl's eyes. "And anyway, we weren't trying to... I told you that we were coming to help you..." The girl floundered, a bitter look on her face. Without another word she opened her book and pointedly went back to reading. Rachael sat back, relishing her small victory.

As the silence deepened she examined the room. It was tiny, barely large enough for the narrow bed, a small dresser, and what looked like a closet set in one wall. In the wall over the bed there was a round porthole, but a brief glance showed only clouds, confirming her theory about the flying ship. The door had a latch and a keyhole. She guessed it was probably locked, though she couldn't actually remember hearing the lock turn when the girl had come in.

A nagging voice in the back of her mind was telling her that while chewing Arsha out had felt really good, it might not have been the best idea. If she was up in the sky, with no way off this ship, she was going to have to deal with being stuck here for a while. There'd be no chance of escape until they put down somewhere, or Justin came for her, and either way she'd be best off knowing as much about the ship as she could. The adults who'd hauled her aboard weren't likely to tell her anything, but Arsha seemed much less guarded. Whilst she'd taken an instant disliking to the girl, that sneaky little voice was telling her that making friends with Arsha was probably her best chance of finding a way to escape.

"Look, I'm sorry," she said, flatly. "I know it wasn't your fault and all."

For a while, Arsha made no sign of having heard her at all. Rachael felt herself growing increasingly irritated, as the girl let the silence play out. She was actually startled when Arsha finally spoke.

"You drool when you sleep."

Rachael glanced down at the pillow, and saw a damp spot in the middle of the impression her face had left. As silly as it was, she felt a colour rise in her cheeks. Arsha closed the book and looked up.

"I saw what Ilona did to you," the girl said. "It wasn't... She shouldn't have done that."

"Thanks," Rachael said, careful not to say more in case she crushed the fragile truce. In the awkward silence, her eyes wandered, settling on the strange lamp sitting by the bed. Something about the light it gave seemed oddly familiar. Next to the lantern she noticed another object on the side table. It was a small silver figurine, carved in the shape of a bird, head tucked under one wing as if asleep. The detail was incredible. She could make out each individual feather. Curious, Rachael reached out to touch the little figurine, but no sooner had her fingertips brushed across one wing than the little bird sprang to life. Silver wings chimed as they spread wide, and the little bird took flight, whirring around the room in a tiny grey blur. Rachael pulled her hand back as if burned, and an astonished gasp escaped her lips.

"Hey, hey, shhh..." Arsha reached up with gentle hands to coax the bird down into her open palm. "This is Penelope. She's a little excitable."

The bird hopped from one foot to the other.

"Is that thing real?" Rachael said. Her heart was still pounding.

"She's a real autom, yeah," Arsha said. "She's Telverian made."

"But it looks so real. Like its almost alive."

"Well, she is, sort of. She only pretends to eat and sleep of course. But aside from that..."

"How's that even possible? She's like an actual robot or something," Rachael said, still staring at the little machine.

"A what?" Arsha scrunched her face up.

"I guess its what we'd call 'em, in the real world... Or, my world, or whatever you call it. But I mean that's only in movies and stuff anyhow. We can't really make, y'know, anything like this. What did you call it again?"

"She's an autom, if that's what you mean. But her name's Penelope. Or Penny is OK," Arsha said, slightly put out.

"Right, yeah." Rachael leaned forward to examine the little bird closely. Penelope hopped back a step and turned to regard her with one pearly bead of an eye. Gently, Arsha began to stroke Penelope's feathers back, the metal seeming to move like something much softer under the girl's fingertips, as the little creature twisted her head appreciatively.

"So, is there anything I can get for you?" Arsha said, as she set Penelope down on the dresser again. "Like, a glass of water, or..."

"I wouldn't mind getting my clothes back, actually," she said.

Arsha smiled.

"They're in the wash... I think. At least I'm pretty sure Milima was joking about burning them. But I've got some of my stuff you can have."

"Um... OK. I guess."

Arsha looked her over for a moment, eyes fixing on her cheeks and then her hair, and she sniffed pointedly.

"Maybe a shower first," she said, sticking her tongue out. Without even thinking, Rachael smacked the girl on the arm, and was rewarded with a delicious yelp of pain. As Arsha rubbed at her arm, scowling, Rachael wondered if she might have taken it a little too far.

"Sorry," she muttered.

"It's OK. I guess I kind of deserved that," Arsha replied.

"A bit, yeah," Rachael said, but she found herself smiling, and to her surprise Arsha smiled back.

"Come on then," the girl said, gesturing towards the door.

Soaking wet and surrounded by clouds of steam, Rachael stood on the porcelain tiled floor of the bathroom, staring at her reflection in the mirror. She hardly recognised her face without the layers of grime that it seemed to have built up over the last year. Her hair, sadly, remained an impossible mat of tangles, and after several painful attempts to pull a brush through it she was forced to give up. She wrapped a towel about herself, and stepped out into the corridor.

Arsha was waiting for her, leaning against the wall with a bundle of cloth folded over one arm. Her little robot pet was sat on her shoulder, and in her free hand she held some kind of large blue crystal set into a silver frame. Flickering lights hovered just above the surface of the stone. As Rachael stared at it in fascination, Arsha looked up, smiled, and pocketed the device.

"These should fit you OK," she said, lifting the bundle slightly.

"Thanks," Rachael said, her eyes wandering to the lanterns that lined the hallway. Like the one in her room, they showed no sign of a flame. Just a glowing light, like a speck of dust floating inside the glass bulb.

"It's a ghostlight," she said, more to herself than to Arsha.

"Yeah. How'd you know?" the girl replied, looking surprised.

"Something Justin told me. I used to see them. When I was little."

"I didn't know you had ghostlights in your world."

"Well we don't... I mean... I guess we do. But it was only people like me that could see them. Or something."

"Oh," Arsha said, apparently at a loss.

"Is that normal then?" Rachael gestured at the lamp. "Using them as lights like that?"

The girl shrugged.

"Yeah. It's better than chemical lamps. I mean they're not as bright, but they last for ages and they don't get hot or smell bad or anything. You just close the shutter when you don't need them. They go to sleep after a bit."

"Right. Yeah," Rachael said, feeling her stomach twist as she watched the little mote of light drifting inside the glass.

The clothes at least didn't fit too badly. Though Arsha was taller, and certainly larger in a few areas than she was, the loosely cut tunic and trousers seemed comfortable enough. She stared at herself in fascination, silver thread gleaming against blue silk. Nothing like the jeans and t-shirts she was used to.

She was still fiddling with the new clothes when Arsha appeared in the doorway.

"They're OK?"

"Yeah. Thanks," Rachael replied.

"So, dinner should be ready, if you're hungry," Arsha said.

Feeling her stomach growl at the mention of dinner, Rachael nodded. As they made their way up the stairs, Rachael found her attention caught by the smell drifting down from the kitchen. They emerged into a surprisingly large dining hall with a long bench table down one side. The rest of the room was occupied by cupboards, counter-tops, a sink and an iron cooking range. Standing by the stove, a woman in an apron was stirring something in a heavy copper pot. Her long, dark braids were tied back with a knotted hankie. The woman looked up as they entered and smiled warmly. As she turned towards them, Rachael's attention was immediately drawn to the tattoo around her right eye. Like the rest of her it had been weathered by age, but the white lines were still clearly visible against her jet black skin.

"Hello. I was hoping you two might be up soon."

"Hey Mim," Arsha said. "Rachael, this is Milima. She's awesome."

"Hey," Rachael said, cautiously.

"Hi Rachael. I hope you're feeling better."

"Yeah. Sure," she said.

"It's OK," Milima said, turning to stir the pot for a moment. "I know you must be apprehensive right now."

"Yeah. Whatever that means."

"Suspicious. I would be," Milima said.

"Guess you've got me all figured out."

The woman gave her a measuring look.

"Well, can you trust us enough to sit down for a meal at least?" she said.

"Food sounds good," Rachael allowed.

"Great," Milima smiled. "Why don't you girls get yourself some plates and bowls, while I get this ready?"

Rachael and Arsha set places, whilst Milima continued to work at the stove. Soon enough Rachael found herself sat on one of the long benches, with a bowl in front of her being filled with steaming hot lentil soup. A wicker basket was set down, piled high with soft loaves of flat bread.

Ignoring Arsha's surprised expression, Rachael devoured a whole loaf before even starting on the soup. It was thick and rich, full of spices that she couldn't even name, and it tasted better than anything she had eaten in a long time. Milima's eyes widened in alarm as the woman returned to the table.

"Slow down girl. You won't have room for the stew."

Spoon half raised to her mouth, Rachael looked up in confusion.

"I'm sorry," Milima continued, wiping her hands on a cloth. "The soup and the bread were just meant as a starter. It's nothing special I'm afraid, just last night's beef, plus some carrots and okra and what-not."

"She's talking rubbish," Arsha said. "Milima makes the best stew ever."

"Well either way, I'd say it's about ready," Milima said, tucking the cloth into her back pocket. Returning to the stove, Milima retrieved another large pan, which she set down in the middle of the table, steam wafting off the surface.

"Give it a moment to cool now."

Footsteps from the stairs above gave her time to look up as a tall figure entered the room. It took her a moment to recognise the young man from the night before. In the clear light, without the goggles, he had the kind of face that you could spend hours drawing. The delicate line of his jaw swept up towards perfect cheekbones that framed piercing blue eyes and a nose like a razor blade. Her stomach twisted in disgust as she thought of him sighting down the barrel of the strange lightning gun he'd carried.

"Hey Micah," Arsha said, smiling brightly. Her cheeriness only made the angry knot in Rachael's stomach twist a little tighter.

"Hey there little bear," Micah replied. "So did someone say stew?"

Dropping down onto the bench beside Arsha, he reached for a long handled ladle. No sooner had his fingertips grazed the handle than there was a loud 'snap' as Milima cracked a wash-cloth over his hand.

"Hands off, you," she said. "Seven below, you've not even got a bowl in front of you. Were you planning to just eat it out of the pot?"

"Pretty much, yeah," Micah said, grinning as he got up to collect some cutlery from the kitchen. From across the table, Arsha caught

Rachael's eye and gave her a resigned shrug. Rachael looked down at her bowl of half-finished soup again, silently wondering how this could be normal for anyone.

"So," Milima said, as she began to fill more bowls, "will the esteemed professor and his star pupil be joining us?"

Micah shook his head.

"You know those two. Glued to their books. I'll bring something down for them later."

"Speaking of which, I should take a bowl up for poor Abasi. He's been at those charts all day."

As Milima spoke, Micah was already shovelling food into his mouth. An instant later an uncomfortable expression appeared on his face.

"Yes, it's hot," Milima sighed.

"How is it I have this figured out and you don't?" Arsha chided, nudging him gently in the ribs, as Micah swallowed his mouthful and gave them all a boyish grin.

Rachael picked out a chunk of beef and bit into it. Her expression must have said everything, as Arsha nodded at her in agreement.

"Told you," the girl said.

Though Rachael said nothing, she had to admit it was mostly because she didn't want to waste any time on talking. She devoured everything that had been set in front of her, and didn't think twice when Micah leaned over to refill her bowl. She couldn't remember the last time she eaten food that tasted as good, nor in such quantities. As she polished off her second bowl, she felt as if her stomach might burst. A heavy warmth filled her body, and for a moment she found herself feeling perilously at ease. She could happily have set her head down on the table and fallen asleep right there and then.

She was so overwhelmed by the satisfied feeling that she didn't even notice Ilona come in. It was only when the others looked up that Rachael realised the woman was standing only a few feet away from her.

Arsha was already shuffling up to clear a place when Ilona gestured for her to stay still.

"I'll just take a tray down. It's OK," she said, flatly.

Bowls were passed over, and Micah stood to help load up a tray. Rachael watched out of the corner of her eye, pretending to be paying more attention to her food. The woman's eyes were bloodshot, her make-up barely concealing the dark circles around them. She looked as if she hadn't slept in days.

As she was about to leave, Ilona turned to Micah.

"So are you planning on coming down to help us any time soon?"

"Not just yet," he said, apologetically. Rachael caught the way he nodded, very slightly in her direction. Ilona glanced at her, just for an instant, then back to Micah.

"Fine. But we've got a lot of work to do."

"I know," Micah said.

As the woman left he sat back down, his cheerful smile returning. Sipping at a glass of milk, Rachael watched as he began to quiz Arsha about her studies. He seemed to be tutoring her in maths, or something like it, and Arsha wrinkled her forehead as she struggled to answer the problems he tested her with.

"Argh. I'm awful at this," Arsha growled, letting her head drop to the table.

"See, she says this because she thinks it's normal for fifteen year olds to be doing math at a university level," Micah said, giving Rachael a conspiratorial wink. "What about you, Rachael? Are you much good at numbers?"

"Not really," Rachael said.

"That's OK, neither am I really," he said with a genial shrug. "Honestly, if my old man hadn't insisted..."

He didn't bother finishing the sentence, perhaps sensing her disinterest. Rachael pushed her empty plate away.

"What's with all this," she said. "Why is it everyone's so keen to act like we're all best friends now?"

For a moment Micah and Arsha were both silent. They shared an awkward look, as if neither of them knew what to say to this.

"We just wanted to... You know... Make you feel welcome," Arsha said. "I mean, we know things haven't been easy for you."

Rachael shook her head in astonishment.

"You don't know nothing about me, so don't try to pretend you do."

"Hey, we're just trying to..." Arsha began, her tone indignant, before Micah silenced her with a raised hand.

"It's OK. Look, Rachael... We're not trying to pull anything here. I mean, this whole situation has been pretty horrible, for everyone. But you're our guest here, OK?"

Scowling, Rachael looked back down at her plate again. The silence was broken by Milima's reappearance.

"Dessert, anyone? It's buttermilk pie," she announced, either missing the mood of the room, or hoping to break it.

"Did the coolroom break down or something?" Micah said, with a surprised expression.

"I just thought we could all do with some comfort food after the last few days," Milima said. "But, if you don't want any..."

"Hey, let's not be too hasty now," Micah said.

"Just what I thought," Milima nodded, smugly.

Rachael thought she couldn't possibly eat anything more, but as a steaming hot slice of pie was set before her, a cold, raw instinct made her pick the spoon up. It could have tasted like a mouthful of dirt, and still she wouldn't have been able to bring herself to refuse free food. When it tasted as good as this, she knew she was helpless. Another glass of cold milk was poured for her and she dug in.

The conversation continued around her, as Milima bemoaned Rishi and Ilona's refusal to sit down for a proper meal. Micah nodded, reaching for a second helping of pie.

"Not that you couldn't think about getting back down there and helping them," Milima added, jabbing a spoon in his direction.

"Healthy body, healthy mind," Micah said, with a grin.

"Healthy doesn't have this much sugar in it, young man. Not that it'll make any difference to you."

Micah shrugged, prompting a quiet smirk from Arsha. Looking down at her empty bowl, Rachael could feel her head swimming. The room felt too warm, and suddenly everything didn't seem straight. She felt dizzy and flushed, as a wave of nausea seized her stomach. She looked across at Arsha, and managed "Toilet?"

Surprised, Arsha gestured at the stairs.

As another wave of nausea washed over her, Rachael left the room as quickly as she could. Halfway down the stairs she broke into a sprint, and barely made it to the bathroom in time.

There was cold sweat on her brow by the time her stomach had ceased heaving. A voice in the back of her head was screaming angrily at her for letting so much good food slide down a toilet bowl, but she was too dazed to pay it much attention. She was shivering and her throat hurt. She fumbled about the sink, looking for something to wipe her mouth with.

She heard the door open, but felt too dizzy to look up. Gentle hands wrapped a towel around her shoulders. A damp cloth was wiped across her mouth, and then a glass of water was held out for her. She took small sips, swilling and spitting first to get the worst of the taste from her mouth. Gentle hands rubbed at her back, as she swallowed small mouthfuls of water.

"That was my fault," Milima said, quietly. "Stupid of me really."

Rachael said nothing.

"I imagine it's been a long time since you've eaten that much in one sitting."

She supposed this was true. She could have lasted a week on what had been put on her plate that night.

"Are you OK now?"

She nodded.

"All right. Up you come."

Milima helped her to stand, taking her arm like a little girl. She felt a hot flush of anger, and pushed the woman's hand away.

"Hey," Milima snapped. "Claws away."

Rachael stared at the woman, incredulous, feeling her hands clench so tight that the nails bit into her palms. Whatever self-control she had maintained throughout dinner, she could feel the last of it slipping through her fingers.

"I know you're angry, Rachael. Of course you're angry. We've assaulted you, we've dragged you away from your home, and we've done nothing but tell you that it's for your own good. And the worst part is that it's the truth."

The woman spoke calmly, meeting Rachael's furious glare with a steady gaze.

"I can't change that, and I can't imagine I'd feel any different in your place. But I can at least try to make things a little better for you. Will you let me do that much?"

"I can look after myself," Rachael growled.

"Seven keep us, I didn't imagine for a second that you couldn't. Rachael, I know what starvation looks like. How long has it been since you had a proper meal? Since you slept in a real bed? A year or more, I imagine."

"More or less," she said, cautiously.

"I'm sorry," Milima said, her tone softening. "It can't have been easy."

Rachael just shrugged, not meeting her eyes.

"It's not your fault," she said. It took her a moment to realise just what that meant. It wasn't Milima's fault, or Arsha's, or Micah's. None of what had happened to her was. No matter how good it felt, to lay everything on the nearest target, she couldn't escape the awful feeling that Milima was right. Lashing out hadn't gained her anything.

She took a long, slow breath and tried to collect herself.

"Come on," Milima said, gently. "Lets get you back to bed."

She just nodded. She felt exhausted by the day, by the dinner, and by the effort of fighting everything. There simply wasn't any strength left in her. They came to the door of the room where she had woken up just a few hours ago. Her room, now. It was a strange thought.

"Not going to try to tuck me in?" she muttered, sourly.

"Would you want me to?" Milima asked, with a joking look in her eyes.

"Hardly," she muttered.

Milima smiled as Rachael opened the door to the cabin. She stopped in the doorway and forced herself to smile back, just for a moment, before she closed the door. It took all the strength she had left in her just to undress and crawl beneath the covers. She looked up at the starlit sky, barely visible through the narrow porthole, and tried not to think about how badly she had wanted to say 'Yes.'

Chapter 14 - Conversations

Morning light crept in through the port-hole. Rachael watched it crawling down the far wall of the bedroom. She'd spent most of the night tossing and turning, the sheets too warm, the mattress too soft. Sick of lying in bed with only her own gnawing anxiety buzzing away at the back of her brain, she finally pulled the covers aside and got to her feet. Sifting through the clothes that Arsha had left in her cupboard, she found a practical looking pair of brown trousers and a plain white tunic.

Feeling less conspicuous than she had in the brightly coloured silks she'd been wearing yesterday, Rachael decided that she might as well try to find something to eat. She slipped out into the corridor and made her way up towards the mess hall.

At the doorway she paused. Sitting at the table, facing towards the cooking range, was a man she didn't recognise. He was dark skinned and heavy-set, with a tight mat of silver-grey hair. His hands, folded on the table in front of him, were large and muscular.

He was leaning forward over the table, listening intently as Milima's voice came from across the room. From where she was standing Rachael couldn't see the woman, but she could easily hear how agitated she was. The man at the table didn't seem to have noticed her, and Rachael stayed put, not moving a muscle as she listened.

"...and maybe we wouldn't be in this mess if you didn't follow every order damn Rishi gives you without question."

When the man spoke, his voice was cavernously deep, a soft rumbling tone, like mountains moving.

"We did the right thing Milima. Rishi wasn't the one who covered up a prediction, and he didn't open a Seed in the middle of London. At least the girl is safe with us now."

She heard the clatter of a pan being slapped down on the iron cooking range.

"Even though the man who's supposed to be our friend still won't tell us why she's so important," Milima snapped. For a moment the man at the table said nothing. The sound of clattering cookware ceased.

"Abasi what is it?" Milima said, her voice quieter, but no less angry, like the sound of a knife being sharpened. "What aren't you saying?"

The man glanced away for a moment.

"Do you think we should just hand her over to the Guild?" he replied.

"Seven, Aba, you know I don't. The damage is done now. We're responsible. And that poor girl... She's been through hell. You can see it in her eyes."

Rachael's throat felt dry, but she forced herself not to make the slightest movement.

"So she stays with us," Abasi said.

"You're still not answering my question. Why did we ever go chasing off after this girl in the first place?"

"Someone had to. Guild doesn't know what she is. And Lord Bhandari knows all too well."

"And what exactly is she?" Milima said, her soft tone becoming, if anything, even sharper. "I expect all this secrecy from Rishi, but not from my own husband."

From his expression, it almost seemed as if the man was unable to speak. As if the words had simply caught in his throat. There was something in his eyes, like sadness, or even fear. Then she heard Milima's voice, trembling with concern.

"Oh Abasi, no. Of all the things for you to get caught up in again..."

"It was my choice," he said, firmly, but with an unmistakable catch in his voice.

"The hell it was," Milima hissed angrily. Rishi had no right, dragging you back into that madness. He knows damn well what you went through."

As the woman spoke, she stepped forward across the room, now in Rachael's view. Her anger was written plainly on her face.

"Melaku, love, it was my choice," the man said, heavily.

"Don't do that," Milima snapped. Don't use that name just because you know I'm angry with you."

"You never let me use it any other time," Abasi said, the words curiously soft for a man with so heavy a voice. As she watched, Milima's expression seemed to melt. The woman stepped forward, leaning over the table to kiss the man on his forehead.

"Almost never," she said with a smile. Then she seemed to take notice of something. "But I don't think Rachael wants to hear us talk about that," Milima added, laughing.

The man quickly looked up, masking his alarm with a cheerful expression.

"Good morning Rachael," he said. "How are you feeling?"

Not really sure what to say, she just shrugged.

"I'm Abasi Bira," he said, standing up to walk around the table towards her. "I'm the captain of this ship."

He offered his hand. She took it, her tiny fingers entirely enclosed in his grasp, but his touch was almost too gentle, as if he was afraid he might break her. His skin was rough and calloused.

"Rachael, if there's anything at all you need," he said, "don't hesitate to ask me, OK?"

"Sure," she nodded.

"Well, I should go check on our course," Abasi said, turning to nod to Milima as he left.

"So," Milima said, getting to her feet, "Do you feel like you could manage some breakfast?"

"I guess," Rachael said.

She took a seat, feeling all too much like an intruder in someone else's home. It was strangely quiet, just the sound of Milima humming softly as she bustled in and out of a larder on the far side of the room. Soon a bowl of yoghurt and an open jar of honey were set down in front of her, followed by a mug of tea poured from a large pan that was simmering away on the stove. Then Milima poured another tea for herself and sat down across the table from her.

Cautiously, Rachael mixed a little honey into her yoghurt and started to eat. She kept expecting Milima to say something, but the woman just sat in silence, sipping her tea and staring off into the distance.

"You not gonna ask how I'm settling in or something?" Rachael said at last.

"I don't know. Do you feel very settled right now?" Milima said, taking another sip of her tea.

"Not really," she mumbled, staring down at her plate.

Milima just nodded, without saying another word.

As the woman drank her tea, Rachael toyed with her spoon, and listened to the distant hum of the engines.

"Honestly," Milima said, watching her from over the rim of her mug, "if it was me in your position, I'd be looking for the first chance to get off this boat. Even out here in the middle of nowhere. It's easier to be lost on your own terms than on someone else's, right?"

Rachael scowled, and sipped her tea, trying not to meet the

woman's eyes. The taste of cinnamon, liquorice, and a host other spices flooded her mouth. For a moment she gagged at the sweetness.

"I know you don't have much reason to trust us," Milima continued, "and I don't expect that you should. After what you've been through recently, I can't imagine trusting anyone comes easily."

"Jesus, could you not?" Rachael growled. She could feel herself losing her cool, but she was past caring. "Stop trying to pretend like you know what I been through. Like you ever had to sleep in the rain or dig food out of rubbish bins cause you're so hungry you'd eat the first thing you found. Like any of my life even matters to you."

Her voice rising to a shout, Rachael slammed her cup down so hard that it spilled, throwing the contents across the table. In silence that followed, she heard the slow drip of the tea splashing on the floor.

She was fuming, staring the woman right in the eyes, feeling her hands shake against the tabletop. Milima looked back at her with a strange calmness.

"Shouldn't I care?" she said. "Suppose you're right. Suppose I've never known anything like the hardships you have. Should I not care about the things you've been through, just because they've never happened to me?"

Rachael searched the woman's eyes, not even sure what she was looking for. Some sign that she was being lead on, that it was all a trick to win her trust. Some glimmer of a lie. As Milima stared back at her, she saw only a stillness. Calm, patient, and kind. At last, Rachael looked away, unable to hold the woman's gaze any longer.

"Sorry about the mess," she mumbled.

"It's fine," Milima said. She saw the hint of a smile as the woman stood up and went to get a tea-towel. As Milima began to mop up the spilled tea, Rachael found herself staring down at the table. The woman stood up and went back to the counter, where she began filling a bowl in the sink.

"What's it mean?" Rachael said, over the sound of the pouring water. "That mark, around your eye?"

Milima turned to look at her with a thoughtful expression.

"It means I was a soldier," she said.

"You were a soldier?" Rachael's eyes narrowed. "Did you fight in any wars?"

Milima nodded.

"I'm from the Herdlands, Rachael. It's all we've ever known."

Before Rachael could ask what the woman meant by this, she heard a movement in the hall and then Arsha appeared in the doorway. She was noticeably subdued as she entered the room. Her hair was a mess and she looked as if she hadn't really slept.

"What can I get you to eat, love?" Milima asked as she set a mug of tea down in front of the girl. Arsha shrugged, face mostly hidden as she lifted the mug in both hands and took a large gulp. Rachael began to eat a little more of her yoghurt, as Milima brought another bowl out for Arsha. The girl picked up her spoon, but seemed to do little more than push the contents of the bowl around.

Rachael scraped her bowl clean, whilst Arsha ate barely half of what was in front of her before pushing her bowl away. With a tutting sound Milima scooped up the girl's leftovers. Though she said nothing, Rachael couldn't help but notice the quiet look of concern in the woman's eyes.

"Arsha, love, how would you like to show Rachael around, give her a proper tour of the ship?"

Arsha looked up at Milima with a puzzled expression.

"I've still got chores," she said.

"Oh don't worry about that. I'll see to the dusting today. You look after our guest."

Rachael tried not to think about how much the word 'guest' chafed at her. The sneaky voice in the back of her head reminded her that knowing her way around the ship could turn out to be very useful.

"I'd like that," she said, "if it's alright with you."

"Sure," Arsha said, with that same thin smile. "We can start down in the hold, I guess."

The hold was enormous, and incredibly dull. Rachael looked out over the rows of wooden crates and barrels covered in netting and saw nothing of interest. Still, she decided she would have to come back later and look for hiding spots, or something useful in the cargo.

The hold occupied the front half of the ship, whilst the back half was divided into decks. The lowest deck seemed to be the sleeping quarters, eight cabins lining a narrow corridor, four to a side, with the bathrooms and laundry near to the back of the ship; the stern, as Arsha insisted on calling it. Staircases at either end lead to the decks above. As they made their way up what Arsha referred to as the 'aft stairwell', Rachael noticed that the two bedrooms furthest back seemed larger.

"Captain's quarters, for Abasi and Milima, and Dad's room," Arsha explained.

"So how comes he gets a bigger room all to himself?" Rachael said. Arsha made a frustrated sound.

"He does all his work in there. It's mostly full of books anyhow."

"He's in there now?" Rachael said.

"No, he's up on the bridge, I think. With the others," she said.

Following the stairs up past the dining room, which Arsha referred to as the 'mess hall', they came out in front of a large door, made of steel, with big wheel locks like something on a submarine. To their right, another narrow staircase continued upwards.

"That leads out to the deck," Arsha said, gesturing at the door. "The stairs go up to the bridge. I think Micah has the tiller right now."

"The tiller?"

"It's the wheel that steers the ship," Arsha said, with an exasperated sound.

"Oh. The steering wheel. You could have just said that," Rachael said, feeling just as frustrated as Arsha sounded. "Why do you gotta call everything weird stuff, and then act like I'm some kind of idiot for not knowing what everything's supposed to be?"

"Because that's what it's called," Arsha sighed. "You'll get used to it."

"Yeah, well I'm not exactly planning on sticking around that long," Rachael snapped.

"All right, you don't want to be here, I get it already," Arsha replied, her voice rising as she threw her hands up in aggravation.

"You think?" Rachael snapped back at her. "Hey, here's an idea, let's head up and ask your dad how long he's going to keep me prisoner for. What do you think he might say to that?"

"Fates, would you just stop? You're acting like he's the bad guy, and you haven't even met him."

"Exactly. I got knocked out, kidnapped, hauled away, and the guy who's supposed to be doing all this 'cos its what's best for me won't even give me a damn explanation. I been here a full day now, and I ain't even met the guy, but you want me to be grateful for that? Well screw you, and screw him," Rachael yelled, feeling her nails digging into her palms.

"Shut up. Just shut up." Arsha's voice rose to a shriek. "You're so horrible. He's going to go to jail because of what he did for you, and you don't even care. You don't care about anyone but yourself."

The words hit her like a blow to the chest. Rachael felt herself stagger back a step.

"He's what?" she said, blinking. For a moment Arsha just glowered at her.

"I heard Milima saying it yesterday," she said, her voice dropping to a low snarl. "Him and Abasi, because of what they did. Dad's probably going to prison, and Abasi will lose his ship... All because they broke a few stupid rules trying to rescue you."

"Good," Rachael heard herself say.

It was as if the word was past her lips before she even had a chance to think about it. She saw the shift in Arsha's expression, felt something inside herself recoil at what she had just done. Then a wave of white hot anger seemed to rush through her, surging up from her gut and spilling out over her tongue.

"Well it serves them both right. Someone should have to pay for all this. For all of what's happened. They had no right to do none of what they did, and now they're both getting what they deserve."

For a moment, the silence was deafening, as the girls stared at each other. When Arsha spoke, her voice was barely more than a whisper.

"You fucking bitch."

Rachael could only stare as Arsha turned on her heel and stormed away, vanishing down the stairs to the lower deck. Moments later she heard more footsteps from the stairway leading up to the bridge, and then Micah appeared, looking worried.

"Hey, what's happening here?" he said.

"Nothing. Nothing's happening," Rachael said. For a moment he regarded her silently, as if trying to decide whether or not to press the point.

"Well?" she snapped, her patience giving out on her. "You got something to say?"

He scowled, but said nothing. Rachael turned away, taking the stairs two at a time, just as Arsha had done. She soon found herself down on the bottom deck, in the empty corridor between the cabins. It was strangely quiet. Even the distant sound of the engines barely seemed to register. She pressed her fingers to her temples and leaned back against the wall.

"Christ almighty," she muttered to herself, "you really screwed that one up."

After a while she got to her feet and took a breath, trying to steel herself against what she knew she had to do next.

Arsha's room was empty, but a glance towards the far end of the corridor told her where the girl had gone. The door to the hold was slightly ajar. In the dim light she wandered through the stacks of supplies. Compared to the cramped confines of the rest of the ship, the hold seemed vast. The smaller vessel, suspended in its cradle above her, seemed a little like a beached whale. She saw the name painted on the side. 'Zephyr'. She wondered what it meant.

At the far end of the room she spotted a ladder leading up to a small loft space. When she reached the top she found a small nook, formed where the walls of the hull met at the nose of the ship. Two portholes and a single lamp provided light to a space that had been mostly filled by a beaten up old couch and a pair of well worn armchairs. Arsha was huddled up against one arm of the couch, eyes red, wetness glistening on her cheeks.

"Go away," she said.

"Look, I just wanted to say I'm sorry," Rachael said. Slowly, she eased herself down into the nearest armchair. "I didn't mean it, what I said. I was just... I didn't mean it."

Arsha's eyes seemed to study her for a moment.

"Yes you did."

"Yeah. Alright." Rachael pulled her knees up. "Maybe I did a bit. But it wasn't right to say it, so I'm sorry for that."

"Fine. What's it matter anyway, if you're sorry or not? Dad's still going to go to prison, and Uncle Abasi's still going to lose his ship, and Micah and Ilona won't have jobs, and everyone's going to leave, and I'll just be..."

As her voice choked off into a sob, Arsha wiped a hand across her reddened eyes, leaving a damp smear across her cheeks.

"They shouldn't never have come for me," Rachael said. "Your dad, and the others. Even if they meant right and all, even if I'd wanted 'em to... It weren't worth it. Not for me. Putting all these people through this. Taking all those risks. And putting you in the middle of it and all. He didn't have no right to do that," she continued, growing agitated as she spoke. "Why'd he have you out there nearly getting killed and all that? Why did you have to be a part of it?"

She saw the girl's expression shift slightly, anger turning to resentment.

"Because I asked to. Because I wanted to help you," Arsha said, bitterly.

"Help me? Why?"

"I don't know. Does there have to be a reason to want to help someone?"

Rachael said nothing at first, as she struggled to wrap her head around this.

"Yeah, well, I don't want no help."

"Right, I get it. You're tough." Arsha turned away, staring at the wall. Stranded in the silence, Rachael gazed out of the porthole at the endless blue sky beyond. She wondered how high up they were.

"I guess it must be easier for you," Rachael said, at last. "Asking for help."

"What do you mean?" Arsha said, turning to her with narrowed eyes.

"I dunno, it's just... You've got all these people around you, all this... Family. I never really had that. It must be nice, trusting people. Being able to make friends easy."

Though she couldn't say what sort of reaction she had been expecting, Rachael was completely taken aback as Arsha threw her head back and laughed. It was a sick, bitter laughter that seemed to rattle in her throat, even as her shoulders shook with the force of it.

"You... You really think I know anything about making friends? I grew up on a ship. My dad's an archaeologist. I've never been more than two months in the same place, and most of those were in the middle of a desert somewhere. You know why I really wanted to help you so much?"

Arsha turned to look her square in the eyes.

"Because I honestly thought there was a chance that we might be friends. Fates, how pathetic is that? I mean, seriously. This..." she gestured at the two of them, "This is the closest to making an actual friend that I've ever been in my life."

Silence followed, broken only by the sound of the wind against the hull, as Rachael looked into Arsha's eyes and was met with only a cold challenge as the girl stared back at her.

"Yeah," Rachael shook her head, sadly, "you and me both."

To her own surprise, she found herself smiling at the appalling awkwardness of it all. With everything else that had happened, it seemed like such a foolish thing to get hung up on.

For a moment Arsha just blinked in surprise. Then, slowly at first, she began smiling back, almost as if she wasn't aware of it herself. Quietly, falteringly, they both began laugh. Rachael felt the laughter grow, rolling over her in waves. Each time it came close to fading, the sight of Arsha's expression seemed to set her off again. In that moment nothing else mattered. The past two days, the past few weeks, the past years, all of it fell away, and there was nothing but the infectious joy of Arsha's smile.

"I really am sorry, for what I said before," Rachael said at last, as she wiped her eyes and tried to put on a more serious face. "I'm still not cool with your dad, or nothing, but you didn't deserve me laying all that on you. You've been so nice to me, and I shouldn't have been so mean to you. Especially not with all you've been dealing with."

"It's OK," Arsha said. "I guess you don't have a whole lot to feel good about right now."

"Not so much. But thanks, for trying to help."

"Yeah, well, it turns out you're not completely horrible," Arsha said, still smiling.

"Did... Did you want to finish showing me around?" Rachael ventured.

"Nah," Arsha said, her smile widening. "Let's do something fun."

The heavy iron door made a clattering sound, as Arsha spun the wheel lock. The girl kept glancing over her shoulder, at the stairway that lead up to the bridge. Then they slipped through the doorway, and Arsha swung the hatch closed behind them, careful not to slam it. They had stepped into a room that was nothing more than a few feet of hallway with a door at either end. The outer door, like the inner, was of heavy steel with another wheel lock. Arsha turned to one side and pulled open a set of cupboard doors set into the wall.

"Here, you'll need this."

Arsha thrust a full length coat into Rachael's arms. She pulled out another for herself, and quickly shrugged it on.

Rachael fumbled with the heavy coat. The cloth was stiff, with a prickly texture, laden with buckles and straps. Cursing, she shifted around inside it, but couldn't get the massive thing to sit right.

"How am I supposed to wear this thing? It's huge."

"Give me a minute," Arsha said. "I just need to tighten it up for you."

She set to fussing with the various straps, tightening here and loosening there according to some strange formula known only to herself.

"Try it now."

Rachael shifted her arms experimentally. She had to admit it really did feel quite comfortable.

"See?" Arsha said, a little smugly, as she set about doing up the clasps on the front of the coat.

"Hey, I can handle that by myself. I'm not five," Rachael said, fending the girl off. "Just because I don't understand your crazy adjustable coats..."

Soon they were both safely ensconced, and Arsha pulled back the bolts on the heavy outer door. Then she worked at the brass handle by the doorway, and with a clatter of spinning gears it swung ponderously open. A wall of light burst through the crack and Rachael was hit full in the face by an icy blast of wind. She pulled the goggles on and tugged the collar of the coat up around her face, suddenly glad of both.

Blinking away the spots from her eyes, she looked through the open door. The deck of the ship was as long as a football pitch, bordered on all sides by open blue sky.

"Come on," Arsha bellowed over the roar of the wind, and waved her out onto the deck.

The sun burned down at them from a clear sky. Tiny wisps of

cloud whipped past the ship on either side. Running to the railing that surrounded the deck, Rachael leaned over, hoping to get a look at the ground below. Peering through the rigging that bedecked the underside of the hull she caught only glimpses of a deep blue ocean. It was staggeringly beautiful. She had never even been on a plane before, but she imagined that even that could not compare to standing out on the deck of a ship, seeing open sky all around and below you. Something impossible, incredible, and utterly beautiful.

"Where are we?" she yelled at Arsha.

"We're in the Ways," Arsha yelled back.

"The what?"

"The Ways."

"You're saying that like it's supposed to mean something," Rachael replied, struggling to keep shouting over the wind.

"The Ways are like..."

Arsha grimaced, and gestured towards the tower behind them. At first Rachael thought she meant for them to go back inside, but instead Arsha lead them around the side of the tower and up a small flight of steps, towards the huge tail assembly of the ship. Sheltered below the back part of the bridge, behind the bulk of the tower, the wind died off and they could talk normally.

"So where on Earth are we, exactly?" Rachael said, as Arsha leaned out over the back railing.

"Well, we're not. We left the Hearth... I mean, Earth, like you'd call it... We left there while you were still out. We've been travelling through the Ways for most of a day now. We're heading for Tiras," the girl said, as she fumbled around for something in the mass of rigging that trailed off the ship.

"Is that a country? And what do you mean about leaving Earth?"

"It's not a country really... It's, well... It's a world," Arsha said, as she turned around with a couple of lengths of steel cable caught in one gloved hand. Looking up, Rachael saw that the cables ran all the way from the top of the tail fin and down past the edge of the deck.

"Wait, you mean like..." Rachael paused, as she recalled some of what Justin had told her. "So these way thingies, they're like the places where you can slip between these worlds, right? But I thought they were supposed to be... I dunno... Like stepping through a door or something."

Arsha laughed.

"It's not that easy. If you could walk through the Ways, we wouldn't need ships, I bet."

As Arsha spoke, she reached for the front of Rachael's coat, and fished out several large metal clips on thick straps. She began to methodically attach each of the clips to the first cable.

"So how does it work then, flying through these things?"

Arsha smiled and shrugged.

"Sorry, I really don't know that much about it. You should ask Abasi some time. He's an expert navigator. He knows all about the Ways. But even he says there's lots about them we just don't understand."

"So you have, like, maps or something?"

"Well, something like that. The Ways are complicated. They shift and change. Sometimes the patterns are predictable, sometimes they aren't. So travelling from one place to another, it's not always the same."

"So why's it look like we're over an ocean then?" Rachael said, as Arsha tested the last of the clips. Apparently satisfied, the girl produced another set of clips from her own coat.

"Dad says that the Ways are sort of... They don't have a proper shape. Stuff that you can see and touch. So, they build themselves out of bits of other worlds. Like a whole bunch of random pieces of stuff thrown together," she said, as she began to attach herself to the other cable.

"That's insane. How can all this be hiding, like no one ever sees it? How's no one from my world ever found them?"

"Because you have to know where to look. They're not something you can see. You just have to know where you're going. People from your world, they don't even know the Ways exist," Arsha said, as she tested the last clip.

"Doesn't anyone ever just find one, by accident?"

"Sometimes? Dad says it's very rare, but it does happen."

"And what happens to them after that?" Rachael said.

Seemingly at a loss for words, Arsha just gestured in Rachael's direction.

"Oh. Right," Rachael said. "So... What are we doing here anyhow?"

Arsha grinned and hoisted herself up to sit on the railing, with her back to the open sky.

"Something fun," she said. Before Rachael could ask what she meant, the girl spread her arms, raised her head, and fell backwards off the deck.

Chapter 15 - Falling

Rachael leaned out across the railing just in time to see the cable going taut as it took Arsha's weight. The line followed along the underside of the hull, and the girl slid along it like a streak of lightning, mouth open in a scream of delirious excitement.

Rachael's head span as she saw the girl disappear from view. She took another wary look up at the windows above, but saw no movement. The clouds below them parted for a moment, and all she saw was a vast expanse of open water. From this height, she knew she'd never even survive the impact.

She backed away slowly from the edge. She tugged at the clips, wanting to be sure that they were secure, though for the life of her she had no idea how to go about checking them. Taking a deep breath she dropped into a sprint, cleared the railing in a flying leap, and fell into the vast expanse beyond.

For one dizzying moment she was flying. Through the thinning clouds the ocean glittered in the sunlight, and the air seemed strangely still. Then the cable snapped tight, whipping her round violently to face the ship as gravity took hold. Her stomach lurched and the hull went rushing past above her. It took a moment to realise that she was screaming.

The ride bottomed out, and then the arc of the cable drew her upwards as her momentum fell away. She reached the crest of her arc and for an instant she hung weightless. She blinked, and saw the weathered grain of the wooden hull floating just before her eyes. As she was about to fall away again, she felt a hand grab at the sleeve of her coat.

Arsha's mouth was moving excitedly, shaping words she could not hear as the girl gestured at something. Looking about wildly, Rachael saw that Arsha was holding onto a rope ladder that had been bolted to the underside of the hull. There were several, evenly spaced with various ropes and cables hanging around them. She snatched at the nearest rope and held on tight. With Arsha's help she was able to manoeuvre across to a ladder. She watched in a daze as Arsha fiddled with the clips, detaching her from the line that ran along the belly of the ship and affixing her to one that followed the ladder up. Properly secured, they both climbed back up onto the deck, flopping across the railing like a pair of beached fish.

Neither of them said another word until they were back inside and the door was shut behind them. Breathless, Rachael looked over at Arsha, who was still grinning insanely. Her own expression must have looked quite similar. Stripped of her heavy coat, she rubbed the warmth back into her arms, her heart still racing.

"That... was... awesome," she gasped, between breaths.

"I know," Arsha said, still grinning wildly. "I've always wanted to try that."

Still leaning her weight against the wall, trying to catch her breath, Rachael looked up at the girl in horror.

"You what?"

Arsha at least had the decency to look embarrassed.

"You mean you've never done that? What if you'd mucked up

with all the ropes and stuff? We could have died."

Arsha shrugged.

"We'd have been alright. We had coats on."

"Coats? What the flip is coats going to do if we're falling from the sky?"

"They're tanglecloth," Arsha said, as if this explained everything.

"What?"

"Tanglecloth," the girl repeated.

"Yeah, and you need to get to the part where you explain what that means," Rachael prompted.

"It sort of... It catches the air, so when you're falling you don't fall so fast," Arsha said, rubbing the sleeve of the coat in demonstration. Rachael ran her fingers over the sleeve, but whilst it did have an oddly prickly texture, she really couldn't see what help that would be.

"So you wear these coats and it's like... Parachutes?"

"I guess," Arsha shrugged. "Most of us use coats. Ilona likes her cloak better."

"So that's why she didn't mind jumping off the building like that?" Rachael said. Then, as she considered this, a thought occurred to her.

"Hold on... Even if we had these parachute coat things on... We'd still be falling into the middle of all that, y'know, not really real ocean stuff, right?"

"Uh... Right," Arsha said, her expression slowly shifting from amusement to horror. "Oh Fates," the girl moaned. "I didn't think of that."

Unable to keep herself from smiling, Rachael squeezed Arsha's shoulder.

"Well, I guess it's good you didn't muck it up then," she said.

Still looking slightly bewildered, Arsha pushed the inner door open. Rachael's smile vanished as the widening opening revealed a tall, dark skinned man with jet black hair that was shading to grey. He had removed his heavy goggles since Rachael last saw him, revealing features that were lean and angular, his eyes deep set and narrowed in a look of fury. Glancing over at Arsha, Rachael watched as the girl's expression fell.

"Girls. I think we'd best sit down and have a talk," he said.

It took barely an instant for Rachael to compose herself.

"Sure. Yeah. Let's talk," she said. The man nodded towards the stairs, and they made their way down and through into the mess hall. He gestured for them to sit as he busied himself at the stove. Arsha looked as if she might burst into tears. Rachael just leaned back against the wall with her arms folded.

"Rachael, would you care for some tea?" the man said, with an almost unearthly calm.

"No. Thanks," she said, curtly.

Eventually he sat down with two steaming mugs, setting one in front of his daughter. Then he sat and sipped his tea. Arsha pulled her cup close, but didn't drink. The girl seemed as perplexed as Rachael felt.

"How are you feeling?" the professor said, setting his cup down. He seemed to have regained his composure, his expression calm, almost pleasant. She studied his face, trying to figure out just what he was playing at.

"Fine," she said. "Peachy."

"Well, I'm glad you've both found a way to entertain yourselves," he remarked. "You and I, young lady, will be having a stern discussion about that later," he added, looking at Arsha. The girl stared down at her tea, cheeks burning.

"I suppose you have a lot of questions," he continued, looking up at Rachael again. "Why don't you let me answer a few."

"Sure. Great. We'll start with 'When do we get back to London?'"

"We don't. Right now, it's simply not possible for us to bring you home again." He paused, for a moment. "Nor do I expect it ever will be," he added, heavily.

"Right. Kind of figured as much. So, did you have a reason for kidnapping me, or was it just for kicks? I mean, it's not like no-one's going to pay much for me," she said.

"You're not a prisoner," the professor said, patiently.

"But I can't go home?"

"No. Not any more. 'Home' is not a safe place for you right now. Not least because the men who actually tried to kidnap you will not have given up yet. Their father, Lord Manindra Bhandari, is a powerful Guild councillor and a man of considerable reach and influence."

"That's a nice excuse. You're all real good at finding reasons why I shouldn't mind being beaten up, hauled off and made a prisoner and all."

She saw how the man's knuckles tightened as she said this. It felt good, knowing she'd hit a nerve.

"Rachael, I understand that you're upset. I'd expect as much, given how we've treated you. What Ilona did was completely unacceptable. But I hope you can see that we were working with a very limited set of options. You were in danger, and we had to get you out of there as quickly as possible."

Rachael felt her hackles rising as she took a quick step forward, fists clenched at her sides.

"Oh right, great job there. You tried to kill the only person who'd ever really looked out for me, just as we were about to..." She stopped herself in time, some fragment of her rational self quietly reminding her that it might not be good to let on exactly what Justin's plan had been.

"Just about to what?" the professor said, sharply. "Burn the whole city to the ground?"

Rachael's eyes narrowed.

"We had a plan. We were going... Somewhere safe. Somewhere we'd be alone. We didn't need you."

"You had a plan? Rachael, do you have the slightest notion of what you and your friend have unleashed on that city you called home? Should I suppose that you already know what kind of monstrosity has taken root there? Did you perhaps consider how many millions would die and decide that you found that cost acceptable?"

His voice was icy cold. He did not shout, but the steel in his words told her he was deadly serious. Her head span, and she took a faltering step backwards.

"Bullshit," she spat. "You're just making that up."

"He's not," Arsha said, her voice seeming very small. "Rachael, he knows about this stuff. He really does."

"What stuff?"

"The Seed," the Professor said. "I suppose that boy told you it would take you somewhere else. That it was a way out."

The venom had gone from his tone, and he suddenly seemed tired, saddened even.

"Yeah. That's what Justin said alright. So what did you mean about... People dying?"

The professor pressed the tips of his fingers together, and closed his eyes.

"I'm sorry. I shouldn't have..." He paused, and Rachael felt the tension singing in the air like a plucked string. "There are things you wouldn't have... Couldn't have known. You had no way of understanding the consequences of your actions, and you should never have had this kind of responsibility forced upon you."

"Responsibility? For what? What is this about?"

"The rift that the Seed opened. The... The gateway, that your friend no doubt tried to take you through."

"It was a way out of there."

"Or a way in. Rachael, what you did created a connection between your world and the deepest and most chaotic parts of the Dreaming. You weren't to know. You were like a child playing with a gun. No one's surprised that it went off in your hands."

Rachael stepped closer, fists clenched at her sides. She could feel herself shaking.

"What? What did I do?"

"You opened a rift between your world and the Deep Wild. A

place of chaos and power. Untamed, uncontrollable, unimaginable. The rift will strengthen, and the influence of the Dreaming will continue to spread around it. It will grow, unchecked, unless we can find a way to stop it, and it will transform or destroy everything it touches."

She said nothing. There didn't seem to be anything left to say.

"I truly don't blame you for what you did, Rachael. You were lost, alone, and frightened. You acted out of desperation and fear. Someone offered you a way out and you clung to it, because you had nothing else. For that smallest of sins you now carry an appalling responsibility. It isn't fair, and it is precisely what I had hoped to protect you from."

She shook her head, horrified at what she was hearing.

"You don't blame me? You don't blame me for being run down like I was some kind of animal. For being chased by killers and monsters? Everything I been through, and the best you got is you don't blame me?"

She stared at them both with a look of absolute disgust.

"Screw you," she said, before she turned and stormed out of the room.

She took the stairs two at a time, heading down, and then kept on walking until she found herself standing at the door to her room again. She slipped inside and closed the door behind herself. She fell down onto the bed and rolled onto her back, propping her feet up against the wall. Staring up at the thin sliver of blue sky that she could make out through the porthole, she silently wished for a glimpse of dark wings in the distance. For some tiny clue that he was still out there, searching for her.

Hours passed as she lay on the narrow bed, staring up at the ceiling, anger churning her insides. She couldn't say for sure how long it had been when there was a sharp tap on the door. As it opened she looked up to see Ilona step into the room. Watching her dispassionately, the woman didn't say a word as she set herself down in the chair beside the bed, legs crossed, hands folded on her knee.

Rachael's eyes narrowed as she studied the gaunt figure. Ilona's hair was tied back in a loose knot, but a few strands had come loose. Her eyes still looked sunken and bloodshot. Her skin was almost unnaturally pale.

"Alright, what? You come to have a go at me as well."

"I am told I owe you an apology," Ilona replied, with no sign of emotion.

"Right. This oughta be good."

"It's hardly an everyday occurrence, I assure you."

"Do you always talk like you've got a stick up your arse?" Rachael snarled.

Strangely, Ilona smiled, just for a moment.

"So what do I do? To make it up to you. Let you hit me? Hurt me like I hurt you?"

"You know you don't exactly sound very sorry."

"Should I be?" Ilona replied, calmly. "You attacked someone I care about. I stopped you. Was that wrong? Are you upset because I cared less about your safety than Micah's? Because you are less valuable to me than he is?"

"Right. I get the blame for everything that happened down there, but you get to smile and say you done nothing wrong."

The woman made a tutting sound.

"If you're referring to what happened with the Seed, I hardly think you are solely to blame for that."

Rachael turned away, fixing her eyes on the wall.

"I'm getting kind of sick of hearing that. It's all my fault but no one blames me. Like I'm supposed to feel better because I only went and killed a million people by accident."

"We all made choices down there. Yours were only a tiny part of what occurred," Ilona said. She paused, as if considering something. "But you do blame yourself, don't you? Even though everything that happened was far beyond your control, you still blame yourself. Not me, not Rishi, not the Bhandaris, or your shifter friend. You somehow imagine it was all your fault."

Rachael said nothing.

"Believe me, Rachael, we all make mistakes enough to carry a lifetime of regrets. Don't burden yourself with more."

Slowly, she turned her head just enough to see the woman's face. Ilona's expression was a mask, blank and unreadable. It struck her that the woman was much younger than she acted. Probably even younger than Micah was.

"I thought you weren't supposed to care about me?" Rachael snarled. "You trying to be friends now or something?"

Another humourless smile flickered across the woman's lips.

"I don't really do... Friends. But then I don't really do many apologies, either."

"So why are you still here?"

"Because you still haven't told me what I should do to make it right. Let me know when you decide," Ilona said. The woman stood, brushed down her skirt, and left without another word.

As the door closed, Rachael threw herself back down on the bed, fists clenched in empty frustration. From the corridor she caught the muffled sound of voices. Then the door opened again and Arsha leaned in, a nervous smile hovering on the girl's face.

"Hey. You should come upstairs. Uncle Abasi has some news for everyone."

Too tired to argue, Rachael rolled out of bed and followed the girl up to the mess hall. They arrived to find everyone else already assembled. Micah and Rishi were sat at the table, the professor drumming his fingers in agitation whilst Micah yawned and stretched. Milima was sat across from them, sipping a cup of tea. Ilona stood against the wall, arms folded, expressionless. At the head of the table Abasi stood, leaning back against the wall.

The girls slipped into the room. Arsha went to hover over her father's shoulder whilst Rachael stayed in the doorway, waiting to see what was going to happen next.

"Fates, Abasi, whatever this is, can we please hurry it up?" the professor said, still drumming his fingers.

"Now that everyone's here," Abasi nodded. "After we entered the Ways over London, I put out a call to an old friend of mine with a few connections among the Wardens. I just received his reply. He tells me that a week ago three ships set sail, heading for the Hearth. For London. They were acting on intelligence received from the Chamber of Foresight, indicating an imminent event. Something that would threaten the integrity of the Veil. The Inquisition is directly involved in a massive control and containment operation. This morning, the Wardens received the first report back from their people on the ground. They know that a Seed has awakened."

Abasi paused, for a moment.

"My friend was good enough to forward me a copy of this report. It's dull reading, of course, but I think we're all more interested in what it didn't say. Even though they've supposedly collected intel from several Guild agents stationed across England, there is no mention of either our ship, or the Jyoti. None at all."

"What does that mean for us?" Micah said. Beside him, the professor looked thoughtful.

"It means," Rishi replied, "that they're covering up any mention of our involvement or the Bhandaris'. Manindra's work, I'm betting."

"Why?" Milima said. "What does Manindra gain by keeping us out of this?"

"Yeah," Micah added, "I can't see a guy like him doing us any favours."

"Manindra's got enough pull on the council to have the Wardens turn a blind eye to this whole thing, but if we were brought up on charges then our version of the story would come out in the courts. They'd have to bring a full case against us, and that would mean exposing all their intel to outside scrutiny. It would soon become obvious that something else was being covered up. If Manindra wants to keep his family out of this, he has to protect us at the same time," Rishi said, his features twisting into a kind of mocking smile.

"Fates, that must burn."

Abasi simply nodded.

"So that's it?" Micah said. "We're in the clear?"

"It's not a definite yes, but..." Abasi's smile grew. Milima set her cup down and lowered her head until it touched the table. Micah leaned back and breathed out a sigh as Arsha threw her arms around her father's neck with a squeal of delight. Rishi actually laughed as he pulled his daughter into his lap and kissed her hair. Rachael could even see Ilona's shoulders settling a little, as if a weight had been lifted. For a moment there seemed to be no thought on anyone's mind but sheer relief.

As the excitement settled, she was surprised to hear the words coming out of her own mouth.

"So what happens now? What happens to me?"

Immediately, the room stilled. The professor looked up at her with a saddened expression, Arsha's face still pressed close to his.

"I suppose that's what we have to decide now. We still can't take you home, Rachael. And you're not safe here. Not yet. Just because Manindra has decided that hiding what his men did in London is worth more than getting us in trouble, doesn't mean he won't come after you. And there's the Guild to consider. They may not be coming after us directly, but if they find out that we have a refugee from the Hearth on board they can still take you into custody. It's the Inquisition's role to see to the care and disposition of all Hearth refugees... Even those that don't very much want to find themselves in the Guild's care. And after what happened in London, I imagine at least a few members of the Inquisition would be quite interested in learning more about you."

"Right. So I keep running. Trust me, I'm good at that."

"That might do, for a little while, but believe me when I say that Manindra Bhandari has not forgotten about you. As a refugee you will have few, if any rights within the Guild lands. He could probably kidnap you in broad daylight and simply claim it was Guild business. With Manindra's connections, I doubt anyone could challenge that claim."

"And you got a better plan?" Rachael said, sharply.

"Trust me, Rachael, I've certainly given it some thought. The best way to keep you safe, both from Manindra and from the Inquisition, is for you to become a Guild Citizen."

"And how does that work then?"

"Simple. I adopt you. I have standing in the Guild, and I would have no trouble getting the appropriate paperwork in order. You'd sign a few documents and by all Guild law you would be my daughter."

"And what if I don't want to?" she said, not quite able to meet his eyes.

"Don't want to what?"

"Be your... Your daughter."

He calmly steepled his fingers.

"It's just a piece of paper, Rachael. That's all I'm asking for. The choices you make with your life, those are yours to make. But you're more than welcome to stay here with us, if you want to. We can look after you. Keep you safe. We can give you a life here, Rachael. A home, and even a future. Will you think about that? Can you, at least, give us a chance?" the professor said. She saw cautious smiles from around the room. People trying to be welcoming.

The whole time Arsha didn't say a word, but there was a look in her eyes that the girl couldn't hide. Something wildly hopeful.

It was hard to look at them all, to meet their eyes and see their nervous yet expectant faces. It was hard to swallow that cold lump and force the words out into the deep silence that filled the room.

"Alright. I'll think about it."

The professor nodded, wetting his lips.

"Thank you."

The meeting seemingly over, the crew began to file out of the room, breaking off into smaller conversations as Rachael held her place by the wall and watched it all impassively. Arsha smiled as she passed her on the way to the door.

"I'll be in my room if... If you want to hang out or anything," the girl said.

There was a curious fluttering in her stomach as Rachael felt herself smile back.

"Yeah... I might do that," she said.

Arsha turned and slipped out the door. The professor was the last to leave, and it wasn't until he was at the door that Rachael finally blurted out the question that had been buzzing away at the back of her head.

"Why'd you come for me?"

He turned back to look at her, as if unsure what she meant.

"Why you?" she continued. "I know why Justin came. And this Manindra guy, he thinks I'm valuable or whatever. I get that. But what's your deal? Why did it have to be you that came all this way, broke all these rules, put all these people around you in danger? Because as far as I can see it, none of them know either."

"Because you were in danger. Whatever the cost, whatever the risk... It was the right thing to do. I know you might not agree, but that's the honest truth," he said, softly.

"I don't buy it. Everyone's got an angle. Nobody does a right thing just 'cos," she said, eyes narrowed.

"Do you really feel that way?"

She said nothing.

"Well, maybe it's time someone started," he said, with a smile that didn't quite seem to touch his eyes.

Chapter 16 - Rooftops

They were flying low, the ocean stretching out on all sides. There was the smell of salt water on the wind, and a soft mist that settled on her face as Rachael stepped out onto the deck. Arsha was standing at the prow, leaning back with her hands holding onto the railing. Her face was turned upwards, a soft smile on her lips as she basked in the sunlight.

"Hey," Rachael said, leaning against the railing beside her.

Arsha turned to her and smiled.

"Morning," she said.

It had been over a week since she'd first woken up in the small cabin that was now her home. She'd kept to herself, for the most part, watching life aboard the ship go on around her. When Arsha wasn't studying or busy with chores, the girl had often joined her in the small loft at the front of the hold. At first they'd spoken very little. Arsha read while Rachael doodled in her sketchpad or watched the view through the portholes. Eventually their faltering attempts at conversations had come more naturally. Arsha was eager to know more about her world, about London, England, and everything else, and she seemed just as eager to answer Rachael's questions about the ship and its crew.

"So... What's happening?" Rachael said, looking around at the empty deck. Instead of answering, Arsha pointed at the horizon, where a craggy outline was barely visible through the fog. Rachael leaned forward over the railing, squinting into the sunlight. Slowly the cliff-face began to take shape, dark lines emerging from the fog, capped with a faint haze of greenery. A deep cleft in the stone wall allowed a river to burst forth, crashing down several hundred yards in a spectacular waterfall that churned the surf into a a violent foam of white. Atop the cliff she could make out a town, spreading out to either side of the cutting formed by the river. The buildings twisted and wobbled as they rose into the air, adjoined by sky-bridges and buttresses, the river gorge criss-crossed by larger bridges held up by ropes and cables. At the near edge of the settlement the buildings hung right out over the edge of the cliff, long wooden piers jutting out into empty space. There were cranes and signal towers, their lights flashing as they guided another vessel in towards its pier.

"Welcome to Westfall," Arsha said, smiling.

They pulled in about half an hour later. Micah and Milima arrived on deck, throwing ropes to the dock-hands who tied off to the large iron loops spaced along the pier. The pier shuddered and groaned as it kissed the hull, the slender scaffolding seeming like it could barely stand up to the Triskelion's mass. Still, it held fast, and as the propellers wound down the sudden quiet was filled with the distant sounds of Westfall.

She could see people moving through the sky-bridges, and along the streets and the dock fronts. There were horses and carts laden down with crates, sacks and barrels, trade goods headed for warehouses, or out to the docks to be loaded. The air was thick with the smell of machine oil, pine wood and manure.

"This is... This is real," Rachael said, almost to herself. "I'm really in another world, aren't I?"

Arsha nodded, not entirely sure what to say.

"I guess this is all just normal for you. I mean, I guess it's pretty normal looking, really. It's just..."

"Did you want to take a look around?" Arsha said.

Rachael nodded.

They were heading for the gangplank when Rachael heard Arsha's father calling her name. She turned to look back as he strode across the deck towards them.

"I'm sorry pet, you won't be doing any shopping today. You both need to stay aboard."

"What? But why?" Arsha said, looking mortified.

"Arsha, we still have Manindra's people and the Guild to worry about. I can't have either of you wandering around right now. Better for you both to stay on the ship. We're just here to resupply and do some maintenance."

"Dad, I've hardly left the ship since Skytower, and this the first time Rachael's ever been anywhere like this. You cannot be seriously making us stay aboard," the girl said.

"Arsha, I've already explained myself. Now both of you need to go back inside. Rachael, I hope you can at least recognise that I'm doing this to protect you."

"Sure," Rachael mumbled, not feeling the slightest bit thankful. Arsha just looked sullen as they trudged back inside. With little else to do, as the rest of the crew made their way out into the town, they ended up down in Arsha's room.

Lying on her bed, Arsha stared at the ceiling as Penelope flew agitated little circles over them. Rachael sat by the door, playing with the strange device that Arsha referred to as a 'holographer'. It seemed to be some kind of camera, but one that could project images in three dimensions. Raising the viewfinder to her eye, Rachael centred it on Arsha's mechanical pet and took a picture.

"It's not fair. I just wanted to show you around was all," Arsha moaned. The girl had begun to drum her feet on the wall in obvious agitation.

"He like that a lot?" Rachael said, not looking up. "Not listening to anyone else?"

"No," Arsha said. "I mean... Not normally. It's just everything that's happening now..."

"Don't see how that's your fault," Rachael said, careful not to meet the girl's eyes. "Guess he just didn't trust you to keep me out of trouble."

She heard Arsha kick the wall just a little harder.

"It's not like that," the girl protested. "He does trust me... And I trust him. I do."

"Right," Rachael said quickly. "Sorry. Didn't mean nothing by it."

Arsha sat up and leaned forward, pulling her knees up to her chest.

"It's not that he doesn't trust me," she said. "It's just... He still treats me like a kid, you know? Like he always has to make all my choices for me."

"So..." Rachael paused, as the sneaky little voice in the back of her head began to wonder just how much of a push the girl would need. "Maybe you need to prove that you can. Make your own choices I mean. Maybe he needs to see that he doesn't have to be telling you what to do all the time."

"That'd be nice," Arsha said. Rachael raised the holographer and took another picture.

"Fates, I hate this," Arsha muttered. "I wish we had something to do."

"I know what you mean," Rachael said. "I really wish we could have taken a look around this place. It's like... It still don't seem real, this thing about these worlds and stuff. I wanted to see it for myself, you know?"

"Yeah," Arsha nodded, glumly.

"It wouldn't even have to take long, would it?" Rachael said, keeping her face hidden behind the holographer, as she focused it on the porthole behind Arsha's shoulder.

"Not really. We could have taken a walk through the main market and been back in an hour."

"Like, they'd hardly have missed us," Rachael nodded.

"Yeah." Arsha settled her chin on her knees.

"So," Rachael paused again, not sure if the girl was ready to be convinced or not, "what if we just did it? You know, took a look around, got back here before anyone noticed?"

"You mean... Sneak out?"

She could hear the nervousness in Arsha's voice, but also the excitement that lurked beneath it.

"Yeah. No harm in it, right? Everyone's out doing stuff anyhow. We could be real quick about it," Rachael said, doing her best to sound nonchalant.

"We can't," Arsha said.

"Why not? Because your dad never lets you do nothing for yourself?"

Arsha said nothing.

"You said it. He still treats you like a kid, right? Like he doesn't even think you can handle wandering about a little town like this by yourself. It's rubbish, that is."

"He's just trying to keep us safe," Arsha said, though she knew it didn't sound very convincing.

"Sure, I mean I get that he means well, but he's acting like we can't look after ourselves. I don't know about you, but I never needed no one looking out for me, you know?"

"Right," Arsha nodded, cautiously. Carefully, Rachael set the holographer down, deciding that it was now or never.

"So what do you say?"

The market was a riot of sights, sounds and smells, a constant press of people and a cacophony of voices, arguing prices, hawking wares, and holding conversations against the din. People in an array of brightly coloured clothes pressed in all around them as they darted through the throng. The smell of cooked meat wafted off the open grills, mingling with the overwhelming scent of cardamom, chilli, coriander, and other spices Rachael had no names for. The air was hot and humid, and sweat gleamed on skin of a thousand different hues.

Sneaking out had been easy, in the end. With most of the crew out around the town, it had only been the professor and the captain left on the ship. From the stairwell that lead up to the bridge they had heard the sound of the door to the captain's ready room closing, the men's voices suddenly muted. After that there was nothing to stop them as they darted across the docks and disappeared between the high walls of the warehouses, making their way deeper into the town.

Moving along the market stalls, Rachael stared in bewilderment at the items for sale. Stalls filled with cutlery, tools, clothes, boots and shoes, nets, ropes, pocket knives, and thousands of other everyday objects that still seemed strangely different. At the same time, there was something curiously familiar about it all, like a distorted version of the open air markets in London.

Eventually they took shelter from the crowds in a small café, where Arsha bought them both coffee and ice-cream.

"How do they keep it cold?" Rachael asked, poking at hers, thoughtfully.

"They have a cold-room," Arsha said, as if the answer should have been obvious.

"A cold room?"

Arsha shrugged.

"It keeps things cold."

"Well... Yeah," Rachael said, making a face. "But how?"

Arsha wrinkled her nose, apparently struggling to recall the answer.

"Uh... Thaumic manipulation through etheric transference?" she said at last.

"And that means...?"

"Honestly? I really don't know," Arsha said, with an embarrassed smile. Rachael laughed.

"Jeez. There's just so much... stuff, you know? Everything's different," she said.

"I think I'd do worse trying to survive in London," Arsha replied.

"I dunno. I guess, it's different, but it's the same, y'know? Like, it's all so strange, that it just makes it even more surprising when I actually recognise something. Like, I just figured when we walked into the café that you'd order some... schnozzberry juice, or something. Not coffee."

"Well... it's not really coffee, like you have. I mean, it tastes the same, but we make it out of a kind of animal droppings," Arsha said. "See, there's this beetle, and it..."

For a moment Rachael's eyes flicked down to her coffee. Then she looked back up at Arsha, whose deadpan expression was already cracking.

"Ass!" Rachael muttered, flicking some ice-cream at her as the girl burst out laughing. Then Arsha flicked a small blob back and Rachael yelped as it splattered across her nose. There was coughing sound, and they both turned to see the woman behind the counter giving them a disapproving glare.

Having narrowly avoided getting kicked out of the café, the girls headed back out into the bustling street. They investigated a few more stalls, and Arsha helped her to pick out some new clothes to add to the hand-me-downs from her own wardrobe. Between her new purchases, and what she'd packed before leaving the ship, her backpack was bulging by the time they were done.

They were just finishing up at the last stall when Arsha suddenly tugged at Rachael's sleeve with a nervous expression. Turning, she caught sight of the tall figure in a tan coat moving through the crowd. Micah.

"What do we do?" Arsha hissed.

"Hide," Rachael replied. "Come on."

She lead Arsha past the stall, weaving through the vendors and quickly slipping out of Micah's sight. Soon they found themselves in one of the narrow alleyways that branched off from the square. It was quieter there, only a little light squeezing down between the tall buildings as the crowds bustled past the mouth of the alleyway.

"The others will be out looking for us as well, I bet," Arsha said, a little breathless.

"Likely, yeah," Rachael said, betraying little sign of concern as she continued down the alleyway. Arsha followed her, seeming nervous, but curious. It wasn't long before Rachael found a stack of crates and barrels under a sloped roof. She scrambled up, catching the edge of the rooftop and hauling herself over.

"Hey, what are you doing?" Arsha hissed.

"Exploring," Rachael said with a shrug. "Come on."

Arsha turned to look back at the crowds in the square. Then she looked up at where Rachael was perched on the edge of the roof. She could see the conflict in the girl's expression. The nervousness in her eyes, as she threw darting glances back towards the streets, where Micah would be waiting to take them back to the ship. For a moment, Rachael considered simply leaving the girl there, or suggesting that she head back. She knew it would be easier, but something inside her seemed to rebel at the thought. It was strange how much she'd grown to like having the girl around. As Arsha's eyes met hers, Rachael held out her hand and smiled.

For a moment Arsha stared at her, nervous excitement written clearly on her face. Then, all of a sudden, the girl scrambled up onto the crates and took her hand. Rachael helped her onto the roof, and the two of them began to make their way over the slates, feeling loose tiles shift under their heels and trusting against all reason that their next step wouldn't send them tumbling into the street below. Soon they were picking up speed, and as Rachael vaulted over a narrow alleyway, Arsha seemed to follow without hesitation. Butterflies sang in her stomach as she sailed over a cobblestone street, rubber soles skidding on the tiles. She turned just as Arsha landed, feet only barely catching the edge. For a moment the girl flailed, arms pinwheeling, before Rachael caught ahold of her.

"You OK?" Rachael said. In her excitement, it took her a moment to realise that Arsha was laughing.

As Arsha grinned foolishly at her, Rachael felt an answering smile on her own lips. Soon they were flying over the rooftops, slipping down into alleyways and scrambling up rusted drainpipes. Arsha was an eager student, as Rachael showed her what lines to follow, where to look for handholds, and where it was safe to step. They began to vault larger gaps and seek out taller buildings to scale, roaming far from the centre of the town as they continued to explore.

Eventually they began to tire. Perched on a rooftop on the outskirts of town, they lay back and caught the mid-afternoon sun. Patchy clouds drifted past, occasionally shielding them from the sun. The river rumbled on through its cutting, heavy and low, like a distant train passing.

Rachael opened her bag and pulled out her sketchbook. With a few quick strokes, she let the shape of the skyline play out across the page. Curious, Arsha leaned over to look.

"You're really good," she said. "You must have practised loads."

"I guess." Rachael shrugged. "It was just something to do, y'know?"

Arsha nodded, and for a while they just sat in silence, as Rachael sketched.

"So what do you think? About the other stuff my dad was saying?" Arsha said at last. "You know... About you living with us."

Rachael shrugged, eyes still focused on the page in front of her.

"I dunno. I mean... What am I supposed to think? How's anyone know when this is all going to be over? And after that..."

Her voice trailed off, leaving only the sound of her pencil tapping against the page.

"It's just... I've been talking to him about going away to the Guildhall. It's like a, you know, a boarding school. So I can get ready for University. He said that if things settle down by then, he'd be OK with paying for you to go as well, if you wanted to."

Rachael turned to look out over the streets as Arsha spoke, her voice nervous and soft.

"I just thought it'd be nice, having someone I know there," Arsha said.

"Know?" Rachael said, unable to keep the incredulity from her voice. "You've known me a week. I spent most of the first day unconscious."

"So I know you don't snore too much," Arsha said with an awkward smile. "They put you in shared rooms at the Guildhall, that's really important."

It was a poor attempt at a joke, but Rachael still found herself smiling as Arsha grinned foolishly at her.

"Honestly," Arsha continued, "I'd just kind of figured I wouldn't know anyone, and... And I'd probably just be too weird for people or something, and it'd be awful. So, at least if you were there, we'd both be weird together or something."

There was an awkward silence, as Arsha waited for her to say something. It was hard to know what to say, especially knowing what she was about to do. She couldn't escape the feeling that she owed the girl some kind of explanation, even though it was hard to pin down why she felt she owed Arsha anything at all.

"Honestly," Rachael said, "I never really thought about my life having things like boarding schools and stuff."

"Yeah. It's kind of scary, isn't it," Arsha said.

"It's not that," Rachael said, turning to look over the horizon again, a nervous pit slowly forming in her stomach. "You talk about the future like it's your whole life. You know, getting educated, getting a job, all them things that... You just don't understand. It's not like that for me. When I think about what's next, all I'm thinking is 'How do I make it through today?' Because tomorrow, I'll be thinking the same. That's all I got now."

"But it doesn't have to be," Arsha said.

"You're saying that like I made a choice, or something. Like I wanted my life to be this way," Rachael snarled. "God, I know you mean well by it, but you're talking about us going off to some fancy school together and being bestest friends forever and it's like you're speaking Martian. Arsh, you're nice. I do like you. But I'm not sticking around. You gotta understand that."

It was clear from the girl's nervous expression that Arsha still hadn't grasped her meaning.

"Well, even if it's only for a few years..."

Rachael said nothing. She knew she was running out of ways to avoid saying what she needed to say. Slowly she began to pack away her sketchbook and pencils.

"We really should get back. Dad's gonna be furious by now," Arsha said.

"Yeah, I know. I'm sorry about that. You can tell him it was my fault when you see him, OK?" Rachael nodded as she shouldered her backpack and got to her feet. As Arsha turned to look at her, it was clear that she'd finally caught what was happening.

"You're not coming back. You planned this, the whole time," she said. Rachael fought back the urge to laugh.

"I didn't plan nothing. It's just.. I take the chances that I get, you know? It's the only way I made it this far and all. Only way I know how. It weren't your fault or nothing. You seem like a really nice person, really. I think... I think we might have been good mates, if things hadn't been... You know..."

For a moment Arsha just watched her in nervous silence. She almost wished the girl would look away. It seemed like that would easier.

"If... If you're planning on taking one of the ships, you should probably go for the one on the farthest dock," Arsha said, quietly. "They're Arvingian, they usually don't mind taking on travellers and such, if you're willing to work."

"For real?" Rachael said, feeling surprised and grateful.

Arsha nodded, and lowered her eyes, staring down into the

streets below. Slowly, the girl pulled her knees up in front of herself. Though she had to get moving, Rachael found herself watching Arsha's miserable expression, wishing there was something she could do about it.

"Thanks," she said, softly. "Are you sure you'll be OK? Facing up to your old man I mean."

"Yeah, I'll be fine. Besides, he's my dad. I kinda... I feel really bad that I made him worry, y'know?" Arsha said.

"I dunno," Rachael said, checking the straps on her backpack once more. "Doesn't seem fair that you should get in trouble just 'cause I made you sneak out."

"Well it's not like you forced me. Besides, I really did have a lot of fun today," Arsha said, forcing a smile. Once again Rachael reminded herself that she needed to get moving. Once again, something about the girl's eyes seemed to pull her back.

"You really meant all that, didn't you, about going off to school together and all?"

Arsha nodded.

"If you wanted to stay. My dad really did mean it too, about wanting you to be part of our family. I know it's not really much of a family, but..."

The girl tailed off, her eyes settling on some point in the far distance again. Rachael settled down onto her haunches, giving in to her curiosity for a moment.

"You said before that it was always just you and him, right? No mum."

"No mum. Or I never knew her at least," Arsha said.

"What happened?"

Arsha considered the question. Rachael heard the town clock chiming in the distance as she waited for the girl to answer.

"She died," Arsha said at last. "It all happened during this big expedition, some place called Fallen Peak. They were supposed to be out there for years, working with one of the Outsider kingdoms. She was a researcher on the team, and I guess they got together and

I was born. But then there was this big storm or something, and a lot of people died. He made it out with a few of the others from the expedition, but she didn't."

"So he took care of you, all on his own."

"Until he started travelling with Abasi and Milima, yeah. At least, that's how they told it. I don't remember any of it though. I was just a baby, I mean. I asked about her, of course. He told me a bit, but I could see how much it hurt when he tried to talk about her, so after a while I guess I just stopped asking."

Rachael nodded, a strange feeling growing in the pit of her stomach. As the silence deepened, Arsha slowly rocked back and forth in quiet agitation.

"You know, if you're leaving, you should probably make it quick. Those other ships will start casting off soon," the girl said.

Rachael found herself turning a curious thought over in her head. Something that she hadn't ever expected.

"Yeah. And your dad going crazy looking for us and all," she said, quietly. Arsha nodded.

Rachael felt the strange thought beginning to crystallise. She found herself thinking of the tiny little loft, with it's battered old couch and chairs. Of the room they'd given her, small but cosy, with a bed that was soft and warm. Of Milima's smile as the woman shovelled another helping of food onto her plate. The way that Micah laughed so easily. The smell of the ship, the creak of it's oak beams and the snap of the sails.

She got to her feet, tightening the straps on her backpack again.

"Guess the sooner we face the music the better then," she said.

Arsha gave her a puzzled look, not quite sure what was happening. Rachael almost wanted to laugh as she saw the girl's confused expression.

"Well, you coming or what?" she said. "If I'm sticking around you gotta help me take some of blame, yeah?"

For a moment the silence between them seemed like the loudest thing in the world. She could hear the carts rattling through the streets, the sound of voices rising up from the market squares, the squawking of birds overhead, all of it humming through the air like the first note of a song. Then Arsha smiled, and Rachael couldn't help but smile back. Together the girls slipped down from the rooftop, and made their way back towards the docks.

Chapter 17 - Distance

As they arrived back at the ship, they noticed a commotion ahead. A crowd seemed to have formed around the dock where the Triskelion was berthed. At first Arsha thought they wouldn't even be able to make it to the ship, but Rachael took her hand and lead her through the crowd, slipping through gaps and shouldering people aside with a few mumbled apologies until they were through.

As they cleared the last of the crowd Arsha let out a horrified gasp. At the foot of the dock, where the Triskelion was berthed, were half a dozen men in long grey coats, rifles slung across their backs and swords hanging from their belts.

Up on the deck she saw Abasi and her father speaking to a lean, dark haired man, his coat jet black, trimmed with silver filigree. He was flanked by what she took be another four guards at first, until she saw their spindly bodies and blank faces, plates of creamy white porcelain set over skeletons of brass and steel. They stood perfectly still, perfectly straight, like statues.

"Who's that guy?" Rachael whispered.

"He's an inquisition agent," Arsha said, wetting her lips nervously. "That's what the coat means. All the other men are Guild soldiers. Greycoats."

"You can tell all that from the coats?"

"Black for inquisition, grey for anyone else who's officially working for the Guild."

"Like a police uniform?" Rachael said.

Arsha nodded. The conversation seemed to be winding down between the three men. They shook hands, and the man in the black coat gave them a curt nod as he left. It was only when the inquisitor's back was turned that she saw a flicker of anger in her father's expression.

As the man walked away the mechanical figures sprang smoothly into life, forming up around the man in perfect formation.

"Those things are alive?" Rachael gasped.

"They're automs," Arsha replied. The inquisitor reached the foot of the ramp and the greycoats fell in line behind him as he marched towards the crowd. As the entourage approached a space immediately formed. Rachael pulled them back into the press of bodies as people jostled each other to move aside. Soon they were invisible behind the onlookers as the man and his soldiers passed them by. Even buried in the crowd, Arsha could hear the soft clicking of the autom's feet against the cobblestones, the sound seeming to cut through everything.

"So, they're like your bird then?" Rachael said, still staring in the direction of the passing entourage.

Arsha grimaced.

"Sort of. These ones are used as servants and stuff."

"Is that bad?"

Arsha shrugged.

"Dad says people only use them as guards when they don't trust real people to follow orders."

"They're not armed."

"Well... They don't really have to be. Automs that big can break a sword in one hand. Or, you know... Your arm."

"Oh."

Then Arsha felt a movement in the crowd behind them, and turned to see Milima standing over them. The woman said nothing, but her eyes followed the procession as it disappeared into the streets of Westfall. When the inquisitor and his guards had vanished from view, Milima turned her eyes back to the girls. Arsha could already tell that her furious expression wasn't solely directed at their visitor. Milima nodded towards the ship and gestured for the girls to head in.

Soon they were sitting around the table in the mess hall. Abasi and her father were at one end of the table with Rachael and Arsha sat across from them, whilst Milima stood in the doorway. On the table in front of where her father sat there was a letter with a wax seal, now broken.

"I suppose I expected as much," her father said, looking at Rachael as he drummed his fingers on the table. With her arms folded in front of her, Rachael glared back defiantly.

"Milima must have scoured half of Westfall looking for you two," he continued. "Ilona and Micah too... They were at the outskirts when they heard you were back. I suppose they'll be with us soon. As he turned his eyes towards her Arsha could already feel his disapproval, and his disappointment.

"Good of you to make them do all the work," Rachael snarled back at him, not backing down even a little.

"The 'work' Abasi and I were constrained by involved keeping a representative of the Inquisition from dragging you off in a pair of shackles. If you're wondering why I was so adamant that you both stay on the ship, that would be one of the reasons why. I understand you have little reason to respect my instructions, but you might perhaps try to make it a little easier for me to keep you safe. And Arsha, I'm even more disappointed in you. I can't imagine why I spent good money on a sending stone for you if you're not going to answer it when I call."

"Hey, leave her out of it," Rachael interjected. "It was me that talked her into sneaking out."

"And I agreed, so it's still my fault. I'm really sorry Daddy," Arsha said, a hollow sensation filling her stomach as she stared down at the tabletop.

Her father scowled.

"All right. We'll talk about this later," he said. Arsha gave a quiet nod. There was a loud 'clang' as Milima dropped a kettle onto the stove.

"So if that's settled," the woman said, "why don't you tell us what our visitor wanted, Rishi?"

A scowl flickered across her father's face, but only for an instant.

"Our 'visitor' was Sir Reuben Ben Mahir. He's following up 'certain lines of inquiry' regarding the recent events in London, and wanted to ask a few questions," he said, bitterly.

"So Manindra didn't pay off the right people after all?" Milima said.

"I don't know. Ben Mahir is an odd character. Something of a renegade from what I understand. I have a feeling he got hold of the official story and smelled a lie. Now he's interested in our angle, and Manindra's."

"What if we just told him the truth?" Arsha said. "That it was all Lord Bhandari's fault. That we were just trying to stop him."

"No matter how noble our intentions may have been, Arsha, the fact is we still broke a lot of laws doing what we did. And, more troublingly, right now we are the only witnesses to what exactly Manindra was doing in London... Just as the Bhandari boys are the only witnesses to what we did. Reuben doesn't seem to be much interested in whose side anyone was on... In fact I rather think he believes Manindra and I were working together on this."

"Why would he think that? You hate Manindra," Arsha said.

"Manindra and I have a history, yes. That's rather the problem. All Reuben sees is two men with a past connection, now both complicit in the same crime. To anyone looking at this from the outside, it is the rather obvious assumption."

"What I'd like to know is how Sir Ben Mahir even knew to find us here," Milima said.

"Manindra told him," her father said. "All Reuben would say was that Lord Bhandari 'had word of our last known destination'. Presumably his boys sent a message from the Jyoti with our heading when we left London. It wouldn't take much to infer that Westfall was the most likely stop-off."

"Really? Manindra told him?" Milima asked, surprised. Her husband nodded gravely.

"Yes. Speaking to Lord Bhandari was, naturally, the young inquisitor's first step in his investigation. Manindra was most cooperative. Fed the man a pack of lies and then sent him our way. He even asked young Sir Ben Mahir to pass this along."

He picked up the letter from the table.

"He wished to inform me in person that he's heard about the 'unfortunate business' I was recently involved in, and wishes to invite me to visit him on his estate, to see if there's some way he can 'assist' in rectifying the situation."

"Seven, he's practically written your confession for you. Reuben's read this, I suppose," Milima said.

"As any good inquisitor would. He was nice enough to reseal it after he was done, of course. Manindra's poisoning the well; strengthening the appearance of a connection between us so that I couldn't even try to testify against him if I wanted to. At this point, if he goes down for this, Abasi and I go with him."

"The gall of the man," Abasi growled. His wife just shook her head.

"It's all part of his long play. Mark my words. He's keeping me from going to Reuben or anyone else in the Guild, at least until he can get whatever he's after. That might involve Rachael, though at this point I'm not even sure if he still needs her. It definitely involves the Seed. That I'm certain of."

"Certain? Rishi, you're guessing at best. We have no idea what the old man's real plan is," Abasi said.

"True, it is mostly guesswork, though not without reason, and I certainly wouldn't mind filling a few of the details," her father replied. "Which is exactly why we're going to accept Manindra's invitation."

This time, as looks of shock passed across every face in the room, Rachael pushed her chair back and leaped to her feet.

"Hold on. Are you telling me this is the guy who sent those bastards to hunt me down, and now you want to go and have a sodding dinner party with him? What the hell?" she yelled, slapping her hands down on the table. Arsha flinched at the sudden outburst.

"Yes, that's exactly what I plan to do," her father said. "The last thing Manindra expects is for me to take him up on this. And, right now, his home is just about the safest place we could be. Manindra is the most dangerous man I have ever known, but he is possessed of a twisted sense of honour. He would never allow any form of 'unsavoury' business to take place in his own home. He will extend us every courtesy for as long as we are under his roof, and in turn I might learn a little about what he's really up to. If we're going to stay ahead of this man, we're going to have to take some risks. Believe me, I don't relish the thought of going back to that place, but it's our best plan right now."

A shocked silence followed this announcement. Rachael stood in stunned silence, eyes wide, fists clenched at her side. Eventually Abasi cleared his throat.

"Rishi, I don't suppose there is any chance we can dissuade you from this madness?"

Her father shook his head, determination etched on his face.

"I suppose I'd best set a course for Firecrest then," Abasi said with a sigh.

Shaking her head, Milima got up and went to lift the squealing kettle from the stove.

As afternoon turned to evening, Ilona and Micah returned to the ship and another argument followed as they both tried to dissuade her father from accepting the councillor's invitation. Abasi oversaw the loading of the last supplies and they finally cast off.

The days passed slowly. To Arsha's surprise, Rachael began to pitch in on the chores, making light work of her punishment for sneaking out. In their free time, the girls retreated to Arsha's room, or the loft over the cargo hold. Most of the time they spent chatting, meaningless small-talk punctuated by questions about their strangely divided worlds. Other times they simply sat together in silence, Rachael sketching whilst Arsha read.

After four days of this routine, Arsha found herself peering out of the porthole as the sun crested the horizon, looking out over a landscape she had never seen before.

Below the Triskelion forests of green rolled out in every direction, brackish marsh waters glistening from beneath the canopy. Rising up from this verdant landscape were vast mesas, sheer sided and flat topped. As she looked closer she began to spy clusters of buildings on each of the mesas they passed. Long and winding bridges connected them like islands. The bridges seemed almost impossibly thin, supported by needle fine spires that reached down into the marshes below. Soon she could make out larger towns and the smoke clouds that signalled steam trains passing along the bridges.

In the distance she spied their destination. Easily the largest of the plateaus, it stood at the centre of a criss-crossing web of bridges, all of them descending into the sprawling city that covered the mesa from edge to edge. Already she could feel the ship beginning to descend.

After a hurried shower Arsha came back to her room to pack her bag and almost bumped into Rachael as she stepped back out into the corridor. The girl had a bag slung across her shoulder. They gave each other a nervous look. Arsha was about to step into her room when she heard Rachael speak.

"So... I spoke to your dad..."

Arsha paused with her hand on the door, giving Rachael time to say whatever she was trying to say.

"Look, this... This adoption thing. I told him it was OK. I just thought you should know."

Rachael paused for a moment, as if there was something more she meant to say.

"I'll see you upstairs," she said, eventually. The girl turned and walked away, quickly disappearing up the stairs.

By the time Arsha had packed and joined the others up above, Abasi was already bringing them alongside the pier. She found Rachael out on the deck, watching as the dock hands tied the ropes off, and the gangplank was drawn over. Rachael seemed even more closed off than usual. Arsha almost felt as if she had only imagined their brief conversation below the deck.

They made their way down from the docks and into the heart of the city. Clattering steam-wagons filled the roads, loaded with goods and passengers, belching out thick smoke that filled the air above them. A wide central boulevard lead them down towards the train station, where they were met by a serious looking gentlemen dressed in finely tailored layers of red and gold silks.

"Professor Chandra?" the man said, his tone sharp and precise.

"Yes, that's me," her father nodded. The man gave a half-bow.

"Your carriage is this way, sir."

Judging by her father's expression, Arsha suspected he wasn't at all surprised, as the man lead them over a small footbridge towards a far platform where a single train car waited, hooked to a shining steel engine that was idling with a low hum. The car itself gleamed with gold leaf and red lacquer, the sides lined with tall windows. The man produced a key on a long silver chain and unlocked the door for them.

Inside was a long open space with a dining table in the centre and cluster of comfortable looking armchairs towards the front.

Heading towards the very back of the carriage, Arsha and Rachael settled themselves on one of the long couches, where they had a clear view from the window. There was a heavy 'thump' as Micah dropped himself down onto the couch opposite them. Arsha just caught the look of disapproval from her father, and from Ilona, as Micah pulled his feet up, put his head back and closed his eyes. She wondered how he could be so relaxed, knowing where they were headed. She could sense Rachael's nervousness as well, as the girl fiddled constantly with her backpack. The train began to shudder into motion and it wasn't long before they were out of Firecrest, and there was only the vast expanse of the forests and marshlands beneath them.

Rachael's eyes were fixed on the window, staring out into the distance. With little else to do, Arsha pulled a deck of cards from her bag and began to shuffle.

"Hey look!"

Arsha leaned over, trying to see what had caught Rachael's attention. They were riding over a wide, flat plateau that seemed to be devoid of any habitation. Just endless open plains that stretched around the tracks on either side, a few herds of wild horses grazing here and there.

"Look at what?" she said.

"The horses, genius," Rachael said, pointing. Near to the carriage, one of the herds was on the move, galloping at full speed, the wind flicking their manes back. Arsha made a face.

"You're kidding me," Rachael said, catching her expression. "How can you not like horses?"

She shrugged.

"I just don't."

"But look at 'em. They're flipping beautiful."

"I dunno. Micah tried to teach me to ride one time, and it was awful. I fell off like a hundred times. And they're big and grumpy and they smell awful."

Rachael barely seemed to be listening any more. The girl had turned away from the window, her eyes fixed on the dozing figure on the couch opposite.

"Micah, you know to ride?"

Micah's eyes flickered open.

"Hm? Oh, yeah. Sure I do."

"Serious? How did you learn?"

Sitting up a little, Micah shrugged.

"Just something I learned as a kid. We had a bunch of horses on my family's estate."

Rachael almost seemed to recoil at the words, as if they had a foul taste.

"Estate? For real. Like, is your family loaded or something?"

Another shrug.

"They're pretty well off, yeah. Merchant banking mostly."

Apparently deciding that she wasn't interested in hearing any more, Rachael turned to look out the window again, her eyes fixed on the distant herd, white streaks moving across the green fields.

Soon they were out over the marshes again, and then they began to make out the mesa that they were travelling towards. Though smaller than Firecrest, it was still large, covered in fields and forests. Nearer to they could make out the walls of a sprawling complex that might have been one building or many. Below the light coloured walls of the estate, part of the cliff face seemed to have been gouged away and the space was occupied by a sprawl of buildings. She saw crowded rows of houses deeper in, ranging down to larger warehouses at the edge of the cliff where the railway seemed to meet some kind of station, a broad platform that jutted out from the cliff itself.

The train began to slow as they pulled in to the station. As the carriage came to a halt a pair of men in dark red uniforms approached.

"Come on, time to go," Micah said. With their luggage in hand, they joined the others at the front of the train car, just as the door opened. They were the last out, and as they gathered on the simple wooden platform Arsha could already see her father talking with a pair of uniformed men. Further back, she could see a pair of steam carriages, like the ones that had filled the streets of Firecrest.

Arsha and Rachael found themselves in the second carriage, along with Micah and Ilona. Her father was joined by Abasi and Milima in the first carriage. Through the glass, she could make out some sort of discussion taking place.

The carriages rattled into life and began rolling through the warehouses, past what appeared to be workshops and other kinds of industrial buildings.

"Fates, have they turned this whole place into some kind of factory?" Ilona muttered.

"Refinery, more like," Micah said. "Saw some tracks carved into the cliff-face below. They're probably carting stuff up from down there in the marshes. Firecrest makes a lot of its money from the metal deposits down there. But this operation all looks pretty new. Most of these buildings were thrown together fast, and not too long ago. Can't really say why the Bhandaris would be so eager to set up their mining operation on their doorstep though."

"Deranged paranoia? The delusions of an ageing control freak?" Ilona said, not hiding the bitterness in her tone.

Micah shrugged.

"Maybe. From what I hear it's the oldest son, Dayaram, that runs most of the family's business matters these days. At least publicly. Who knows how much of that is just his dad giving the orders though."

"How do you know so much about this?" Rachael said.

"I did mention the part where I'm from a merchant-banker family, right?" Micah laughed. "It was pretty much our job to know what everyone's up to."

The carriages began to follow a winding switchback road up the cutting, towards the high walls of the estate above. Below them the smoke and lights of the town began to look tiny. Eventually they crested the bluff and found themselves on a long, straight avenue lined with tall poplar trees.

The walls of the estate were grand and imposing, with a pair of wrought iron gates that were set into a broad archway. The gates swung open as they approached, and the carriages pulled to a halt in a wide open flagstone courtyard. Uniformed men opened the doors and gestured for them to step down. Long, covered passageways lead off in each direction, presumably connecting to other parts of the complex. At the centre of the courtyard stood a pool of crystal clear water, surrounding a plinth from which a marble statue looked down at them with a commanding gaze. The figure was ancient, the features worn away almost to nothing, but Arsha thought it looked vaguely feminine.

Approaching them was a tall, gaunt figure, dressed in a familiar looking coat of red and gold. Leather boots clicked against the hard flagstones as the man walked. At his waist hung a basket hilted blade in a ruby encrusted scabbard. The woman on his arm was almost as tall as he was, and she had a sharp, lean face, with piercing eyes, and hair that fell down over her shoulders in a wave of black curls. Her sari was all the colours of a flame, brilliant silk and satin of red, yellow and orange surrounding her like a halo of fire. Rubies glittered on the gold chain that ran from nose to ear.

"Professor Chandra. Captain Bira. Welcome to our home," the man announced as they approached, his voice much softer than his appearance had lead Arsha to expect. Her father turned to face him with a cold expression.

"Dayaram," he said, with the barest hint of a nod. "It's been a while."

Chapter 18 - Amber

The man in the red and gold looked her father over with a cool gaze, as if he was studying an apprentice's craftsmanship.

"I trust your journey was not too trying?"

"We had a little trouble on the way, but nothing we couldn't handle," her father replied, smoothly. "Now, this must be... Vaneeta, yes?"

Her father smiled politely in the woman's direction. She inclined her head ever so slightly, as Rishi and Abasi offered perfect half bows. The smoothness in her father's voice, and his pleasant smile, reminded her of how he sometimes acted around the men on the university board. Though she'd seen him put on the facade before, it always left her feeling a little unsettled, as if she was watching a different person who had stolen her father's face. Across from him, Dayaram and Vaneeta's faces seemed like perfectly arranged masks, pleasant on the outside, but with eyes that seemed all too hollow within.

Abasi and Dayaram shook hands, their grip perhaps a little too firm, and then her father began to introduce his crew. Micah bowed and kissed Vaneeta's hand, and Ilona, her features set in almost uncanny mimicry of Vaneeta's, allowed Dayaram to offer the same courtesy.

"My wife, Milima," Abasi said, as Milima nodded at Dayaram and Vaneeta in turn, pressing her hand to her chest, just over her heart.

"And you must be miss Chandra," Vaneeta said, smiling sweetly as Arsha remembered herself and bowed politely. She was sure she must have looked horribly awkward, but no one remarked on it. She wished she had Ilona's easy way with high class manners.

"And of course, the young lady herself," Dayaram added, turning to address Rachael. "You must excuse us, young miss. We were not informed of your name."

"I'm Rachael. Barnes," Rachael said, obviously feeling uncomfortable with their expectant gazes.

Dayaram simply nodded and gestured for the group to follow him toward the archway at the far end of the courtyard. As they walked, Arsha and Rachael slipped into the back of the group, side by side.

"That was weird," Rachael whispered as they walked. Arsha just shrugged.

"It's sort of this thing everyone has to do. I think all the big families just have this game going or something, to see who can sound the most sincere without meaning it," she said.

"Father is in his study," Dayaram was saying to her dad, at the front of their procession. "He's been informed of your arrival, and hopes you will join him for lunch. He regrets that he could not greet you all in person, but he is an old man, and tired."

Her father nodded politely.

"You may inform Lord Bhandari that I will be pleased to join him. There is much that I wish to discuss," he said, as Dayaram lead them under the archway, into a long tunnel lit by a myriad of hanging ghostlamps.

"What was with that thing Milima did back there? Like, when

everyone else was shaking hands and stuff," Rachael said, as the soft gloom of the tunnel enclosed them.

"That? Oh, uh, it's a Herdlander thing. Most people don't like shaking hands with them, so they do that instead," she said.

"Why? I mean, why don't people want to touch them or whatever?"

Arsha considered this for a moment, feeling slightly confused by the question.

"I guess it's just, y'know, because of what they are."

"What they are?" Rachael repeated, perplexed.

Arsha just shrugged.

"Outlanders."

They emerged from the tunnel into a sprawling garden. A path of white gravel was laid out between green lawns. Vibrant sprays of brightly coloured flowers seemed to burst forth from every side. The air was thick and warm like a heavy blanket after the coolness of the tunnel. Beyond the nearest rooftops, Arsha could see towers and sloped roofs that rose up in grand tiers.

"God, I could spend all day running around this place," Rachael said, eyeing the vast expanse of the rooftops.

At the far end of the garden, steps lead up to the front of a colonnaded building with a large pair of double doors. As the group approached the doors swung wide, revealing a grand entrance hall.

"Rooms have been prepared for you in the South wing. Our home is yours, should you wish to wander the grounds or make use of any of the facilities. The servants will attend to anything you require."

"Thank you, Dayaram. You are too kind."

"Not at all, Rishi, not at all. I can show you to father's study now, if you wish. Vaneeta will see that your companions are settled in."

"If you would," the professor nodded.

"Oh, when you are done speaking with my father," Dayaram added, "he has asked if young miss Barnes might grant him a few moments of her time."

Rachael looked up sharply, and Arsha saw her father's civil mask crack just a little, before he recovered himself.

"I'm afraid that's simply out of the question," he said, with the appearance of perfect calm.

"Oh? I rather thought it might be her decision to make," Dayaram replied, with a raised eyebrow. He turned to regard Rachael directly, his features carefully neutral as he waited for her reply. Arsha tried her best to hide her curiosity, as she waited to see what Rachael would say.

Rachael looked over at her father, as if trying to decipher what was going on behind his cautious mask. Then she looked back to Dayaram.

"Sure," she said. "I'll hear what the old man has to say."

They found themselves being lead through broad and well lit corridors that were covered in deep carpets of red and gold. The winding passageways eventually brought them to what Arsha imagined was one of the more secluded wings. Trying to remember the route was a nightmare. The estate seemed to have been built upon itself in layers, some of it surprisingly new, some of it very old.

Eventually they arrived at their rooms, where servants deposited their baggage and politely inquired after any needs they might have.

"It's like one of them fancy hotels," Rachael whispered. "Everyone's being polite because they have to be."

Arsha just nodded. They had been put in a shared room with two single beds and a small en-suite bathroom. Windows looked out onto the gardens, perfectly manicured and surrounded by a high stone wall.

Rachael began to poke around the room as Arsha sat down on the bed and watched. When they heard a whispering sound, both girls turned to look in unison.

The door had been left slightly ajar, and through the crack they could see two pairs of eyes watching them. Small, rounded faces with nervous expressions. Two young boys, the oldest not more than six as best she could guess.

Surprised, she raised a hand and waved.

"Hi there," she said, gently. If anything, the boys eyes grew even wider. There was another flurry of whispering, and then the door was pushed open and both boys stepped nervously into the room.

"Hi. I'm Arsha. This is Rachael," Arsha continued.

"I'm Mohan," the older one said with a sudden energy, proudly slapping his chest. "This is Jeevan. He's my brother."

"And do you boys live here?"

"Of course we do. We're the hairs to the family."

"Hairs?" Rachael said, looking perplexed.

"I think he means 'heirs'," Arsha said, with an embarrassed smile.

"That's what I said," Mohan said, pouting.

"I guess that means the stiff bloke we met before would be your dad, huh?" Rachael said.

"He runs everything here. And my granddad is a... is a guild council... uh... councilman."

The boy seemed immensely pleased with himself. Silently, Jeevan stood a little behind him, clutching at his older brother's trouser leg. In his other hand the boy had a small stuffed doll, some kind of winged lizard.

"So who's this then?" Arsha said, smiling as she gestured at the doll.

"It's a dragon," Jeevan announced, proudly holding it aloft. Immediately detaching himself from his older brother, he flew the 'dragon' in a lap around the room, as the girls both watched and laughed.

"It's probably just a Rake, actually," Arsha whispered, leaning close to Rachael so only she would hear.

"What's that then?" Rachael whispered back.

"Big winged lizard. They fly in packs, and they hunt herd animals and stuff. Abasi hates them, because they attack stuff that threatens them. You know, big flying things like our ship. So whenever we see packs of them we have to put in to port, or fly slow and close to the ground so they won't attack us."

"So, how's it you don't just call them dragons?"

"Well, they're not. There aren't any dragons. Not any more."

"Oh," Rachael said, seeming both disappointed and perplexed by this discovery. Jeevan continued flying his doll around, making angry growling noises as the 'dragon' attacked their legs. Then both boys looked up in surprise as the door opened. A young man stood in the doorway. Another brother, she guessed, perhaps ten or eleven. It was hard to tell with boys.

"Mohan. Jeev," the boy hissed, sharply. He made a gesture, and his brothers looked up with disappointed expressions, but made no move. His first effort having failed, the young boy strode into the room, grabbed both of their hands and lead them out of the room, ignoring their protestations. From the doorway he threw a sharp glare back at the girls, before the three of them disappeared.

"That was weird," Arsha said, after a moment's pause.

"A bit, yeah," Rachael nodded.

"It's so sad. They're just innocent little kids. They've got no idea what their family is really like."

"Won't stop 'em from turning out just as bad," Rachael replied. Arsha turned to look at the girl with a mortified expression.

"You don't know that," she said. Rachael just shrugged.

"People can't change what they come from."

Not sure how to respond, Arsha said nothing as Rachael continued to poke around the room.

"What about where you came from?" she said, quietly. "What were they like? Your parents?"

Rachael stood at the window, staring out into the garden. For a moment Arsha wondered if she simply hadn't heard her.

"It's just you've never really talked about them," she added, cautiously.

"What's to talk about?" Rachael said, still not looking at her. "They weren't my real parents."

"What do you mean?"

For a moment it seemed as if Rachael was turning something over in her head, as if she wasn't sure what to say, or maybe just how much to say.

"Justin told me," she said, at last. "My real mum, she lives way out in this dream thing. Honestly, I didn't really understand much of it. Point is, the people what I grew up with, they were never really my mum and dad."

"Did they know?"

Rachael shook her head.

"So they still loved you. Just because you weren't really their daughter, doesn't change that."

Just for a moment Rachael turned away from the window, to give her a disdainful look.

"Love me? Arsh, they thought I was crazy."

Arsha could think of nothing to say, as Rachael turned back to the window, her eyes fixed on something in the far distance.

"They thought I was crazy and they didn't know how to fix it," Rachael said, her voice growing softer. "You know if it hadn't of been for me, they might have made it work. Dad might never have left, and Mum might never have..."

She fell silent again. The only sound was the clock on the wall, counting out the seconds as Arsha stared at her hands, and wondered what to do. She almost jumped in surprise when Rachael stepped away from the window.

"Screw this," the girl said, "let's have a poke around."

Trying not to let her nervousness show, Arsha followed Rachael out of the room, still trying to think of something to say. As they turned the corner, the pair of them very nearly crashed into the tall figure walking quickly the other way.

"Woah. Girls, hi," Micah said, clearly as surprised as they were.

"Fates Micah, you nearly scared us to death," Arsha hissed, feeling her heart pounding out a drumbeat on her ribcage.

"Sorry, about that," he said. "Anyway, I was looking for you two."

"Why's that?" Rachael said, eyes narrowed.

"I was having a little wander around the grounds. There's something I want to show you," Micah said, nodding in the other direction.

"What is it?" Arsha said.

"Just trust me," he replied, with his usual boyish grin.

Before long they found themselves outside of the manor walls, walking down a rough path that cut across the open fields of the estate. Though there were uniformed men at the last gate, no one made any move to stop them. A soft wind blew over the mesa, making the long grass whisper as they walked. Micah had brought lunch with him, roti and fresh mango juice, which they ate as they walked. Even though the spiciness of the food made her eyes water, Rachael still asked for a second roti, wolfing it down in three bites as if it might have less time to burn her tongue. Micah went ahead of them, eventually leading them to the crest of a gentle slope which they could not see beyond. Silhouetted against the blue sky, he turned and beckoned to them.

As they crested the hilltop, Arsha looked down and saw what Micah had meant to show them. A worried expression creased her face, and she felt a nervous fluttering in her stomach.

"Horses," Rachael gasped.

There were three of them, slender and beautiful, grazing in the sun as if nothing in the world could bother them. Already Micah was approaching the nearest of them, a reddish-brown mare that was a little shorter than the other two. Very gently he whispered to the animal and stroked at its mane. For a moment the creature tensed, seeming nervous, but he slowly calmed it, speaking softly and stroking its neck and flank. Eventually, he lead the horse over towards the girls.

"Girls, this is Amber, and Jamal tells me that's Ruby, and Opal."

"Who's Jamal?" Arsha said.

"Huh? Oh, he's the stable-boy. I went out for a smoke and we got chatting."

"Hi Amber," Rachael said, sweetly. She seemed enraptured, gazing intently into the horse's huge brown eyes. Arsha found herself becoming more fascinated by Rachael's demeanour. The girl was always so guarded, like she was expecting a fight. It was strange to see her speak and act so softly.

"Can I?" Rachael raised a hand, gingerly, towards the horse's nose and looked up at Micah excitedly.

"Sure. She's friendly."

With something between terror and delight, Rachael ran her fingers down the horse's long snout. It sniffed, sharply, and Rachael pulled her hand back in alarm.

"Stroke, don't tickle," he said. "She's a big girl, you won't hurt her." Micah demonstrated, running his own hand along the mare's snout, quite firmly. Amber leaned into his palm, appreciatively.

"Here," he said, dipping a hand into his bag and producing a small apple, red with spots of green.

He showed it to Amber, who devoured the offering greedily. Clearly fascinated, Rachael tried it herself, giggling as Amber's thick tongue slapped at her palm, and soon all three horses were gathered around, jostling the girl for treats as Rachael laughed. Arsha stood back, watching.

"So," Micah said, "you girls want to go for a ride?"

Rachael turned to look up at Micah with an incredulous expression. The girl seemed genuinely speechless.

Whatever objections Arsha held, they were worthless against Rachael's expression of pure delight. Before long Micah had rounded up all three of the horses and brought them back towards the stables outside the manor walls. He saddled the beasts quickly, setting about the straps and buckles with a practised hand, all whilst Rachael prodded him with a hundred questions. Arsha could scarcely believe the change that had come over the girl.

Eventually the horses were saddled and ready, and Micah set about helping each of them into the saddle. Rachael took a shot at vaulting up onto Amber's back, but she couldn't seem to find the right place to grip, and the girl quickly ended up on her ass, looking embarrassed. Arsha covered her mouth to keep Rachael from seeing her laughing. Still, she caught the scowl that was thrown in her direction.

"Alright, let's try this," Micah said, helping Rachael to her feet. Then, with scarcely any warning, he grabbed the girl by the hips and hoisted her up into the saddle. Rachael's look of surprise made it even harder for Arsha to silence her laughter. As Micah turned away, Arsha couldn't help but notice how red Rachael's cheeks were, or the way the girl's eyes followed Micah as he walked.

"Your turn," he said, standing at Arsha's side. "Come on now, you've done this before. Put one foot up, and I'll help you up the rest of the way."

"Yeah, and the last time I fell off and got mud all over myself. And the time before that I scared the horse so bad it ran off," Arsha said, pouting.

"OK, yeah, try not to do that again," Micah said, chuckling.

That first step was almost impossible. Arsha finally forced herself to lift one leg and set the ball of her foot into the stirrup. Then Micah lifted her by the waist, just enough that she could throw her leg across the saddle. When Opal shifted under her, a jolt of terror ran down her spine and she felt sure she would fall. At the last second she grabbed at the front of the saddle and held herself in place.

"OK there?" Micah said. Looking down at him, she forced herself to smile.

"See... Not so scary," he said, smiling back.

Arsha glanced over at Rachael, who was trying very hard to hide how nervous she was. The girl's knuckles were white on the reins. It was oddly reassuring, knowing that she wasn't alone in that.

"Just sit tight there," Micah said.

Taking the reins from them, he held one in each hand and began to walk, leading one horse on either side of him.

"Just concentrate on sitting right. Hold the pommel if you need to balance better... That's the little ridge at the front of the saddle. Rachael, keep your back straighter. You have to keep your shoulders over your hips. That's right. Arsha, press your legs in more. Grip with your calves. Come on, you've done this before."

They walked back out across the fields, Micah reciting a soft litany of instructions as the horses plodded along at a gentle stroll. Arsha found that her nervousness slowly faded as her attention was consumed by the awareness of her own body and that of the creature that carried her. She realised, with a little jolt of surprise, that she could feel Opal's heartbeat pulsing up through her ribcage. She could feel the slow expansion and contraction of the horse's chest as it drew each breath. Occasionally the mare would let out a sudden snort and Arsha would feel a ripple run down her back. There was something strangely beautiful about being so completely connected to another creature, so aware of every tiny movement of her body.

They started to get the hang of it, and before long Micah gave them the reins and mounted up on Ruby to ride with them. Arsha fell off once, and Rachael took several tumbles, mostly from trying to pull Amber into sharp turns that the horse was all too willing to comply with, whether her rider was ready or not. No matter what, Rachael was on her feet the moment she hit the ground and springing eagerly back into the saddle. As they began to master bringing the mares up to a gallop and back down to a walk again, Arsha saw a look of delight firmly root itself on Rachael's face. She seemed entirely lost in the moment.

Eventually Arsha began to slacken off a little, easing her horse into a slow trot as Micah focused his attention on correcting the finer details of Rachael's posture. Soon enough the two of them set off on a proper run, leaving Arsha to take a breather by a narrow creek. Opal lapped at the water as Arsha rested in the saddle.

As she gathered herself a little, she heard the approaching sound of hooves. When she looked up it was not Rachael and Micah she saw, but a stranger on a black horse. As he drew closer, she realised the boy was about her own age. He had wavy hair and bright, attentive eyes. He was good looking, she had to admit, though it was not hard to see the Bhandari family resemblance in him. She felt a chill when she noticed the rifle slung over his shoulder, and the brace of dead birds hanging from his saddle. Hawks, she realised.

"Hey, you there," he called out.

"What?" she said, turning Opal to face him.

"Arsha, right? Where's your friend? The refugee?"

Arsha scowled.

"Rachael? She's riding. With Micah."

It seemed important to add the last part, somehow. The boy nodded.

"They'd best stay close to the house. Father wouldn't be happy if anyone got hurt," the boy replied, lip twisting in a sneer.

"Yeah. Right. I'll them that," Arsha said, still scowling. Seeming to sense her mood, Opal backed off a pace and snorted loudly in the boy's direction. He nodded again, and glanced down at the mare.

"Be careful with that one. Never got broken in properly. She can be a bit dangerous. Little too much spirit."

Arsha felt a scathing smile creep across her face.

"Good thing she's with me then," she said. The boy gave a derisive snort and wheeled away. He was a distant shape against the horizon when she heard Micah and Rachael approaching. Rachael looked breathless, but deliriously happy, and Micah had a healthy glow about him.

"What was that about then?" Micah said, nodding at the distant shape of the boy on his horse.

"One of the Bhandari boys. I didn't like him much," she said.

"Huh. Yeah, that'd be Vasuki I'm guessing. I met him with his dad at a function one time. He was an obnoxious little... Well, yeah," Micah said. "Anyway, we should probably head back. I'm starving."

Arsha turned to look over at Rachael.

"You had fun?"

The girl just nodded, clearly too out of breath to even speak clearly.

Micah was right about the time. The sun was getting low, and the sky was slowly reddening. Micah took the lead, as Arsha and Rachael followed a little way behind him, their horses walking side by side.

"Hey, thanks for doing this," Rachael said. "I know you weren't really having the best time out there and all. I just... I really appreciate it."

Caught off guard by the curious sincerity in Rachael's expression, it took her a moment to respond.

"No, it's OK," she said. "I'm glad you had fun."

Rachael smiled.

"Yeah, I did."

Arsha caught the way Rachael's gaze settled on Micah's back, his sweat soaked tunic plastered to his shoulders, and she couldn't keep herself from smiling.

"Admit it. You like him," Arsha said.

Rachael's cheeks glowed crimson as the girl scowled.

"I never... Shut up," the girl stammered, as Arsha grinned at her.

"Not even a little bit?" she said sticking her tongue, as Rachael stared down at the reins.

"Yeah, I mean, he's OK if you like tall, muscle-y guys with perfect cheekbones," she said, quietly.

As Arsha struggled to hold back her laughter, Rachael looked at her with narrowed eyes.

"What, and you've never thought it?"

Arsha just shrugged.

"Not really... I mean I've known him since I was, like, seven? He's like a, you know, a big brother or something."

"Right," Rachael said, with a knowing smile. "You live with a guy who looks like that, and you never had even one dirty thought?"

It was Arsha's turn to fix her eyes on the reins, as she felt her cheeks tingle.

"Maybe a little bit," she mumbled.

She caught Rachael's eye, and almost in unison the girls stuck their tongues out. A moment later Micah was looking back with a bemused expression at the both of them, doubled over in their saddles, trying not to fall off from laughing.

The sun continued to dip towards the horizon as a cool wind sprang up. Slowly, the walls of the estate began to rise up ahead of them, and Arsha couldn't help but notice how the light slowly faded from Rachael's eyes as they drew closer. Before long the girl had the same cold, guarded expression that she always seemed to wear.

They arrived at the stables, and Micah helped them dismount as a young man stepped forward to lead the horses away. As they walked through the gates into one of the many courtyards, they saw the tall form of Dayaram Bhandari approaching them. Arsha's footsteps slowed as the man fixed each of them with his icy cold eyes.

"Miss Barnes," he said, his gaze settling on Rachael. "My father will see you now."

Chapter 19 - Manindra

As they were brought inside, Micah took Arsha's hand and lead her away. Rachael was left alone with Dayaram, struggling to match his long strides as he lead her down a corridor flanked by doors on both sides and decorated with elaborate tapestries. They were moving deep into the heart of the complex, and she could feel the air growing cooler as they walked. She had little time to take in the artistry as they moved past, but Rachael couldn't help but notice that most of the tapestries seemed to depict strangely fantastical beings; a man with a body made from cogs and gears, a floating cape with the suggestion of a body within, an androgynous figure holding up a needle and thread, and a lithe woman whose body seemed to be carved of jade all caught her eye, though briefly.

Distracted by the strange images, she was caught by surprise when Dayaram stopped at a door and tapped lightly.

"Come in," a voice called out, less a request than a command.

Dayaram turned the handle and held the door open, ushering her in. Swallowing, her throat unbearably dry, she stepped through into a study that was too large to seem cosy, but dimly lit in a way that felt warm and enclosed. The walls were lined with bookshelves and tapestries. A pair of wing-backed chairs were set in front of a fireplace, where a few large logs glowed a steady red.

In one chair, facing slightly away from her as she entered, an old man sat with his eyes fixed on the glowing embers. His thinning hair flowed down over his shoulders in neatly brushed silver waves, and his grey beard was thick and well groomed. He wore a long, loose fitting tunic and trousers of white linen. His bare feet were propped up on a small footstool, toes wiggling in front of the fire.

He looked up as she entered and smiled warmly. She heard the door close and looked back to see that Dayaram was still with them.

"Ah, Miss Barnes, welcome. Please, please, sit down," the old man said, gesturing at the chair opposite his. His voice had a hoarse, soft quality to it.

She took a seat, as Dayaram knelt by the fire to add some fresh wood. Sheets of red and orange flame leapt up from the grate, and a crackling sound filled the room.

"Ah, that's better," the old man said.

Dayaram moved to the small table between them, where a large silver tea tray had been set down.

"Tell me, my dear, do you take milk and sugar?" the old man said, with a genial air.

For a moment she said nothing, watching his expression as he patiently waited for her answer, willing that placid mask to crack. The fire popped and hissed, and she heard the gentle chiming of a silver teaspoon against the sides of the cup as Dayaram prepared his father's tea.

"Ah, thank you, Darry. You really should have let the servants handle this, my boy. You do trouble yourself so."

"It's no trouble father."

Accepting the cup, the old man turned to look at her again.

"Milk. No sugar," she said, stiffly.

"No sugar? Well there's a surprise," he said, smiling at his son. "A child who doesn't have a sweet tooth. You know, my boy Rakesh takes three sugars in his tea, and against all reason he's still as thin as a rail. He gets that from his mother's side of course, just like his brother here." He sighed, gently. "Poor Naveen takes after myself. No wonder he exercises so much."

The old man gave his son another warm smile, and patted the man's arm gently.

"Now, why don't you give us a little time alone, eh?"

"Just call if you need anything father."

"As always."

Dayaram turned and swept out of the room, closing the door softly behind himself as the old man sipped his tea.

"Ah, that boy. He'll smother me with love."

"Yeah. It's really touching," Rachael said, trying not to sound too sardonic.

"Oh it's quite alright my dear, you needn't pretend to feel anything other than contempt for me. I extend you these courtesies because I am an old man and it pleases me to do so. You're quite welcome to take that cup and throw it at the wall if you'd prefer. I'm sure the thought crossed your mind."

He wiggled his eyebrows conspiratorially at her. For a moment her fingers tightened around the handle of the tea-cup, which rattled against the saucer. She watched a little trickle of tea spill down the side and pool in the saucer.

Gently, with great care, she set the cup and saucer down on the table and moved her hands to her lap. Manindra said nothing, but Rachael caught his self indulgent smile as he sipped his tea again.

"Thank you, by the way, for agreeing to speak with me. I do appreciate having a chance to clear the air a little. Ah, manners. I haven't even introduced myself."

He set the cup down, and folded his hands across his belly.

"I am Lord Manindra Bhandari of House Bhandari, and I am quite delighted to meet you young lady. You have, I must say, caused more than a little bit of a stir around here."

"Is that what you call it when your boys try to kill someone."

"Ah, so dramatic. It was only your companion we tried to kill, my dear. We had no intention of harming you in any way. You are far too valuable. For all his remarkable talents, the boy was expendable, and something of a problem I'm afraid. I have little sympathy for problems."

Manindra smiled as he spoke, but there was an edge to his tone, like a razor. Perfectly precise. He was trying to get a rise out of her, she knew. As soon as Rachael saw it, she felt a coolness spread through her, as she settled in a familiar space, where the thinking part of her seemed to have stepped back from what was happening, watching from a distance. It was difficult, to keep her hands from forming fists, keep her expression from turning to a snarl, but she forced the anger down, buried under an icy coldness that seemed to numb her whole body.

Instead of meeting his gaze, she let her eyes wander about the room. The tapestries depicted the same figures she'd seen out in the hallway, but one in particular drew her attention. A woman whose body seemed to be comprised entirely of golden leaves, her face concealed behind a white porcelain mask that left only the mouth and chin exposed. Rachael felt a shudder of recognition, as she remembered a ride in an empty train carriage that seemed a lifetime ago. She could almost hear a voice like dry leaves whispering her name again.

"Fascinating, aren't they?" Manindra said. There was a curious softness to his tone. "I wonder, how much has Chandra told you?"

Rachael scowled, and Manindra's eyebrows rose a little.

"Not enough, I suspect," he added. As the old man continued to gaze at the figures, her curiosity finally got the better of her.

"What are they?"

"We call them the Dreamwalkers, though they've had many names throughout the ages. They are ancient, as old as human civilisation. These depictions have been found throughout the ruins of the Ur."

He seemed to notice her look of confusion.

"The first people," he continued. "Or at least, the oldest recorded civilisation, and certainly the first to find the means to travel beyond the Hearth, and out here into the Borderlands. There is much we still don't know about our oldest history, but we do know that after the Ur discovered the ways, they left the Hearth behind, and we suspect it was they who created the Veil, in order to prevent anyone from following them."

Manindra's eyes remained on the tapestry for a moment longer, before he turned to regard her again.

"I suppose you'd like to know why I asked to speak with you?" he said, taking another sip of his tea.

Rachael shrugged.

"Because this is the part where you tell me your evil plan, right? That's what bad guys are supposed to do."

She was actually surprised when the old man burst out laughing. Tea slopped over his hands and he carefully set the cup down, smiling as he wiped himself clean with a small white handkerchief.

"Oh my. You're blunt. I like that," he said, with a gleeful smile. "Well then, if you must know my dear, my evil scheme is thus: Having learned of the present danger through some close allies of my own, I sent my boys to London to find and capture you, preferably before you could awaken one of the Seeds in the middle of the city you call home, and unleash a nightmare on untold millions of innocents."

Despite the lightness in his tone, there was a cold edge to Manindra's expression. Something hard and sharp, like a knife. She forced herself to meet his gaze, in spite of how badly she wanted to look away.

"Right, because you're so big on caring about other people."

He shook his head, sadly.

"Children think in such simple terms. I will gladly admit that I did all these things for purely selfish reasons. Gaining control of the

Seed would have allowed me immeasurable influence with the Guild Council. Of course, in doing so you would have been spared the awful responsibility of destroying an entire city. So tell me, precisely what harm would have been done if I had succeeded in my nefarious plan?"

"Your men attacked us," she replied, struggling not to sound petulant. "They had guns, and... That thing. That animal."

"None of which would have been necessary if you had not proven to be such a remarkably elusive quarry, young lady."

"You didn't have to..." she began, before he cut her off, coldly.

"Yes. We did. You should be thankful that I consider you so invaluable a resource, my dear. Had the Inquisition found you first, they might well have placed far greater importance on preventing you from ever reaching the Seed in the first place. Perhaps the bullet that found your shifter friend might have been aimed at you instead."

A sick sensation roiling in her stomach, Rachael swallowed hard, trying not to let the queasiness show.

"Maybe it should have," she said, quietly.

Manindra shook his head and looked down at his cup.

"Well, what's done is done. What I want, my dear, is the Seed. Controlling it would stop the danger it poses, and would grant me a powerful bargaining tool. My own motives may be of no interest to you, but perhaps you might take this chance to undo the harm to the city that raised you. If you were to refuse Professor Chandra's offer of adoption... If you willingly give yourself over my care... I have the resources and the knowledge to close the rift and safely contain the Seed itself. All we need is you."

"And what happens after that?"

"You remain in my care. You are too valuable, and too dangerous, to be granted freedom. But I can keep you from falling into the hands of the Inquisition, who will, I imagine, see you as little more than a curiosity to be studied. You will live here on my estate as my ward. I cannot imagine you will want for anything."

"Yeah, no thanks mate. I'll pass."

"Tell me, do you really imagine you have much choice in this matter?"

Rachael said nothing, deciding it was better to hold her tongue as Manindra watched her with a pitying expression.

"Ah, but of course, you still imagine you have a third option. Rishi hasn't told you."

"Told me what?" Rachael said, eyes narrowing.

Manindra sighed, heavily.

"That was cruel of him, to let you hold on to a false hope."

Still regarding him with a wary gaze, Rachael held her tongue, waiting to see what the old man had to say for himself.

"The young man who was with you in London... Doubtless he told you that you were connected to the Dreamwalkers in some fashion. To one, in particular I imagine."

As Rachael tried to mask her surprise, Manindra turned to regard the tapestries again.

"The Lady of The Falling Leaves," he said, casting a glance back in her direction. "You recognised her image. Tell me, did he offer to take you to her? Was the Seed perhaps to be your means of finding her realm?"

Rachael said nothing, but she had no doubt that Manindra had already found his answer in her silence.

"My dear child, you have been chasing a phantom," he said. "The Dreamwalkers are all long dead. Every last one of them. Their deaths are recorded in every Ur ruin we have uncovered. Their history was written into their walls, crafted into the architecture of their cities. Every Guild scholar knows it."

He gestured towards the books that lined the study walls.

"I will show you a hundred texts that all say the same. You will doubtless find the same books on Rishi's shelves, if you care to look."

Finally, she could not contain herself anymore.

"So what?" she snapped. "You honestly expect me to believe any of that? You gonna convince me that Justin was just lying to me this whole time?"

"Not lying. Merely mislead," Manindra replied, calmly.

"You really expect me to buy that?"

"Tell me," he said, leaning forward a little, eyes bright with curiosity, "your young friend. Did he claim to have met the Lady of The Falling Leaves in person. To have been to her realm?"

"He..." Rachael paused for a moment, skewered by the old man's question. "He went there in his dreams," she finished, with none of the fire she had felt surging through her only a moment before.

The old man regarded her sadly.

"Dreams, my dear, are the substance of all true magic. The same magic that would have granted him his particular abilities. Fatework, it is called."

"He said it had been years," Rachael said. She meant for the reply to sound forceful, but the words came out like a mumbled excuse.

"Time moves strangely in dreams. I'm sure you've experienced this for yourself. Even memories are just dreams of a different sort," he said. "Did it not all seem just a touch too convenient? For someone like yourself to discover that she was secretly the heir to an ancient legacy? A lost princess, perhaps? Was the young man to be your knight? Your prince? Wasn't it just a little too perfect, to learn that there was a new life waiting for you, just beyond the other side of the curtain?"

His voice was soft, almost kindly. In the silence after he spoke, Rachael heard the crackling of the fire in the grate, as the old man sipped his tea.

"So what am I then?" she said. "Cause you still went to a whole lot of trouble. And that Seed thing still did something."

"There is a grain of truth in what you were told. You are an heir to the legacy of the Dreamwalkers, if distantly. Some tiny part of your lineage doubtless traces back to their kind. Enough to make a connection. Growing up in the vicinity of a buried Seed saw to the rest. The Seed was searching for someone to awaken it. It found you."

He sighed, again.

"You are an echo, my dear. Nothing more. Your connection to the Seed is, indeed, quite valuable. But there is no one waiting for you beyond that gate. The Lady's halls are abandoned and empty."

Calmly, Manindra leaned forward in his chair, regarding her intently.

"You and your young companion have been manipulated from the very beginning, and as a result you now have the blood of an entire city on your hands," he said. Uncomfortable with his icy gaze, she looked away.

"Like you care," she snarled. "You think you're any better?"

"Because I am selfish?" Manindra said, seeming entirely unsurprised. "Everyone is selfish. Anyone who pretends to act only for the good of others is a liar and a fool. I seek power and influence, and I offer a chance to wash your conscience clean. Both of us selfishly saving the lives of millions."

Rachael turned to look at him again, her eyes cold and hard.

"Doesn't sound like much of an offer to me," she said.

"What else would you seek?" Manindra said, raising an eyebrow. "Freedom? The only freedom is power, and that is something you have never known. You were born powerless, and you will die powerless. You will always be caged, girl. It might as well be a gilded one."

Rachael said nothing. Eyes narrowed, she met his gaze, and forced herself not to look away.

"Tell me," Manindra said, softly, "is Rishi Chandra really any different? Has he offered you anything that I haven't?"

"He said..."

She began to protest, and faltered. Now that she thought about it, it seemed hard to pin down just what the professor had promised her.

"I see," Manindra said, with obvious disappointment. "Well, run to him, if you wish. He will fight for you, I have no doubt of that. As with all things, Rishi will fight this to the bitter end. And I will destroy him, utterly and without mercy. I will ruin him and everyone he holds dear. His daughter, his friends, the crew of that charming little ship he rides about on; they will all suffer to protect you. And it will not make the slightest bit of difference."

Manindra's voice was like the sound of a blade being sharpened, and Rachael felt no doubt at all that the man believed every word.

"Why would I care for what happens to any of them?" she spat back at him. "I don't owe them nothing."

"Really?" Manindra leaned back in the chair and smiled. "Then why sacrifice yourself for them?"

Still smiling, Manindra nodded to her.

"Think on it, young miss. I thank you. This has been most enlightening."

Rachael made no move, didn't say a word as the old man touched a small crystal inset into the table, which made a gentle chiming sound. She sat in awkward silence while Manindra sipped his tea, until the door opened and Dayaram stepped in. Looking up to see his son standing in the doorway, Manindra shook his head sadly.

"What on earth do I pay all these servants for, dear boy?"

Dayaram just smiled as he awaited his instructions. She couldn't help but notice that when Dayaram smiled, it was only his lips that moved. His eyes remained as cold as ever. Especially when he smiled at his father.

"Well if you will insist on being my personal adjutant, Darry, would you be so good as to see the young lady back to her companions," Manindra said.

"As you wish father," his son nodded and turned to her, holding the door open. She got to her feet, taking one last glance at the old man as he stared contentedly at the fire. Then she turned away and followed Dayaram out of the room.

They walked through the long corridor once more, as Rachael felt the figures on the tapestries staring down at them.

"He scares you, doesn't he," she said, softly. Dayaram made no sign that he had heard. "That's why you want to be so close to everything. You're trying to see just how bad he's lost it. Just how dangerous he's gotten."

Still Dayaram walked, without a word. They crossed the entrance hall, and approached a large set of double doors. He stopped, with one hand on the door. Before he could turn the handle, Rachael looked him in the eye.

"Believe me," she said, "it's as bad as you think. It really is."

When he spoke, his words were like steel scraping over ice. There was coldness in his eyes, but she also suspected just a hint of fear.

"So long as you remain a guest in our house... Young miss... You would do well to mind your words."

Dayaram opened the door and ushered Rachael through into a spacious dining hall. As she entered she saw that everyone else was already seated. Only Manindra had yet to join them. However her attention turned quickly to the two figures she had not expected to see at the table. Even without their long red coats, Rakesh and Naveen were easy to recognise.

Naveen had his hair tied back, and was sat by Vaneeta's side, chatting with the woman in a hushed tone. Closer to, Rakesh was sat back from the table with little Mohan and Jeevan sat on his knees, bright eyed and laughing as the young boys both did their best to shout over each other.

Rachael didn't dare move. She watched them both, trying to make sense of what she was seeing. She couldn't seem to match Rakesh's smiling face to the haggard look he had worn when she last saw him, standing on top of the Shard Building with a sword clutched in one hand. Then the man looked up at her as his nephews continued to bombard him with questions. His smile remained, but saw something dangerous behind those eyes. Something hard, like steel. Then the moment passed, as Rakesh returned to answering the torrent of questions that Mohan and Jeevan assaulted him with.

Dayaram lead her to the table, seating her by Arsha's side before taking his place just to the right of the head seat. She noticed that the professor was seated to the left, and wondered if that was important. Then the doors swung open again, and a hush fell on the room. Manindra Bhandari entered, his steps slow and measured as he surveyed them all. A nervous Vaneeta swooped in to gather up her young boys as Rakesh and Naveen stood to their feet. Their expressions now quite serious, both men went to meet their father.

"My boys," Manindra boomed, suddenly beaming as he clapped a hand on both of their shoulders. It was funny, Rachael thought, how the old man could be half a foot shorter than both the young men, and yet seem to tower over them. Watching closely, she saw the look in the old man's eyes as he regarded both of his sons carefully. A look of deep disappointment. There was a brief conversation that she could not make out. Then all three of them went to take their places at the table. Rachael felt a knot tightening in her stomach. She wondered if she would be able to eat anything at all.

As dinner began, all but the oldest of the boys were ushered away to the kitchen. Only Vasuki remained, seated between his uncles. Rachael couldn't help but notice the sour glances he kept throwing in their direction. A strained but polite conversation filled the room. Rachael began to hope that she could stay quiet and be ignored, but it wasn't long before Manindra turned his attention to her. Smiling delightedly, the old man bombarded her with questions about where she had come from. He seemed genuinely delighted by ideas like 'the internet' and 'mobile phones'. She mumbled brief answers as best she could. It was difficult to endure the barrage of questions without wanting to grind her teeth and simply refuse to speak any more. Throughout it all Manindra listened attentively, seeming for all the world like a kindly grandfather.

When dessert finally arrived, she felt too exhausted by the conversation to even lift a spoon. She was desperately thankful when other conversations began to overtake the old man's questions. Finally Manindra excused himself, and this seemed to signal that they were free to go. She noticed that the old man's sons followed close behind him as he left the room. Too tired to put much thought into what that might mean, Rachael slipped down from the table and made her way out onto the balcony.

She leaned out over the railing and found herself looking down over the town below them. There was a gentle breeze, but the air was still unpleasantly warm.

She heard the door, and looked across her shoulder to see Micah stroll out onto the balcony. He leaned against the stone railing and stared up at the sky. Rachael found herself uncomfortably aware of the shape of his face, the strong line of his jaw captured in the glow of the ghostlamps that swayed above them.

"Hey," she said, turning to sit on the balcony. Her throat felt dry.

"What's up?" he said, apparently unconcerned by her precarious perch.

"Nothing, I just," she paused, trying to gather her thoughts, "you know... Needed some fresh air."

"Yeah, me too."

He nodded, and went to stand at the railing beside her. Reaching into his pocket, Micah produced a small cloth bag, from which he extracted a slightly crumpled looking roll-up.

"Here, give us one of those then," Rachael said, as Micah put the cigarette to his lips and struck a match.

He laughed.

"Oh no, not a chance. Filthy habit," he said, taking care to blow the smoke away from her.

"Mate, I grew up on the estate, yeah?" she said, doing her best to sound nonchalant. "I've smoked ciggies before."

"Yeah, I'm sure," he said. "I'll get to watch you cough your lungs out, and then you can watch as Milima murders me. 'Lona will probably help too."

"I won't tell," she said, pouting just a little.

"Not happening, kid. Nice try though."

With a sigh, she slipped down off the railing and turned to look at the view. In the far distance she could make out the lights of Firecrest. Below them the streets around the estate were lit by the orange glow of the furnaces.

"Fates, you see it like this, it's almost beautiful," Micah said, softly.

"It's a bit like home," she replied. Micah just nodded as he took another drag. For a moment she found herself staring down at the railing, trying to work her way around the lump that had formed in her throat.

"Hey, um, I wanted to say thanks, for today," she said. "It was... It was really fun."

"Nah, don't worry about it," Micah said. "I was going stir crazy anyhow. I've never been good at being cooped up, you know?"

Rachael nodded.

"Yeah. Me too."

"Well, maybe I'll take you out again tomorrow, if the professor's crazy enough to have us stick it out here."

"I... I'd really like that."

"Just, don't get your hopes up, OK?" he said. She was surprised by his look of concern, though she couldn't really say why.

"Yeah, I know," she said. "It's just... I really was crazy about 'em, you know? Even when I started drawing, it was all just pages and pages of horses. Whole books of 'em. I mean, I knew it was stupid. Rich girls get horses, not dirt poor scabbers living on the estate."

She looked up at the tall windows above them.

"Guess some things are the same wherever you go."

"Seems like it," Micah said, nodding.

"I suppose where you grew up must have been a lot like this."

Micah turned to look back over the structure that loomed over them.

"Yeah, yeah it was. I mean, different, but the same."

"So why'd you ever want to leave for?"

"I guess I've never really gotten along all that well with most of my family," Micah said. "They're good people, but I just never really..."

He tailed off, staring out into the distance.

"I think getting away from that place was the best thing I could have ever done. Yeah, I had it easy there, but I felt... Trapped, you know? When Rishi came along, offered me this chance, I didn't hesitate."

Micah looked down at the stub of his cigarette, barely anything of it left, and made an amused sound.

"Go on then, let's see you give it a try."

As he held out the cigarette stub for her, Rachael hesitated a moment before taking it. Pinching the cigarette to her lips, she breathed in and felt a choking wave of hot smoke sear it's way through her lungs. She could see him barely holding back his laughter as she spluttered and coughed. She could feel her ears burning.

"Fates, give me that back," he said, still smiling bemusedly as he took the stub from her hand and flicked it into the darkness. Rachael watched the tiny ember sail down into the night, like a microscopic shooting star. Rachael watched it go, desperately trying not to meet his eyes. To her relief, Micah just carried on talking as if nothing had happened.

"Look, this stuff with my family... I'm not trying to say it's anything like what you've been through. I know I've always had it easy. Even living on the Triskelion, even when I'm freezing to death or sweating my ass off on one of the professor's expeditions, I still chose this, you know?"

He grinned, suddenly.

"Honestly, I only complain so much because it gets up Ilona's nose."

"Jesus," she muttered, "what even is it with you two? Like, are you a thing or something?"

"Oh Fates, no. No, no, no, no. Ilona is..." He shook his head. "You know what, I'll get back to you on that one when I figure it out, OK?"

Micah paused for a moment, looking off into the distance again.

"But I care about her a lot," he said. "All of these people... I know it's awful to say it, but they've been more family to me than anyone I was born with."

"Yeah," she said. "That... That kinda makes sense."

"It's not who you're given, you know? It's who you find. That's what counts," he said, his smile strangely subdued. He gave her shoulder a squeeze and turned away from the railing.

"Hey, Micah," she called after him. He stopped, and looked back.

"Thanks. Really."

"Don't mention it."

He smiled and slipped through the door, leaving her standing in the warm night air. She closed her eyes and listened to the sound of the wind.

Chapter 20 - Cinnamon

Rachael tossed and turned, unable to get to sleep. It was too warm inside, the air too humid. In the bed across the room from her, she could hear Arsha's soft breathing as the girl slept on in spite of the heat. Eventually Rachael slid out of the bed and pulled on a dressing gown. She slipped out of the room and padded down the corridor, hoping to find a glass of water. In the dark, the unfamiliar corridors all seemed alike, and she found that she could not remember the way to the bathroom. Instead she ended up at the end of a narrow hallway, looking up at a small and winding staircase. Curious, she followed it, and found herself in some kind of greenhouse. Arranged around the edge of the room, stone planters overflowed with a brilliant array of flowers. The scent of them filled the air, almost overpowering her. A glass dome gave her a perfect view of the stars. By the planters were three low marble benches, like those she saw sometimes in the older parks in London.

Taken in by the strangeness of the place, she sat down and stared up into the deep black sky. She wondered if the stars were the same here as back home. In London you almost never saw any stars.

She'd been staring up into the inky blackness for some time, when she heard a sound, like someone tapping at the glass. At first she could not make out where it was from. Looking around, she finally saw a small shape against one of the window panes.

It was a raven. For a moment, she wondered what a raven was doing in a place like this, let alone why it would be tapping at the glass. She barely had time to consider the question before the answer came to her, and her heart nearly stopped dead. She rushed to the glass, where she saw the tiny latch that the raven was tapping at. She fumbled at the mechanism and finally pushed the window open just wide enough for the bird to slip through, swooping by faster than she could follow. She turned just in time to see the cloud of oily black smoke reforming, a tall shape barely inches away from her.

Then he was standing there, his long coat draped around him, face flushed as if he had been running, hair matted with sweat. Gently, as if she was something fragile, his hands went to her shoulders and he looked at her with an expression of wonder.

"Rachael. Thank God you're OK."

She blinked in surprise, unable to form a coherent thought. All she could think of was the shape of his face in the moonlight, the colour of his eyes, the feeling of his hands around her shoulders.

"I've been following you for weeks. I wasn't even sure what I was doing half the time; I was crossing worlds, moving through impossible places, and I just... It was like there was something inside, telling me how, telling me which way to go. Like it was pulling me towards you. I almost caught up with you just as their ship was leaving that town on the cliff-face. I was exhausted and starving... I... I had to stay and find food. Then I finally found this place, and I was so sure you'd already be gone... God Rachael, when they took you..."

Justin's words seemed to flow past her like falling rain. Her fingers traced the shape of his face as she moved into him. Their lips brushed, and then met. It felt natural, like something that had always belonged to her.

It was a while before she became aware of her surroundings again. His smile was warm, and just a little bit surprised. His arms encircled her waist as if holding her up. She decided that was probably for the best.

"Don't you dare try to pretend you were expecting that," she whispered.

"Not exactly," he said. "Imagined. Hoped for."

He stroked back a misplaced strand of her hair. She was certain her cheeks must have been glowing.

"Imagined?" she said, raising an eyebrow. He just smiled back at her. Rachael wondered if she was imagining the sense of relief that was flooding off of him. If, perhaps, she was only seeing her own feelings reflected back at herself. It didn't matter. At the moment, nothing seemed to matter any more.

He leaned in and kissed her again, their lips only touching lightly this time. She could feel the tension in him as he pulled away and looked her in the eyes.

"I'm sorry you had to wait so long, but I'm going to get you out of here. We'll leave tonight."

"Justin," she began, but he cut her off.

"I did some scouting out around the town below, before I came here. There are trains that come in every four hours. Bunch of stuff gets loaded and unloaded. From what I heard they keep running all through the night. We can sneak aboard the next one and get back to that big city. I think we'll be able to stow away on a ship or something from there."

"I... I guess. Can't you just fly us out together? I thought you said that it was easier, out here. For you to change."

"It is, a little, but it's... It's not enough. To do what I did before... I'd need some kind of power, like the Seed."

"You really think you can get us away?"

He squeezed her shoulders, giving her a fiery look.

"Rachael, it's the best way for you to escape."

"I... Justin..." She faltered and looked away.

"Rachael, don't be scared. I'll be with you."

She stepped back a little, and his hands fell away from her shoulders.

"It's not that. It's... These people... They're not what we thought."

"Rachael, whatever they've told you, it's lies. All of it. They're acting nice to win your trust. They're just as greedy and cold hearted as everyone else. Why else would they bring you here, to the same people that were hunting us in London? Do you really believe they're going to let you leave here? That they aren't just arguing for a better price? Rachael, you know where you belong."

Her laugh was mirthless, something tired and strained.

"Look, even if you think they might help you, do you honestly think you're better off with them?"

He watched her calmly as she let this thought sink in. She looked up into his earnest eyes and reached out to touch his face, as if reassuring herself that he was really there. Whatever doubts she had felt, whatever questions Manindra or Rishi had managed to plant in her mind, she felt them all melt away. Just looking into his eyes was enough.

"No. You protected me. You... You went through so much, just to find me."

"I made you a promise. I'm going to keep it."

"Thank you," she whispered.

"You don't have to thank me. Just listen; the next train comes in a few hours, so I'll have to hide until then. Get back to your room and wait there. I'll signal you when it's time to go."

Seeing that she understood, he kissed her one more time. Even with her eyes closed, she could feel his body dissolving into smoke beneath her hands. Only the ghost of his lips remained against hers as she heard the fluttering of wings. Then he was gone. She opened her eyes and looked around the moonlit room, silent and empty. The fragrance of the flowers filled the air.

She turned and caught a sudden motion by the stairs, then the sound of footsteps. She made it to the top of the stairs in time to see Arsha at the bottom, halfway around the corner.

"Hey," she hissed, as loudly as she dared. For a moment Arsha just froze. Her eyes were large and frightened in the moonlight as she looked up at Rachael. Slowly, the girl drew a breath. Rachael carefully unclenched her fists and let her shoulders relax.

"How much did you see then?" she said.

"Not much, I guess," the girl mumbled, shifting back against the wall, her hands clasped behind her back. "I'm sorry. I heard you get up and I thought you might want to talk. So, I followed you up here, and..."

Rachael's anger had already abated. Taking a step back from the edge of the stairs, she settled herself down on one of the benches that encircled the floor of the solarium. Cautiously, Arsha walked up the steps and sat down on the bench next to her.

"That was Justin, right?"

Rachael just nodded.

"He's been following us?"

For a moment, Rachael wasn't sure if she should answer.

"I won't tell my dad," Arsha said. "I promise."

"Yeah. He's been following us since London. And now... God, Arsh, I don't know what to do. He wants..." She paused, not sure if she could go on. "He wants me to go with him."

"Where to?"

"I'm not sure exactly. I guess we'll have to head back to London, somehow. To get back to that... Gateway."

"The Seed. You're trying to find a way out into the Deep Wild, right? To where your mother is."

Rachael nodded.

"Yeah. This seed thing, it can take us there. We'll be safe. That's what he told me."

"You trust him?"

"I do."

"When... When are you going?"

"Now, pretty much," Rachael said. "Well... Assuming you don't say anything about it."

Arsha gave her an indignant look, almost as if she was offended by the suggestion. Rachael smiled.

"Thanks Arsh. Really, thanks."

"It's OK," Arsha said. She spoke quietly, her eyes fixed on the floor. "Just tell me one thing. Do you trust him? When he says that... That he can keep you safe. That he'll get you home. Do you believe he can do it?"

"Yeah. I do. It's... Hard to explain. I'm not good at, y'know, trusting people. Not so much. But with Justin... The way he talks, you just know he believes it, every word he's saying. Like, really believes it. You feel like nothing in the world could stop him. Just look at all he did to find me. Because somehow he really believes I'm worth that. He nearly died to keep me safe. I have to believe in him Arsh. If you can't believe in someone like that, what can you believe in?"

Rachael looked up to see Arsha watching her with an uneasy expression.

"You really care about him, don't you?" the girl said, quietly.

"Yeah. I do," Rachael nodded.

"Was that... Was that the first time you've kissed him?"

It was such a strange question that Rachael couldn't help but smile.

"Yeah. It actually... It was kind of the first time I've kissed anybody," she said. She was relieved to see that Arsha at least looked surprised. "Back when I was still going to school and stuff, I always used to make out like I was, you know, experienced like," she continued, looking down at her hands. "Like I'd been with all these guys and stuff. But it was all just this... This thing. Like, if I kept acting like I'd been there and all, I could just keep pushing them away."

"Why?"

She shrugged.

"I'm not exactly much of a people person, right?" she said.

Arsha smiled.

"You might have mentioned it," she said, sticking her tongue out.

"I guess with your dad flying around all over the place, you never had much time for boys and all?"

"Not much," Arsha said, but there was something in the way she smiled that caught Rachael's eye.

"Get out," she said, laughing. "Come on then, share the goods, girl."

Arsha's started nervously tugging at her fingers again.

"It was just this one guy, actually."

"Oh, now I have to know," Rachael said.

"Not a chance," Arsha shot back, sticking her tongue out.

"After I told you all that about Justin? Come on."

"Fine," Arsha said, pouting. "But... You can't tell my dad. Or, any of the others, I guess, but they'd just tease me and stuff. I think Dad would actually have a heart attack. He still acts like I'm ten."

Against the face of everything else that had just happened, it seemed like such a ridiculously small secret to keep. All the same, Rachael nodded, solemnly.

"So, we were stopping in Tairk for a few days. It's out in..." Arsha seemed to catch herself, about to rattle off the name of another place Rachael didn't know. "It's this big desert. The three main cities, they're all in this area called the Hive, because it's this massive plateau of rock that got carved up into a kind of honeycomb by the wind. We were there a few days, and my dad just sort of let me explore after we got to know the place. I just kind of went out walking... I mean I stayed to the safe parts, but I was pretty much just going wherever. I got hungry, so I found a café and had something to eat, and then as I was walking out I heard this sound coming from the alley by the café. It was music... So, I sort of poked my head around the corner, and he was sitting there, playing a... He called it a 'haran'. It's this sort of stringed instrument they have there."

Rachael clapped her hand over her mouth, but could scarcely hide her delighted smile.

"Oh sweet Jesus, he was a guitarist," she nearly squealed. Arsha blinked in confusion.

"A musician, like," Rachael explained. "Trust me, boys who play music are always the hottest."

Arsha smiled.

"Yeah," she sighed. "It was something about his hands. I just kept thinking that he had really pretty hands. He was so caught up in what he was playing, I don't think he noticed me at first. I must have looked really stupid, just staring at him like that."

Rachael smiled to herself at that.

"But he just sort of looked amused. And I got all embarrassed and told him I really liked what he was playing, and he shouldn't stop because of me... And I guess we just got talking."

Arsha's eyes were fixed on the ground, but the way her lips curled as she smiled told Rachael everything she needed to know.

"His name was Mikal. He was a Hiver boy... One of the people who'd lived there for forever. He had long hair, all in braids, and the paint marks they wear... But not too much, just around his face and neck. We talked for... Hours. He showed me all around the city, but... I sort of don't really remember any of it. I guess I was too busy looking at him. It got late, so he walked me back to the ship. When we were a few streets away I told him dad might worry if he saw me coming home with someone strange, and we'd have to say goodbye... And when I squeezed his hand, he just sort of leaned in..."

Arsha's expression told her the rest.

"After that I sort of didn't get back home for a while."

"Did you see him again?"

Arsha nodded.

"We were there for another week. I didn't even bother with

breakfast. We just spent every minute together. My dad had to tell me off for coming home so late."

"Can't blame ya."

"Yeah. But we've never been back since. He probably wouldn't remember me."

"Hey, what... Are you crazy? Of course he would."

Arsha shrugged.

"I think it's just as good this way... I'm not really sure what I'd do, if I saw him again."

"Kissing him might be a start," Rachael said, sticking her tongue out.

"Well... After that, I mean," Arsha smiled.

Rachael just shook her head.

"So... What about you and Justin? What was it like, you know, kissing him?" Arsha said, raising an eyebrow.

Rachael could feel herself blushing again.

"It was... I don't know. Exciting. Scary. I didn't really think about it much, but," she gave Arsha an amused smile, "his breath kinda smelled a little actually. I didn't mind so much, but... I guess flying thousands of miles doesn't give you much time to find breath mints, right?"

Arsha giggled a little, putting a hand over her mouth to stifle the sound.

"Like, really smelled, or just a little?"

"Just a little. I wasn't really thinking about it," she shrugged. "But I could feel his heart beating. Like, really loud, you know? What about you?"

"You mean Mikal? He kind of smelled of cinnamon. He worked at the café in the morning, baking the rolls."

"Wow."

"Yeah... But after that, I couldn't eat cinnamon buns for a month. First time Milima put a basket down for breakfast, I had to pretend I needed the bathroom, I got so embarrassed."

"God..." Rachael put her head back against the cool glass, and looked up into the black. "This is so weird. I mean, here I am, who knows how far away from anything normal, in a place that shouldn't even exist, with a girl who lives on a flying ship... And I'm having just about the most normal conversation I've ever had in my life."

Arsha just smiled. Rachael tucked her feet up on the bench.

"Thanks. For trying to be my friend," she added. "I mean I really am happy that I met you. I guess, in a way, everything in my life has been falling apart for a long time now. But you were nice to me, even when I didn't give you any reason to be. So... Thanks."

She smiled, awkwardly.

"Thanks for letting me be your friend," Arsha said, returning the smile.

They made their way back to the room and waited, sitting on their beds, staring nervously at the walls. Rachael kept her bag at her side and forced herself not to recheck the contents every five minutes. The hands on the clock ticked round so slowly that she began to wonder if it was broken.

A shadow flickered across the room and Rachael looked up to see a movement at the window. The raven was perched on the corner of the sill, one eye turned in their direction. Rachael jumped off the bed and pulled the window open. Instead of changing, the bird just hopped back and forth, nodding towards the gardens below.

"OK," she said.

As the raven took flight, she turned to look at Arsha. She could see the nervousness in the girl's eyes. She imagined her own expression could not have looked much different.

Slipping out the window was easy enough. With Arsha's help, she reached the first handhold, and began to scale her way down the wall, until she was near enough to the ground to drop the rest of the way. A movement above made her look up, surprised to see Arsha following her down.

An open expanse of moonlit garden was all that was left between them and the nearest wall of the estate. She turned to Arsha who just nodded, as if showing that she was ready. They dashed across the open ground and huddled into the cover of the bushes, watching for any sign that they had been spotted. Above them Rachael heard the flutter of wings as the raven landed on the wall. Then she saw the cloud of black smoke take form, and suddenly Justin was there, perched atop the wall and reaching down a hand for her.

She turned to look back at Arsha.

"This is it," she said, keeping her voice low. Arsha nodded.

"I wish I could come with you," the girl said.

"No, you don't," Rachael said, smiling, much to her own surprise. "You've got a life here, Arsh. A proper life. And things will be OK, now that I'm not around."

"I know. But I wish..."

Rachael put her hand on the girl's shoulder, cutting her off.

"Just give me a decent head-start, OK?"

"It's OK. I won't tell them where you're going."

"Thanks. I'm going to miss you," Rachael said. It felt strange, saying those words, and she was surprised by just how much she meant them.

"I'll miss you too," Arsha said, biting her lip and looking genuinely miserable. Feeling like she ought to do something, Rachael put an arm around the girl's slim shoulders. Arsha immediately threw both arms around her, burying her face in Rachael's shoulder.

"Hey, give over. You're making me blush here," Rachael mumbled.

"Don't care," Arsha replied, her voice muffled. The girl released her grip and took a step back. "Be safe."

Rachael nodded. Above her, Justin hissed at them.

"Come on. We don't have time." She looked up to see him glaring at the both of them from his exposed perch.

"Alright, I'm coming," she said, reaching up to take his hand. He pulled her up to the top of the wall, and they both turned to drop down on the other side. She caught one last glimpse of Arsha looking up at them. The girl waved. Then they dropped down into the long grass at the foot of the wall and Arsha was gone.

Chapter 21 - Moonlight

They kept moving, following the road down the cliff-face, but staying in the bushes and long grass until at last they could see the glow of the foundries and hear the sound of the train pulling in to the station.

"Come on, we won't have long before they finish loading," Justin said, gesturing for her to hurry. They kept moving down the winding road, and soon they were in amongst the buildings, keeping to the narrow back alleys as they made their way towards the station. It was only by the silhouettes of the cranes looming over the skyline that Rachael had any sense of how close they were. In the gloom, she could almost have been in London again. The buildings had the same feeling of faded industry, though up close they were obviously recently built. Even in the night they could hear the sounds of work coming from the warehouses, getting louder as they grew closer.

Around the station lanterns blazed, burning some form of

chemical that gave a far brighter light than the ghostlamps could. She heard the sounds of machinery and tools at work. Lights flared from the mouths of the buildings around them. She caught glimpses of the men who moved through the pools of light, tough working men, some scarred, all weathered and worn. Some reminded her of faces she had seen before amongst Korban's men. The thought worried her.

They kept moving, until Justin finally gestured for them to stop by a large stack of cargo that was being prepared for loading. Leaning out a little, he nodded at a bridge that crossed over the whole of the train station.

"We'll drop down from there," he whispered. "As the train is leaving."

She nodded. From the looks of things the train was nearly ready to go. They could already see the loaders closing up most of the carriages.

"Alright, let's move," Justin whispered. They dashed across the gap and up the stairs onto the bridge itself. It was little more than a walkway, wide enough for four people to walk abreast, with a railing on either side. The bridge itself was unlit, and in the shadows they could easily wait until their moment. Below, they saw the workers close up the last of the carriages and turn away, heading back towards the warehouses. The hissing of the steam engine suggested that it was preparing to move.

It was Justin who saw the movement in the shadows at the far end of the bridge. He moved with breathtaking speed, flicking out a hand towards the shape in the darkness. Rachael saw something small and shiny fly out of his hand, and then heard the ringing impact of metal on metal. A loud cursing erupted from the darkness and she heard two objects bouncing across the ground.

Then a shape erupted from the shadows, hard and fast, barrelling into Justin like a freight train. She saw him fall, as the heavy-set man slammed him into the ground. She glimpsed the shaved scalp, bisected by a ragged scar. Korban, the mercenary captain.

"Gave me a lot of trouble back Veil-side, you did," Korban growled, as he kept Justin's face pressed against the bridge. "Good men I'll have replace. Good friends I lost. All for... What, this?" He turned to look at her, clearly unimpressed.

"Can't say I see why. Now you, I see why a man would pay money for a freak like you. Damage you did... Impressive."

"You want to be impressed?" Justin grunted. The next moment Korban's hands were clasped around nothing, as Justin's body dissolved. An instant later the dark smoke cloud reformed above him. Justin fell, throwing his hands around the man's neck. Korban reacted with astonishing speed, hurling Justin over one shoulder so fast that the boy didn't have time to shift before he slammed into the walkway.

Korban's hand went to his pocket, but before he could produce whatever weapon he was reaching for Rachael hurled herself against the man's leg, making him stagger back a step. With an almost casual gesture his hand caught her hair, and she was hurled away like a rag-doll, an explosion of pain rippling across her body as she went tumbling down the steps from the bridge.

Breathing hard, she pulled herself up on her hands and knees. Her head was pounding, and every part of her body seemed to be screaming at her. Below them she could hear the train moving, picking up speed. She looked up to see Justin and Korban on their feet, facing off across the narrow bridge.

Justin lunged, but Korban's guard was up and the man deftly parried every blow, even as Justin struck out at him a dozen times or more. Whatever angle of attack he chose, Korban seemed to counter it without effort.

"What, no more tricks?" Korban snarled.

Justin's eyes narrowed, but he said nothing. Once more, he darted in with a strike aimed at Korban's neck. As the man raised an arm to block the blow, Justin shifted. The smoke reformed in the air, the small dark form of a raven striking at Korban's face with its claws and beak. The man staggered back a step, angrily swatting the small bird away. As Justin backed off, Korban looked around, blinking. For a moment he didn't seem to know where his opponent had gone to.

The bird swooped in from behind where the man stood, reforming into Justin's own lanky form, black coat swirling around him as he took shape right behind where the man stood. As Korban wheeled around, an elbow jabbing sharply back in Justin's direction, the boy caught the larger man's arm and pivoted. Korban's whole body seemed to roll across Justin's shoulders, and then the man was flying across the railing, arms spread as he fell towards the train.

She heard the sound of the impact as Korban slammed into the roof, rolling so close to the edge that she was sure he would go over. At the last second the man's hand snaked out and caught a handrail, just barely keeping himself from falling. Already the train was picking up speed, the distance between the tracks and the cliff-face widening rapidly. The man stood to his feet with a look of cold fury on his face, and produced something from his pocket. She supposed it might have been a sending stone. She turned towards Justin and caught his satisfied expression.

Then her eyes fell on the small silver object lying at Justin's feet. It was round and flat, a little larger than a tennis ball. Catching her eyes, Justin noticed it too. Then everything went white. For the briefest moment Rachael saw sparks of blue-white electricity arc out of the tiny object, reaching out towards the metal support struts that framed the pier and framing Justin in silhouette. The shockwave sent her flying backwards into a stack of crates, the impact knocking all the breath out of her lungs. Then she could barely see anything at all, as a wall of hot air washed over her and she heard the deafening sound of thunder.

Blinking, she looked up at a dark sky. Her head rolled from one side to the other. The ringing in her ears slowly began to fade.

She heard the footsteps before she saw him, a figure emerging from the long shadows between the warehouses, his red coat flapping in the breeze.

"No. Oh God no," she mumbled, her tongue feeling like it was too big for her mouth. She made it half-way to her feet before Rakesh's hand caught her by the collar and hauled her the rest of the way up. He could almost have carried her like a doll. She had no choice but to walk or be dragged. She glanced back at the bridge and saw a crumpled heap of black cloth, smoking slightly. It took her a moment to realise it was Justin. She could just about make out his face, eyes halfway open and rolled back in his skull. She felt a knot in her stomach and her legs almost gave way beneath her as she wondered if he was dead.

Rakesh forced her onwards, between the tall buildings and out into the well lit streets.

"You're crazy," she said, her ears still ringing. "Can't just haul me past all these guys like this."

"Why not? We own them," Rakesh said, his tone utterly mirthless.

She already knew that he was right. It was impossible to believe that struggling or crying out was likely to do her any more good here than it might have back in London.

"I'd advise against running," he continued. "My patience with you has entirely run out. You were trouble enough in London, without Korban managing to twice botch the job of bringing you in. I won't let that happen again, and to the hells with father's honour."

They were passing through the lights of the warehouses and workshops, and she could see that they would soon be out on the main street. As she thought about where they might be going, some part of her recoiled from the thought of just going quietly, dragged like a dog to whatever cage Rakesh had waiting for her.

She twisted in his grip, bringing his arm up just enough that she could get her teeth around his hand and bite down hard on one finger. The taste of blood was on her tongue and he roared in pain, pulling his hand away. She didn't waste a moment, darting away into the nearest side street.

Too late, she saw that it was a dead-end. Rakesh was already on her heels, the steel blade of a sabre gleaming in his hands. She ran towards the far end of the alley, looking up for any way to scale the walls, but there was nothing within reach. Just smooth brick walls, nearly impossible to climb.

Then she heard the sound of another set of footsteps. She glanced back to see Rakesh turn at the sound of polite cough.

Ilona's hand snaked out, the silver mesh of her gauntlet crackling with a corona of blue sparks. It was as if she was reaching towards his face with a handful of lightning. Rakesh had scarcely an instant to react, and yet he seemed to simply fall to the side. There was no appearance of balance or control, yet with a strange shuffling of his feet he was suddenly upright once more. Ilona's gauntleted hand grasped at empty air as he struck her across the face with the hilt of his sword with a resounding crack.

Ilona's head flew back, and she scarcely stayed standing, her hand catching at his collar. With a nasty smirk, Rakesh span the sword over in his hand, the blade flashing as he drew it back to strike, but the swaggering gesture gave Ilona a brief moment to recover. The woman's head flicked forwards, the movement so swift as to seem almost graceful, if not for the sound of the impact and the cry of pain as Rakesh reeled backwards, clasping his free hand to his nose. Blood spilled down the man's face as he reeled. Her hands gripping tight about his collar, Ilona did not let him go. Her face a picture of cold fury, she slammed the man backwards into the wall of the alleyway and brought a knee up hard into his guts. Then the gauntleted fist snaked out once more, and with a bright flash of blue and a loud snap Rakesh slumped to the ground. A faint coil of smoke twisted upwards from his collar.

In the silence that followed, Rachael felt the sound of the streets around them come rushing back in. The creaking of the cranes, the clattering of the machinery and the rattle of the distant train. Ilona picked up the sword and hurled it away.

"You're OK?" Ilona said, turning slightly to meet Rachael's eyes, as she flexed her hands. Rachael wasn't entirely sure if it was a question.

"Yeah. Yeah, I'm fine."

Rachael got to her feet, still unsteady, but oddly grateful that Ilona didn't try to help her up.

"Justin... We have to..."

She didn't even try to complete the half-formed thought. She went to dart past the woman and immediately felt a restraining hand on her arm. She twisted in the woman's grasp, trying to wrench herself free.

"Hey, he's OK," Ilona said, sharply. For a moment Rachael just stared at the woman, uncomprehending.

"He's OK," Ilona repeated. "Micah messaged me. He's with him now."

The woman held up her sending stone, as if to somehow prove what she'd said.

"You think I came looking for you on my own?"

As the words sank in, Rachael began to breathe easier. She leaned back against the alley wall, feeling all the strength seem to seep out of her body. Her eyes settled on Rakesh's unconscious form, slumped against the wall just across from her.

"Smug bastard," she muttered.

She glanced up to see just the hint of a smile pulling at the corners of Ilona's thin mouth.

"Aim over the belt, not under. Men like him expect you to go for the cheap shot. They don't tense right," Ilona said. "Micah taught me that."

"Thanks," Rachael said, not taking her eyes off of Rakesh's face. There was a black mark where the last blow had struck him, and his collar was singed. Ilona seemed to follow her eyes.

"When it was you, I used a half-charge. Didn't feel like being nice to him."

"You've got a weird idea of nice, y'know?" Rachael said.

"I've been told that before," Ilona said. This time, she really did smile. Rachael smiled back. It was a curious feeling.

"So, what now?" she said.

"That depends on you," Ilona replied, her expression serious as she looked Rachael in the eye.

"You're really giving me a choice, or just saying that?" Rachael said.

"Does it matter? It's still your decision to make, whether or not I choose to respect it."

"You've got a really funny way of thinking about stuff."

Ilona said nothing, apparently waiting for her question to be answered.

Rachael leaned back and looked up at the sky. She could hear the faint sound of the train tracks shifting and the howling of the wind against the cliff-faces.

She let out the breath that it seemed she had been holding the entire time.

"I'll stay," she said.

Ilona simply nodded as she raised her sending stone. The call was brief. Not long after, Micah appeared in the mouth of alleyway. He had Justin's limp form slung across his shoulders, the weight barely seeming to bother him.

"Fates, girl, you scared the life out of us," he said as his eyes met hers.

"Sorry," she shrugged, looking away. He turned to look at Ilona and the fallen man.

"You're OK?" he said. Ilona just raised an eyebrow. "Yeah, kinda figured," he replied. "Asshole deserved it too. Come on, we should get going. We need to meet up with the others, fast. I don't think those guys back there really believed I was working for the Bhandaris."

Ilona nodded as Micah walked away. The woman turned to Rachael.

"Coming?"

Rachael nodded as she fell in behind them. Micah lead them on a winding route that seemed to stick to the back streets and side alleys, finally emerging on some far flung part of the plateau. Ahead they could see a platform that protruded from the side of the cliff, iron struts holding up something that she guessed must have been designed as a landing pad. Resting on the platform was a small white boat, just like the ones she had seen flying over London. The memory made her a little uncomfortable.

Up on the deck she could see Abasi at the helm, the Professor standing at his side examining something at the controls. Milima was standing by the front landing strut, with Arsha close at her side. When the girl saw them approach she didn't waste a second in running to meet them.

"Rachael, I..."

Arsha seemed about to launch into a full blown explanation when she remembered that Micah and Ilona were standing either side of her. She paused, and swallowed.

"I'm sorry. I didn't tell them. It was just... When Dad came to find us, you weren't there and I had to explain and..."

"No, it's cool," Rachael said. "If... If Ilona hadn't found me..."

She decided that she didn't want to think about that.

"Is he OK?" Arsha said, looking at Justin.

"He shouldn't be, given what hit him, but yeah. I guess he's survived worse," Micah said. "Never thought I'd see someone still breathing after an arc-mine to the face."

"Hey, move it people," Milima's cry was a sharp whip-crack in the air as she gestured for them to get aboard. Micah went first, handing the unconscious Justin up to the men on the deck and then scrambling up the ladder. At the top he turned to pull the rest of them up. Milima was the last aboard, as the propellers began to spin up. They nestled down on long bench seats that lined the inside walls of the boat. As Rachael sat, Arsha immediately squeezed in beside her. Justin was laid out along the floor, his coat folded under his head.

"I don't understand. What are we doing?" she said to Arsha.

"Leaving," the girl said, with a confused shrug.

"Is this... Because of what we did?"

"Actually, it's because of what I did," she heard the professor say. She looked up to see the man standing over them. As the boat lifted off from the pad he seemed to scarcely think about keeping his balance, calmly shifting his stance with the swaying of the hull. The motion reminded her of people standing on the tube trains.

"What do you mean? How did we even get this boat? Are we stealing this or something?" she said, having to raise her voice over the roar of the propellers.

"Stealing? No," he replied, with a smile that seemed to have no humour in it. "Why, Manindra Bhandari himself filed a flight plan and released this vessel on our behalf. Or, at least, that's what their records show."

"You faked them?" she said, already realising that it wasn't really a question.

"Yes. Luckily for you and your friend here, we were never really planning on staying for long."

"When he says 'we'..." Micah interjected, with an aggravated look.

"Yes, some warning might have been nice," Milima added with a scowl. The professor just nodded calmly.

"I'm sorry. It was necessary. Having you all know what I was up to might have given me away. I wasn't even sure for myself exactly how all of this might go down."

"So, what, you just came to talk to this guy and then run off? What for? What did you find out?" Rachael said.

The professor's eyes met each of theirs in turn as everyone watched him, waiting for his answer. His whole manner suddenly seemed very cold. There was something about him that reminded her of the way Rakesh had acted.

"From Manindra? Very little. The man is more deranged than ever. But I learned a great deal from the files I stole from him. Whatever hope any of you held that we might have reasoned with this man, abandon it. Manindra is entirely beyond reason."

There was a long pause, as everyone digested this.

"So... What happens now?" Micah said.

"We keep running. For now, it's all we can do. I'm sorry. I really don't have a better answer."

He turned away, walking to the prow of the boat where could look out ahead. Peering over the edge of the hull, Rachael could see the lights of the town and the estate receding below them. Far off, Firecrest was an ember in the darkness.

Chapter 22 - Scars

Rachael felt a curious sense of deja-vu as she sat watching Justin sleep. Then she realised that it wasn't this she remembered, exactly. Rather, that this must have been how it seemed to Arsha, watching over her on that first day aboard the Triskelion. Without realising it, she had sat herself in the same chair with the same lantern resting on the table between them.

She glanced down at the sketchbook on her lap, the pencil in her hand poised to add the last few details to a portrait of Justin's sleeping face. She felt a nervous twinge in her stomach, knowing that she would have to hide the picture from him. He seemed so calm, so at ease. So vulnerable. It was nothing like the way he'd seemed when she first met him.

There was a slight rap on the door, and it eased open as Arsha peered in.

"Hey."

"Hey," Rachael replied. "So your dad let you out?"

"He... He didn't really say anything about it. It seemed like he should have been angry, but it was all just so confused."

Rachael gave the girl a cautious look.

"And you're sure he's not just... You know, waiting to drop the hammer later, or something."

"He's not like that," Arsha said, shaking her head, with a sad smile. "Besides, I asked him."

"Oh."

"He... He just kind of looked at me, and then he said 'You have to make your own choices now.' Like, there wasn't anything else he could say."

"Well that's good," Rachael said.

"Yeah," Arsha replied, clearly not feeling it.

Gently, the girl closed the door behind herself as she slipped into the room. With nowhere else to sit, she settled down against the wall and tucked her knees up.

"It's all... Different. I keep wondering who he is," Arsha said.

Rachael looked meaningfully at the sleeping boy in the bed, before Arsha shook her head.

"I meant my dad."

"Oh."

"I just don't understand how he could get tangled up in all this. I'm not saying he's perfect or anything, but he's my dad, you know? He's nice and funny and kind, and he makes me feel better when I'm upset, and he listens even when I want to talk about dumb stuff that no one else cares about, and he helps me with all my stupid hobbies and things, and..." She drew a breath. "And now I have to believe there's this whole other person, who I never knew about, all this time?"

Feeling uncomfortable, Rachael looked back down at her sketchbook.

"I'm probably not the best person to ask about that," she said. "Feels to me like everyone's just faking it, you know? Like, if we somehow lie to ourselves enough about what we are inside, it might stick. Everyone's just covering up the ugliness."

She glanced across at Justin, seeing him, for a moment, with blood dripping from those soft lips.

"That guy, Rakesh, he called Justin a monster. But the things him and his brother did, it was all just as bad. Worse, even. With Justin, at least you see the ugly. He wears it on the outside."

"And you're OK with that?"

Arsha hugged her knees to her chest, shivering slightly.

"We're all ugly. Manindra was right about that part. We're all selfish and mean."

"And what about you. If everyone else is so horrible..." Arsha said, sharply.

"Your dad said it. Manindra said it. There's a whole city dying because of me. I guess you don't get much more ugly than that."

Whatever Arsha might have said, it was forgotten when Justin stirred in his sleep. Eyes flicked open and then he sat up sharply, looking about with a wary expression.

"Hey... Hey, Justin, it's me," Rachael said, grabbing him by the shoulder. His eyes met hers, and she saw him draw a calming breath.

"Rachael... What happened?"

"It's... Look, we're safe, OK?"

He looked around, taking in the cabin and then Arsha. She gave him an embarrassed wave.

"Safe, where?"

"You're on the Triskelion," Arsha offered.

"The what?"

"It's the ship they took me on. Arsha's dad, and the others."

His eyes narrowed.

"What happened?"

"After that guy came after us... He knocked you out with one of those lightning things. But Ilona found us."

"And now we're here? With the people who kidnapped you?"

"It's not as simple as that."

"Really? Because it seemed pretty simple when they shot at me and hauled you off," Justin snarled, sitting up on the edge of the bed, the sheet falling down to ruck around his waist.

"Look, I'm not saying I didn't think the same thing," she said, her voice catching in her throat. "It weren't easy or nothing. But... I think they really mean it. I think they want to help us."

"And how long did it take you to decide this? Because you seemed fine with my plan last night."

"I know, but... After what happened. After that man came after us again. Justin, we'd barely made it ten feet and we were in trouble. I don't know what I'm supposed to do here, but it seems like these are the only people who are really trying to help us. I mean, Ilona is a total bitch and she still came for us."

He leaned forward, taking her gently by the arms, looking into her eyes with that same fierce intensity that she had found so startling at first.

"Rachael, this is insane. We had a plan. We know where we need to go and these people are not going to help us get there, no matter what they say."

"You don't know that. And what good's it us running off, with your plan and all, if we never get there?"

"What makes you so sure of this now?" he shot back at her.

She had no answer, but he must have seen the way she glanced over at Arsha.

"Oh. Right. I guess it's all the same as long as you have someone to cling onto," he said.

She pushed him away, shoving the chair back hard against the wall as she got to her feet. Arsha had to scramble aside just so that Rachael could pull the door open and force her way out into the corridor.

She found her way to the loft over the cargo hold. As she reached the top of the steps she was struck by just how easily this little space had become a refuge. Sitting back on the old couch, she found herself untensing just a little. Glimpsed through the porthole, wisps of cloud drifted past.

She heard his footsteps on the cargo hold floor, then the creak of the ladder. At last he stepped into sight, his eyes drawn to the portholes ahead. It took him a moment to see her, lying back on the couch. She looked up at him with defiance in her eyes, but she didn't say a word. She was more than happy to let him make the first move. For a moment he stood there, awkwardly, his eyes soon turning towards the view through the windows once more.

"I'm sorry," he said.

She nodded. An acknowledgement, nothing more.

"I shouldn't have said that."

"You're right. You shouldn't have."

He sat down heavily in the chair opposite her.

"So... What do you want me to do?" he said.

"Does it matter?" she growled. He simply gave her a look, patient, expectant.

She closed her eyes for a moment, trying to find some sense of what she was doing.

"I think you should meet him. The professor. See what you think."

"I can't promise I'll like him," Justin said.

"I don't know if I like him yet. But I think he really wants to help us."

"There's plenty of bad people that know how to act like they mean you well."

"Just... Trust me," She said.

"Alright."

They found the professor on the bridge. After some fussing with the charts he had been examining, he agreed to sit down. They made their way down to the mess, the three of them sitting around the dining table.

Justin was clearly agitated, one foot tapping out a quiet but insistent rhythm against the wooden floor as Rishi settled himself on the bench across from them.

"So. You'd be Justin," Rishi said, with a cautiousness that Rachael hadn't entirely expected.

"And you are? Rachael just calls you 'the professor' or something."

"She's not the only one," he said with a dry smile. "My name is Rishi Chandra. I'm a professor of archaeology, officially. In practice, my studies stray into the more... Esoteric."

"Meaning?"

"Meaning I have learned a great deal about the mysteries of our world. About the passing of the Ur and the legacy of the first Dreamers. About creatures like you," Rishi said, with a deadly serious look in his eyes. Rachael found herself wondering if she had made a serious mistake.

"Creatures?" Justin said.

"You can't possibly imagine that you are still human, after what you've done to yourself," the professor replied. There was no venom in his tone. He seemed almost genuinely curious.

"Why not? I'm better, stronger, more powerful. What about that makes me anything less than human?"

"I didn't say 'less than'. But as long as you remain changed as you are, you'll never be entirely human. It's the inevitable result of what you've done to yourself. Or, perhaps, allowed someone to do," Rishi said, with a probing look. Justin seemed suddenly uncomfortable.

"Well, that's beside the point," the professor said. "Tell me, when Rachael found the Seed in London... Was that your doing?"

"You mean, was it my fault?" Justin said, carefully.

"Did you suggest it?"

"No. I only showed her what she could do. Rachael's choices are hers to make. Not yours."

"But you were sent to London, to find her, yes?" Rishi continued, his tone level, though his eyes were fixed on Justin, unblinking.

"Yes."

"By whom?"

"By the woman I serve."

"I see," the professor said. Though he seemed calm, Rachael could see the tension in him.

"What is this? Rachael told me I should talk to you, because she thinks you're on her side. So why does it feel like I'm being interrogated here?"

"Because protecting Rachael is foremost on my mind... And I have serious concerns about just how much danger you may have put her in."

Justin's hand slammed the table hard enough to make Rachael's ears hurt.

"I put her in danger?" he exclaimed. "And what were you doing when you snatched her off of a roof-top? When you chased after us with your ships and your guns? And that... That thing that your people unleashed on her?"

"What exactly do you mean?" Rishi said, his voice eerily calm.

"A hollow man," Justin said, icily.

Rishi's eyes narrowed and he turned to look at her.

"Really? They used a hollow man to track you?"

"They? Like you weren't a part of that," Justin said.

"Justin I told you he wasn't," Rachael said.

"What, because he says so? Rachael, he's lying to you. Did you see any sign that they weren't working together? Did any of his people actually try to stop those guys back there? Did they keep me from getting shot? Or were they shooting at me too? Did they come to save you when that thing was chasing you? Did they do anything to protect you at all? You're a prisoner here, you just don't know it."

"Ilona rescued me from Rakesh. After you were knocked out on the docks, she was the one who saved me," she said, coolly.

For a moment Justin stared at her, fuming. Then he jumped up from the table, his hands twitching with nervous energy.

"I suppose you think this is all some elaborate trick," Rishi said, calmly.

"Shut up," Justin snapped.

"Jesus, would you just believe me for once?" Rachael said, slamming her hand down on the table.

"Why? So he can tell us more lies. I'm done with this. And you should be too," he said, turning towards the door. He was nearly out of the room when Rishi spoke, softly, but with a chilling edge to his voice.

"I know what you are, Knight of the Autumn Glade."

Justin stopped and looked back.

"I know what you are, and I know who you serve. I know the stone ridge where you took your oaths upon the setting sun, and I know about the secret halls beneath the roots of the Bower Castle where you were unmade."

"How can you know that?" Justin said, eyes narrowing.

"Because I have studied the oldest things in this world. I know who you serve, and I know what she is. I wonder... Did she ever tell you just how she came to be scarred?"

Justin stared, but said nothing. Slowly, calmly, the professor stood and walked towards the younger man.

"Justin... Are you sworn to protect this girl?"

"Upon my life," Justin said, swallowing hard.

"Then we both have the same intent. There is a great deal you have been misled about, but I promise you this; I mean Rachael no harm, and that makes me one of the only friends you are likely to have."

He held out his hand, eyes fixed on Justin's. Slowly, cautiously, Justin reached out to take it.

"When the time comes," Justin said, "you'll let her go. Go home, where she belongs."

"That will be her choice to make, and only once she knows enough to make it."

Justin's regarded the man suspiciously.

"There is much about your Lady of the Falling Leaves that even you do not know," Rishi continued, sternly.

Justin regarded the man carefully.

"Fine," he said. Then he turned and walked out of the room. For a moment she was torn. A part of her wanted to stay, to ask the professor exactly more about what he'd said, but already the man was walking away from the table, the conversation clearly ended.

She caught up with Justin in the hallway. Her hand caught his sleeve and he turned to look at her, eyes as cold as ice. His look softened as he recognised her, but he said nothing. There didn't seem to be anything to say.

The day passed slowly. They spent most of the time hiding out in the loft over the hold. Neither of them spoke much, and the time crawled past. For a while, Arsha joined them, but the girl seemed nervous around Justin, almost as if she was about to flinch every time he moved.

They skipped dinner, sneaking food down from the pantry to share a meal in silence in the hold. Finally they each retired to their rooms. Rachael laid down, stilled the ghostlamp, and tried to sleep.

There was no light through the porthole when she woke, brought to by a gentle rapping on the door. Feeling groggy, cold and uncomfortable, she crawled out from her bed and slipped the door open a crack.

It was Justin, in his tattered jeans and t-shirt, bare feet resting on the wooden floor.

"Can I come in?" he said, glancing around the corridor as if worried he might get caught.

"Yeah. Sure," she muttered, opening the door wider. He slipped into the room, as she fumbled about for a dressing gown. Feeling more comfortable with the gown pulled around herself, she settled down on the bed beside him.

For some reason her heartbeat seemed louder than usual. She folded her legs under herself and looked him in the eyes, as if there might be some clue to why he had come.

For a moment he said nothing. Instead he just looked at her with a puzzled expression.

"So, are you going to say anything. Because I was trying to sleep," she said, her voice hushed.

"Have you really thought about this?" he said, calmly.

"About what?" she said, her eyes narrowing.

"Where we're headed. These people. You need to start asking yourself some serious questions about who your friends are," he said with an infuriating calm.

For a moment she looked away.

"I don't know how I'm supposed to answer that," she said. "They don't... Nobody ever told me how I'm supposed to handle something like this. Justin, it's impossible. I'm... I'm in a place that no one like me has ever been before, and even to these guys, with their flying ships and magic thinky crystals, I'm supposed to be something no one's ever seen before. If they don't even know what they're doing... How should I?"

"Then why are you handing your safety over to them?"

"Because I've got no one else."

She could see it the moment the words left her mouth. How deeply they cut him.

"I see," he said.

"No, Justin, you don't," she said, reaching out to put a hand on his shoulder. He looked at her as if being touched was the last thing he could ever want, but she held on regardless. "You keep trying to do this all on your own. You keep trying to be the only one who can help me, but it's not working. This is too big. It's too much for the both of us. We can't just run around on our own, thinking it's OK."

"Really? Because you didn't seem to think that before."

"Because I was being stupid. Because I was too scared of everyone and everything around me to see that people were trying to help me."

"You were being smart. You never should have trusted these people."

"Justin, I... I can't keep thinking like that."

"Then I guess I'm no good to you any more," he said, moving to stand. She caught his arm, pulling him back down.

"Will you just shut up for a moment? Just... Just stop it. All of this. You can't fight them. You can't save me. You can't do all this on your own. But I can't neither. I need you here. Because I'm scared, because I'm alone, and because you're one of the only people who's ever made me feel safe."

The look of surprise on his face was priceless. Feeling strangely distant from herself, almost as if she was watching her own actions, like a stranger, she slipped an arm around his shoulder and pulled herself close enough to let his lips brush against hers. Then his hands found her shoulders, and she felt herself falling backwards against the pillow. She could hear her heart pounding in her ears. She slipped a hand under his shirt, fingertips pressed against his chest, catching the echoes of a matching rhythm. The room was too hot.

He was careful not to rest his weight on her. A hand slipped around her waist, fingertips tracing the bumps of her spine. The cord of her gown seemed all tangled up. She could feel the muscles moving beneath his skin. She drew a deep breath as he pulled away for a moment, like coming up for air. His lips were pressed against her throat. For a moment she imagined long canine teeth, dripping with blood.

"You should get back to your room." She said, softly. He raised his head up to look her in the eyes.

"You don't want me to stay?" He said, meaningfully.

"I really do. But... I'm not ready for this. And it's taking everything I've got to say no."

There was just a moment when he hesitated. At least, she supposed that it must have been only a moment, though it felt like forever. Then he nodded, his hands gentle as he let her go. He went to the door and slipped it open, peering out first to check the corridor.

"I'm here. If you need me," he said. She nodded, drawing the covers up over herself. Then the door closed and he was gone.

Morning crept in through her window. She crawled from her bed and made her way to the shower, both saddened and relieved that she didn't catch sight of Justin in the corridor.

Stepping out of the shower, she almost crashed into Arsha. The girl's eyes were half closed. She looked up at Rachael in groggy surprise.

"Hey? Sleep well?"

"Uh, yeah," Rachael said, feeling her cheeks reddening. She quickly turned away, leaving the girl to the shower as she went to get dressed.

She made her way up to breakfast, finding Micah and Ilona seated across from one another, pouring over a set of notes as they sipped at their cups of tea. Steam wafted up from a basket of fresh cinnamon rolls, and Rachael grabbed one as she sat down.

Micah looked up and nodded.

"He's out on the deck," he said. Caught with her mouth full, she couldn't ask who, but she already knew the answer.

On the deck she found Justin still in only his jeans and t-shirt, despite the chill wind. It was too loud to call out to him, so she just stood by the doorway and watched.

He was repeating a set of forms, flowing from one motion to the next with a liquid grace. He looked like a dancer, the way he carried out each motion so smoothly. It took her a moment to realise that his hands were set in such a way that he might be gripping something. Something like a sword.

She watched for what seemed like a long time, until he finally noticed her. He seemed surprised but she just smiled, tugging the coat tighter about herself.

"It's OK. Keep going," she tried to yell over the wind, but standing out in the centre of the deck there was no way he could hear her. He started walking her way, just as the door swung open beside her.

Arsha came out, bracing against the headwind and looking up at both of them in surprise. Then the girl gestured for them to follow her around the bridge tower. With a shrug, Rachael let her lead on. In the lee of the tower, shielded from the wind, they could just about talk normally.

"So, Dad says we're about three days out from Cauldron now."

"Cauldron... You said that's where your old house is, right?"

"Yeah, that's right," Arsha shrugged, the movement mostly lost under the heavy coat.

Rachael was pondering this when Justin gestured at something in the distance. A slim object was emerging from the clouds. It was a ship, small and sleek, painted jet black with stripes of green and silver.

"That's an Inquisition ship," Arsha said, eyes widening. Rachael felt a cold sensation in her stomach.

The ship seemed to be getting closer, its trajectory bringing it towards that of the Triskelion. Then she noticed something else. The sound of their propellers was descending, from a high pitched humming to a bass roar, the sound of each rotation becoming more distinct.

"We're slowing down," she said. Arsha nodded.

"Come on," the girl said, gesturing inside.

As they heaved the inner door open and burst through into the corridor they found the professor waiting for them.

"Daddy, what's going on?" Arsha said.

They all saw him pause before answering.

"It's the Inquisition. Sir Reuben Ben Mahir."

"Who?" Arsha said.

"From that town with the waterfall, remember?" Rachael said, recognising the name.

Arsha's eyes widened in alarm.

"But, you said they weren't going to do anything. That Lord Bhandari had covered it all up." The words jumbled as they spilled out of Arsha's mouth, nervous panic widening the girl's eyes. Her father stepped forward and put a gentle hand on her shoulder.

"Things have changed, love."

"So, what's... What's happening?"

"They're demanding we allow Sir Ben Mahir and his men to come aboard. He's going to speak to myself and Abasi. For now, I want all of you to stay out of the way. Head on up to the bridge where the others are."

He turned to look at Justin.

"If they find out you're aboard... If they have even the slightest idea of what you are..." he said, his expression hard edged.

Justin nodded, calmly.

"I can be invisible."

"I'd imagine so," the professor said.

They all watched as he slowly dissolved, the dense black smoke coalescing down into the tiny form of a rat, which scurried away, disappearing from sight.

"Yeuch," Arsha muttered under her breath.

"It's OK," Rachael shrugged. "Takes getting used to."

"OK, both of you get out of here," the professor said, gesturing towards the stairs up to the bridge. Rachael went as instructed, but Arsha stopped to put her arms around her father, pulling herself tightly to him.

"I'll be OK, love," he whispered, stroking back her hair.

She nodded, not looking up. As Arsha broke away to follow her up the stairs, Rachael saw that there were tears in the corners of her eyes.

Chapter 23 - Bound

The slender black skiff touched down lightly on the deck. They watched from the windows of the bridge as four guards disembarked and took up positions. Then Reuben climbed down, followed by the same collection of porcelain figures that she had seen following him in Westfall. His automs. She shuddered at the sight of the mask-like faces. The figures moved with a steady and unnatural grace.

Below, Rachael could hear the inner door open. The professor and the captain were there to greet Sir Ben Mahir, all polite deference and custom. Rachael wondered how they could stand it. The procession soon made its way below decks.

Not a lot was said on the bridge. People moved about, looking awkward and uncomfortable. Micah fiddled with some charts. Arsha sat to one side of the room, eyes downcast, looking nervous. After what seemed like an age, Reuben finally left, taking his dolls and his men with him. Not long afterwards, Abasi appeared on the stairway, regarding them all with a sour expression.

"We should head to down to the mess. Come on," he said.

Rishi looked up from the head of the table as she came in. She was the last to arrive. Everyone else was either sat at the table, or, in Micah and Abasi's case, leaning against the walls.

"Where's Justin?"

"Hiding," Rachael said, with a shrug. "Like you asked him to. You want to try to find him, go ahead."

The professor shook his head in dismay.

"Right. Wonderful. Well, if he's listening, he's listening," he said, with obvious frustration.

"What's all this about?" she said.

"Have a seat," he replied, somewhat testily. His sour mood seemed to be reflected by the whole room. She stepped inside the doorway and leaned back against the frame with her arms crossed. The professor's attention returned to those at the table around him.

"Abasi and I have been summoned to appear before an Inquisitorial hearing, to investigate our crossing of the Veil and the events in London which followed."

Around the room, a breath seemed to be let out. Not of relief, but a sense of something expected, and feared. Even Ilona's eyes seemed downcast.

"Sir Reuben Ben Mahir is bringing this case on behalf of the Inquisition and the Chamber of Foresight. I am given to understand that Rakesh and Naveen Bhandari have likewise been called to give witness and stand against charges," Rishi continued, his tone calmly matter of fact. It was only the tightness of his knuckles that revealed the tension in his body.

"Sir Ben Mahir wished to inform me of my rights, and demanded to know what my involvement was in this matter. Fortunately, I did not meet him empty handed. The documents I... borrowed... from Manindra's estate will demonstrate that Lord Bhandari received communications from persons within the Chamber of Foresight before dispatching his sons to London. If we are very, very fortunate, we'll get to watch Manindra's allies throw him to the wolves, if only to keep themselves from getting dragged down with him. And if we're even more fortunate, we'll get out without any of it falling down on us."

There was a palpable sense of relief around the room, but Rachael couldn't help but notice the grimness of the professor's expression. The tension had not left him.

"We are to make haste to the Citadel," he continued. "The Dawning Light has been commanded to escort us there without delay. There will be no unplanned stops or deviations. Abasi will liaise with the captain of the Light to receive directions for our course. Upon arrival at the Citadel, the Triskelion will be grounded until further notice and Abasi and myself will be placed in voluntary custody for the duration of the hearing. They have called an emergency court, which should should begin session as soon as we arrive. If the winds favour us, the journey should be about five days."

He stopped, and looked around the room.

"Does anyone have any questions?"

There was a long silence, before Micah raised his hand.

"Voluntary?" he said.

"Voluntary," Abasi replied, "meaning 'Or you'll be in a whole lot more trouble if you don't.'"

"Right. Got it," Micah said, glumly.

After that, there were no more questions. Slowly, people began to file out of the room. There as a tense, nervous feeling in the air. She let most of them pass by, not meeting anyone's eyes as she tailed the others out of the room.

Standing at the top of the stairs she looked back and saw that Arsha was still in the mess hall with her father. Through the narrow doorway she could make out the pair of them standing close together, and could just about overhear their conversation.

"Daddy, what's going to happen to you?" Arsha said, her voice so quiet that Rachael barely heard it.

"I don't know sweetheart," he said. "But with any luck this will all blow over in a few days, OK?"

"And what if it doesn't?"

He paused, unable to answer for a moment.

"We'll figure it out."

Arsha looked away. He reached out a hand to stroke her cheek, wiping away a dampness from around her eyes.

"We're going to get through this sweetheart. I just need you to be strong, for a little while."

Suddenly she threw her arms around him, and pressed her face into his chest.

"I don't want to be strong. I want my daddy," Arsha gasped, her voice muffled by his shirt.

He pulled her close, and for a moment neither of them moved. His face was buried in her hair, and Rachael thought he might have been saying something, but it was too quiet for anyone but Arsha to hear.

He straightened up, resting his hands on her shoulders.

"I have to go make some preparations. If you need me..."

Arsha nodded. Her eyes were wet with tears.

"I love you, and I'm proud of you," he said, kissing her forehead. The girl nodded, and stepped away. Arsha's eyes were lowered as she walked out of the room, as Rachael found herself awkwardly caught looking on. Arsha looked up as she passed Rachael on the stairs, with a sullen, hurt expression. She passed by without a word. Feeling as if she should apologise, or at least explain, Rachael followed just in time to hear Arsha's door slam.

For a while she stood by Arsha's room, hand half-raised to knock. Finally she gritted her teeth and rapped on the door.

"Go away," came the muted reply.

She sighed and turned to leave, but she couldn't seem to bring herself to walk away. She turned back and tried the handle. The door opened. Steeling herself, she stepped into the room and closed the door behind her.

Arsha was sat on her bed, legs tucked up in front of herself, face hidden by her folded arms. From her perch on the dresser, Penelope looked up and gave a shrill chirp.

"I told you to go away," the girl mumbled.

"I know," Rachael said, awkwardly. "But... I wanted to say that I'm sorry. For listening in there. And... You know. For everything."

Arsha said nothing. Not even a sign of acknowledgement. Feeling deeply uncomfortable, but unable to bring herself to leave just yet, Rachael cleared a small space and sat down with her back against the door.

A long silence stretched between them, as Rachael waited for Arsha to make some sign of movement. After watching her for a while, Penelope fluttered down from the dresser and hopped across the floor towards her, her movements quick and cautious. Gently, Rachael reached out to brush the little bird's feathers back.

"You should hate me," Rachael said, at last. "All this... I've really mucked things up for you all."

"It's not... It's not like that," Arsha said, not looking up.

"It's OK. I'd hate me," she said, staring at her hands. Arsha lifted her head, enough to look her in the eyes. The girl looked furious.

"Why do you do that?" Arsha snapped. "Why do you always try to make everything about you?"

"I didn't..." Rachael barely had time to begin before Arsha cut across her.

"Your fault, your problems, you that's got it harder than anyone else," she thundered.

"I was trying to apologise," Rachael replied, sharply.

"Oh, good. You're sorry. I'll let everyone know, Rachael's sorry, so it's all OK now. No problems."

As Arsha threw up her hands in a gesture of frustration, Rachael was already on her feet. She stormed out, Penelope's angry screeching following her down the corridor.

She stalked back to her room and threw herself down on the bed.

She heard a soft movement, somewhere down low, a scratching sound close to her feet. She lifted her head from the pillow in time to see the swirling smoke cloud reforming. Then Justin was sitting there at the foot of her bed. He reached out to take her hand.

"Where the hell did you get to?" she muttered angrily, pulling her hand away.

"Hiding. Watching," he said.

"See anything good?"

"Saw you fight. It wasn't fair, what she said to you. The things that you've been put through, because of them..."

"Yeah. But it weren't fair what's happening to her, either."

He just shrugged, and let his hand rest on the back of her ankle. She rolled over, to look at him properly.

"Thanks," she said, softly.

His only reply was to give her leg a gentle squeeze.

The sky was an ugly grey. The sun had not yet crested the horizon, but the first light was filtering through, giving shape to the patchy clouds. Rachael and Justin stood out on the deck, leaning against the railing. She had borrowed one of the heavy coats from inside, though she left the straps undone. He had his own long black coat on. Around them the high stone walls of the canyon rose up to meet a sky turning to first light. Craggy grey stone was split by long bundles of creepers that hung down into the emptiness below. Far below, the river was a dark streak through the canyon.

For a long time, they stood in silence, faces raised skyward, until a flicker of motion caught their eyes. Rachael drew a sharp breath as she caught first sight of the broad-winged silhouette wheeling in the sky.

The Rake was a slender thing, much more so than she had imagined. A kind of lizard with featherless, leathery wings and a long neck and tail, it seemed to twist and writhe, worming its way through the air. It really did look an awful lot like some kind of dragon.

There were others that she began to make out. A flock, she had been told. She could see them now, their weaving flights bringing them close before darting away. She saw a smaller one try to nip at another, like puppies at play. It was perhaps a trick of the perspective, but they seemed smaller than she had imagined.

Over a sullen and dismal dinner the night before, they had been warned about the flocks that had been sighted in the area. Abasi had shared the news with a despairing shake of his head, as if the whole thing was some kind of sick joke.

Flying low through the canyon, and slower than usual, they were safe enough. Abasi had wanted to halt until the flock passed, but they were told that Reuben's people had insisted they keep moving. And yet, despite all the downcast faces, some tiny spark of excitement had flared inside of her.

A movement above the flock made her gasp in surprise. The rakes had seemed small, but now she saw why. A vast black silhouette passed over the rest of the flock, its wings vast enough to cover all of them if they would fly close enough together. One wing, she noticed, seemed to have a large hole in it.

She watched, enraptured as the mother played amongst its children for a while, seeming to gather them all in before turning on a wing to glide off into the distant sky, rays of sunlight momentarily glinting through the mother's injured wing. The little ones followed in her wake, and soon Rachael lost sight of them in the light of the rising sun.

"I can't stay," Justin said.

Shocked, she turned to look him in the eyes, hoping for some sign that he was playing with her.

"Why? After all this time you spent looking for me..."

"This is just a cage, Rachael. What good's it going to do if I'm just joining you inside the bars?" he said.

"You can't just believe they might want to help us?"

"Maybe they do. But I don't think they can. This professor, he seems to think he can keep you hidden away, or play some game with their courts, make everything OK with a few pieces of paper. You remember what those men did back in London. Rachael, these people don't listen to pieces of paper. They have guns and bombs and absolutely no remorse. They are not going to behave because someone tells them to."

She turned away for a moment, letting her eyes wander across the canyon walls that penned them in on both sides.

"So what, we just keep running?" she said.

"Eventually. I can't take you with me," he said, heavily. "I'm too weak now. But if I bide my time, if I wait for the right moment... It will be easier, if they can't watch me. If I'm the one moving in the shadows. This place, where they're taking us... There's power there. I can feel it already, even this far away. So I'm leaving, but I'll be watching. I promise you that. I won't let any harm come to you. And when the time is right..."

She turned towards him, and saw the fire burning in him. The intensity of his conviction, as his eyes locked on hers.

"Justin, I really don't think this is the right idea," she said, shaking her head.

"I'm sorry," he said, raising his shoulders in a helpless gesture. "I just don't have a better one."

"Please, don't go."

Her hands found his, fingers entangling as if she could pin him in place.

"This is the only way to get you out Rachael. It's the only way to bring you home."

He paused for a moment, his eyes studying her face.

"Stay strong, OK?" he said.

"Sure. Right. I'm good at that." She said, biting off the words as if they had a foul taste.

He stepped in close and his lips were on hers, his fingers brushing her hair back. She wanted to seize that moment and hold it forever. But he let her go and stepped away. Smiling, self-assured once more, he sat back on the railing, spread his arms and threw himself over the edge.

Unable to help herself, she leaned over, just catching sight of the outstretched wings of the hawk as he swooped downward into the depths of the canyon.

A stack of crates collapsed with a satisfying crash, tumbling over one another and spilling across the floor of the hold. For a moment she stood and watched them settle, tension still singing through her body. Her foot hurt. The first few kicks had barely shifted the stack.

"Feel any better?" a voice said.

She wheeled around and saw Ilona standing in the doorway to the hold. The woman was wearing some kind of loose silk pyjamas.

"It's fine," she mumbled. "I'll clear it up."

Ilona shrugged as she stepped into the hold, letting the door swing closed behind her. She walked across to the far corner, under the loft, where she pulled aside a cloth covering. From a small pile of equipment the woman lifted up a heavy looking sack with a rope trailing from one end. She threw the rope over a hook that protruded from the underside of the loft space and began to pull. As the sack rose Rachael realised what it was. A punching bag. The sight of it brought back a strong memory of the smell of sweat and grime. The sound and the energy of the gym where her father had taken her sometimes.

Still not saying a word, Ilona began wrapping her hands. Then she produced a spare roll of cloth, which she tossed lightly in Rachael's direction.

"What's this?"

"For your hands," Ilona said, flexing hers in demonstration.

Feeling somewhat unsure of what was happening, Rachael pulled off a couple of lengths of cloth and took a shot at trying to wrap her hands up as Ilona had done. It was difficult, working with just one hand, and the cloth wouldn't seem to stay put no matter how she twisted and tied it.

"Here," Ilona said, holding out an open palm. Frustrated, Rachael threw the strips of cloth at her.

"Hand," Ilona said, almost as if she was commanding a dog. Seething, Rachael held hers out as instructed. Ilona began to weave the bindings deftly until they were fully secure.

"How does it feel?" The woman said. Rachael flexed her hands carefully, still not sure what they were doing.

"Good. Now, come here."

Ilona went to stand at one side of the punching bag, bracing it. Rachael had seen how this was done. She stood across and raised her fists. She found herself wondering if there was a proper way to stand. Ilona said nothing. Not sure of what else to do, Rachael threw a punch. Then another. Soon they came thick and fast, the bag responding with a satisfying thunk as each of her blows connected. She punched and kicked until she felt ready to collapse from exhaustion. Finally, gasping for breath, she dropped to the floor of the hold.

Ilona crouched at her side.

"Better?"

Rachael shook her head.

"Not really," she gasped.

"Good," the woman said, with a fleeting smile. "I'd be disappointed if all this fuss was over something that could be solved by punching a sack a few times."

Despite herself, Rachael felt a smile flicker across her own face. Ilona stood and held out a hand. Rachael took it, and was lifted to her feet.

"OK, take a break. You brace," she said, nodding at the bag. Following the woman's instructions, Rachael stood with her hands properly placed against the sackcloth. Standing across from her, Ilona settled down on the balls of her feet, hands raised in clenched fists. For just an instant the woman glanced up, as if to make sure she was paying attention. Then she fell into a series of strikes that flowed from one to the next with no apparent effort. Even with the weight of the bag, Rachael felt herself recoiling with each blow.

"I guess I was doing it all wrong," she said, when the woman was done.

"Yes," Ilona said, without elaboration. Rachael felt herself bristle a little. "Would you like to learn?" the woman continued.

"I... Yeah. I would," she said, surprised.

"OK. Set your feet like this."

Ilona demonstrated, and Rachael did her best to follow the woman's movements. Slowly, Ilona began to draw deep breaths.

"Breath from the diaphram. That's good. Shoulders back a little. Rest your weight forward, on the balls of your feet. Now bring your hands up. Fists lightly clenched, thumb on the outside. Like that."

"Are you going to show me how to throw a punch or something?" Rachael said.

"No, I'm going to show you how to take one," Ilona replied, with a flicker of a smile.

"Oh come on."

"I'm serious," Ilona said. "You're small, so avoiding a blow is always going to be better than taking one, but you still need to know how. Being able to get away from a fight is much more important than winning one."

"So, you wanna teach me how to fight by hitting me a bunch?"

"Don't worry, you get to start. Hit me as hard as you can. In the face."

For a moment, Rachael hesitated. Again, there was a flicker of a smile.

"Scared?" Ilona said.

Without even thinking about it, Rachael swung. Her fist connected with the woman's jaw, but as Ilona rolled with the blow, there seemed to be little effect.

"Try it again," Ilona said. Rachael did, with just as little effect.

"Where'd you learn all this stuff," she said.

"Various teachers," Ilona replied. "Anyone I could find."

The woman stepped forward and began to adjust Rachael's

stance, light touches helping to shift her weight and position.

"Why?" Rachael said, as Ilona shifted her foot forward very slightly. As the woman straightened up, there was a coldness in her expression, even more so than usual.

"Because I was weak. And I didn't want to be," she said. "Now, watch what I do."

The instructions continued in the same clear, clipped tones. Two hours later, muscles burning, hands aching, and her head swimming, Racahel collapsed against a heavy barrel. She could feel tiny bruises swelling up in a dozen places. Ilona had pulled her punches, but only a little.

"I think that's enough for now," Ilona said. The woman held out a flask and Rachael took it, greedily gulping the water down.

"That was brutal," she gasped. "How do you even manage that?"

"Practice," Ilona said, with a shrug.

"Right, practice. You just woke up one day and decided to be a total badass."

The woman shrugged again and picked up a towel. Rachael looked down at her hands, her knuckles raw and stinging, even through the bindings.

"I wish I was strong like you," she said, quietly. "All I do is run."

Ilona watched her for a moment, with a thoughtful expression.

"I didn't just wake up one day," she said, speaking slowly, picking her words with care. "Someone... Someone hurt me. After it was over, I knew I could never let it happen again. Whatever you think you admire in me... The person I am... I was never really given a choice." Ilona paused for a moment. "But then, I suppose, neither were you."

As if nothing had happened, she began to undo the wrappings on her hands. Her face had returned to the same blank, vaguely disinterested expression she always wore.

"This time tomorrow?" Ilona said, without looking up. Her voice was so carefully devoid of emotion that they might as well have been talking about the weather.

She found Arsha in the mess. Breakfast seemed to have come and gone. The girl was sitting with half a cinnamon roll on her plate and a full cup of tea by her hand. She seemed to have lost all interest in her food.

Rachael set herself down across the table. Arsha made no sign of having noticed her. Rachael waited patiently as Arsha drank her tea and picked at her half finished roll. Finally the girl emptied her cup and made to stand.

"Where are you going then?" Rachael said.

Arsha gave her a cold look.

"Why do you care?"

"Look," Rachael said, tersely, "this is stupid. I'm stupid, you're stupid, and this whole thing is stupid, so can we just stop it?"

Arsha said nothing, but she stayed seated.

"I don't know how to stop being... Me," Rachael continued. "And I get that I'm pretty much the last person in the world anyone would want to hang around with, but right now, I figured you could do with a friend... Even if it's a shitty one. And I figured I owe you that much at least."

For a while Arsha just stared down at her plate. The girl's hands were clenched tight, knuckles pale.

"I know this really sucks for you," Rachael said. "And I can't do nothing about it, just like I can't do nothing about where I am right now. But I wish I could, because you don't deserve this. You're probably the nicest person I've ever met, and it's not fair that you should have to deal with all this when you never did nothing to deserve it."

She waited for some sign of response. At first the girl said nothing, but slowly her hands unclenched. Then Rachael heard a strange sound, like rapid breathing, and the girl's shoulders began to shake. It took a moment to realise that Arsha was crying. Tears rolled down the girls cheeks, splashing onto her plate.

Rachael's throat felt dry. Her words were all gone. Slowly, she reached across the table and placed her hand over Arsha's. Instantly, the girl's fingers closed around hers.

They sat that way for some time, until Arsha's tears stopped and the girl wiped her eyes dry, sniffling quietly.

"I'm sorry for being mad at you," she said with an apologetic smile.

"Don't be. I'm sorry for making you mad," Rachael said, returning the smile.

"Thank you."

"Any time."

Chapter 24 - Glass

It was well past midnight, the sky outside velvet black and studded with pinpricks of silver, when Arsha found herself standing outside the door to Rachael's bedroom. She tapped lightly for the second time. She almost jumped when the door opened. Rachael was wearing a dressing gown over her nightie and a look of confused surprise.

"Hey, what's up?"

"Can I come in?" Arsha said, glancing up and down the corridor, reassuring herself that no one else was up.

"Yeah, course."

Arsha slipped inside as Rachael closed the door and dropped back down onto her bed.

"What's up?"

"There's something I need to tell you," Arsha said, biting her lip.

"About what?" Rachael said.

"About... About how this all started. Everything that happened, I mean."

"Like, the stuff with me and your dad, and all?"

Arsha nodded.

"Did... Did my dad tell you why he came looking for you?"

"Sort of. Said it was the right thing to do or whatever."

Arsha paused for a moment, biting her lip.

"That's not the whole story," she said. "There's some stuff that he couldn't tell you... But I think I should. I think you need to know."

"Know what?"

"In our world, there are people who... We call them Seers. They can see the future, in a way. It's like, glimpses, and jumbled up stuff. Dreams."

After a moment Rachael nodded, as if the idea wasn't so surprising.

"That's why my dad came to find you. One of these Seers... She shared a prediction with him. A dream that she'd had. They're not supposed to... In fact it's... It's a really bad thing. I mean, really, really bad. If anyone ever found out... That's why he couldn't tell you. To protect her."

"Right. But he could tell you?" Rachael said, raising an eyebrow.

"Not exactly..." Arsha paused again. "I kind of listened in."

Rachael looked surprised, and just a little impressed.

"The point is, this prediction... It was about the Seed... But it was also about me and you. She saw us both standing together, in the middle of London... We were holding hands, she said. There was a boy with us... She talked about him being made of smoke and shadows..."

"Justin."

Arsha nodded.

"I think so. There was a bunch of other stuff, that didn't really make a lot of sense... But she said something about a choice. And about our hands being wrapped up in red string."

"Red string?"

"Yeah. It didn't really make a lot of sense to me either, but since then I've been reading some stuff... My dad's library has a lot of books about Fate and stuff. He doesn't let me read that stuff normally, but with all that's happening, he's been pretty distracted, and after we did the ritual to talk to you... I got looking into what red string might mean, if it was something to do with magic, or Fate."

"And?"

"Well, I found this thing, in one of these books. I was looking at stuff about the Herdlands, because Milima said that they still do real fatework out there. And there's this ritual they do, where two people join themselves together. They call it blood-binding. It's a way of tying your Fates together. Connecting yourself to someone else, permanently."

"Like, blood brothers, right? You cut your hands and stuff?" Rachael said. Arsha blinked at the girl in surprise.

"Yeah, that's right. How did you know?"

"It's just, like, one of them things from stories and stuff, y'know? Like, a couple of kids from my block done it because they thought it would make em well gangster and all, but then one of them, his hand went all manky, because they done it with a piece of glass."

"Well, I guess it's the same sort of thing, but, you know, we'll be careful to disinfect the knife and clean the wounds properly so we don't have to worry about stuff getting infected. They really did it with a piece of glass?" Arsha said, looking at the girl incredulously.

Rachael just shrugged.

"That's so stupid."

As Arsha shook her head in despair, she saw Rachael's expression shift.

"Wait, hold up..." Rachael said. "So you actually want to do this?"

Arsha looked down, her fingers tangling together, as her stomach suddenly twisted around on itself.

"I mean, we're sort of sisters already, right?" she mumbled. "With my dad adopting you. But it seems kind of sad that it was just some pieces of paper and stuff, and I thought this would make it real, you know? And that stuff in the prediction about red thread and all... I think this is what she meant. That we were supposed to do this."

To her surprise, Rachael laughed.

"Oh my God, you're actually serious. I can't believe you're actually serious."

"Fates, do you have to?" Arsha snapped. "Yes, I am serious."

"Jesus, I'm sorry Arsh," Rachael said, suddenly serious. "Honest, I didn't mean to be harsh or nothing. But I just don't see why... Why you'd wanna' do something like this. I'm not being funny but it's a bit much isn't it?"

Arsha stared down at her hands, fingers twisting into knots.

"Because they're going to take you away," she said, her voice little more than a whisper. "The Guild, or Manindra, or someone, they're going to take my dad and they're going to take you, and I can't stop it, and you're going to be alone, and I know you can handle it, I know you're not scared and you'll make it through because you're the strongest person I've ever met... You're stronger than I could ever be..."

Her eyes were blurry, and she could feel tears running down her cheeks.

"But you shouldn't have to," she continued. "You shouldn't have to go through all this, and you shouldn't have to be alone. No one should have to be alone."

Arsha looked up and saw that Rachael was staring at her, eyes wide with astonishment.

"Of course I'm scared," Rachael said, quietly. "Jesus, Arsh, I'm terrified. It's like, every time I think I have something to hold onto, it all changes again. Like everything I'm reaching out for keeps getting snatched away from me, and I'm just falling. I'm falling, and I don't even know when I'll hit the bottom."

Rachael stared at the floor, chewing her lip as Arsha looked on in silence, too stunned to think of anything to say.

"I can't figure you out," Rachael whispered. "You're always so nice to me, and I gave you so many reasons not to be. I don't get it. I don't get why you care. Why any of what happens to me should matter to you. I don't know why you'd ever want to do this."

"I'm sorry," Arsha said. "I guess I can't really explain it either. I like you. You're smart, and you're funny, and I feel happy when I'm with you. You're an amazing person, and you don't deserve everything you've been through. Isn't that enough?"

Rachael said nothing, her eyes still fixed on the floor.

"I'm not trying to force you," Arsha said, gently, reaching out to brush a hand across the girl's shoulder. "Whatever you decide, I'm going to be here for you. No matter what."

When Rachael looked up again, there were tears in the girl's eyes. Sniffing, she wiped a sleeve across her face.

"Alright. I'll do it."

"Are you sure?"

Slowly, Rachael smiled, her cheeks glistening with tear tracks.

"Yeah. I'm in."

For a moment they just smiled at each other.

"But I can't promise I'll be much cop as a big sister, OK?" Rachael said.

"Big sister? Where'd you get that idea? I'm the older one, remember?" Arsha said, laughing.

"Oh, what, by like six months? That doesn't count," Rachael said, with an obviously feigned look of incredulity. Arsha smiled and stuck her tongue out.

"Oh, it so does."

"Yeah? Well if I'm gonna be the little sister, you know that means I get to annoy the heck out of you all the time, right?" Rachael said.

"Oh dear," Arsha said, smirking, "however will you manage that?"

Rachael laughed.

"Alright. You win," the girl said, still smiling. "You know you can be a real brat sometimes, right?"

"You're damn right," Arsha said, sticking out her tongue again. "I'm an only child. I'm good at getting what I want."

Rachael's smile faded.

"Yeah, well, lucky for some. I was an only child too."

For a moment there was an uncomfortable stillness in the air. She could hear the creaking timbers, and the hum of the propellers, as Rachael stared at the wall, biting her lip. Gently, Arsha put her arms around the girl and pulled her close. She felt Rachael's arms around her, squeezing tight, as she leaned in to whisper in the girl's ear.

"Not any more."

It was eerily quiet in the hold. Ensconced above the large room, in the pool of light that a single ghostlamp cast over the loft, the girls knelt on the dark oak floor, facing each other in nervous silence.

Carefully, Arsha undid the bag she had brought, and produced the contents one by one. Dried herbs and salt, a flask of water, a small wooden pot, bandages and safety pins, three small clay bowls, some matches, and a wooden handled kitchen knife.

Arsha crumbled the dry herbs into the three bowls and set a lit match to each one in turn. A powerful aroma filled the room, as the herbs began to smoulder, a dull red glow creeping through the papery leaves. Then she picked up the bag of salt and began tracing a swirling three point pattern on the floor between them. She could feel her hands shaking as she tried to keep the lines even. Several times she had to glance at the image she had copied out of the book to make sure she was getting it just right. Finally, she placed the wooden bowl in the centre of the pattern and filled it with water from the flask.

"What happens now?" Rachael asked, quietly.

"Start by taking deep breaths," Arsha said. "Don't force yourself, just breathe, deep and even. Focus on your breathing, on the sound of your heartbeat. Let everything else fall away."

She spoke evenly, trying to keep her voice calm and reassuring, the way Milima's had been. Her own eyes were half-closed, but she could see enough of Rachael to watch the girl's breathing slow.

"Concentrate on the sigil... The pattern in the circle. It's like a map, for your mind. It shows you where you need to go."

Arsha noticed that a sheen of sweat had already appeared on Rachael's forehead, and realised that her own face was feeling flushed and damp. The air smelled bitter and sharp, as she breathed in the thick smoke. She swallowed. Her throat felt dry.

"Hold the sigil in your mind. Focus on it. Let everything else fall away."

Already, Arsha could feel as if she was floating, as if her body was made of clouds.

"Fall. Fall inside of yourself. As if your own mind was the whole world and you were just a tiny dot, floating deep inside of it."

Arsha could feel her blood pounding in her ears. The walls of the room seemed to fall away, leaving a dark and empty space around them both.

"Now I want you to picture a door. Any door. Imagine it however you like. When you can see it clearly, you're going to reach out and open it."

They sat in silence. Then she heard Rachael's voice, a whisper so quiet that she could barely make out the words.

"I can't."

Rachael's eyes were still closed. Her knuckles stood out white against her tightly clenched hands.

"It's OK," Arsha said, softly. "This is just part of the ritual. Opening the door is part of creating a connection. You let me in. I let you in. We become a part of one whole."

"I know. I know," Rachael said, her voice tight. "But I can't. I can't open that door. I know... I know what's behind there. I can't go back to that."

"You're not going back Rachael. I promise you, you're not. You're moving forward. That's why I want to do this with you. I want this, for both us."

She heard the girl take a deep breath.

"It's OK," Arsha said. "When you're ready."

"OK," Rachael whispered.

It took a moment, to centre herself again, trying to resume the calm even tones she had been using.

"Close your eyes, open the door, and step through. This is the space between us. The connection we share. This is real. Do you see me there?"

"I can see you."

As she spoke, Arsha pictured her own door. It was the door to her bedroom, battered old oak-wood chipped and scarred in a hundred tiny but familiar ways. She could almost feel the brass handle turning in her hand. It opened, and she stepped through into the darkness, where Rachael stood, facing her. She saw the tears on Rachael's cheeks and the fear in her eyes. She wondered if it was real or just her imagination.

"OK," she said. "Hold out your hand."

The knife gleamed in the darkness, as Arsha drew it across the skin of Rachael's palm. She watched the blood well up around the cut and begin to drip, slowly, from the edges of her palm. She heard the soft splash each drop made as it fell into the bowl of water.

Arsha then held out the knife, handle first, and offered her own hand, wishing that it wouldn't shake so much.

When the blade met her palm she gasped in pain. It was as if Rachael was drawing the tip of a red hot poker across her skin. It took everything she had not to pull her hand away. She bit her lip so hard that the taste of blood flooded her mouth. Distantly, she heard the knife clatter to the floor, but all she could think of was the pain. Tears flooded her eyes.

"It's OK," she heard Rachael say. "I think I know what happens next."

Carefully the girl pressed their bleeding palms together, clasping Arsha's hand tightly in hers. Their mingled blood dripped down from their hands, falling softly into the bowl. Arsha felt a warmth and a tingling throughout her whole body. She seemed to be surrounded by endless light, and she was intensely aware of Rachael's breathing, her pulse, her heartbeat. As the sound of it thundered in her head, she felt the words coming back to her.

"Repeat... Repeat after me. Forever to this binding we submit," she said, hearing Rachael echo the words back to her. "Bound in body, bound in mind, bound in spirit, bound in fate. In blood we forge our souls to share as one."

Blinking, Arsha opened her eyes again. Rachael's hand was still clasped in hers. The water in the bowl was a pale red. The mounds of crushed herbs had burned out. The smell of blood and smoke filled the air. There were tears glistening on Rachael's cheeks.

Rachael's eyes flickered gently open, and they looked at each other as if they were both expecting something to happen. It felt as if something should have changed, but the room was the same. It seemed that they were the same too.

"Did it work?" Rachael said, cautiously.

"I don't know," Arsha said, before breaking into a nervous smile. "I've never done this before."

"Right," Rachael laughed, softly. "I guess, maybe... I guess I was expecting something more... Magical."

"That wasn't enough for you?" Arsha said, drying her eyes with her free hand.

Rachael blushed and looked away.

"Yeah. I guess it was," she said.

Gently, Arsha lowered their clasped hands into the bowl of water, carefully washing away the blood. She expected it to sting, but it didn't really hurt very much at all. When they withdrew their hands from the water, her breath caught in her throat. Where there should have been a gaping wound, there was barely a mark. Only a tiny scar, a single thin line across the palm, like it had healed years ago. She examined Rachael's palm, and found the same. Only a slim trace of a scar.

"I guess it did work," Arsha said, softly.

"Yeah. It's weird... After all the other things I've seen, I shouldn't really be surprised by this."

"Why not?" Arsha said. "I am."

Still staring at her hand in amazement, Rachael began to stand up. She was halfway to her feet when her legs seemed to give way, and she fell backwards against the sofa. Arsha covered her mouth, trying not to giggle.

"Shut up. I'm just dizzy," Rachael growled, but there was a smile on the girl's face. As she settled onto the couch, Arsha slowly cleared away the remains of the ritual. Carefully she poured the bloodstained water back into the flask, and packed away everything into the bag. Then they made their way back down the ladder, slipped through the corridor with soft footsteps, and dumped the last of the evidence down the toilet bowl.

Eventually they arrived back at Rachael's room. The girl fell down onto her bed, leaning back against the wall with a dazed expression. Arsha stood, awkwardly twisting her hands together as the ghostlamp flickered.

"Alright... Good night..." she said, half mumbling the words.

"Hey, come here you," Rachael said, holding up her arms in a beckoning gesture. A little confused, Arsha sat down on the bed beside her, and immediately Rachael's arms slipped around her shoulders, pulling her close. Her head fell against Arsha's chest, eyes closed. It struck her that she had never seen the girl quite so defenceless.

"Thank you," Rachael whispered, her voice so soft that Arsha almost couldn't hear the words. Arsha said nothing at all, as they lay together, arms tight around one another. The ghostlamp settled and dimmed, as Rachael's breathing settled. Slowly, Arsha pulled the blanket up over the both of them, and laid her head back. She could feel her sister's heartbeat, soft and slow, as her shoulders rose and fell with every breath. Outside the porthole the night darkened and the propellers droned on, their gentle hum lulling her off to sleep.

Standing out on the deck, they watched the Citadel approaching, lit from behind by the rays of the morning sunlight which reached out across the rolling white dunes of the desert below. At first all they saw of the Citadel itself was a smudge on the far horizon. Slowly it grew closer, larger and more menacing. As they watched the shape resolved itself into an island of rock hanging in the blue sky, completely unsupported. The sunlight gleamed on the spires of crystal that dotted the dunes, far around it.

They stood at the prow, leaning against the railing. Rachael was still wincing from her morning training with Ilona. For three days now she had been spending every spare moment down in the hold, practising under Ilona's watchful eye. With time to spare, Arsha had buried herself in her various projects. The harmonic had finally come together, but when they'd turned it on they found only the Citadel wave, with blandly neutral music and coldly mechanical announcements. They had promptly turned it off.

They watched in silence as the sun continued to rise. Eventually the Citadel was near enough that she could make out the shape of the buildings, rising up in staggered waves towards the centre of the structure, where a single tower stood far above all the rest. It was so slim and fine that the whole thing seemed to be hanging from the sky on an invisible thread, connected to that needle point. Concentric rings of walls, dotted with towers, rose up like a wedding cake around the outer perimeter. At first she thought the tiered structure looked like a castle, but as it grew in size the sense of scale became clearer, and she began to see that it was closer to being a city.

Below where the island floated, shapes emerged from the desert, the tiered and misshapen skyline of a much larger city, tall spires that reached for the sun and crowded rows of buildings that lined narrow streets and broad avenues. All of it had taken on a warped and misshapen appearance. Sand had built up in great waves around the base of the buildings, and most of the structures had a twisted, half-melted look to them.

The city below gleamed in the dawn light, but the Citadel itself shone like the sun. The dazzling rays of sunlight reflected off every wall, as if every surface was a mirror. As the distance closed, Arsha finally saw that every part of the Citadel, from the lowest edge of the outermost walls on upwards, appeared to be some kind of clear stone or crystal, tinted aqua green like jade. She drew a sharp breath as the realisation set in. It was made of glass. Every part of the Citadel, every brick and stone, was made of glass.

It was beautiful. As soon as the thought entered her head, she hated herself for it, but she couldn't shake it. The Citadel was elegant, radiant and utterly awe inspiring, and she hated it. Still she watched as they approached, the ship sinking lower until they were below the level of the island. Vast openings lined the lower reaches of the island on which the citadel rested, lit by strings of lanterns along their inside walls, looking like tiny sparks of light in the darkness of each cave mouth. As the ship approached one of the openings, it almost seemed as if it would be too small, but the cave continued to grow as they drew closer. Every time she thought she had judged the perspective correctly, the shape of the Citadel turned out to be even grander than she had imagined. The whole island was vast, and each of the caves could easily accommodate ships much larger than the Triskelion, the vessel seeming tiny against that great dark opening. As they entered the tunnel, Sir Reuben's sleek black ship followed them in.

Darkness overshadowed the deck, with only the lights on the walls to guide them. They moved slowly, the propellers beating out a steady rhythm. Up ahead she could see light. She looked down to see that Rachael's hands, like her own, were tight against the railing.

Then she looked up, and felt her breath catch in her throat. The ship emerged into an enormous cavern, too large for her to even begin to guess at its scale. The walls of the cavern were some kind of rough hewn crystal, and deep beneath their surface a million lights glimmered in the darkness, like stars. Walkways and piers protruded from all around the walls.

They floated upwards, turning slowly to orient towards one of the many docks. The ship drifted in gently, guided by Abasi's steady hands as Sir Reuben's vessel manoeuvred towards the pier beside theirs.

Just as they were making the final approach she heard the door to the deck open, as Micah and Ilona emerged.

"Hey. Best you two stand clear," Micah called out to them. He nodded in the direction of the slender figures moving their way. Even from a distance Arsha saw the blank faces and the eerily synchronous movements. Automs.

Without any sound, a group of half a dozen of them began to tie the ship off, first throwing ropes over and then calmly leaping a gap of maybe eight or nine feet. The deck shuddered slightly under the impact as each of the figures landed. Micah took a couple of steps forward, tension making his shoulders rise under his long coat.

When the automs were done they returned to the pier, standing a little way off as if waiting for instructions. Soon Abasi, Milima and her father all emerged onto the deck. Both of the men had the same look on their faces, like they were steeling themselves for what came next.

Across from the Triskelion, Reuben emerged from his ship with his mechanical bodyguards in tow. He walked calmly, as if he had all the time in the world. Already she could see that more guards were coming to join him, two lines of men in long grey coats filing down onto the docks from the walkways above. When all his men were assembled, Reuben nodded and turned towards the deck of the Triskelion.

The crew seemed to have gathered into a loose cluster on the deck, and somehow she and Rachael had ended up at the centre of it. She wondered if that had been by intention. As Reuben approached, her father looked him in the eye.

"Well, shall we get this over with? Or do you need more men?"

Reuben nodded to the nearest of his guards. The officer stepped forwards, holding up a pair of metal cuffs. Arsha felt a lump growing in her throat.

"Professor Rishi Chandra, you are to be bound by law," the officer barked. "Will you consent to be bound?"

With a cold look, Rishi held out his arms, fists clenched, wrists exposed. There was a soft 'chink' as the cuffs were locked into place.

"Captain Bira, you are also to be bound by law. Will you consent?"

She saw Milima squeeze her husband's hand, before the tall man stepped forward and offered his wrists as her father had done. Again, the soft 'chink'.

"You will be escorted to a place of holding. Is there anything you require before we leave?" the officer said.

"I will have my effects brought over, if required," her father said, with obvious restraint.

"Very well," Reuben said, before turning to nod at the commander of the guards. With a sharp salute the officer turned and began to march off. Falling in line to either side of Rishi and Abasi, the men began to march after him. She saw her father turn, just briefly, to look back at her. She couldn't say for sure if it was sadness or resolve that she saw in his eyes. Perhaps it was a little of both.

As the men walked away, she felt Rachael reach out to take her hand. The girl's grip was firm, and she held on as tight as she dared. It felt as if her sister's hand was the only thing holding her up.

Instead of following, Reuben paused and then turned to look at Rachael.

"Since I imagine the young lady here is unaware," he said, obviously addressing the adults present, "I should remind you all that as a Hearth refugee she will be required to present herself for a routine medical examination before she may enter the Citadel proper. The Citadel is a closed environment, and we cannot risk the outbreak of some unknown Hearth malady."

"We'll see to it," Milima said, coldly. "Will that be all."

"For now, Mrs Bira. Thank you."

With a slight nod that Arsha imagined was supposed to be a half bow, Reuben Ben Mahir turned on his heel and walked away after the guardsmen, his automs moving in perfect time with him. Already she could barely make out her father between the white-coated guards as they made their way up the winding slope that lead towards one of the many tunnel mouths. Then they were gone, slipping away into the darkness of the tunnels, headed for the city above. No one said a word as Arsha stared at the place where her father had been.

Chapter 25 - Blood

A carriage pulled up, the horses snorting and flicking their tails as they drew to a halt. Arsha watched as the door opened and Micah stepped out to help Rachael down.

"Thanks," the girl said, giving the man an awkward half smile as he boarded the carriage again. Micah smiled back and closed the door. Then a whip cracked, and everything was covered by the sound of the carriage clattering away.

Arsha was sat at the prow, head resting against the railing, her legs dangling over the front of the ship. The cavern floor, far below, was shrouded in darkness. Above, the lights in the roof glittered like stars. The sound of the carriage faded, and then all she could hear was Rachael's footsteps echoing through the still air as the girl walked towards her. She pulled her legs up and turned to sit with her back against the railing, as Rachael sat down beside her.

"Hey," she said.

"Hey," Rachael nodded. "Micah went back to go watch some more of the hearing."

"What was the examination like?" Arsha said.

"Horrid," Rachael replied, "all needles and weighing and stuff. Blood tests, all kinds of things. And the whole time they had me sitting in this stupid white nightie thing with no undies on or nothing."

Arsha pulled a face.

"Sounds awful."

"Yeah, well it's done now. They said I'm all OK. No germs or whatever."

"Well, that's good."

"So, this hearing of theirs... It's been going three days now. How much longer is it gonna be?"

"Tomorrow. They're going to make all their closing arguments and stuff. Either way, it's all going to be over after that."

"We're not going to win. Are we?"

For a moment, Arsha didn't say anything. She leaned her head back onto the railing and stared up the lights above them.

"None of them want to say it, but... It's not going well. Micah's quiet and Ilona is just more... Intense. She's always that way, when she can't solve something."

"Yeah. I figured. I guess that means they're going to take me away after all," Rachael said.

"I know," Arsha said, feeling a lump in her throat. "I don't want them to."

"Thanks," Rachael said. There was a long pause before she added "And your dad... I guess they're going to lock him up too."

Unable to even form the words, Arsha just gave the barest of nods.

"I'm sorry," Rachael said.

"He'll think of something. He never gives up," Arsha said, feeling all too much like she was trying to convince herself. "For you too. I know it. He won't stop fighting until we have you back."

"It's OK. I know how it is."

Arsha reached out and took the girl's hand.

"You know I'm not giving up on you, right? Not ever. We promised."

Whatever Rachael might have said in reply, it was lost when they both turned towards the sound of another carriage approaching. It was larger and more elaborate than the one that had brought Rachael back from her examination, and it was painted all in white.

The carriage doors opened and four men in long white coats disembarked. Though Arsha didn't recognise the braiding and trim on their sleeves and shoulders, she knew that even Citadel guards didn't normally wear such elaborate uniforms. They were followed out by a young woman with a boyish face and short cropped hair that was pulled close to her scalp in rows of tightly woven braids. The woman wore a half cloak of green and gold cloth, and beneath the dark leather of her armour there were flashes of blue silk. A sword hung from her belt, the hilt and scabbard simple and unadorned. The last figure to emerge from the carriage was dressed head to toe in a full white robe, with a hood that covered their face. The hem of the robe was trimmed in a deep red, and it was marked all over with the golden sigils of the Chamber of Foresight. Arsha had never even seen the marks in person before, only in her father's books. The figure moved calmly, with a stately and feminine grace, as if her feet were only brushing the ground. The guards took up a formation around the two women, strangely tense despite how little danger there seemed to be. They approached the ship without a word spoken between them. The guards kept a slight distance, as if actually touching the person in the flowing white robe might be a terrible thing.

At the foot of the gangplank the short-haired young woman made a commanding gesture, and two of the guards turned to stand watch on the dock. Then the robed figure ascended the walkway to the deck, the remaining pair of guards flanking her. Approaching the prow, she stopped a few paces from them. Arsha felt herself holding her breath. In the shadows of the deep hood she could make out a dainty chin, skin the colour of honey.

It was eerie, how quiet everything was. When the woman spoke, it was with a voice like music, clear and gentle, that sent a shiver of recognition down Arsha's spine.

"Good evening ladies. I wondered if I might come inside."

Feeling as if she had only just come to her senses, Arsha leapt to her feet and gestured politely towards the main door.

"Thank you," the woman said, her head inclining slightly below the hood. Hearing the voice again, Arsha felt her suspicions growing even surer.

She lead the way as they headed inside, Rachael staying close beside her with a bewildered look on her face. At another gesture from the short haired woman, the remaining guards took up positions just outside the door. From their faces it was clear they were not happy about something. As Arsha and Rachael got the heavy door open, the robed woman turned to her companion.

"Rukiya, these people are old and dear friends. I'd like to speak to them alone, please."

The shorter woman looked surprised, perhaps even horrified by this suggestion.

"My lady, I can't."

"Rukiya, please. Just do this one thing for me."

Lips pressed in a thin line, Rukiya nodded, clearly even unhappier than the guards were.

"I'll stay by the door, but not outside. I won't let them put half a foot of steel between us."

A sigh.

"Agreed."

No happier, the shorter woman nodded as Arsha led them all inside. True to her word, Rukiya took up a position just inside the inner doorway, as the robed woman followed them down to the mess. Sitting alone at the table, Milima looked up as they entered and her eyes immediately widened in astonishment.

"By the Seven... Seeker, I am so sorry. No one... We weren't told of an official visit..." Milima blurted out, jumping up from the table. Arsha saw Rachael's eyes widen in surprise, clearly taken aback by the sight of Milima seeming flustered.

"Milima, please. It's quite alright," the robed woman said. "This is not what you think."

Calmly, the figure drew back her white hood, revealing the face that Arsha remembered from her father's sending. She felt butterflies dancing in her stomach as she tried to keep her expression calm.

"My name is Maya. I'm a good friend of Rishi Chandra, and I am very grateful to finally meet you."

"Can I... Can I offer you anything?" Milima said, still clearly nervous and confused.

"Tea would be lovely, thank you," Maya said with an angelic smile, as she settled herself at the table.

Milima nodded and turned to set a kettle on the stove.

"I... I suppose you know Rishi's situation," Milima said, as Rachael and Arsha took seats across the table from Maya.

"Yes, and your husband's too. I've been sitting in on the sessions. Milima, I am so very sorry. I know this must be awful for you all."

"We'll pull through," Milima said, with a faltering attempt at a smile. "Seeker... I don't meant to impose, but is there anything you can tell us about what's going to happen at the hearing tomorrow? Anything you might have heard?"

"I'm afraid there's very little I can tell you," Maya said. "Beyond my own suspicions."

Milima nodded, unable to hide her disappointment.

"I have heard a little about Reuben Ben Mahir," Maya continued. "He's an earnest and forthright young man, by all accounts, just like his sister. Very eager to prove that his family's influence had nothing to do with being granted his appointment, whatever the truth of that might be. And he's gained a reputation as something of... A troublemaker, I suppose. He's embarrassed more than a few nobles already, exposing dirty secrets and a few shady dealings. I couldn't say if he actually believes in what he's doing, or if it's just more Guild politics, but he's certainly ruffled a few feathers. But going after Manindra... I really don't think he knows how dangerous an enemy he is making. That worries me."

"Well it's about time somebody stood up to the man. Honestly, Maya, the thought of Manindra Bhandari finally getting what he deserves is the only silver lining I can see in all of this," Milima said, as she set a steaming mug of tea down in front of the woman. For a while Maya just stared down into the surface of the liquid, as if seeing something there.

"Manindra's plans don't fail," she said. "They just get... More dangerous. The man has no concept of defeat. He is entirely possessed of the certainty of his own importance, his... His 'right' to the things he has set his eyes on. There is nothing in this world that he does not believe he can bend to his will. It's just a matter of how far he will have to go to make it happen. So yes, that worries me. Manindra is never more dangerous than when he has been defeated."

With a heavy sigh, Milima set herself down at the table. Maya raised her cup, blew gently on the surface, and took a long sip.

"I'm sorry, I don't mean to seem ungrateful. I appreciate your insight, Seeker, I truly do," Milima said.

"You're carrying a lot right now, Milima. I understand."

"And being a terrible host. I'm afraid I'm not really sure what we can help you with, though. Rishi and Abasi are both in holding, and it's just myself and the girls here on the ship right now."

"Actually, my visit concerns the young ladies. I wondered if you might permit me to speak with them alone for a little while?"

"Uh... Certainly," Milima said, taken aback. "If it's alright with the girls, of course."

Confused, Arsha glanced at Rachael, who looked just as perplexed. The girls both nodded.

"Wonderful," Maya said. Then, with a glance upwards, at where Rukiya was no doubt still holding guard on the floor above, she added "Is there somewhere we might..."

"If you're looking for some privacy, Rishi's library is at the end of the hall," Milima said quietly.

"Thank you," Maya said with a warm smile. As the woman stood, Arsha jumped to her feet and lead the way. Her father's library was located at the very back of the ship, past the stairwell and just above the engine room. She opened the door and let the others step into a room that would have seemed large if it was not almost completely filled with bookshelves. Each shelf was filled to the brim, the books strapped into place with leather bindings. In the centre of the room stood a round table with four chairs and a single ghostlamp at its centre.

Arsha closed the door and turned to see Maya standing in the centre of the room, hands folded in front herself. The woman's poise and grace seemed entirely flawless. Rachael stood a little to one side, looking nervous, unsure of what to do with herself. As Arsha stepped towards the table Maya moved towards her.

"May I?" the woman said, reaching out to take her hand. Dumbstruck, Arsha just nodded, as Maya held her palm up between them. Then she realised what the woman was looking at, the thin line of the scar standing out clear against the skin. Maya's soft fingertips brushed across the raised line.

"You did this yourselves?" she said. Arsha nodded. "Very well done. This is a strong binding. Any fateworker would be proud."

"How... How did you know?"

Maya smiled.

"Red string. It took me a while to puzzle it out, of course, but two nights ago I dreamed of a hand clutching a bloody knife. The rest was easy to put together."

Arsha nodded, not saying a word.

"Oh there's no need to be so cautious my dear. I assume you already know about the prediction I shared with Rishi, yes?"

Arsha blinked.

"How did you...?"

"You recognised my face, darling. The moment you saw me. Your father refuses to even keep a holo in case he lets slip that we stay in touch, and that was first sending I'd made to him in ten years. The only way you could recognise my face is if you'd found a way to listen in. Rishi is too careful for anything else."

"I... Yeah. I did, a bit. I'm really sorry," she said, lowering her eyes. Maya's hand settled lightly on her shoulder.

"It's done now, and for the best I suspect. Have you told Rachael yet?"

Arsha nodded.

"Good," Maya said, smiling.

"So... Is that what this is about?" Rachael said. "This prediction stuff and all?"

"In a way. We should sit," Maya said, gesturing towards the table. Still feeling a little dumbstruck, Arsha followed Rachael, taking a chair beside her. Maya sat down across from the two of them, folding her hands on the table.

"So... What else can you tell us about your prediction? About what's going to happen?" Arsha said. Her throat felt dry.

"Very little I'm afraid. Most of it is still fairly opaque to me. I've been having visions ever since, but they've been confused, fragmentary, very little that I can piece together. That's the nature of predictions, I'm afraid. Mostly the Chamber collects these pieces, cross-references them with what the other seers have seen, and builds up a larger picture. Seers very rarely have a complete prediction on their own. The intelligence that the Chamber passes on to the Guild council is usually gathered from hundreds of seers across thousands of visions, and even then the results are generally murky at best. But, the truth is, these last few weeks, I've been keeping most of what I've seen to myself. I fear there's something rotten at work in the Chamber, and I can't escape the feeling that whatever I've been seeing... That it wasn't meant for them."

"Won't you get in a lot of trouble for that?" Arsha said.

"Perhaps. But that can't be helped."

"You don't seem all that worried," Rachael said.

"The life of a Seer is a little hard to explain. I know this all must seem very strange to you, Rachael. In this world, people with abilities like mine... The Guild needs us, but it also fears us. We live very constrained lives. I have not left the Citadel since I was 12, and I will probably remain here until the day I die. After a while you grow used to the idea of living in a cage. It certainly leaves you with very little to be afraid of. I might lose a few privileges, perhaps, but I'm too valuable for anything worse than that."

"That's..." Arsha began to say.

"...Awful," Rachael finished for her.

Maya simply spread her hands, palms upward, in a helpless gesture.

"There is one thing that I am absolutely certain of," the woman said. "Something has started here, something much bigger than what we can see now. The two of you are standing together at the eye of a storm. The choices you make now could change everything. The fate of worlds will be reshaped by what you two have done, and what you continue to do now. I know that's an awful responsibility to place on you both, and I wrestled without myself about whether to say anything at all, but... But I know that no matter what else happens, you are going to need each other. You must find strength in each other, because soon there is going to be very little else left to you."

Arsha turned to look at Rachael. Her sister looked just as nervous as she felt.

"I was wondering before," Arsha said, "how do you know my dad?".

"I'm his little sister," Maya replied in a matter-of-fact tone.

Arsha's eyes widened.

"Sister? Dad never mentioned having any brothers or sisters."

"No, he wouldn't have. We're not related by blood. Rishi was my father's ward. You know about the wreck that killed his parents, I suppose?"

Arsha scrunched her nose up, confused.

"Dad told me that he grew up with his granddad, after his parents died."

Maya nodded.

"I know. You have to understand, Arsha, he had his reasons for lying. After everything that happened, Rishi wanted nothing to do with our family. The truth is, I envy him, being able to leave it all behind so easily. Even sequestered in the Citadel here, I've never really felt like I was far enough away from my father."

"Your father?"

Maya paused, her shoulders settling in a heavy sigh.

"Manindra. Manindra Bhandari."

"That crazy old..." Rachael interjected, seeming to catch herself just in time.

Maya just nodded.

"I was the youngest. I think even as a little girl I recognised the madness in my father... And how it had infected my brothers. In a way, it infected Rishi too, but there was a kindness in him that my father could never quite find a way to cut out. Not like he did with Rakesh and Naveen. As for Dayaram... I don't know. Whatever part of himself he managed to hold onto, he's buried it deep inside. He plays the dutiful son so well that he's forgotten how to be anything else."

"No... I can't believe that. How could my dad be anything like those people?"

"For all the poison in his heart, there is much in my father to admire, Arsha. Much that your father learned from him. Rishi is driven, resourceful, determined, inspiring, and fearless. All things my father taught him. Our parents shape who we are, whether we like it or not, but that doesn't mean that we can't decide what kind of person we will become. Rishi has gone to the ends of the earth to cut away my father's influence from his life, and he has become a very different man from the one that Manindra wanted him to be."

"But why didn't he ever tell me this?"

"Why do you think? Rishi never wanted you to have anything to do with my family. Arsha, believe me, I couldn't agree more. If I could somehow erase that part of myself, I gladly would. If there was a surgeon's knife that could cut deep enough to extract every last trace of him, I would hold it myself, and I would smile with every cut."

"He still shoulda let her know," Rachael said. "It weren't right, keeping that from her."

"Perhaps. Rachael, I'm not trying to pretend that anything about Rishi is perfect. We are all flawed creatures. He's made the best choices that he can, given the circumstances. We're in no position to judge him."

Rachael said nothing, obviously holding back whatever thoughts she had on the matter.

"Is there... Is there anything else you can tell us? Anything at all?" Arsha said.

Maya considered this for a moment.

"This is a marvellous library," she said, at last, looking around the room in apparent wonder. "I suppose Rishi must have a copy of the Guild laws and statutes here somewhere."

Arsha looked around, uncertainly.

"I guess," she said.

"Volume Three, if I recall correctly," Maya said. "There is a chapter on the subject of lineage and inheritance. You'll find some interesting notes on the subject of blood-bonding, and how it relates to Guild law."

Arsha scrunched her nose up, trying to figure out what the woman meant by this.

"I thought that kind of thing was, you know, forbidden," she said.

"Oh yes. The practice of fatework, in all forms, is highly regulated within the Guild. However the results of that practice are another matter entirely."

"So what Arsh and I did..." Rachael began, tailing off with a nervous look.

"Would, to my understanding, be recognised by Guild law as no different from any other blood tie. If Reuben means to snatch you away from your family here by having your adoption annulled..."

"It wouldn't matter, because she'd still be my sister," Arsha said, hearing the excitement in her own voice.

"By Guild law, that will make Rachael every bit as much your father's daughter as you are, entitled to all the same protections. Reuben might try to argue it of course, but there's enough precedent that I imagine Miss Karvonen... Sorry, Ilona... Will be able to tear him to pieces. I'm sorry, I know this doesn't help your father... Believe me, I am every bit as worried about Rishi as you are, Arsha... But at least it is something."

"Thank you," Arsha said. She turned to look at Rachael, and saw the nervous relief in the girl's eyes, barely concealed.

"Thanks," Rachael said, not quite able to look Maya in the eye. "Really, thank you, for all of this."

"You're both welcome, of course," Maya said. "Now I really should be going. Rukiya will only let me stay down here so long."

The woman smiled and got to her feet, smoothing the front of her robe down.

"Hey," Racheal said, "you won't... You won't get in too much trouble for all this? Will you?"

"A little. But I'll be fine. Honestly, I think Rishi will be more angry at me than anyone else will."

"Why?" Arsha said.

"Because your father is one of kindest men I have ever known, and he's never stopped trying to protect me, from myself and from everyone else. But sometimes little sisters just have to get in trouble."

Maya smiled again, and just for a moment Arsha saw Rachael smiling back, as if amused by something the woman had said. Then Maya turned and let herself out.

"Remember, Volume Three," the woman said as she closed the door.

Chapter 26 - Whispers

It was early in the morning when the carriages came for them, rattling through streets that were filled with what Rachael at first took to be fog. It took her a while to realise that there wouldn't be any fog in the city. They were riding through thin wisps of cloud.

The city was neatly arranged, with six long spokes radiating outwards from the central tower. Their carriage joined one of these main streets and proceeded towards the tower itself. The thin spire looked down over everything else in the city, a slender needle of glass that seemed uncomfortably similar to another building, a world away. Rachael assumed that they would turn away onto a side street as they neared the city centre, but instead they continued right up to the very base of the tower and the cluster of buildings that surrounded it. The building they arrived at was larger than a cathedral, with a high domed roof and a long colonnaded entrance hall that stretched out towards them. An impressive set of double doors crested steps of milk-white glass, flanked by rows of grey-coated guards. Impressive as it was, even this immense structure seemed insignificant against the vastness of the tower that overshadowed it.

The courtyard was filled with people, dressed in a dazzling display of coloured silks and gold and silver embroidery. She supposed the crowds were all here for the last day of the hearing, just like they were.

As they stepped down from the carriage their guards formed up around them, leading them in a procession towards the wide steps. She saw people in the crowd turning to look. Some pointed or whispered, and she became increasingly sure that she was the focus of at least part of their attention.

At the doorway another set of guards checked paperwork and waved them through. They entered into a large foyer. Curved staircases followed each wall, leading up to a balcony above. Wall hangings were arrayed in every colour imaginable, each adorned with an elaborate symbol in gold and silver thread.

Groups milled about the room talking amongst themselves in hushed voices. Micah laid a hand lightly on her shoulder, keeping her close. She glanced up at the others, unable to avoid noticing the way Milima's face seemed to slip into a worried frown. Arsha seemed to notice as well, moving close to the woman's side. Milima slipped an arm around Arsha's shoulder and gave them all a weak smile.

"I'll be OK," she said. Even Ilona reached out to touch the woman's arm, the small gesture of comfort seeming to speak volumes.

Rachael turned away and studied the crowd, endless unknown faces milling around her. Then her eyes fell on one face that she recognised, and a cold shiver passed down her spine.

Manindra Bhandari stood amidst a small gathering, his long white hair tied back in a braid with a ruby clasp, his weight resting on an ebony cane. Naveen stood with him, dressed in red and gold like his father, a sword hanging at his waist. He had a hard scowl on his face.

The crash of a gong resounded through the foyer, turning every eye upwards to the balcony where a man in a grey robe stood.

"Ladies and gentlemen, if you will please proceed to the Hall of Whispers and take your seats."

The doors below the balcony swung wide, and the crowd began to move in their direction. Ilona lead the way as their group joined the stream of people filing through the large double doors. Rachael followed at the back, not feeling particularly eager to see where any of this was going. As she was being jostled by the throng, she was surprised to feel a sharp tug at her sleeve. She looked back to see a woman in a familiar looking white robe standing a little behind her.

"Maya?" she whispered.

The lady nodded. Maya's bodyguard stood at her side, staying in step, eyes razor sharp. She gave Rachael a stern, measuring look.

"Rachael, I just..."

Maya seemed unsure of what to say. The cool confidence the woman had shown a few nights before had now vanished entirely. A pair of older men ducked past them, carefully avoiding the seer, though their curious eyes took in the scene.

"I'm sorry," Maya said, with a deep earnestness. "Rachael, I'm truly sorry. You have to believe that. What's going to happen in there..."

Confused, Rachael tried to catch a glimpse of Maya's face under the hood as if she might find some explanation there. More people were flowing past them, an exaggerated care in the way they avoided even brushing Maya's robes.

"Go. Be with the others," Maya gestured, apparently unable to bring herself to say anything else. Though she wasn't happy about leaving without a clearer answer, Rachael saw the way Rukiya's eyes fixed on her, like something dangerous. She gave the bodyguard a curt nod and slipped away, joining the crowd that filed into the chamber.

As she entered the hall, she found herself at the top of a flight of steps leading down to an open floor. A dais occupied the far side of the chamber, supporting an imposing desk and a high backed chair, whilst all around her tiered seating filled the remaining space. A balcony above encircled half the chamber, seeming to offer more seating. Above it all a high domed ceiling of stained glass allowed sunlight to pour down onto them.

The domed glass had been divided into smaller sections, each depicting a person, strangely stylised. Some were hard to make out, others more clearly depicted, but Rachael immediately recognised the figures she had seen on the walls of Manindra's home. Her eyes quickly settled on the form of a woman in a flowing dress, surrounded by a swirling cloud of autumn leaves. Her face was concealed by what appeared to be some kind of mask. For a moment she could almost hear a voice like dry leaves whispering her name again. It was only when a tall man jostled her as he passed that she remembered where she was standing.

To the left of the room, a couple of rows from the front, she could see Manindra sitting with his son. Further down, in the very front row, she saw Reuben Ben Mahir with a couple of men she didn't recognise. To the right, a set of seats appeared to have been reserved for them. Already she could see the others waiting for her. Micah gestured, ushering her into the row ahead of himself. The long bench was hard and uncomfortable.

She glanced across at where Manindra and Naveen sat. The old man's self-indulgent smile never faltered, but his son scowled at everything in the room as if it might be a threat. Just like the way Rukiya had been looking at her. She was thankful that at least Rakesh wasn't there too.

As the last group entered the chamber, she barely paid attention until she saw the long grey coats of the guards who flanked the two men walking between them. Rishi and Abasi strode between the tiered seats, shoulder to shoulder, cold eyes seeming to issue a challenge to anyone watching. It was only as Abasi saw them seated at the front that his expression softened. He almost seemed to want to reach out past the guard who stood at his side, to grasp his wife's hand. Rishi, however, seemed to barely notice them. There was only the briefest flicker in his eyes as they met Arsha's. A moment of something that almost seemed like shame. Then the two men were brought to their seats at the centre of the chamber, just in front of the open floor that surrounded the dais.

In the nervous silence her eyes returned once more to the image of the woman in the glass, surrounded by the swirling golden leaves, the sunlight making the whole image glow.

A few minutes later, a man in grey entered and sounded a gong.

"All rise for Lord Inquisitor Kadima," the man declared, his voice ringing out across the hushed chamber.

As everyone in the chamber stood, Rachael followed their example. Her eyes flickered to Ilona's face, the cold mask that seemed to give nothing away. She tried to let the same blank expression settle on her own features, to become an empty space, devoid of emotion. Anything to keep her stomach from twisting itself in knots. She felt Arsha's hand brush against hers, and with scarcely a thought she slipped her fingers through her sister's.

A tall man entered the room, walking slowly to the dais where he took his seat behind the large desk. His hair was a tight mat of greying curls, and he was dressed in long black robes hemmed in blue and gold. His face had the square roughness of a heavy stone, skin the colour of jet.

The gong was struck again and the man cleared his throat, a rough, rasping sound that resounded through the silent chamber. When he spoke, his voice creaked like oak timbers, old but strong.

"Ladies and gentlemen, you may be seated. This court of inquiry shall now be called to order."

As people took their seats, a hush settled over the courtroom.

"This court has heard the arguments presented by all parties, and reviewed all material evidence pertaining to this matter. We have deliberated on the arguments and the facts presented to us, and we are ready now to pronounce judgement in this matter."

The man paused for a moment to glance down at his desk, where Rachael supposed he must have had papers laid out.

"We have heard, from Sir Reuben Ben Mahir, a charge of conspiracy against Lord Manindra Bhandari and Professor Rishi Chandra. That these two men conspired to gain unlawful access to information held by the Chamber of Foresight, and put that information to the purpose of capturing and containing a forbidden artefact, namely one of the Seeds which was discovered in the city of London, beyond the Veil. Sir Ben Mahir contends that, in doing so, these individuals and persons associated with them and working under their direction enacted multiple breaches of the Accords during the events which transpired in London."

A pause, as the Lord Inquisitor cleared his throat.

"After reviewing the evidence brought by Sir Ben Mahir, and certain documents provided by Professor Chandra, it is the finding of this court that Lord Manindra Bhandari was indeed in possession of materials that should have remained the sole purview of the Chamber of Foresight, without clear cause or remit. For this matter, he shall be censured, and his family's estates, titles, and privileges revoked, immediately and forthwith."

A murmur reverberated through the room, a thousand whispered conversations springing up at once.

"On the actions of Professor Chandra and Captain Bira," the Lord Inquisitor continued, his voice rising above the din, "we must first address the question of their crossing the Veil without papers of travel, and without apparent cause. Whilst I have serious questions..."

The Lord Inquisitor fixed Rishi with a steely gaze.

"...As to precisely what sparked Professor Chandra's sudden interest in this matter, I have seen no evidence that he obtained access to information from the Chamber of Foresight, no matter what Sir Ben Mahir or House Bhandari may contend. However the fact remains that Professor Chandra and Captain Bira are responsible for crossing the Veil without the permission of the

Wardens. On this matter, Professor Chandra has informed this court that this decision was entirely his responsibility, and that he wilfully coerced Captain Bira into compliance."

Rachael heard the sharp gasps from those seated around her.

"Oh Abasi..." Milima said, under her breath. "How could you let him..."

"That idiot..." Micah growled. Though Ilona said nothing, Rachael saw the way the woman's fingers curled, as if ready to make a fist. She turned to look at where Rishi and Abasi sat. The professor's eyes were cold, almost lifeless, but Abasi looked as if he wanted to throw up.

"Thus, this court has no recourse but to find Professor Chandra entirely culpable in this matter. As to the charge of conspiracy, though the prosecution has dwelt for some time on the history shared between these two men, this court must acknowledge the following... First, that the fostering of Rishi Chandra under House Bhandari is a matter of record. Second, that Rishi Chandra was formally disowned by House Bhandari, and all ties between House Chandra and House Bhandari were severed some twelve years past. Third, that the prosecution has failed to bring sufficient evidence to demonstrate any further collusion. Thus, we can find no cause sufficient to prove any charge of conspiracy."

"Are you following any of this?" Rachael said, turning to look over at Arsha. The girl nodded, her eyes wide. She seemed unable to actually form a reply.

"In the matter of the breach of the Veil enacted by Professor Chandra, this court declares that Professor Chandra shall immediately be stripped of privilege, his papers of travel removed, and his house be fined the sum of ten thousand Guilders."

Again, the rising chorus of whispers from around the chamber. For a moment it appeared the Lord Inquisitor had finished, until the man seemed to remember himself.

"One other matter has been brought before this court's attention. In the matter of the care of the child Rachael Barnes, a refugee from the Hearth, Sir Ben Mahir has moved to take the child into custody as material to the matter of the awakened Seed. Professor Chandra has claimed the child as his adopted daughter, and refused to present her to the Inquisition. However in light of these penalties issued against Professor Chandra, this court must deem that he is longer a fit or suitable guardian. The adoption of Rachael Barnes by Rishi Chandra is hereby annulled. The child shall be granted to the care of the Inquisition until suitable arrangements can be made for her."

The way the old man spoke the words, it seemed almost like a dismissal. As if she had been hardly worth mentioning. No matter how she had tried to prepare herself for this, she could still feel her hands shaking. Then a voice rang out, loud and clear across the courtroom.

"Lord Inquisitor, I... I need to say something."

Arsha stepped down from the seats as she spoke, crossing to the centre of the chamber with quick, nervous steps. In the sudden silence all eyes were on her. For a moment the old man didn't say a word. He just regarded her curiously, as if he had never seen a teenage girl before in his life.

"Speak your piece, child," he said at last.

"Lord Inquisitor, you can't take Rachael away. Even if my dad can't adopt her, she's a member of this family now."

"Child, no matter how you may feel about this, the law is the law. If you have nothing germane to bring, you must clear the floor."

The Lord Inquisitor spoke with the slow and patient tones of an old man addressing a little girl, too young to realise her own foolishness.

"Lord Inquisitor, this is a... A matter of law. Rachael is my sister. Bound by blood and fate. According to the precedents set by the Dunforth trials, Guild law recognises the practice of blood-binding as..." The girl faltered, for a moment, pausing to catch her breath. "As being of equal weight to the ties of family established by birth or marriage."

For a moment, no one seemed to know quite how to react. The general tenor of the courtroom seemed to be one of confusion. People were glancing at each other, as if to see if anyone knew what the words were supposed to mean. Rachael caught the professor's expression, frozen in disbelief. The man's knuckle's were pale as he gripped the railing in front of him. In Manindra's eyes she saw a look of quiet curiosity that left her even more unsettled.

Gathering himself, the Lord Inquisitor regarded Arsha very carefully, as if his eyes could pierce through any lie she might try to tell him. Standing her ground, Arsha held up her palm, showing off the thin scar. Sensing her cue, Rachael jumped down from her seat before anyone around her could react and stepped out onto the floor with her own hand raised high, the matching scar clearly shown.

In the silence, a single word was spoken.

"Arsha..."

Rishi's astonished gasp seemed barely a whisper, but it still echoed loud in the hushed room.

The Lord Inquisitor drew a long, calming breath.

"Very well. A fateworker shall be called upon to determine the veracity of your claim to be blood-bound. If it is confirmed, I shall reconsider my previous judgement. Does the prosecution have any point to bring in this matter?"

He turned to regard Sir Ben Mahir. The younger man slowly unfolded himself, striding out onto the floor.

"Yes, Lord Inquisitor, we do. The prosecution accepts that Rachael Barnes and Arsha Chandra are now bound by blood. We must, therefore, move that both children be immediately placed under our care. If, as she claims, Arsha Chandra has indeed been blood bound to miss Barnes then we can only conclude that miss Chandra is, herself, irrevocably contaminated."

"Contaminated?" the Lord Inquisitor said, raising an eyebrow. "Sir Ben Mahir, I do hope you mean to explain yourself."

"Yes, Lord Inquisitor. I have here the results of the medical examination performed upon miss Barnes before her admission into the Citadel. Under our discretion, pursuant to Guild laws and articles volume seven, section thirty-two, the results of this testing were made available to our own experts, who have provided their formal conclusions which I also have here, signed and witnessed. I will, of course, make all of these documents available to the court upon request. However, if you will permit me to summarise, what we learned from examining the child's blood was... Well... Baffling to say the least. None-the-less, our best alchymists agree on one thing with absolute certainty; whatever this girl may be, she is not human. Or at least, not entirely. As such we must attest that she stands outside of the protection of Guild law. Even the bonds of blood."

For a moment, Rachael felt as if she wasn't sure which way was down. She caught the incredulous expression on Arsha's face, as the girl turned to look at her.

"We have not yet fully determined the precise nature of the child's altered heritage," Reuben continued, "but it is quite likely that her inhuman ancestry is connected to the situation now unfolding beyond the Veil. As such, the Inquisition demands that she be turned over to our custody for further study. Naturally, if Arsha Chandra has truly bound her blood and fate to Miss Barnes', we must contend that she is likewise contaminated, and must also be rendered into the care of the Inquisition."

"No!" Rishi cried out, leaning out halfway across the railing in front of him, eyes wide with horror as the guards pulled him back.

With a deeply disgruntled look about him, the Lord Inquisitor regarded Ben Mahir for a long moment.

"Very well. This court accepts your recommendation. Rachael Barnes and Arsha Chandra shall be given to the care of the Inquisition, pursuant to the ongoing investigation into the matters occurring beyond the Veil."

"No, you can't take her! You can't take my daughter!"

Rishi's cry resounded through the room as he vaulted the railing. He was moving across the floor before the guards could react. He ran to his daughter, snatching up her hands in his. Rachael could see the way he stared at the pale line across the girl's palm, as if not able to believe it.

"Oh Arsha, why did you do it? Why?"

Arsha turned to look at her father, with eyes that seemed ready to fill with tears.

"I had to, Daddy. It was the only way."

"No, Arsha, no, you foolish girl, you never should have..."

The words tumbled out of his mouth, crashing into one another in his confusion, as two guardsmen caught him by the shoulders and dragged him back, kicking and thrashing.

"Get that man out of here," the Lord Inquisitor snapped.

The professor continued to shout as he was hauled out of the room, a stream of violent curses against the Lord Inquisitor, Reuben Ben Mahir, and most of all Manindra. His eyes flickered between them, spittle forming around his mouth as he shouted himself hoarse, all the while twisting in the iron grip of the guardsmen.

As Rachael watched, his eyes met hers, furious and wild. For a moment he seemed to not even recognise her. When he did, the expression that passed across his face chilled her. In those wild eyes, what she saw was an accusation. Her own feeling of shame was immediate, and momentary. She realised that he was wrong. She had not stolen his daughter from him. She had not put him in this place. He was the one. The one who had taken her away from everything she had known, who had committed the crimes that he was now facing the penalty for, who had made his own daughter a part of it all. He was the one who had failed. After all his promises, he had done nothing to protect her. She was going to be locked away from the world, and the only one who had done a thing about it was Arsha.

As the guards hauled Rishi out of the chamber and the doors slammed closed behind them, she saw figures in grey coats moving towards where she was sat. Others came to stand at Arsha's side, gesturing for her to follow them.

Ignoring their instructions, as the nearest of the men tried to make her step clear of the seats, she looked up at the glass dome above, some impulse making her long to see the sunlight. The figures in the stained glass window stared down at them all impassively. In their glass eyes there was no pity, no comfort. But as she watched, the window darkened. For a moment she thought the shadow must have been cast by a cloud, but then she recognised the shape.

The shape of outstretched wings.

Chapter 27 - Wings

For a fraction of a second the window seemed to bulge inwards, and then there was only an expanding cloud of coloured glass raining down upon the marble floor as Justin burst into the hall. With a great sweep of his wings he halted in the air, hanging for a moment before he dropped down to land on the magistrate's podium. There was a crash of splintering wood as claws the size of cart-wheels tore into the platform. Rachael saw the Lord Inquisitor scrambling away, feet tangling in his long coat. Majestically, Justin swept his wings outwards. The wind buffeted the whole chamber and Rachael stumbled back a step. Then his lungs swelled and he let out a deafening cry that rattled the glass in the remaining windows.

Silence followed. Towards the back of the room she saw a pair of grey-coated guards standing with their swords drawn, but clearly unwilling to approach. She wondered how long they would have before more came, with guns.

Justin surveyed the silent chamber once more. The vast black form of the bird dissolved down into the shape of a young man in a flowing black coat. He swept his hair back and grinned, amused, arrogant, entirely sure of himself. In the face of those sparkling gold flecked eyes her fear vanished. The courtroom continued to empty, people pushing past each other in their panic. At the doors she could see more guards struggling to get into the room, but they were fighting the press of bodies. When the centre of the chamber cleared she remained alone, as Justin walked calmly towards her.

Then she realised that she was not alone. Standing beside her, Arsha reached out to take her hand. The girl looked frightened, but she held her ground.

"I wasn't sure..." Rachael began to say to him, a guilty feeling twisting her stomach.

"Yes you were," Justin said. "I'll always come for you. You know that."

He spoke calmly, but as his eyes fixed on hers she saw the turmoil behind that gaze. The uncertainty. The hurt. She had doubted him, and he knew it.

"I believe it. I believe it now," she said, uncomfortable with the tacit admission.

"It's OK," he said, a little of his affected arrogance slipping away. "I shouldn't have left you..."

"Just... Shut up," she said. His eyes flickered towards the guardsmen now pushing their way through the crowd at the door.

"We should go," he said.

"Yeah."

"And her?" he nodded to Arsha. Rachael turned to look her sister in the eye.

"It's your choice," she said, keeping her voice as level as she could. To her astonishment, Arsha barely blinked. The girl's eyes were cool and hard.

"I'm not saying goodbye again. I'm with you. No matter what," she said. Still, Rachael couldn't help notice the way she avoided looking at Justin when she spoke.

"OK," Justin said. "Let's go."

Glancing back, Rachael noticed Manindra and Naveen. When the rest of the court fled, they had remained. So too had the crew of the Triskelion. Micah, Ilona, Abasi and Milima all watched them from the tiered seats. Not one of them said a word, but Rachael got the feeling they were holding their tongues, waiting to see what happened next. Even Maya had remained, lurking at the very back of the room, Rukiya standing before her with her blade held firmly in one hand.

Naveen also had his sword drawn, and was edging forwards slowly. His father stood back, with an expression that seemed almost awestruck.

Justin looked at Naveen's towering form, and just shook his head. "Don't," he said.

Though she could see his hands trembling, Justin's eyes remained fixed and calm. Watching the way he projected that cool demeanour, Rachael found herself achingly aware of how desperately she had missed him.

A clatter of heels against the marble alerted them to the guards breaking through into the chamber. They had lightning ballistas cradled in their arms. Taking advantage of the moment, Naveen advanced a step and Rachael saw that even Ilona half-raised a hand, as if to level the arc-gauntlet that she had been forced to leave behind.

Justin's reaction was immediate. He stepped between the girls, a hand pushing each of them back a step.

"The podium," he said sharply. She didn't have time to ask what he meant, as instantly he began to change. A heartbeat later the giant raven dominated the chamber once more, claws gouging thin lines into the marble floor.

Turning to glance back, Rachael saw what he meant. The magistrate's podium stood high above the courtroom floor. From there they would be able to climb onto his back. Taking Arsha's hand, she dashed up the steps as Justin moved towards the guards.

He let out another ear-splitting cry, and as the guards staggered he swept his wings forward in flashing arcs of glistening black feathers. Naveen darted forward with an angry roar. A wing-tip caught him in the chest, hurling him across the chamber. There was a painful sound as he struck the far wall and fell to the floor. His sword clattered to the ground. Micah was scrambling over the benches, unarmed but still making a beeline towards herself and Arsha. It was strange how easily she expected his thoughtless heroism. She felt a momentary surge of relief when Ilona tackled him, pinning the man to a bench, clear of the fighting.

The other wing swept through the guardsmen, not striking any directly but flooring them all with the clap of air that followed hard in its wake. Rachael felt a rush of excitement as she saw weapons knocked from hands. One man kept his grip, and from a prone position he pointed the lightning ballista upwards to fire. Justin simply reached down with his curved black beak and plucked the gun from the man's hands. There was a snap, and two halves of the weapon fell to the ground.

Forcing herself to look away, despite the giddy rush she felt at seeing Justin so thoroughly demolishing the grey coated guardsmen, Rachael clambered up the podium, hauling a dumbstruck Arsha with her. As they clambered onto the Lord Inquisitor's desk, she glanced back and saw that the old man had not left the room after all. Below the back edge of the raised dais he was huddled against the wall, a frightened look in his eyes. It almost seemed impossible that it could be same man who had commanded the entire chamber into hushed silence with every word. Now Rachael saw the way his skin sagged around his eyes, the way his wrinkled hands shook. He looked up and met her gaze. She wanted to turn away, ashamed of seeing him like this. She wanted to say something cruel. Something comforting. Something proud. There were no words that could encompass everything she was feeling. She turned to look at Justin, as he swept his wings back once more and ruffled his feathers, the gesture making her think of the way he would flick his hair back.

A guard made to scramble for his gun. The clack of claws against marble seemed to send a clear enough message. The chamber belonged to Justin. He turned his head back and forth, sweeping his gaze about the benches, daring someone to answer his challenge. The room seemed to hold its breath. Micah had ceased struggling, though Ilona still kept his arm pinned behind back, her eyes watching Justin cautiously. Abasi and Milima watched with the same cautious expressions. Only Manindra seemed curiously unafraid. In his eyes she saw only a burning hunger. He seemed not even to have noticed that his son lay in a crumpled heap at the back of the chamber.

Then Maya stepped forward. As she pulled her white hood back, Rachael saw the sadness in her eyes. When the woman spoke the whole world seemed to ring like a bell. Rachael staggered, nearly falling off the podium. She saw Justin shaking his head, as if trying to stop the sound from hammering in his ears.

Again Maya opened her mouth, but no words came out. Or at least no words that she could hear. She knew somehow that the woman had spoken, but the words seemed as if they would not fit inside her head. Again there was something that went beyond sound, making the whole world shake. Her stomach churned and her head swam. Everything seemed to be moving slowly, as if the air had turned to syrup.

Again Maya's mouth opened, the soundless words forming. Blood red tears were tracking down the woman's face. Rachael heard Justin's shriek of pain, slicing through the ringing echoes in her head. Black smoke boiled off of his body, and he seemed to flicker like an old television. Like he was there and not, at the same time. For the briefest of instants, instead of the vast form of the raven there was only a boy, on his knees, screaming in pain.

Then the raven lunged, curved beak darting forward. In the blink of an eye Rukiya was there, pushing Maya away. Rachael saw blood as Justin's beak closed around the woman's leg. He flicked his head up, tossing Rukiya aside like a doll. Sprawled on the floor,

Maya looked up at him with eyes wide in terror as Justin drew back his head to strike again.

Rachael felt her mouth moving, shouting at Justin to stop. For a moment, he hesitated. Then Maya's lips moved. This time she did not speak the words. She shouted them, at the top of her lungs. Rachael's head swam, and she felt herself falling, tumbling down from the podium onto the cold floor of the chamber. When her head stopped swimming, the raven was gone. Justin lay on his side, curled into a tight little ball of pain, his black coat spilling out around him. Hazily, she noticed that the floor was still covered in brightly coloured shards of glass.

She looked up to see Maya standing over her, swaying unsteadily. The woman fell to her knees, drops of blood falling from her chin. She felt the woman's hand cradling the back of her neck, lifting her head a little. Enough for them to look each other in the eyes.

"I'm sorry. I saw what would happen if I didn't," Maya said, her voice barely more than a whisper, "and I couldn't imagine anything that could be worse. I'm sorry, Rachael. I'm so sorry."

She heard the words, but they seemed like something distant, like a conversation overheard. Just a fading echo. It seemed as if all the sound had been sucked out of the world. She wanted to lash out at the woman, punch her, kick her, spit on that delicate face. But it was all so pointless. All her rage seemed to float around her, empty and useless. Her arms and legs felt numb. Her chest seemed to have a weight pressing down on it.

She saw the guards gathering up their weapons, saw them close in from all sides. Maya was lifted to her feet, carried away by men with nervous expressions. She saw the men coming to take herself and Arsha. She didn't fight. She couldn't. Her legs didn't seem to work any more. One of the men hauled her to her feet and began to drag her away. She couldn't tear her eyes away from Justin's face, that look of agony turning to shame. She saw tears forming in his eyes as his hands clenched tight, knuckles showing white. Then they passed through the doors, out into the streets, and everything seemed to pass in a blur.

She saw the tower hovering above them, seeming to sway and bend until she realised it was the tears blurring her vision. She saw clean white hallways of frosted glass. Stairways cut into the substance of the tower, leading them upwards. A room, a bed.

She passed in and out of consciousness. Doctors came and went. Cuts were bandaged. Needles poked into her flesh. Strange devices flickered and hummed. Whispered conversations as notes were scratched onto sheets of clean white paper. More injections, and she faded out again.

Eyes finally crept open on a small room that seemed to have been hollowed out from the milky green glass of the tower. It was hard to make the shape of it come into focus. The angles all seemed to be slightly wrong. She was surrounded by crisp white linens. The bed was carved from some kind of pale white wood.

Slowly, she got to her feet. Her clothes had been left folded on a chair by the door. She felt stiff and sore, like she'd been lying in bed for days.

A simple curtain covered the doorway. Rachael pulled it aside and stepped through into another hauntingly sterile room. A large window seemed to blend into the walls around it, as if the glass had simply been worn thin in that spot. White lace curtains framed the window on either side. Four chairs had been arranged around a small table. The furnishings were simple, all of them carved of the same sale pale white wood. Across the room from her stood a second doorway, just like the one she had come through.

Standing at the window, Rachael looked down into the streets below. The sun shone down from a clear blue sky, and for a moment the lifeless city seemed almost beautiful. Though they were higher than the tallest buildings around them, she could still make out the people and the carriages clearly. She wondered if one of them would be carrying the crew of the Triskelion back to the ship. She decided that by now they were probably already gone.

She looked down at her hands, and saw that they were shaking. In the silence, she heard the soft shuffling of bare feet on the smooth floor. Rachael looked up as Arsha slipped through the curtain that covered her door. The girl paused, surprised.

Neither of them said a word. There was a scraping sound as Arsha pulled a chair away from the small table and fell into it. Rachael turned to face the window again, watching the carriages drift through the streets.

"Do you think they'd bring us something to eat? If we asked?"

Arsha's voice was hoarse and thin, barely a whisper.

"Maybe," Rachael said.

From the corner of her eye she could see the way that Arsha stared at the blank tabletop. The girl seemed to have been hollowed out, like a perfectly carved model of herself.

"So, what now?" Arsha said, at last.

Rachael blinked in surprise.

"What now?" Arsha repeated.

"What do you mean, 'what now?' Like I'm supposed to know?"

Arsha lifted her head just a little, looking at Rachael with a helpless expression.

"You must have some kind of plan, right?" she said. "That's what you do. Even when you were with us on the ship, I know you were thinking of ways out the whole time. I don't know how to do this. I'm not like you. You've survived so much."

Rachael felt a kind of sick laughter curling up from somewhere deep inside. She shook her head, as her fingertips brushed the smooth surface of the glass window.

"Yeah, I have a plan. Give in. Let them win. Whatever happens now I can't do anything about it, so I'm going to close my eyes and hope the worst part is over quick."

"How can you say that?"

Arsha's voice was a stunned gasp. Again Rachael felt that sick, bitter sound of laughter welling up from inside.

"Because that's what surviving is. It's getting by, holding on, keeping some tiny little part of yourself moving. That's all. Your dad tried to win, Justin tried to win, and none of it mattered a damn. People like Manindra and Reuben always win, and the people who fight them just get stepped on. So screw your dad and whatever fight he's got with the old man, and screw Maya, and all the rest too."

"He's your dad too," Arsha said.

"Whatever. I just want it all done with," Rachael turned away and pressed her forehead to the glass, feeling the warm sunlight against her skin as she closed her eyes.

The sun was setting when they heard the sound of the door opening. No knock, just Reuben standing in the doorway, speaking softly to one of the guards. Then the door closed and for a moment he stood in silence, looking about the room.

His eyes turned to the table, where food and a jug of iced water had been left for them by the guards. Fresh bread, sliced ham and beef, salad, and small bowl of fruit. None of it had been touched. He looked to each of them in turn, waiting for a reaction. Eventually he shrugged, pulled up a chair and sat down at one end of the small table.

"How are you both feeling?" he said, his voice soft, almost gentle. "The apothecaries tell me you're mostly recovered."

Silence greeted him. Neither of the girls even bothered to look at the man as he picked an apple from the bowl in front of him.

"You should eat, really. It's going to be a while before we see fresh fruit like this again."

He bit into the apple, chewing slowly, the sound of it filling the room.

"I am very sorry about what happened. The seer has been taken into custody, of course. I'm told that the fatecraft she used is very, very old, and very powerful. Naturally, the Chamber denies any knowledge of how she could have come to learn such a thing."

He took another bite.

"Ah. Your shifter friend has also been taken into custody."

At the mention of Justin, Rachael looked up at the man, her eyes cold.

"What did you do to him?"

For a moment Reuben said nothing, studying his half finished apple as if it fascinated him.

"He's alive and well. Better than he was a few days ago, in point of fact. Our fateworkers have put a binding on him to prevent any further use of his... Abilities. But he's in no danger."

"That supposed to be some kind of threat?" she growled.

"Of course not," Reuben said, exasperated. "I'm not here to bully you, Rachael. What I want is to put an end to this. I want to find some way that we can assure your safety, and the safety of all the people within the Hearth."

There was a pause. Her throat felt dry.

"Because of the Seed," she said.

"Yes. Because of the Seed. Because in all of their ridiculous feuding, your adopted father and Lord Bhandari have allowed this rot to continue to fester, while more and more innocent people suffer."

"Feuding? You were the idiot that thought they were working together." Rachael snapped.

"Young lady, I am well aware of just how much those two despise each other. I'm an Inquisitor, it's my job to know when I'm being lied to."

"Then why'd you go after her dad so hard back there, if you knew he was only trying to help?"

"Whatever Chandra is trying to do here, it certainly isn't helping. I had only one goal in that courtroom, and that was to see to it that neither of those men had any more part in this. They've both done more than enough damage already."

"What do you mean?" Arsha exclaimed. She had been so quiet that the sudden outburst seemed to catch both of them by surprise. "My dad's been doing nothing but try to stop what's happening in

London. If you and Manindra hadn't been chasing after him all this time, he'd be there right now trying to stop the Seed and everything else that's happened. This is your fault, because you wouldn't trust him, and because you didn't stop Manindra from getting away with all the awful things he was doing."

Watching the girl's eyes, Rachael could see that she was holding back tears. Arsha's mouth was set in a hard line, her anger barely masking everything else she was feeling.

Reuben sighed.

"I wish I could believe that, young lady. I really do. I know you think the world of your father, and I'm sorry that I have to be the one to tell you this, but he doesn't deserve the faith you have in him."

"How can you say that? You don't know anything about him," Arsha snapped.

"Yes, I do," he said, heavily. There was another pause. He seemed to be gathering his thoughts. "A mentor once told me that a guardsman looks for where the crime is. An Inquisitor looks for where a crime isn't. A broken window, a tavern brawl, these things are easily solved. But the absence of a crime... How do you investigate that?"

He let the question hang in the air for a moment, though it was clear he wasn't expecting an answer.

"I have been taking an interest in your father's activities for a very long time now," Reuben continued. "Ever since I was a junior officer in fact. He's covered his tracks well, mostly with Lord Bhandari's help. Bhandari, you have to understand, has always kept himself at a remove. He prefers to work through others. Your father was one of his finest agents. Nothing we've ever been able to prove, of course. Barely any evidence at all. Mostly it was the signs of where evidence wasn't. The inconsistencies and alterations. References to forbidden archives, redacted statements, trails of paperwork that lead back on themselves in endless circles. A lot of missing crimes. So I kept picking at the threads. A little here, a little there, but it all adds up, given time. And in that time I have begun to get a very clear picture of what kind of man your father is. What he and Manindra have done."

"What do you mean?" Arsha said. Rachael caught the note of growing uncertainty in her voice.

"I mean Fallen Peak. I mean the trail of bodies they left getting there, and getting back again."

"You're lying," Arsha snapped at him. "He told me what happened at Fallen Peak. I was born there. He nearly died getting me out alive."

"Yes. I've heard his story. How the expedition was marooned. How he fell in love with one of the researchers working for him. How she died in a storm that wracked the outpost. How they finally managed to get one of the ships flying again, with only half a dozen of them left alive. How the hardship of the journey caused most of his remaining crew to lose their minds. I've heard it all. And it's a lie, every bit of it."

"How do you know that?" Arsha said.

"Because I've been there. Because I wanted to see for myself what could have been so important that so much effort was spent to conceal it. Do you know what I found? Nothing. Or, very nearly nothing. Manindra and your father were out there for seven years. Stranded, supposedly, with a crew of sixty all told. That many people, living in one place for that long... There should have been a mountain of evidence. But what I found was the signs of a simple temporary encampment. No struggle. No disaster. They were there for perhaps six months at the most. The only sign of any struggle was the outpost itself... Or, what was left of it. The whole thing had been reduced to a smouldering crater. So for six and a half years I can offer no account of where Manindra and your father went to. Six and a half years, during which sixty people died or were lost, and an ancient Ur citadel was reduced to ash and rubble, with no clear answer as to why or how."

"That's not true," Arsha said, her voice on the edge of breaking.

"I'm sorry," he said. "I know this isn't fair. I wish there was time to explain. To help you understand what's happening here. What has been happening for many years now. But even if we had all the time in the world, I don't imagine this would be any easier to accept."

He drew a heavy breath, and emptied his glass.

"Unfortunately, every moment the Seed continues to grow, and the walls of reality around it weaken. Soon it be strong enough to tear the Veil apart, and unleash an unimaginable chaos on all of the Hearth. The apothecaries tell me you're both well enough to travel, which means we have to make our move now. I came here because I felt you both deserved an explanation for what is happening, and because I would really prefer to do this with your cooperation. We think there is a chance, a slim chance, that the Seed can be made dormant again. That's why we need you, Rachael. Because you awakened it. And Arsha... if you are now Fatebound to her, then we may well need your assistance as well. My ship is being prepared as we speak. We'll set sail for the Hearth within the hour. My men will come for you then."

"And what if we don't help? What are you gonna do then?" Rachael said.

He shrugged helplessly.

"Whatever we have to. I'm sorry, Rachael, but there are billions of lives in the balance here. Against that cost, to sacrifice a few... Even a few million..."

"What do you mean?"

"If nothing else can be done... If the Seed cannot be contained... Then we will bring fire. We will burn every part of it away, and the whole city with it. And then we'll pray that's enough."

She said nothing. There was a scraping sound as he pushed his chair back. At the doorway he paused, and turned to look at them both.

"I'm sorry for what I had to do to your father. For what it's worth, I believe there is good in him. None of us are born monsters."

Arsha's eyes were red with tears as she looked up at the man with a hateful expression.

"Just go away," The girl whispered, her voice hoarse. Slipping an arm around her sister's shoulders, Rachael said nothing, but the look she gave the man made it clear that she felt the same. With a dejected nod he turned and walked out the door. It closed behind him with barely a sound.

Chapter 28 - Iron

True to Reuben's word the guards came for them within the hour, watching with impassive stares as they were herded out of the room. They were lead through the hallways of the tower, up and up, to a room that was lined with windows from floor to ceiling. They could see the city spread out below them, so neat and orderly that it looked less like a city and more like a piece of clockwork. Like a watch, made all of glass.

Jutting out from the side of the tower was a long pier, to which a ship had been moored. They immediately recognised the slender shape, black with green and silver trim.

A pair of large doors lead out onto the pier, and they were marched out towards where Reuben stood waiting on the deck. He gave the guards a satisfied nod and gestured for them to head inside. Dock hands untied ropes and adjusted parts of the rigging as the ship made ready to sail.

Inside, the vessel was every bit as polished and precise as

without. The soft grey walls and white oak floors were a stark contrast to the weatherbeaten look of the Triskelion, yet it did not feel the slightest bit welcoming. They were guided to a spacious guest room which they were clearly meant to share. The guards remained outside, and Rachael heard the sound of the lock turning as the door was closed.

Tired and frustrated, she dropped down onto one of the beds. It all felt so familiar, despite how strange it should be. Another cage, as beautifully gilded as the last.

Arsha stood by the door looking nervous and confused. Rachael couldn't bring herself to say anything. She just lay back and closed her eyes, as the ship swayed into motion.

The journey was an empty succession of silent hours spent staring at the same four walls. Their meals were brought to their room by the guards. Their plates were collected an hour later. They were permitted to use the bathroom, one at a time, always accompanied. They woke up, ate in silence, passed empty hours, and slept. They said little, none of it meaningful. Sometimes they invented games or read some of the books that lined the room, but neither of them found the slightest joy in any of it.

Rachael began to relish sleeping. It was an escape from the agonising greyness that filled each day. In her dreams she would catch glimpses of Justin's face, the smell of his body, his hair, the feel of his hands on her skin, the touch of his lips against hers. Always she woke with an aching feeling, as if reaching for something distant. Sometimes she dreamed of London, but those dreams were brief, flashes of fire and crumbling towers of rusted iron, black smoke blinding her, filling her lungs until she fell to her knees, gasping for breath. Then the dream would pass, and she would wake to sheets soaked with sweat, white lines scored into her palms where her nails had dug in.

It might have been the seventh or eighth day when something else woke her. She sat up in her bed, in a room dimly lit by a single slumbering ghostlight. She could hear the sound of the engines humming through the walls, a softer note than the Triskelion's, but nothing seemed amiss. Then she heard other sounds. A muted shout. A sudden thump. Footsteps on wooden floors, hard and heavy. Glancing at the other bed she saw that Arsha was also awake. Just the girl's face could be seen, peering out from under her sheets, looking at Rachael as if waiting for directions.

Then the sound of a gunshot rang out clear and sharp. Two more followed, in quick succession.

Rachael didn't waste a moment. Rolling out from the covers, she hit the floor and immediately ducked under the bed, gesturing for Arsha to do the same.

"Rachael..." Arsha hissed. Before the girl could say more, Rachael turned and pressed a finger to her lips. Arsha swallowed and bit back whatever she had been about to say.

The sound of shouting grew closer. They heard something heavy slam into the wall from outside. Another pair of gunshots rang out, deafeningly loud. Then the lock clicked open. The door swung wide, as the light from the hallway framed a figure in silhouette. Rachael slid back deeper beneath the bedframe, already beginning to realise what a futile gesture it was. Across the room she could just make out Arsha staring at her from the darkness under her bed.

Footsteps, slow and measured as the man crossed the room. A swaying pool of light accompanied him. He wore heavy looking boots and his trousers were patched and grease-stained. Standing between the beds, the man dropped to one knee and set the ghostlamp down on the floor as he glanced to either side.

Rachael recognised Korban's face immediately. His gaze almost seemed to slide over her, fixing on her face only long enough for her to be sure that she had been found. Then he rose to his feet and turned to survey the room again, as if they were little more than incidental details.

"That's both of them. Bring them to the bridge," he barked to the men outside the door. Then he turned and stalked out of the room.

More men entered, and rough hands pulled them out from their hiding places. Between the two broad shouldered thugs she could see Korban talking to someone, his voice too low for her to make out clearly. Then Korban stepped aside and her breath caught in her throat.

Justin's eyes were cold and impassive as he nodded silently in Korban's direction. His hands were folded behind his back, as if he was a soldier standing at ease. It was only as Korban turned away that she caught a glimmer of anger in Justin's expression. As she met his eyes he glanced away immediately.

She called out his name, but he didn't seem to be listening, and as she tried to run to him one of the guards caught her shoulder. Holding her put, the man thrust a dressing gown into her hands.

"Let's have you decent first," he growled.

Feeling her cheeks burning, Rachael slipped the dressing gown on as the men watched impassively. A semblance of dignity observed, the men proceeded to march them both out of the cabin.

The blood splattered walls were the first thing she set eyes on as they stepped through into the corridor. Two crumpled heaps of cloth turned out to be a pair of dead men, their clothes soaked through with blood, faces ashen and still. She couldn't even make out where they had been shot. The blood had drenched everything, splashing onto the walls and spilling out over the ground. Someone had taken the time to throw a couple of sheets down.

Arsha doubled over, heaving out what remained of her dinner. The sound of the girl retching seemed to come to her from a long way off. The walls were spinning. Rachael reached out a hand to steady herself, and when she brought it away she saw that her fingers were smeared with red. There was an acrid smell in the air. She supposed it was gunsmoke.

"Why? Why did you have to kill them?" Arsha sobbed, barely able to get the words out. Rachael turned to see Justin watching them both with those same cold eyes.

"What the hell is this? What did you do?" she snarled.

"What we had to. You should be happy, Rachael. I promised I

would come for you, and I did."

He knelt down and tore a clean strip of cloth from the clothing of one of the dead men. Then he went to Arsha's side, gently lifting the girl's chin to wipe the spittle from her lips. Rachael watched, scarcely able to believe it was really him.

Arsha's eyes focused on his and she recoiled, slapping his hand away. Rachael saw the hurt expression on his face, but she couldn't even say why it mattered to him.

"What is this Justin? Why are you with these guys? They tried to kill you, remember?"

He looked up at her, sadly.

"They're not what we thought, Rachael. Manindra saved me from their prison. He showed me what he really is. We were wrong about him, this whole time."

She couldn't even understand what he was saying any more. She stared at him, feeling like she was falling, spinning through the air. One of Korban's men gave them a hard look.

"That's enough talk. Get moving," he growled.

They were marched towards the stairs at the end of the hallway. Half-stumbling, unsteady on their feet, they were forced to ascend until they emerged onto the bridge of The Dawning Light.

Like everything on the ship it was a study in clean white lines and silvered edges, now smeared with blood, riddled with bullet holes and scorch marks. Strewn across the floor were the shattered remains of Reuben's automs. She couldn't say what had been used to destroy them, but Korban's men had certainly been thorough about it.

Reuben Ben Mahir was sitting in the captain's chair, but it was clear that he wasn't the one giving orders anymore. Manindra stood with his hands clasped at his back, Korban standing to his left and Rakesh on his right. More of Korban's men were standing around the edges of the room, their weapons held loosely but with obvious menace.

In the stillness Manindra sighed.

"I am deeply sorry that it came to this, Reuben. Your father is a great man. This will be a terrible blow to him."

"Are you insane?" Reuben said, almost seeming to spit the words out. He leaned forward in his chair, red faced with anger. "This is open war. The whole Guild will be after you for this. My family will see you dragged before the Inquisition in chains."

"Yes, I am quite sure they will try. However it's rather too late for that now, don't you think?"

Manindra spoke with an icy calm, and Rachael saw how Reuben shrank back a little, his confidence already waning.

"Fates, Manindra, what can you possibly hope to gain from this now? The Seed is awake, whether you like or not, and it's tearing open the Veil around it. Whatever secrets you meant to unlock from the thing, they are buried under a sea of rust. The whole city is contaminated," Reuben stammered, his hands tightening around the arms of his chair. "If we don't put a stop to it now, the Hearth will descend into chaos."

"You think I mean to study it?" Manindra said, incredulously. "To put an ancient wonder in a box and poke at it until it reveals some meagre insight? If I give my son a sword, I do not mean for him to study it, I mean for him to use it."

"Use it? Manindra, you can't actually be planning to open a gateway in the middle of the city. The Dream will coming flooding through, the damage will be irreversible."

"A regrettable outcome. If we had been able to secure the Seed and the girl we might have forged our gateway somewhere safely secluded. Alas, Rishi's meddling put an end to that."

Reuben's eyes seemed to grow even wider as he stared up at the old man in disbelief.

"But why? What could you possibly hope to find out there that was worth condemning an entire city to die?"

"Our salvation, my boy. There is a darkness coming, and she is the only thing that can stand in its way."

"She...?"

Reuben looked perplexed, but Rachael had the uncomfortable feeling that she already knew what Manindra meant. Then Reuben's eyes narrowed, as if a piece of a puzzle had just fallen into place.

"So that's what you were doing at Fallen Peak. Looking for one of the Dreamwalkers."

Manindra gave him a measuring look.

"Seven years, and you really think that all we did was look?" he said, pausing for a moment as if to let the words sink in. "The gateway was destroyed during our return, unfortunately. One of Rishi's little parting gifts. I have been forced to wait a very long time for a chance like this."

"You told me they were dead," Rachael said, unable to restrain herself any longer. "All of them."

Manindra's eyes flashed with cold anger as he turned to look at her.

"Yes. I lied. Never give away the truth when a lie will suffice."

"So I am connected to them," she said.

"Unfortunately for you, my dear, I only told you some lies. Yes, the Lady of The Falling Leaves still lives... But you my dear are not her daughter, her descendant, or anything else of the sort."

"Only you just said yourself that you're nothing but a lying sack of shit," Rachael spat. "Tell him, Justin. Tell him it's not true."

As she caught Justin's eye, his gaze remained cold, but only for a moment.

"Rachael..."

He shook his head, sadly.

"I can't. I'm sorry, he's right. You're not her daughter."

For a moment her breath caught. She almost felt as if she had been struck. It was strange that, even after everything that had just happened, she could still feel betrayed.

"But you told me..."

"Rachael, I promise I didn't know. I was tricked, just like you were."

"Tricked..."

She stared at him, coldly.

"By Chandra," he said.

"For what it's worth my dear, you companion truly was deceived," Manindra said, with a barely concealed smile. "Chandra's plan was most resourceful. It took me years to puzzle out precisely what he'd done. After our return from the Deep Wild, he knew that his daughter could not be safe within Guild lands. Any of the great houses would be eager to lay their hands on the child of a Dreamwalker, even if the Inquisition didn't snatch her up first."

As Manindra spoke, he turned to look at Arsha. The girl took a step back, seeming to shrink under the man's commanding gaze.

"His daughter..." she said, her voice seeming quite small. "What do you mean?"

It almost made her angry, the way the girl could seem so genuinely perplexed. She could feel the last pieces falling into place, as a cold certainty clenched at her stomach. Arsha turned to look at her, eyes wide and frightened.

"What does he mean, Rachael?"

When Rachael spoke, it was almost like she was hearing the words from a far distance. She felt numb. Disconnected. Like a passenger in her own body.

"He means you, Arsh. It was you all along."

"But how?"

"That was the question that tore at my mind for many years," Manindra said. "At first I suspected a warding, but no ward could ever have been that effective. Besides, a warding might have kept you safe from the rest of the Guild, but I knew the truth. No, he needed something more permanent."

"He traded your fates," Justin said, his voice hollow. "That's what lead me to you, in London. That's why the Seed called out to you."

Manindra nodded.

"A very old piece of Fatework. One that I had almost forgotten existed. He took all of your mother's power from you, and gave it to your ersatz sister here. Severed from your legacy, you were of no more use to me, and concealed beyond the Veil the recipient of your power would have been almost impossible to find. It wasn't until my spies in the Chamber of Foresight picked up word of the Seed that we were able to narrow our search."

"You mean your daughter told you," Rachael said, coldly.

"Not wittingly," Manindra replied, with a cruel smile. For a moment no one spoke, as Manindra turned to look over at Reuben again.

"Ironically," he continued, "in your attempt to stymie young master Ben Mahir, your blood rite undid your father's hard work, returning to you the Fate which you had been so cruelly denied."

He turned to look back at Rachael, lip twisting cruelly.

"In that, at least," he said, "this worthless vagabond proved to have some value after all."

A haunting silence fell across the room. Rachael could feel her hands clenching at her sides. Part of her wanted to scream. Part of her wanted to launch herself at the man, to tear him to pieces with her bare hands. And yet, she did nothing. That cold, numb feeling had seeped into every part of her body. She seemed to no longer be in control. She felt powerless, immobile.

When Reuben spoke, his voice was soft, almost pleading.

"Manindra... Lord Bhandari... If this is true, if one of the Dreamwalkers still lives, then we must proceed with caution. That kind of power could be incredibly dangerous. Please, let me bring this to the Inquisition. They have resources that could help you. This is a matter for the entire Guild."

Manindra turned to look at him, and shook his head, sadly.

"But as you pointed out mere moments ago, my boy, I am rather beyond reasoning with the Guild. For your father's sake I had hoped that you at least might be saved, but I think that has proven a forlorn hope."

He sighed, and turned to his son.

"Rakesh."

"Sir," Rakesh nodded.

"Make it clean."

"As you wish," Rakesh replied. At his gesture, two of Korban's men stepped forward as Reuben began to rise from the chair, a panicked expression on his face. The men caught him by the shoulders and began to force him from the bridge, in spite of his struggling.

Manindra turned to Korban and continued to speak, over the sound of Reuben's terrified pleading. "Get everyone back aboard the Jyoti, then scuttle this vessel. Be thorough. Nothing may remain."

As Reuben struggled, one of the guards calmly smashed the man's nose in. A fountain of blood came gushing down Reuben's shirt, spilling down onto the floor. Manindra turned to look with a disapproving glare. Then they were gone, and Rakesh calmly followed them out.

"We'll lay whitefire charges from bow to stern. She'll burn to cinders before she touches the ground," Korban said, barely seeming to have noticed the interruption. A moment later one of his men spoke up.

"Commander, we just received a message from the Jyoti. The Triskelion set sail from the Citadel, not long after we did. Looks like they've been following us."

"Good," Manindra said. "I'd hate for young Rishi to miss out on all of this. Just keep us far enough ahead of them, Commander."

Rachael felt Arsha clutch at her arm unsteadily, looking as if she might be about to throw up again. Even Justin, despite his outward calm, was clearly uneasy. She could see it in his eyes.

An awful silence settled over the bridge. Then Manindra turned to look them over with an imperious gaze.

"Make haste, gentlemen. London awaits us."

They were lead out onto the deck. Drifting close by, matching speed with the The Dawning Light, was a sleek white vessel with a stripe of crimson across its flank. The name 'Jyoti' was painted on the prow in letters of gold.

A rope bridge connected the decks. They were lead across, empty sky beneath their feet as the bridge swayed and clattered. Once inside they were shown to separate rooms. Rachael was thankful for that. As the door closed and the lock clicked shut, she fell down on her knees by the narrow bed, pressing her face into the sheets. The soft linen grew wet with her tears as she screamed until her throat was raw.

Three more days passed. She did not bother to dress. She refused showers. She ate when she was told to. In the empty hours she sat and stared at the far wall, as everything around her seemed to turn to grey.

After three days, they came for her. Clothes were pressed into her hands, and she put them on without any thought. Then they brought her out onto the deck. The ship was still, hanging over a familiar landscape. Manindra stood at the prow with his son at his side. Justin and Arsha were already waiting. She walked towards the railing, her movements wooden and lifeless, and looked out at the city below.

London was not the same. Somehow, she had held in her mind the idea that this one thing would not betray her. The streets that she had known so well could not possibly be reinvented like this.

What she saw was a kind of elegant, impossible chaos. The entire skyline had been overwhelmed by a forest of rust red towers that stretched into the sky like frail and gnarled fingers, desperately reaching for the clouds above.

One needle of twisted metal towered above all the others, a slender spike of iron that seemed to pierce the sky. It was impossibly tall, the highest towers of Southbank seeming like dots beside it. It took her a moment to recognise a shape in the water, at the tower's base. The twisted remains of Tower Bridge, half sunken in the Thames. The tower had grown from the spot where the Shard once stood. Nothing of that fine sliver of glass remained.

"Did we do all this?" she said, looking over at Justin. Immediately she wished she hadn't spoken. In the shock of it all, she had forgotten that he wasn't hers anymore.

She was surprised to see him turn to her and nod.

"God... It's horrible," she said.

"No. It's beautiful," he said, his eyes shining with earnest intensity. "We've changed the world. Everywhere, everyone will know about this. They can't hide, they can't forget about it. It's too big, too strange. It's... Impossible."

"Why would you want that?" she said.

"Think about it Rachael. No one will ever suffer the way we did. They'll finally understand. They'll see the world as it is."

She said nothing. She had nothing to say. She just stared at her city, so monstrously transformed, not sure if she was astonished or appalled.

She noticed the sound of the ships engines rising in pitch. They were descending, the prow beginning to gently incline towards the tallest of the spires. Towards the Seed.

Chapter 29 - Fire

They were loaded onto one of the slim white skiffs, like the one they had used in their flight from Manindra's estate, and Rakesh took the controls. Two guards went with them, but Korban remained aboard the Jyoti. Rachael was grateful for that much at least. She was less happy to see Justin setting himself down across from where she and Arsha sat.

The little skiff lifted off from the side of the larger vessel, and they began to descend towards the tower. She wondered if anything of the Shard remained. Far below, she could see that the tower of rusted iron seemed to have pushed the buildings aside, pushed up through the ground itself. It was like something that had grown. Whatever stood there before, it must have been completely destroyed. She wondered if this was the Seed they all talked about. Or maybe it was what grew from the seed. It was all so confusing.

Perhaps two-thirds of the way towards the top of the tower she saw vast archways that lead within. The mouth of each archway was easily large enough to accommodate their tiny vessel, but further in the passageway narrowed sharply. Rakesh set them down on the platform below and they disembarked. Manindra took the lead, as the guards flanked them on either side. Somehow Justin ended up between herself and Arsha, as Rakesh brought up the rear.

The narrow passageway ended in a round chamber, maybe twenty feet across, with no apparent exits. The only other opening was above them, the chamber stretching upwards into the distance, the ceiling so high that she couldn't even make it out at all.

She wondered what the point of this place was. It seemed to be nothing more than a large and empty alcove. Then she noticed the tracks running up both sides of the chamber, their insides line with teeth, like gears. A moment later she felt the room shudder, and the ground shifted slightly. Then, with the sound of heavy machinery lurching into motion, they began to rise.

As the platform gained speed, she felt Justin move closer to her.

"I'm sorry," he said, his voice kept low enough that only she would hear it over the clattering of the gears. "If I'd known, Rachael... I would have told you, I swear. But I'm going to get you out of this. That's the deal I made with Manindra. We help him, he lets you go."

"And Arsha?" she said, her voice a sharp hiss.

"She goes with him. To her mother. She'll be safe, I promise."

"If you gave a damn about either of us, you wouldn't have let none of this happen," she said.

"Rachael, there's nothing else I can do. The Guild men... They put a binding on me. I can't change. There's nothing I can do to help. Look, just... Just do as he says. You'll be OK. We'll all be OK."

Rachael said nothing. Moments later, the platform rattled to a halt. A corridor seemed to encircle the tower in either direction, light streaming in through tall windows that lined every inch of the outer wall. Ahead of them stood a grand archway and a darkened tunnel that she imagined lead toward the centre of the tower. Inevitably, it seemed, that was where they would be going.

Manindra lead them into the darkness, their footsteps echoing off the walls as they proceeded together. The way was only barely lit by the lantern that Rakesh carried. Finally, the tunnel came to an end. The chamber they entered was vast, an open circular space that was wide enough to hold a cathedral, and rose up into a high domed ceiling formed from curved spars of iron. Between the ribs of the dome it was filled with a smoky black glass that barely let any light in, save for where it had chipped and cracked away, allowing shafts of brilliant sunlight to punch through into the dark of the chamber. The floor was hard sheet iron. Everything was covered in a fine patina of rust.

At the centre of the room lay a vast pit that seemed to descend into the depths of the tower. In the middle of the pit stood a pillar, connected to the chamber by a single footbridge without railings or handholds. No guardrails lined the pit either. Just a sharp edge and a sheer drop. The pillar rose up in its centre to form a plinth, as if a statue might stand there. However the plinth was empty. There was only a shimmering in the air above it, like a heat haze.

"Is that it?" She said, unable to keep the question to herself.

"That's the gateway," Justin affirmed. "But it's not open yet. It doesn't have a destination."

"So where does it go?" she said.

"I don't know. Nowhere, I guess," he said.

Closer to, just between themselves and the bridge, was a smaller platform, more like a lectern. Like everything else it was made of rusted iron, seeming less like something crafted and more like it had grown from the floor. The top spread out like the branches of a tree, and the base melded into the floor just like roots. At the centre was a crystal, small enough to hold inside your palm, every facet a deep black.

"Gods but isn't it beautiful?" Manindra said, spreading his arms out to encompass the whole chamber as he strode towards the centre.

For a moment the old man seemed content to simply revel in the magnificent decay that surrounded him. Then his eyes settled on Justin.

"Well my boy, shall we begin?" he said, smiling broadly.

Justin nodded. Rachael found herself wondering if she only imagined his apparent unease.

"You're going with her, aren't you?" Rachael said, as Justin turned towards her. "To your Lady... To her mother."

Again that silent nod.

Arsha looked at them both with a frightened expression.

"I don't want to go, Rachael. Not without you."

"It's OK, Arsh. You're going to be OK. He'll look after you." She turned to give Justin a cold glare. "He promised."

"Children, my patience has its limits," Manindra said.

"Sure. Whatever," Rachael snarled. She turned back to Justin. "So what do we do?"

"The Seed," Justin said, nodding in the direction of the lectern like shape. "It's waiting for you."

Slowly, she approached the lectern, looking down into the heart of the black stone as she set her hands to either side of it. He was right, she could feel something inside it. A sense of something, vivid and powerful. Like a heartbeat.

Manindra turned to look out across the narrow gap. His back was turned to her, and his hands moved in front of his chest. It took Rachael a moment to realise that he was unbuttoning his coat. Rakesh stepped forward to take the long garment. Calmly, without any sign of apprehension, Manindra continued to remove his shirt.

As the garment was pulled away Rachael's breath caught in her throat. The whole of Manindra's back had been covered by a single massive scar. It was a circle, bisected by a single line. The flesh of the scar was an angry red, and she was sure that the pattern must have been burned in. She wondered how it could possibly have happened, how painful it must have been. The shape could only have been deliberate.

"Thank you, son," Manindra said, gently patting Rakesh's arm as the younger man stepped to one side.

Sensing that it was her cue, she tore her eyes away from Manindra's mutilated skin and looked down at the stone again.

"Alright," she whispered, "let's see if you're listening."

Almost instantly she could feel the pulsing energy within the stone respond, seeming to reach out to her. She pictured a doorway opening. A flicker of light appeared over the platform in the centre of the pit. It was only for an instant before it vanished again. Even that tiny flicker seemed to draw something out of her. Suddenly her whole body felt numbed with cold.

"Yes. That's it," Manindra said, the excitement in his voice breaking through her concentration.

"I don't know where it should go," she gasped, her breath seizing in her throat. She could feel herself shivering, the iron lectern under her hands barely keeping her upright as her knees shook.

"You know the place," Justin said. "Imagine it, just like I told you."

Her hands still shaking against the lectern, she closed her eyes and pictured the place he had described to her when they had sheltered in that burned out building, what seemed like years ago. Open fields, leaves turning golden. High mountain-tops in the distance. She pictured a white horse running through the forest. She could almost hear the hoof-beats.

Her eyes flicked open as the sound suddenly became all too real. Over the platform the shimmering haze had become a swirling storm of fallen leaves that burst apart as the head and shoulders of a sleek white stallion burst through. Manindra threw himself to one side as the horse cantered across the narrow iron bridge, which shook under the creature's hooves. It ran a circle around the chamber as everyone stared, aghast. Nearing them once more, the creature raised its head and whinnied as its body burst into a swirling cloud of dead-leaves that scattered across the chamber floor.

She looked around and saw that the light in the chamber had taken on a faintly golden hue. The black glass above them seemed to flicker with light. She saw wisps of smoke rising up from deep within the chasm.

Eyes bright with a kind of awe-struck wonder, Manindra took one hesitant step towards the bridge. She saw that the old man was trembling with excitement.

"Gods... How long have I waited for this?" he whispered. He almost seemed to forgotten that he was not alone. Rachael wondered if she only imagined the uneasiness on the faces of his guards.

"Come on Arsha. Your mother is waiting for you," Justin said, reaching out to take the girl's hand. When she pulled it away, he caught her by the arm instead. Rachael could see how tight his grip was as he walked her towards the portal. Suddenly Rakesh turned, drawing his sword in one smooth motion that ended with the tip of the blade hovering at Justin's throat.

For a moment Justin just stared at the two men, aghast.

"You were going somewhere?" Rakesh said, raising an eyebrow. The old man didn't even turn to look.

"Manindra, we had a deal," Justin snarled, veins standing out in his neck.

For a moment the old man said nothing, as his son regarded Justin with a cold and contemptuous glare. Then Manindra spoke with an eerie calm.

"Wait until my son and I are through the gateway, then kill them all. Leave the bodies for Rishi to find when he gets here. Return to the Jyoti and inform Commander Korban that his work is done for now. He is to rejoin with the rest of his forces and wait for contact from Dayaram."

An unearthly silence followed. Even the two guards seemed subdued as they acknowledged their orders, a grim silence settling on them both. Rachael felt as if her head was swimming. It was like someone had kicked out a stool from under her feet, and she was just waiting to hit the ground. Then Justin broke the silence.

"You crooked old bastard. You swore yourself to her service. We had a deal," Justin roared. Arsha recoiled, but his grip on her arm didn't falter.

Manindra whirled to face him.

"A deal? What kind of deal did you imagine that was then? What made you think that you could dictate terms to me, boy?" the old man bellowed at him, a colour rising in his face.

"What will you do? Kneel before my Lady with her daughter's blood on your hands?" Justin spat back at the man.

"Which one, my boy? The bastard spawn, or the poor imitation you so nobly tried to protect? Which of these two broken creatures should I cast at her feet as my offering? I do not mean to return to her court a servant. I mean to be her king. And I will not walk into her castle with the child of her false lover at my side," Manindra roared, his face crimson.

"That's what this is?" Rachael gasped. "This... All this... It's because you got turned down? Because she chose him instead of you?"

His eyes flashed livid fury as he turned to stalk towards her. She took a step back, only to feel a hand clamp down on her arm, as the nearest of the guards caught her in a steely grip. Then Manindra was upon her. Barely seeming aware of what he was doing, the old man snatched the pistol from the holster at the guard's hip, gripping the weapon by the barrel as he smashed it into her face.

She reeled back, the whole room spinning end over end as red flashes of pain blurred her sight. She felt something wet on her cheek. Her arm felt numb, where the guard held her tight, not letting her fall. Through the one eye that was not covered by a stream of blood, she saw the old man raise the pistol again.

Arsha appeared from nowhere. She caught Manindra's arm with both hands. Then he struck her across the face with his free hand and she fell to the ground. Justin barely caught her in time. He dropped to one knee, easing her weight down with him, a look of outrage on his face.

"Do you have any idea, any idea what that man has cost me? What he stole from me?" Manindra bellowed, spitting out his fury as he looked over the three of them. "Can you possibly imagine what it is, to stand before the realisation of all your dreams... To stare upon the face of a goddess, to feel her loving touch, to see her eyes as she looks upon you... And then... And then to have all of that snatched away? I watched from the shadows as she took him in, as she let my own adopted son lay his hands upon her perfect form, as she gave herself to him, utterly deceived by his liar's tongue. I saw the boy I had raised over my own blood steal from me everything I had dreamed of. And then, when that was not enough, when even to be allowed to stand in the shadow of perfection was more than I could ask for, he tires of her love, of her perfect devotion and we are forced to flee her courts. The most divine place you can imagine, and I was torn from it by Rishi Chandra's hands. And after all is done that man has the gall to tell me that he has 'rescued' me. That I should be grateful to him. Grateful for crushing everything I have struggled for. And you... You mewling infant, you wonder why I hate him?"

The sound of hard footsteps on the iron floors caught everyone's attention. Eyes flickered towards the arched entrance-way, and in the shadows of the darkened tunnel three figures could be made out, approaching with swift strides. Though barely visible in the gloom, there was enough to make out the professor's long step, Micah's pony-tail flicking out, and the shape of Ilona's cloak.

Manindra's guards turned to raise their rifles, but before any of them could bring a weapon to bear a shot rang out and a blinding flash filled the darkened tunnel. Manindra's cry of pain was loud and sharp as a crimson spray erupted from his leg. He fell forwards and his son barely caught his arm in time to support the old man. Rakesh looked up, furious, as Rishi stormed towards them with a smoking revolver clutched in one outstretched hand.

"You will never touch my daughter again!" Rishi roared, face twisted in fury as his voice echoed through the chamber. Already Manindra's men had their weapons trained on him, but they were being watched in turn. Micah held the lightning ballista tight, the stock tucked into the crook of his shoulder, one eye closed as he kept the weapon levelled. Ilona had the other man covered, her gauntleted hand outstretched in what seemed like an almost contemptuous gesture. But looking closely, Rachael could see the strain on their faces. There was sweat on their brows and a nervousness in their eyes.

Gasping for breath, Manindra's face twisted into a crooked mockery of a smile.

"My lost son returns to me."

Rishi ignored him as he went to help his daughter up, but Arsha fixed him with a furious glare. He stopped, all his assuredness vanishing in the face of his daughter's accusing eyes. She stood up, a little unsteady.

"He told us what you did," Arsha said. "He told us everything. About my mother. About how you used Rachael to protect me. Is it... Is it true?"

He was silent. It took him a moment to meet her gaze, and when he did Rachael saw a sadness in his eyes that seemed as if it had been there for many years. Like an old wound, scarred over now, but still there underneath it all.

"Yes," he said, heavily. "It's true."

Rachael heard the coldness in her own voice when she spoke.

"Why me?" Why did it have to be me?"

"It was chance. Just chance. I took Arsha to a Fateworker I knew... Not one of the Order; a shaman, from the Skivir tribes. I knew there was a way to take Arsha's Fate and bind it to another. One other person, alike enough to fool the weave of Fate, but entirely unconnected to my daughter. What would you have done in my place? To know that all this misery would fall upon the one person you loved more than any other... And that you had the power to take it away, if only you would give it to someone you had never known in your life, and never would."

"You ruined my life to keep her safe," Rachael hissed through clenched teeth, climbing to her feet.

"Yes. To keep my daughter safe. How could I have chosen any differently?"

"It wasn't right," she said, taking a step back, bringing herself closer to the pedestal, and the bridge beyond.

"Of course it wasn't right," he cried, his voice somewhere between a shout and a sob. "Do you think I ever imagined, for even an instant, that it was right? I am not a good man, Rachael. I will spend my whole life bearing the weight of my sins. Why do you think I came for you? Why do you think I went through all of this, trying to keep you safe? This blood is on my hands. It's all that I can do."

She could see the pain there, plainly written on his face, but she didn't care. It was his pain, his way of pretending to be righteous, and she couldn't feel any sympathy for that.

"It's not enough. You don't get to just... Just buy it off. Like it's something you can put right, like there's some way back. My dad walking out, because he couldn't stand that his daughter was crazy? My mum trying to care for me alone, with everything falling apart? And all of it just... Just because of what you done. You think you can fix any of that? You can think you can make that up to me?"

For a moment there was silence. She saw the looks in their eyes as they watched her with horrified expressions.

"I can't change those things, Rachael," he said, his voice heavy. "I can't ever undo them. But I can try to make it better for you, if you'll let me."

"Because you feel bad," she screamed. "Because this is the way you tell yourself you're OK. It's not about me. It's not about what you've done. It's just about telling yourself that you're trying to make it better."

She took another step back, brushing the edge of the pedestal.

As she steadied herself with one hand, she felt the hard black crystal of the Seed. As soon as she touched it, she felt the warmth within. The pulsing heartbeat. It seemed so easy. Like she'd done it before. She felt the Seed answer, as she reached out to it. There was a warm, tingling sensation in her arm. A feeling of something moving under her skin.

She saw their expressions first, the surprise and the fear as the swirling leaves that surrounded the gateway slowly turned to dust. Only a shimmer remained in the air. The link had been broken. When she raised her hand, she saw only a thin covering of rust on her palm, but where the black crystal had nestled on the pedestal there was only an empty niche. She saw the horrified look in the professor's eyes.

"Rachael... What have you done?" he said, his tone hushed and fearful.

"Manindra was right," she said, scarcely bothering to look at any of them. "He was the only one who told me the truth. I never mattered to anyone. I was just useful."

The edge of the chasm was barely a few feet away. Past that, the plinth and the gateway. She could feel a connection to it, beating inside of her. It was like a hole in the world, reaching out to nothing. A road with no destination.

Slowly, Arsha took a step towards her. Justin moved with her, hovering like the faithful protector that he was. It was so strange, seeing that devotion turned towards someone else. She felt it twisting inside, desperately longing to be the one person he wanted to care for. But some part of her saw now what a lie it had all been. It had never mattered who stood in that girl's place. It had never been about her. He just needed someone, anyone to protect.

"You're wrong," Arsha said, looking her in the eyes. "You do matter. You matter to me."

Rachael shook her head.

"You think that, but it's not true. I never gave you anything that someone else couldn't have. I was just convenient. For both of you, that's all it ever was."

She took another step away, and Arsha's eyes widened in surprise.

"Rachael... Your hand."

The change was as sudden as it was natural. She felt the pulse of the Seed quickening inside of her. It was like something drawing breath. There was no pain, even as the blades burst through her skin. Just a sensation of warmth as the rusted iron gauntlet formed itself around her hand. She held it up to the light, flexing her fingers, surprised at how easily it moved. Set in the palm was the glistening black crystal, seeming to glow from deep within. Somewhere in those inky depths, she could feel the Seed pulsing with life.

"Rachael, please. You don't know what it is you're playing with," the professor said.

"Yeah I do," she said, the words coming as a surprise, even to herself. It was so easy. Almost as if she had done it before. She touched the ground lightly, the tip of one gauntleted finger brushing against the metal. Where she had touched, the rust began spreading like fire. She turned to run. The bridge was ahead of her, and then the gateway. She ran, feeling the iron grating of the bridge twist and moan as the rust consumed it. She could hear other footsteps, shouted cries as someone gave chase, but she did not look back. With a terrible sound of crumpling metal the bridge fell away behind her. The heat haze of the gate erupted around her, growing wider, opening up to take her in. She reached out a hand and felt a ripple in the air.

And then she was gone.

Chapter 30 - Howl

It was Arsha who moved first, dashing out onto the narrow bridge, barely a few yards from Rachael's heels. Justin tried to follow her, but as he reached the bridge it was already falling away. As the surface collapsed beneath Arsha's feet she threw herself forward, barely landing on the edge of the platform. The gateway rippled with a blaze of burning light as Rachael passed into the shimmering haze and disappeared. Arsha rolled to her feet and threw herself towards the gateway without any hesitation, as it began to shrink in on itself. Justin felt a howl of rage explode from inside of him as Arsha's outstretched fingertips connected with the haze, and then she too vanished. From across the chasm he could only watch the empty space in the air where the gateway had been.

He was only dimly aware of what was happening around him. He turned to watch as Rakesh sprang to his feet, catching Micah across the jaw with a solid blow that dropped the man to his knees. He saw the professor turn to level his pistol, even as one of

Manindra's guards took aim at him. The man's finger had barely touched the trigger when a bolt of lightning arced out from Ilona's hand. The guard staggered back, even as his companion smashed the butt of a rifle hard into the woman's guts.

It all seemed so distant. So empty. He couldn't understand it, how they could be so focused on their own pathetic squabbles in the midst of all this. The anger began to rise in him. He could feel the blood pounding in his ears. He could feel the wolf in the back of his mind, snarling, howling to be let loose. He felt it strain against the binding, like chains wrapped tight around him.

Then he remembered. High halls, a roof of woven branches. A mask of leaves, hiding a beautiful face. A delicate touch, one finger caressing his cheek. The smell of her, like the freshness after the rain. The change. The way that it had first come over him, how he breathed in as a man and breathed out as a creature. How he had first seen the world through different eyes. How he had known, truly known every cadence of the wolf's cry. How the scent, the deep, true scent of everything had opened up for him. But most of all he remembered the overpowering hunger. The urge to hunt and kill. The savage power of it, the way the smell of blood made the stomach growl with expectation. He felt the bindings strain ever tighter, but in that moment there was only the howling of the wolf as the memory overcame him. It tore through the binding, snarling and howling. He changed without a thought. The distance to the first of the guards vanished in the blink of an eye. Then there was only the smell of fear, the sound of a scream and the taste of blood splashing across his tongue as his teeth sank into the flesh and cartilage of the man's throat. Too soon, too quickly the man's body fell limp. The second guard bringing his weapon to bear, at his master's insistent urgings. Too late, too slow... Too human. The thunder, the acrid smell of burning, the ripple in the air as the bullet passed over him and then the soft meat of the man's thigh, parting so easily around his fangs. The clatter of a fallen weapon and another scream of pain. It was all so easy.

A flash of light as the lightning passed inches from his face. The change came quickly, his thoughts flowing so effortlessly from the wolf to the hawk. Small, swift, sharp. The air rippling around his wings. The lightning streaking past, too slow, too slow. Then the woman's face before him, the perfect moment when her eyes widened with fear. Her eyes, so pretty, so sweet. He let talons flick out, scoring soft skin. Saw her reel back as he beat the air. One eye was a river of blood.

The smell of it brought the wolf out once more. He felt the unyielding iron of the floor beneath his claws. The man in the red coat darting forwards with bright steel in his hands. The ringing sound as the blade cut the air, passing through the space where he had been barely an instant before. Springing to one side, darting, circling. From the corner of his eye he caught the shape of the gun as the professor took aim. Another side-step, fast and low. The thunder rang out but he was too swift, and the man in red made an easy shield to put between himself and the professor's fire.

Steel flashed as he darted forwards, jaws snapping at empty air as the man in red stepped back in a sliding motion. He felt the cold sensation of the blade as it bit into his flank, pain flowering along the length of the wound. Not deep, a scratch, too little to slow him down. Another side-step, darting in to snap at the man's heel. Again the blade flashed, but this time he was expecting it. The slightest twist of the neck to close his jaw around the hand that gripped the blade. The man's cry of pain, overtaken by the ringing of the steel as it bounced across the iron floor and span off into the emptiness at the centre of the chamber.

Once more the thunder rang out. He felt the bullet pass, close enough to tear a ripple of fur in its wake. In an instant he turned towards the sound. The professor. He could smell the man, a smell that made his stomach churn in anger, in hatred. The man had one eye closed, sighting down the barrel of his gun. Too slow. Hind legs coiled and released, the air flowing around him. Jaws wide, longing to taste the man's flesh.

And for a moment that face was all he could see. Blinded by rage, he hadn't noticed the professor's companion throwing himself in the way. With one hand Micah pushed the professor back as his other arm darted into the space where the man's throat should have been. Jaws closed around thick hide, teeth dug into the flesh beneath and a cry of pain rang through his ears. Muscles tightened as he sank his teeth deeper. If he couldn't have the professor he would take this instead, would make the man suffer for stealing his prey. He could smell the adrenaline rushing off the man in waves, hear the cries of pain as he twisted his head back and forth.

When the thunder sounded out again it was as if the whole world rang like a bell. For a moment everything seemed to stop. Then the fire exploded through him, the searing bursts of pain as each shot tore into his body. He tried to run, tried to change, tried will some movement into his own limbs, but his body did not seem to be under his control. It was as if all his strings had been cut. He skidded, tumbled, and for the briefest of moments he was aware of the edge of the chasm. Then, falling, falling down. A gentle lightness embraced him as the world began to fade into black.

Half glimpsed through one eye, Ilona saw the wolf crumple as the first shots struck true. Even as the body hit the ground, Rishi did not stop firing until the impact of the last shot had sent the bloodied grey form tumbling over the edge of the chasm.

Rishi lowered the revolver, a cloud of gun smoke slowly parting around him as he moved towards the edge of the chasm, every muscle tense with caution.

She could feel the heat of the metal beneath her cheek. She felt the ground shudder, as a tremor ran through the building. One side of her face burned as if it had been set alight. She reached up to wipe the blood from her eyes, but as her fingertips brushed her face she felt the loose edge of the skin and the surging fire seemed to burst through her skull.

Dimly, she heard Micah's voice. His strong hands were lifting her upright. She caught a glimpse of his face. There was something comforting about his look of distraught concern.

"Come on now, let me see," he said. Carefully he pried her hands away from the side of her face and studied the damage.

She could feel her breath returning. Her heart no longer seemed as if it was trying to rip itself out of her chest. As she waited for Micah to examine her, another tremor ran through the building. She heard the sound of cracking glass.

Micah's shoulders slumped as a sigh of relief escaped him.

"You're OK. The eye's intact. Fates, there's a lot of blood though."

"It's alright," she said. "Head wounds... Always bleed a lot."

Micah nodded as he shrugged of his coat and pulled his tunic away. The cloth tangled around his shoulders, and he yanked harder until it tore. She wondered if she should buy him another. Bundling up the fabric, he pressed it to the wound. She let out a gasp of pain as the fire exploded into life once more. She forced herself to draw deep and even breaths. Slowly she gathered up the pain and locked it away inside. Hands shaking, she took hold of the cloth and forced it against the gash.

"Thank you," she said, still breathless. Then she noticed his arm, teeth marks scored deeply into the flesh. There was blood, but it seemed as if he hadn't noticed any pain at all. Like a curious child, Micah reached out to poke at the wound. Immediately his face crumpled, and she saw him bite his lip.

"It's OK," he said after a moment, though his breathing was strained. "I mean, it's not too deep. I can still use the arm. Nothing Milima can't bandage up."

"You're sure?" she said, her expression doubtful.

"I'll be fine," Micah said, with a grimace.

"OK. See what you can do for him," she said, nodding at one of the fallen guards. It was obvious from the briefest glance that there was nothing to be done for the other. The sea of blood around his fallen body told it all. Already it was beginning to drip over the edge, into the empty expanse in the centre of the tower.

"And hurry," she added. "I don't think this place is going to last much longer."

The guard's leg was bleeding badly. She watched as Micah did his best to put pressure on the wound, stripping off the man's tunic to use as a tourniquet. It was enough for now, but Ilona could see that he would need a surgeon, and soon. The man's face was pale, his breathing shallow and hurried. Micah caught his eye, clearly trying to keep his expression reassuring.

"What's your name?" Micah said, somehow forcing his usual cheerfulness to show through.

"Wrel," the man gasped. Though his voice was weak, his accent was no less distinctive.

"You're Kalvari?" Micah asked. Wrel just nodded weakly.

"Beautiful place. My father took me there once. Come on, let's get you on your feet. It was a business trip. We were settling some sort of legal dispute in Varashen... Or was it Rannar?"

As Micah talked calmly, keeping the man distracted, Ilona forced herself to her feet and looked around. Rishi was standing by the edge of the chasm, looking down at where Justin had fallen. Rakesh was kneeling over his father, checking the wound on Manindra's leg.

Then Rishi turned and gestured at Rakesh with the still smoking revolver.

"Get him up. You're leaving. Micah, help the other one. He can go with them."

"Professor, I don't know if we should move him yet. Maybe we can sort out a stretcher, or..."

"Get him up," Rishi growled sharply, cutting Micah off. The younger man scowled, but let it be. Rakesh said nothing. His eyes surveyed them all, cold and sharp, but he wasn't about to argue. Instead he turned to his father again.

"Father? Can you stand?"

With a grunt, the elder Bhandari rose halfway to his feet before pushing his son aside. For a moment it seemed as if the old man would fall, but he regained his balance and stood tall.

"I'll tear down the sky before I hand him what's mine." Manindra snarled, glaring at Rishi. The professor didn't even bother to meet the old man's gaze.

"Rakesh," Rishi said, levelly, "I'm giving you a chance. Take your father home."

Rakesh didn't say a word. He just nodded and began walking, forcing Manindra to move with him. The old man didn't seem to have the strength left to struggle. Manindra's eyes burned with hate, but he didn't say another word.

Ilona stepped closer, laying a hand on the professor's shoulder. She heard a rumbling from far below, and the floor shook beneath them. She was sure the tremors were getting stronger. She heard a sound above them, like thick ice cracking.

"Rishi, we should be going as well."

He shook his head.

"Rishi, you can't stay. This place is falling apart," she said, sternly.

He looked around, and her eyes met his properly for the first time since the fighting. There was something wild and desperate that had awakened inside of him. Something terrifying.

"Can't I?" he snapped. For a moment she thought of the sound of the wolf's jaws closing. "My daughter is in there. I'm not leaving until I get her free."

"Rishi, we can't."

"Yes we can. I'll find a way," he snarled, stalking towards the pit. "Go on. Get everyone clear."

"Rishi, please."

Even as the words left her mouth she knew how they sounded. Cold. Disdainful. She had never known how to beg, even when she needed to.

He ignored her, walking towards the pit and the lectern. One hand traced the hard metal around the indentation where the Seed had lain. He barely seemed to notice as the tower shuddered once more.   He ignored her even as she approached, standing at his shoulder.   Finally she laid a gentle hand on his arm.   Another rumbling sound filled the chamber.

"Rishi," she whispered in the silence that followed.

He turned, fury flashing in his eyes, an outraged "What?" forming on his lips.   There was a loud 'crack' as her gauntleted fist struck him across the jaw.   Rishi swayed for a second, and then his whole body simply went limp.   Moving quickly, Ilona caught him as he fell, struggling under his weight.   She pulled the professor's arm across her shoulders and held him about the waist.

"Fates, 'Lona, are you crazy?" Micah yelled at her.

"No," she said.   "But he might be.   You know we can't stop this. We don't even know where to start."

Micah didn't seem to know what to say to that.   He looked at the platform, at the empty air where the gateway had been.   As they both watched, another tremor ran through the building.   Sadly, he shook his head.

"Be safe.   Both of you," he muttered, wretchedly.

"Fates willing," Ilona said.   "Come on."

To his credit, Micah didn't waste time.   He hauled the injured guard to his feet and made for the exit at good speed.

At the archway Ilona turned and looked back one last time at the empty air over the platform.   Once again she heard the rumbling from below.

"I'm so sorry," she whispered to the empty air, as she turned and walked away.

Chapter 31 - Sisters

It was the feeling of cool grass against her skin that pulled her back to consciousness. Her face was pressed to the ground, and she breathed in the smell of the damp earth.

Peering through the grass, Arsha could make out a dark blue sky, half covered in cloud. The sun had already dipped below the rooftops. The air was chill and a breeze gently rippled through the greenery, whispering in the branches of the trees.

She sat up and took in her surroundings. She was in a park of sorts, surrounded by a black wrought-iron fence with the paint all peeled off. She was close to a path that ran across the park, from the gateway nearby to the distant fence, shrouded in darkness. Beyond the fence she saw rows of blocky grey towers, ugly shapes that clustered over the skyline.

There was noise, a constant, distant buzz of movement, the sound of great machines of some unknown purpose, but she could not see any of it. The sounds seemed to come to her from far away. Near to, all was still save for the breeze.

Arsha stood and tried to brush off the mud and wet grass as best she could. She looked around uneasily, but could see no clear sign of where to go. There was no evidence of movement or life. Eventually she picked a direction at random and set off down the path.

Ahead she could make out some lights burning with a yellow haze in the misty air. They illuminated a rough rectangle on the ground, edged with logs and covered in a carpet of woodchips, surrounding various pieces of play equipment. The designs were slightly unusual, but she could pick out familiar shapes. Swings, a climbing frame, a merry-go-round; all rusted and old, the brightly coloured paint peeling and flaking from the metal.

The playground seemed to be empty. Cautiously, she crossed the border of rough hewn logs and approached the swings. The chain jingled as she nudged the seat with one knee. In the fading sound of the chiming metal she felt certain that she heard another, like someone laughing. A little girl, maybe.

Then she heard the creaking of a metal axle. She turned around to see that the merry-go-round was moving. Though there was no one pushing it, the metal frame turned faster and faster. As she watched, a shimmer in the air seemed to form around it. She could make out the shape of two figures, ghostly and translucent. A fair skinned woman with long blonde hair tied back in a pony-tail, holding onto the bars with her feet resting on the lip, leaning back as far as she could go as the wheel span. She had her head flung back, eyes bright with laughter. The other figure was sitting in the centre of the merry-go-round, holding tight to the bars, and staring up the woman in wide eyed wonder. A young girl with a pretty face framed by that same bright blonde hair.

Then the image faded, and the rusted iron wheel began to slow to a creaking halt.

"She loved the merry-go-round. That was her favourite."

Arsha turned at the sound of her voice. Rachael was sat on one of the swings, hands clasping the chains, rocking gently back and forth. She was looking at the empty merry-go-round as if seeing something else entirely.

"Swings was good too. She'd try to push me higher and higher. Kept saying that one day I'd go all the way over the top. But she loved the merry-go-round. She'd make me hold on tight, there in the middle, and push it as fast as she could. She'd be laughing so loud and everyone would stare at her, but she just didn't care."

For a moment Arsha couldn't think of anything to say. It was all so strange and so perfectly ordinary at once. She couldn't escape the feeling that she was a voyeur, seeing things that she had no right to.

"Rachael... Where are we?" she said.

"This is the park, where she always took me. When I was little. She was happy then. But it got worse, the more I got worse. And Mum and Dad kept arguing, fighting. It got so bad, I'd just get out the house. They wouldn't even notice I were gone. I'd come out here for the quiet. Late at night I could be alone, a little."

Looking out over the empty park, Arsha thought, for a moment, that she caught a glimpse of a girl of maybe ten years, sitting alone on one of the benches. A thin jacket pulled tight around her shoulders and a sketchbook on her lap. Then it was gone.

"But he left in the end. Didn't he?" Arsha said, quietly.

Rachael nodded.

"Yeah. I remember, I actually told myself it was good. That things'd be better, with him gone. But I missed him so much. At nights I'd be lying in bed, thinking about the way he smelled when he came back in from work, all covered in oil and stuff from the garage. He'd come in late sometimes and kiss me goodnight. I couldn't understand it, how I could miss him no matter how much I wanted to hate him."

Arsha nodded, her mouth too dry to speak.

"But Mum... She fell apart. It wasn't just the money, or looking after me. It was him. She hated him, and she missed him. Every day. It was..."

Rachael tailed off. Arsha noticed that the girl wasn't looking at the playground anymore, but at something in the distance. One of the tall buildings that formed the skyline, a dark blocky shape eerily reminiscent of a tombstone.

"So then I'd come out here to be alone again. To be away from her. From that place. There were older kids that hung out round here. I started hanging out with them. They'd score ciders and forties. It wasn't much, but I guess it didn't take a lot to get me smashed. I liked it, because it helped me to forget about everything else. Some of the kids liked to run. They'd show me how to do flips and drops and stuff on the climbing frames. Taught me stuff about 'parkour' and all that. We'd get drunk and make each other do stupid dares and stuff. Sometimes, it was like things were all right."

"Is that it?" Arsha said, looking across at the distant building. "The place where you lived?"

"McAllen Estate. It's horrible there. Just four blocks of flats and a little square in the middle. I hated it."

Arsha considered this for a moment, still feeling all too much like she was falling with no safety line.

"I... I think we should go there," she said.

"I can't go back there."

Rachael shook her head firmly. "It's not... I didn't even close the door."

"When?" Arsha said.

"Nothing. It don't matter," Rachael mumbled, her voice barely audible.

"Rach, you have to take me back there. I need to see."

"No. You don't. You think you want to, but you don't. No one wants to see. They just look past you and pretend it's not like it seems. Because it's easier than knowing what really goes on around them."

"So show me," Arsha said, firmly. "You have to take me there. Please Rachael, you have to show me."

"Says who?" the girl snapped back at her with a sudden fire. "I don't have to take you nowhere. I don't care. I don't want you asking all these questions. I don't want none of this."

"Please, Rachael. You have to," she said, hearing the desperation in her own voice.

"Why? Why should I?" Rachael shouted, leaping up from the swing to stand with her fists clenched at her side.

"Because I need to know," Arsha said, the words catching in her throat. "Because I'm your sister and I need to know why you're hurting like this. Because we made a promise."

Rachael looked at her with cold, penetrating eyes. It was a vicious look, taking her measure, searching for some sign of motive. Of weakness.

"Yeah. Sure. Come on then, I'll show you," the girl snarled as she stalked away across the empty park.

Soon enough they moved from damp grass to tarred black roads with faded lines painted across their surfaces. Street signs clustered every corner, some twisted at odd angles or painted over with scrawled markings. Graffiti adorned almost every spare inch of wall. Here and there a withered husk of a tree or a bush grew, all showing signs of mistreatment.

At one intersection Arsha looked to the side to see a mangy looking dog wander across the road. It had a collar, but it could not have been fed properly in weeks.

They made a final turning and the cluster of tombstone buildings stood before them, four identical towers arranged in a square. As they approached Rachael's footsteps slowed. Arsha saw that the girl's hands were shaking. They stopped at the entrance to the courtyard at the centre of the four towers.

Everything was grey. The buildings were some sort of stone, formed seamlessly. From the centre of the courtyard she could see the tiered walkways rising up around them, lined with iron railings, the paint long since peeled. Stairs lead up on each side, all exposed to the open air. Along each walkway she saw a row of doors. Once they might have been blue, but the paint had long since faded away, or been covered by layers of graffiti.

Foul odours arose from blotchy stains on the floors and walls, some obviously recent. The freshest stains were the only thing that seemed new. Piles of shiny black bags overflowed a yellow container, their rotting contents spilling out where the black skin had split and peeled back.

"What kind of place is this?" Arsha said, looking around.

"Council flats. Hundreds like 'em, all over this city. They just sort of stamp 'em out, like machinery."

"Why?"

"It's where you live, if you ain't got nothing else. If you ain't lucky enough to have a good job, or good education, or whatever other bollocks it is they want from you. Right face, right clothes, all that."

Arsha nodded. She'd seen places like this before in some of the larger cities she'd been to. Factory workers houses, built by the dozen in identical rows. Narrow, crowded buildings, sometimes holding a family on every floor, or so her dad had told her. She felt the sting of the memory, and pushed it aside.

"I hated it here," Rachael said. "Next door was always drunk, and upstairs you could hear 'em shouting all hours. Some of the other kids were alright, but most of 'em were right horrible."

She tailed off.

"Well it don't matter. It's not home now."

Suddenly the girl turned, and began to walk away.

"Go see whatever you want to," Rachael growled. "I'm outta here."

As the girl swept past her, Arsha wondered if she only imagined that Rachael was holding back tears. She turned, reaching to grasp at the girl's hand, and as she looked back the way they had come she saw something that seemed to turn her body to stone.

Where before there had been a city, stretching out into the far distance, now she saw only a wall of grey, almost like fog. Something deeply unnatural, utterly impossible. It was like staring at nothing at all. Where it met the street and the surrounding buildings there was only a ragged edge, as if whatever was beyond that grey wall had simply been torn away. Where it touched the surface, the road was crumbling, the fragments flying off into nothingness as if swept up by a violent wind. The buildings too were being eaten by the grey wall. Trees, street signs, all shredded into chaff, an inch at a time.

"What is it?" Rachael said, her voice trembling.

"I don't know," Arsha said. "But it's getting closer."

"What's that mean?"

"I think it's falling apart. This world. Rachael, you created this. Everything here, you made this when we went through the gateway. It's the only thing that makes sense. This can't be the real London... It doesn't even look like this anymore. When you went through, you made this place."

Rachael's mouth pressed into a hard line.

"Alright smart-mouth, so where do we go now?" she growled.

"Inside, I think." Arsha said.

"No. I ain't going back in there. No way."

"Rachael, we have to. It's the only place left."

"Why? Why do you keep... why can't you just leave it alone?" Rachael said, her voice rising to a shriek as she rounded on Arsha angrily. "You keep asking all these stupid questions, keep pushing at stuff and it's not right. You don't belong here and you don't have no right to... I never wanted to go back to any of this. I didn't want to remember. I didn't want to."

Flexing her hands in agitation, Rachael began to pace in circles. She swung a vicious kick at a loose piece of stone, which sailed into the wall of empty grey, vanishing instantly.

Arsha said nothing. She just turned and began walking towards the nearest stairs.

"Hey. Where you going?" Rachael called after her.

"Inside," Arsha said, with a sullen shrug. "Come along if you want to."

"Hey. Hey don't go. Don't leave me out here," Rachael called after her. At first, Arsha kept on walking. Then at the bottom of the stairs she turned and looked back.

Rachael was on her knees, her hands tangled in her hair, face twisted in a look of torment. The girl seemed to be frozen against the hard ground like some awful statue. Arsha slowly walked towards her, stomach twisting nervously as she knelt by Rachael's side.

"I don't know why you're doing this. I didn't want you here," Rachael whispered, her voice hoarse.

"I think you did," Arsha said, gently.

"Why do you keep saying that. Why do you keep acting like I planned all this. Like I ever wanted any of this?"

"I didn't mean that. Rachael, I..." Arsha looked down at the paving stones and swallowed a lump in her throat. "I know you didn't want this. I didn't either. Fates, Rachael... When I think about what happened back there. About those people getting killed. About those men that were after you. About Dad... What he did. It's like my heart's going to collapse, like it'll just crumple in on itself completely. And I can't do anything to stop it. I'm here with you, and I'm trying to make sense of all this. And I need you. I need you to help me find a way for us to get out of here."

Rachael looked up, just enough for Arsha to see her eyes under the tangle of her hair.

"What makes you think I want to get out of here?" the girl whispered.

For a moment, Arsha couldn't think of anything to say.

"Where else am I supposed to go? I tried being part of Justin's world, but I never belonged there. I tried being part of your world, and all I did was make things worse for you. So where do I belong now?"

"You know what?" Arsha said, "I don't know. I'm just some stupid little kid who's spent her whole life hanging off her Daddy's arm. So I don't know what comes after this. Fates, Rachael, I just found out that I'm not even human. How am I supposed to answer something like that, when I don't even know where I belong anymore? But I'm going to find out. And you're coming with me."

Rachael looked up at her, eyes wide with fear. The girl didn't say a word, but when Arsha stood and offered her hand, Rachael took it. They walked together towards the stairs. Rachael lead them up to the third floor, where a long row of doorways stretched out ahead of them. At the end of the row, one door stood ever so slightly ajar.

The crack was wide enough to reveal a glimpse of a filthy beige carpet and a few scattered cigarette ends. As they approached she caught a breath of foul air that slipped through.

"I can't," Rachael said, her voice choking off into a whimper.

Arsha said nothing. She just took her sister's hand in her own, and with the other she pushed at the door, swinging it wide open to reveal the room beyond.

The apartment was vile. The carpet bore innumerable stains. Tiny brown and black circles dotted the fabric, each tailed by a little streak of grey ash like shooting stars. A battered couch with threadbare cushions faced a flashing box full of colours and light and noise. A clock ticked away on a mantelpiece, next to a framed photograph with cracked glass. The photograph showed a woman and a girl. Rachael and her mother, just as they had been when she glimpsed them on the merry-go-round. There was a man with them, his blonde hair cut razor short, a smile on his face. The frame was nearly concealed by a dozen empty cans, each reeking of sour beer. More empty cans littered every surface, and more still were strewn across the floor. Layers of peeling wallpaper covered the walls. In some places the paper had been scratched or worn right through to the plaster.

The woman lay sprawled across the threadbare couch. One arm trailed to the floor, knuckles brushing the carpet. Between the fingers a cigarette had burned to a stub, leaving tiny red marks on her pale skin. The tips of her fingers were stained a dirty yellow. She wore a green sweater, one sleeve rolled up. Her arm was pitted with a thousand tiny scars, and a fresh scab seemed to have formed there just recently. Her mouth hung slightly open, yellowed teeth as uneven as the buildings outside. The lips were painted a deep crimson. Blonde hair sprayed out across the arm of the couch in a shower of gold.

The woman's eyelids were open but the eyes were rolled back, showing only a ghastly white. In spite of how monstrously transformed it all was, Arsha still recognised the face of the woman in the photograph. It was older and harder, but the same shape still lurked beneath the layers of decay.

On the table lay the contents of a small cloth bag. A length of clear tubing, a metal spoon with its neck bent at a sharp angle, a tiny packet of white powder and a clear glass syringe.

She felt Rachael's hand tighten around hers. Nails dug into her skin, and a second later Rachael was doubled over, violently expelling the contents of her stomach onto the pitted carpet. Horrified, Arsha could only stare at the scene in front of her. She could scarcely understand what had happened. She had only the vaguest sense, things half overheard, pieces that gathered together, buzzing at the back of her head like angry wasps that she desperately wished to ignore. She did not want to know, did not want to understand. Everything before her was simply too horrible, too nightmarish to be allowed to be real. She wanted to shut it out, to step back from the room, slam the door and run away from it forever.

Rachael continued to cough and retch. Arsha watched with horrified fascination as the puddle of vomit inched towards her boots.

"Rachael... Oh Fates, Rachael... What happened?" she said, as the girl drew ragged breaths.

"I did. It was all because of me. Dad never sticking around, and everything that happened after. It was me."

Eyes swelling with tears, Arsha fell to her knees, heedless of the vile liquid that squelched into her trousers. Still holding Rachael's hand in hers, she put her other hand to her sister's shoulder and pulled her close, their heads resting together.

"Rachael, you can't blame yourself for this. Not for this."

"There's no one else," Rachael said, her voice cracking. For a moment Arsha could only stare at her, head swimming.

"There's me," she said, at last. "If this really happened just because of you, because you were different, then it wasn't really you at all. It was me. My Fate. My fault. I'm the one to blame for everything that happened. Rachael you know it's true. If you have to hate someone, hate me. Not yourself."

"No. No, it can't be your fault."

Rachael shook her head, her eyes squeezed shut.

"Why not? You said it yourself. If this is all because of what my dad had to do to protect me, then I'm the one who should be responsible."

"But you can't be. It has to be me."

"Why? Why does it have to be you? Rachael, this doesn't make any sense."

Rachael drew a shuddering breath.

"Because I wanted this. Because I wanted her to die. I hated her so much. For what she did. For what she was."

Rachael looked up at her with eyes overflowing with tears.

"It was like she was hardly ever here sometimes. She'd come home in the middle of the night. I'd hear her screaming and crying and throwing things around. She'd drink and drink and fall over on the couch. Most nights I'd wait until it was quiet... 'til I knew she'd gone to sleep. I'd come out and put a blanket on her. Try to clean up some. She pissed herself sometimes. If I could manage it, I'd leave her skirt and stuff in the tub, run some water to rinse it. But she never said thank you. Not even once. Like, it didn't matter. She didn't even care. Or like it was just something I was supposed to do. And then she'd bring these guys home... and they were always horrible. I just hid mostly, stayed in my room. I... I crawled under the bed with my pillows so I wouldn't have to hear. And then she started bringing the needles home instead. And I knew what it was cos the kids on the block all talked about it, talked like they all knew about her. There were stuff they called her... it made me so mad. I'd fight 'em for saying it, kick the lot of 'em in the faces. Got in so many fights. But it just made me hate her even more, because it was true. All the stuff they said about her, the names, it was all true."

Rachael sat back on her haunches and looked up at the body on the couch.

"When I found her... I didn't know what to do. I just... I packed a few things and walked out the door. Didn't even close it after me. I just left her lying there. I just left her."

There was blood on the back of Arsha's hand where Rachael's fingers had squeezed tight enough to break the skin. A darkly glistening red film joined the places where their hands met, the blood slowly thickening, sealing them together as it dried.

"When I found her... when I found her, I thought 'Thank God.' I felt... happy. Cos it was over. Cos it was..."

Tears rolled down the girl's cheeks as the words spilled out in a wretched gasp.

"I was happy. I was happy that she was dead, because I wouldn't have to hate her any more."

Scarcely able to breath, Arsha pulled her sister into a tight embrace, feeling the girl's body shudder in her arms as she gasped and sobbed. Around them the wallpaper peeled and rotted, falling away in damp chunks. The carpet withered back to the concrete floor, which slowly crumbled away. Furniture collapsed into worm-ridden piles. On the couch the woman's body shrivelled, the skin and flesh rotting away until only bones remained, as the cloth of the couch fluttered away on a foul wind that burst in through the crumbling walls. The winds tore the ceiling away, and Arsha saw that the whole building was gone, only the room remaining, falling to pieces around them as the world collapsed into endless grey.

"Sometimes... sometimes I'd come home and find she'd left dinner out. It was just sausages or something with canned spaghetti and stuff. She'd put it all in a bowl with cling-film on. And she'd leave a glass of juice out. Like she was still trying to be a mother." Rachael choked back a sob. "She was trying. She just... She just didn't know how."

Arsha pressed her sister's body closer.

"Rachael... Rachael, I'm so sorry. Fates, I wish there was something I could say. I just..." she paused, struggling to draw breath. "I'm here. I'm here," she whispered, lips pressed closed to her sister's ear. In answer, Rachael shook her head and pushed her away.

"No," she said, her voice little more than a wet gasp. "No, you have to go. It's all coming apart. You can't stay, Arsh."

"I can't leave you here," she said.

"Yes you can. It's still here, the Seed. It's still inside me. I can... I can send you back."

"I don't care," Arsha said. "I'm not leaving without you. You're coming back with me."

"I can't," Rachael sobbed. "Don't you get it? I belong here. You were right. This is where I was meant to be. I tried. I tried so hard to get away. To be somewhere else. Be someone else. But it weren't real. I kept trying to escape, but I just kept bringing myself back here. 'Cause I deserve it. All of this. This place. This life. This fucking city. I was so stupid thinking I could ever have anything else."

Rachael wiped a hand across her face, blinking back her tears as a trail of snot ran down her chin. Her eyes turned to the grey wall, where the motionless form on the couch had been.

"It's not like no one'll miss me none. And it'll be better for you, with me gone. All I ever did was make things worse."

Rachael turned to look at her again, a twisted portrait of a grateful smile spreading across her face.

"It's OK," she said. "You don't gotta pretend you understand. You're lucky, not understanding. You shouldn't have to."

Rachael trailed off, the smile fading.

"You never shoulda had to see this. You never shoulda cared about me. I didn't deserve that."

"Shut up. Shut the hell up," Arsha said, her voice half choked by tears. Her hands tightened around Rachael's trembling shoulders. "Of course I don't understand. I can't... I can't even try to understand. It's too big. It's too awful. It's like it won't fit inside my head."

She gasped for breath, her body shaking as tears streamed down her face, the grey wall hovering at the edges of her vision.

"I can't pretend I know what it was like."

Her hands moved to frame her sister's face, tears running slick between her shivering fingers as she set her eyes on Rachael's and did not blink.

"But I know that I'm not leaving you. Not now, not ever. And don't you dare tell me no one would miss you, because just thinking about losing you hurts worse than anything. I don't care what you think, I'm not leaving you behind. You're my sister and I love you. So please... Please... Come home."

Rachael looked up at her, eyes wide with fear and doubt, and just for a moment Arsha saw the briefest hint of a nod. Then everything fell away, and nothingness swallowed them completely.

Chapter 32 - Broken

The iron floor was rough and hot against her skin. Rachael was lying on the hard surface of the platform, aching all over. She could see sunlight, streaming in through the spaces left by two broken panes in the black glass ceiling above. She wondered what had broken them. The air had an acrid smell to it. A foul tasting slime coated the inside of her mouth. Her eyes felt raw, and each breath she drew was hoarse and ragged. Her arms and legs seemed to be too heavy to move.

A tremor ran through the platform. She heard the building groan around them as more cracks appeared in the black glass panes. She eased herself into a sitting position, knees curling to her chin. She saw that her left hand was still bound up in the heavy iron gauntlet, the plates moving clumsily as her fingers curled. For a moment she held the strange object up to the light, watching in curious fascination as she clenched and unclenched her fist. She could feel her heart pounding against her chest, and a sick feeling coiled up tight within her stomach. She had the curious sensation of being a passenger in her own head, watching everything with a strange detachment, despite the constant urge to fill her lungs and scream. Everything was too loud, and too hot. Whisps of smoke curled through the air, making her cough.

Arsha was lying beside her, sprawled out across the platform. Rachael wasn't even sure if the girl was breathing. She forced herself to reach out a hand, pressing trembling fingertips to the girl's neck. She imagined she should be searching for a pulse, but when she touched Arsha's skin, she felt a breath drawing inward, throat swelling as the girl's eyes flickered open. Arsha coughed as Rachael pulled her hand away.

Arsha sat up and looked at her, blinking away tears.

"You're here?" Arsha gasped.

"Yeah," Rachael managed. "Yeah, I'm..."

She tailed off, not sure what she was supposed to say. None of the words in her head seemed to fit. Then her sister's arms were around her, her face buried in the girl's hair as Arsha pulled her into an embrace so fierce and strong that it crushed the air out of her lungs. Without even meaning to, Rachael found her arms encircling her sister's body, holding tight as if she were the only solid thing left in the world. She felt tears rolling down her cheeks, as her breath came in short gasps.

She couldn't say how long they held each other, as she felt Arsha's chest rise and fall with each breath, her heart pounding through her ribcage as tears ran down her shoulder, mingling with her sweat.

"Thank you," Arsha said. The words were a faint murmur, the girl's face still pressed against her neck.

"For what?" Rachael said.

"For coming back."

Arsha's grip loosened a little, and the girl sat back to look at her with eyes red from crying. Arsha wiped a hand across her face, and her eyes settled on Rachael's left hand, encased in iron.

"Oh Fates, Rachael, your hand. Is it OK?" the girl exclaimed, seizing the gauntlet with both hands.

"Uh... Yeah, I think," Rachael said.

"Can you take it off?" Arsha said. Looking down at the strange device, Rachael could still see where parts of seemed to have emerged from within her arm, the skin parting around the blades of iron.

"I don't think so," she said.

"Does it hurt?"

She shook her head, as Arsha continued to stare in horror. Rachael shifted uncomfortably and turned to look at their surroundings. They were both sitting at the foot of the plinth, just below where the gateway had been. The twisted remains of the bridge hung from the far edge of the pit that surrounded the platform. Black shards of glass littered the platform, along with larger pieces of iron debris. The whole tower was swaying gently, the metal groaning as tremors ran up from below.

Arsha followed her gaze, noting the disarray with an expression that slowly shifted to alarm. As the girls took stock of their situation, the platform suddenly shook, and a thunderous roar echoed up from somewhere far below.

"We're stuck here, aren't we?" Arsha said, looking at the broken bridge.

Rachael gave her a gloomy look.

"Yeah, I think so. Serves you right for coming after me, I guess." She saw Arsha's expression. "Sorry. I didn't mean it like that."

"We're getting out of here. Somehow." Arsha said, firmly.

"Your dad left us."

"He must have thought we weren't coming back. He wouldn't have... he's probably coming back with the ship," Arsha said, her lower lip trembling slightly.

Another bellowing reverberation ran up the tower. Moments later they both heard a movement above them, a little like the crackling of ice-cubes in a glass. She looked up to see a maze of cracks slowly spreading across several of the black panes above them. Arsha let out a shriek as shards of black glass rained down towards them. They shielded their faces as broken splinters flew at them from every direction. Rachael felt the shrapnel biting at her skin, and she saw one shard draw a neat red line across Arsha's forearm. As the black rain stopped they looked up at each other, blinking, breath coming in short gasps. Arsha clutched at the cut on her arm, blood oozing between her fingers. Another tremor ran through the chamber, and they both heard a groaning sound from up above.

"Oh Fates," Arsha whimpered as she looked up. High above them, one of the long spars that formed the skeleton of the dome began to shudder and twist.

"Arsh, I think we're in real trouble here," Rachael said, touching her fingers to a cut on her face. Blood was already running down her cheek.

With a terrible moan the huge metal beam began to tear free, appearing to sag at first, until the end snapped loose and the whole beam began to fall directly towards them. It seemed to happen so slowly, so gently that at first Rachael didn't even feel scared. It took a moment for the perspective to snap into place. The iron beam was huge, maybe a hundred feet from end to end and wider than two grown men, and it was hurtling down towards them.

"Rachael..." Arsha whispered hoarsely, scrabbling to her feet. They both took faltering steps backwards as the huge mass of iron hurtled towards them. The platform was barely twenty feet across in all, and they had no way off. They could only guess where the falling beam would land. Huddling close to each other they moved towards the edge of the platform. Rachael reached out and took her sister's hand, squeezing it tight.

It was Arsha who saw that they had guessed wrong. She threw herself forwards, dragging Rachael with her as she dove across the platform. Just behind them Rachael felt the colossal weight of the iron spar as it passed just inches from their heels. The beam struck the platform like a sledgehammer. The whole building shook, and Rachael was thrown forwards on a wave of air that hit like a thunderclap. She slammed into the ground, skidding forwards on her elbows as the edge of the platform rushed towards her.

She couldn't stop in time. As she was about to plunge over the edge she felt Arsha's hand tighten around hers, and a moment later the whole of her weight seemed to focus itself like a solid blow against her shoulder. She dangled halfway over the lip of the platform, restrained only by Arsha's tenuous grip on her arm. All the air seemed to have been sucked out of her, and no matter how she wished she could pull herself back, all she could seem to do was stare into the vast drop below. The pit seemed to go down forever, nothing but blackness below her.

She felt the platform shift underneath her body, and it took a moment to realise that it was Arsha pulling her clear of the edge, inch by inch.

"Thanks," she gasped, blinking in confusion.

"Come on, we should go," Arsha replied, gesturing towards the fallen beam. It took Rachael's befuddled mind a moment to grasp what she meant. The beam had landed across the chasm that surrounded the pillar, joining it to the rest of the chamber.

Beneath their feet the platform was shaking violently. The impact of the beam seemed to have cracked one of the supports, and the whole thing felt like it might collapse any second. Arsha quickly leapt up onto the beam, turning to help Rachael up as they both struggled to keep their footing.

They ran the length of the beam without even daring to look down at the fall below. Terrible shuddering groans emitted constantly from the entire chamber as their feet pounded against the iron spar. It held just long enough for them to drop down onto the floor of the main chamber. As they fled the room a sickening crunch resounded through the air and the platform gave way, crumbling down into the pit with the massive beam sliding in after it. Arsha turned back to watch, eyes wide, until Rachael grabbed at her sleeve.

"Come on, let's go," Rachael screamed over the constant groaning of the building. Another ceiling pane crazed with a spider web of cracks and began to disintegrate, raining black razor shards into the hall. They ran out of the sagging arched doors and into the dark corridor beyond.

Emerging at the far end of the tunnel, they found themselves blinking in the sunlight that streamed in through the shattered outer windows of the tower. As their sight returned, they looked out on the rusted city and saw a sea of crumbling towers beginning to sway and topple. Parts of the buildings were falling away, raining down into the dark mists below. Many of the towers seemed to be crowned in a glittering haze; falling shards of black glass sparkling as they caught the light.

The tremors were nearly continuous now, the building shuddering and groaning beneath their feet. There was a gaping hole where the elevator had been. Daring to lean out a little over the edge, Rachael glimpsed the twisted remains of the platform, far below. From the look in her sister's eyes she could tell that her expression had said enough.

"There might be another way down, I guess," Rachael said, not really feeling it. Arsha did not reply. Her attention had been drawn to something outside of the tower. As Rachael followed the girl's eyes she found her gaze settling on a tiny but rapidly growing black dot, skimming over the rooftops. Arsha began waving frantically. At first nothing seemed to happen, but then Rachael saw that the dot was turning, coming closer. Soon enough, she recognised the shape of the Zephyr, blew light crackling around its floatstones as the propellers blurred. Arsha let out a whoop of joy.

"See? They're coming for us. I told you they'd come," she said, punching the air in excitement.

The Zephyr closed the distance quickly, on a path that would take it right past the floor where they stood. She could see Micah at the wheel, whilst Ilona stood at the prow, watching them through some kind of lens. Arsha ran right up to the edge of the building, holding on to a window frame as she eagerly watched the vessel approach.

The building shifted again, beginning to slope forwards at an alarming angle. Tremors continued to shake the room, and Rachael was certain that she feel them growing in intensity. She could barely keep her footing as the ground swayed underneath them, seeming to move further with each pendulum swing. An awful realisation settled on her.

"Arsh. He can't stop. The building's coming down Arsh. Nothing's staying still. They can't stop for long enough."

Arsha turned to look at Rachael, eyes widening as this thought sunk in. Slowly, the girl began to back away from the edge.

"Arsh, we have to jump," Rachael said.

"No. We can't. No," Arsha stammered, helplessly.

"We have to. It's the only way out."

Arsha looked out over the edge, and Rachael could see the fear in her eyes.

"Arsh, go. Go now."

Arsha shook her head and backed away from the edge.

"Arsha, jump!" Rachael screamed as she pushed the girl with both hands. Off balance, Arsha was forced to run with her down the sloping floor as the entire building lurched forward.

They jumped.

For a breathless moment the emptiness took them, and there was only the wind. The Zephyr seemed to slide beneath their feet, smooth and graceful. She saw the two figures on the deck looking up at them, faces aghast.

For a moment, everything seemed still.

Rachael came down hard on the back of the deck, her momentum carrying her into the back railing, pain exploding across her shoulders as she crashed into a heavy coil of rope.

Arsha missed the back of the deck by inches. Rachael watched in horror as she fell past the ship, reaching out to grab at the railing which was just too far away. She saw Micah letting go of the wheel to reach out towards her, too late to catch Arsha's hand. She saw the look of hopeless and desperate terror in her sister's eyes, fingertips outstretched to grasp at nothing. And then she looked down at the city below, the shape of the buildings hazy and indistinct. Distant, but inevitable.

Without a thought Rachael snatched up one end of the rope, heavy and rough against her palm, and in one smooth arc she dove across the railing.

She straightened her body out, pointing her toes like a diver, trying to gain as much speed as possible. The wind whipped her hair into her eyes and tore at her clothes, the sound of it roaring in her ears. Below her, Arsha's expression was caught between terror and wild hope. Rachael plunged towards her, the heavy rope trailing out behind her in the freezing air.

With her free hand she reached out, the darkly gleaming metal fingers of the gauntlet outstretched as she slowly closed the distance. The drop below them was long, long enough that they could scarcely even see the ground, but the distance was growing shorter all the time, and Rachael wasn't sure how much rope she had left. Arsha reached out her hand and their fingertips brushed, but could not quite catch. She reached out again, the distance closed a little more, and she got her hand around Arsha's wrist, iron fingertips digging into the girl's skin. Arsha grabbed her arm with both hands, squeezing tight. Even through the metal plating, Rachael could feel how tightly the girl was holding on. Barely a second later the rope ran out.

For a moment it seemed as if she felt nothing at all. There was sickening pop and then sudden, searing agony. Her hand had become a distant thing, something that didn't belong to her anyore. The rope flew out of her grasp as her arm flopped uselessly, dislocated at the shoulder. For a moment all she could do was scream.

Eventually the pain subsided enough for her head to clear, and she realised what had just happened. She was falling to a certain death, and she had no way out. The sudden surge of adrenaline cleared her head a little, and in her terror she couldn't even think of the pain. She looked at Arsha, who looked back at her with tears streaking her eyes.

"You shouldn't have come after me," Arsha yelled at her, over the wind. For a moment Rachael was stunned

"How can you even say that?" she yelled back. Arsha bit her lip, but didn't reply. Then Rachael realised that what she saw in the girl's eyes wasn't just sadness, but gratitude.

Tears were welling up in her own eyes. She didn't even dare to look down. She didn't want to know how long they had left. For a moment, she felt a wild hope that they might just stay like this, forever. As she stared into her sister's eyes, she felt her breath catch in her throat.

"Arsha," she gasped. "Your face..."

Creeping up from Arsha's neck, like frost on a windowpane, was a fine pattern of rust, as if the skin itself was corroding. She looked down at Arsha's arm and saw the rust growing across her body, seeming to spread from where Arsha's hand touched the rusted metal plating around Rachael's fingers. Where their palms met she felt a burning heat, and whisps of dark smoke seeped from between their clasped hands. With her free hand Arsha touched her face and flakes of rust fell away, the skin a raw pink underneath, as if she had picked away a scab.

"The seed," Rachael said, her voice hoarse, barely audible over the wind.

Arsha's mouth opened in a gasp of pain, but no sound came out. The back of her shirt exploded.

Rachael watched as twin shapes tore free, like they were being carved out of the air. Leaves of iron, paper thin and nearly eaten through by rust, piled onto one another, layer upon layer, forming a long, sweeping pair of wings. As they thickened, taking on substance, they caught the wind and Arsha's body jerked upwards with the sudden deceleration. Their hands slipped apart and the force of their separation sent Rachael spinning. Desperately she looked about, trying to control her fall, but Arsha had disappeared from her view. As she tumbled through the air, trying to catch sight of the girl, her eyes fixed on the ground rushing up towards her. She had barely seconds before she hit. All other thoughts left her mind, and she closed her eyes. For a moment, she wondered what it would feel like. For a moment, she thought she saw her mother's face.

She felt something crash into her chest, knocking the wind out of her. It was a few seconds later that she opened her eyes again and saw the ground growing steadily more distant. She turned her face to one side, and looked directly into Arsha's eyes.

She felt Arsha's grip around her waist slipping, and flung her good arm around the girl's neck, holding on for dear life. Wings of rusted metal, whispering like dead leaves, seemed to rip the air apart with every stroke, strong and fast. They gained speed, climbing higher as Rachael looked around and let out an exultant shout of joy.

"Oh God, I love you so much," she screamed, laughing in delight. Looking back over Arsha's shoulder she saw the spire continuing its slow collapse. Fragments of rusted metal and glass showered down in a thickening rain, shattering on the ground as it cracked and shifted. Chunks of pavement upended, deep rifts forming around the base of the building as it toppled. The top of the tower crumpled and then exploded outwards in a spray of twisted metal as a dark shape broke free. Wings spreading wide enough to black out the sun, Justin wheeled in the sky far above them. Rachael's breath caught in her throat as she watched him circling. She felt Arsha's hands clutch tight as the shadow passed over them. Then he was climbing higher and farther, his vast form growing small as he soared into the distance. Solemnly, Rachael watched him leave.

The Zephyr was descending in a sharp dive, levelling out as it passed below them. Looking down, Rachael could see three figures on the deck staring up at them. Wings beating hard, Arsha descended, visibly straining at the effort of holding them both aloft. At first she seemed to be coming in smoothly, until it became clear that she had no idea how to actually stop. They hit the deck and rolled, tumbling together across the wooden floor. Rachael's arm smashed into the ground as they tumbled and the pain in her shoulder exploded, drowning out everything else.

"Rachael? Rachael, can you hear me?"

She supposed she must have blacked out for a moment. Ilona was staring down at her, half her face covered by bandages that were already showing dark stains. She could see blood matted in the woman's hair.

"Yeah... Yeah, I'm here," she mumbled. Ilona sighed in relief, and for a moment she swore that a smile crossed the woman's face. Two fingers were pressed against Rachael's throat, feeling her pulse. As Ilona counted silently, Rachael looked across the deck to where Arsha stood with her father, their bodies pressed close together. Her face was buried against his chest and tears were streaming down his cheeks. Her long wings trailed across the deck behind her, fluttering gently in the breeze. The back of Arsha's shirt had been shredded, the tattered remains soaked with blood. Where the wings protruded from the girl's back she could see the ragged edges of the torn flesh. It looked very painful.

As their long embrace ended, Arsha looked up and saw her watching. Then the girl was running towards her, stumbling as her wings dragged on the floor so that she half knelt, half fell at Rachael's side, hands framing her face. Tears streaked through the patches of red rust that covered Arsha's face, cracking around her smile.

Smiling, Rachael went to reach out towards Arsha with her one working hand, only to pause as she caught sight of angular metal plating that encased it. The gauntlet almost seemed like a part of her now. She could barely even feel it. She hesitated, hand half-raised towards her sister's cheek. Then Arsha raised her own hand to clasp Rachael's, palm to palm. Arsha squeezed her hand, the gesture barely felt through the metal.

The clouds enveloped them, a wall of grey suddenly closing around the tiny vessel like a fist, before tearing open again as a brilliant blue sky was revealed above them.

The moment the Zephyr was above the clouds and on an even keel, Micah left the tiller and ran the length of the deck in three long bounds. Arsha turned to meet him, shrieking as she was lifted off her feet and swung round in a crushing embrace. For a moment her wings flared out over them both like a canopy, bare metal gleaming in the sunlight. Micah set Arsha down again and took a step back, an expression of pure astonishment on his face. With one hand he stroked at a wingtip. Iron feathers rustled softly as Arsha giggled in surprise.

"That tickles," she exclaimed.

"Really?" Micah's eyes widened. He tried it again, smiling as Arsha giggled.

"That's amazing," he said.

Experimentally, Arsha spread her wings out and then pulled them in close. Even tucked in tight to her body, her wings still arched high over her head, the tips brushing the ground.

Looking around, Rachael could see that everyone was now staring at Arsha. Ilona's expression was equal parts surprise and concern, but on Rishi's face Rachael saw something else entirely... Something like fear.

"Alright, let me take a look at that shoulder," Ilona said, suddenly breaking the silence as she turned towards Rachael. The woman quickly unbuttoned the top of Rachael's blouse and pulled back the collar to examine the swelling, prodding at the bruise flesh with the tips of two fingers. A fire burned where she touched, as Rachael gritted her teeth, unable to keep from letting out a slight whimper.

"It's dislocated. I'm going to give you something for the pain. We'll set the joint back into place as soon as we're landed," Ilona said, calmly.

As Ilona disappeared into the hold and Micah returned to the helm, Arsha and her father slipped away to the other side of the deck. Rachael watched their hushed conversation with a vague curiosity. Arsha's smile seemed to have faded, leaving a coldness in her expression. For a moment the professor turned to look in Rachael's direction, and beneath his apologetic eyes she saw that same coldness, anger concealed there like a movement in the darkness. Her fault, perhaps, that his daughter had risked so much to save her. The thought twisted like a knife in her stomach.

Then Ilona emerged from below, returning to Rachael's side with a small black leather bag which opened to reveal gleaming rows of medical implements. Sifting through the contents, Ilona produced a glass bottle and a brass handled syringe.

"For the pain," she said.

"No I'm... I'm OK. I don't need nothin," Rachael said, shaking her head quickly.

Ilona's eyes narrowed for a moment, and then she continued to fill the syringe, tapping the side to check for air.

"I said I'm fine," Rachael snapped, jerking away from the needle. The movement twisted her arm, and blinding pain seized her. It seemed to crash over her body in a wave that left her trembling and breathless. As her vision cleared, she saw Arsha kneeling at her side. Without a word, Arsha reached out for Rachael's gauntlet covered hand. As Arsha wrapped her hands around the cold metal, Rachael met her eyes. The girl looked at her steadily, concerned, but without pity. Rachael saw only a calm assurance. Ilona was looking at them both with an expression that was equal parts curious and frustrated. Rachael could feel Micah and Rishi watching them as well, but Arsha ignored them all.

"I was there, remember?" Arsha said. Swallowing the lump in her throat, Rachael managed a faint nod. She winced as the needle pierced her arm, but her eyes stayed locked on her sister's. As the needle slid free, she felt Arsha squeeze her hand, clasping it tight.

She gave an answering squeeze as she let her head fall back against the railing. A heavy sigh passed her lips as she stared up at the clear blue sky.

Chapter 33 - Home

They caught up with the Triskelion a little way outside of the city. Ilona watched from the prow, the cold air numbing the tender flesh around her damaged eye. The Zephyr drifted in to settle gently on the deck. The ladder was lowered and Micah descended first to help the girls down.

Milima appeared and with promises of bandages and clean clothes she ushered the girls inside.

Micah and Rishi set to stowing the Zephyr. Ilona tried to help, but she could already feel herself flagging. The ropes slipped from her hands, fingers feeling thick and clumsy. She could see that both men were trying their best not to say anything. They wouldn't dare tell her to stop, but they were both thinking it.

She turned away, trying not to stumble as she made her way inside. In the silence of the corridor she paused to find her breath. Then she heard the door swing open again and sharp footsteps from behind. She turned to see Rishi standing a few feet away. His eyes fixed on hers, trembling with cold fury.

"I'm sorry Rishi. I truly am," she said. "It was the only way to..."

"To what?" he snapped, cutting her off. "I just don't understand it Ilona. Why would you try to keep me from saving my own daughter? What could you possibly..." he floundered, unable to find words large enough for all the force of his anger.

She looked at him in stunned silence.

"How can you even ask me a question like that?" she said at last.

"It seems to be the only question worth asking, right now."

"Rishi, I didn't keep you from saving Arsha, I kept you from killing yourself chasing something impossible. She's alive, she's unhurt, and so are you."

"'Unhurt.' You'd dare to call that 'unhurt'?" he said, his voice little more than a cold hiss.

"I didn't have a lot of good choices in front of me," she said, feeling her hands shaking at her sides. "Maybe you could have done something. And maybe you would have just killed yourself trying. I couldn't bear that, Rishi."

She reached out to touch the swelling on his cheek, where her fist had struck him. The metal of her gauntlet had broken the skin, leaving a tiny crack, freshly scabbed.

He slapped her hand away.

"What could possibly make you think I'd care about my own life when my daughter was in danger?"

For a moment, all she could do was stare at him. The silence hung between them like a chasm. She felt a dizzying sensation of vertigo welling up inside, as if she was standing at the edge of that chasm, staring down. Before he could react, her hand slid around the nape of his neck and she leaned in to press her lips against his. Just for a moment, she was certain that he forgot to breathe.

She pulled away, with a feeling like electricity running through her fingertips.

"I didn't do it for you," she said.

She turned away, taking the steps down the lower deck as

quickly as she dared, forcing herself not to break into a run. Even that small restraint left her as she dashed to her room and threw the door closed behind herself. She leaned back against the hard wood and pressed her hands against her eyes, tight enough to keep the tears locked in.

Arsha felt as if she was floating on a soft cloud. She was lying on the table, stripped to her underclothes, whilst Milima gently washed away the blood, muck and rust from her back. She had been given a dose of nightroot, a little milder than the one Milima had mixed for Rachael after setting her arm. Arsha tried to recall her studies about the drug, but all she saw was the illustrated page, the words sliding into one another. She recalled that it caused light-headedness. She wondered when that would begin. Across the room, her sister was already fast asleep, deep in the drug's embrace.

The cuts on her face had been closed with ointment and her arms had been bandaged. They hurt, but the pain seemed distant now. She felt hypnotised by the sound of the cloth being submerged and squeezed out, the soft rippling noise of water falling on water, gentle and clear. The contents of the bowl had turned translucent red. Milima rinsed out the cloth once last time, before lifting the bowl and pouring it out into the sink. There was a soft clatter as she began to mix up another concoction.

Arsha closed her eyes and gently flexed her wings out. Feathers of beaten metal, each fading to rust at the edges, shimmered as they moved under the ghostlamps, and the gentle chiming of metal on metal filled the room. It was such an impossibly strange feeling. Like an extra pair of arms. She couldn't even say where she ended and the wings began. Perhaps there was no difference.

She looked up and saw Milima watching her.

"They scare you. Don't they?" Arsha said.

It was only for an instant that Milima looked away. Just an instant, but Arsha already knew what it meant.

"It's OK, if they scare you. I saw the way everyone was looking at me, when they thought I wouldn't notice. Everyone's a little scared. Even Daddy was scared."

She paused for a moment, not really sure if she was talking to Milima anymore, or just to herself.

"I think... I think he was the most scared of all."

Slowly, Milima set aside the small bowl she had been holding. She knelt down in front of the table, her face level with Arsha's.

"They don't scare me. Not exactly. But it's not easy, Love, seeing how much you've changed," Milima said as she reached out a hand, fingers almost brushing the beaten metal. Almost, but not quite. "Not just this. You. I can see it in your eyes, Love. I know that look."

"What look?" Arsha said.

Milima's hand cupped Arsha's cheek, as the woman's strong face seemed to crumple. Tears welled up in the corner of Milima's eyes as her hands settled on Arsha's shoulders.

"Maybe they do scare me, a little. But they're beautiful, just like you."

As Milima stroked her hair back, Arsha couldn't help noticing the faded line of a scar that ran down the woman's arm. It was one of a few that she knew Milima carried.

"You got that a long time ago, didn't you?"

Milima paused for a moment and glanced down at her arm. Then she smiled.

"If by 'a long time', you mean 'before you were born', then yes, but it's not as if I like to admit it."

Arsha looked down at the bandages around her arms.

"Does it still hurt?" she said.

"No. Not any more," Milima replied.

Rishi stumbled through the doorway into his room, and nearly fell into the chair by his desk. There was blood on his fingertips, grease under his nails, and the smell of gun-smoke in his clothes. His muscles burned, his head ached, and through it all he could still feel the ghost of Ilona's kiss on his lips. He pressed his hands to his temples and tried to block out the pain.

It took him a moment to register the knock at the door. He didn't even have the strength to answer. It opened anyway, and Abasi stepped into the room, closing the door behind him.

"Thank the Fates, you're OK," he said, running a hand across the thick grey stubble that crowned his head.

"OK. Is that what you call this?" Rishi said, staring up at the wall.

Abasi shook his head, gently.

"Alive's a start."

"Doesn't feel like it."

"I don't suppose it does."

After a moment, Rishi leaned forward just enough to prise open the bottom-most drawer of the desk, and fish out a half empty bottle of whisky. Trembling fingers fumbled at the cork, as the bottle nearly slipped from his hands. Then Abasi wrapped one hand around the neck of the bottle.

"Let me get that," his friend said, easily prying the cork loose. Abasi took a long swig before passing the bottle back. Rishi almost smiled as he pressed the mouth of the bottle to his lips and felt the amber liquid burn its way down his throat.

"What happened in there Rishi? I got the bones of it from Micah, but..." Abasi paused for a moment. "You actually shot the old man?"

Rishi said nothing, but Abasi must have read something in his face as he took the bottle back.

"Fates, you really did. Bastard had it coming at that. Pity he lived," Abasi added in a growl, before taking another swig.

"I imagine I'll get in enough trouble just for that," Rishi muttered.

"It sounds like Manindra has more trouble to worry about. I saw the Jyoti high-tail it out of here with at least three Guild ships in pursuit. Thank the Fates for that, or we'd never have slipped away in the chaos."

Abasi held the bottle out for him, but Rishi just shook his head. He felt his shoulders begin to shake as he slumped forward over the desk, unable to hold himself up anymore. His head in his hands, he felt ragged breaths tearing at his chest.

"Fates, Abasi, I've really made a mess of this. I think she really hates me now."

"You mean Arsha?" Abasi sighed, gently. "Of course she hates you. She's your daughter and she's fifteen. There isn't a fifteen year old girl alive who doesn't hate her father as madly as she loves him."

Rishi choked back a bitter laugh.

"No. This is different. All these years, she's never really known who I am. Now she's finally learning, and it's going to break her. It's going to break me."

"You're wrong, Rishi. Arsha knows better than anyone who you really are. I think she knows you better than you know yourself. You look at yourself and you see who you've been. But when she looks at you, she sees the man you are. I'm not saying it's going to be easy for her to forgive your past. That... That might take some time. But she'll never stop loving you. Never."

Rishi said nothing. In silence, he stared at the wall. Calmly, Abasi sifted through the detritus of his desk to find a couple of empty glasses, into which he poured a generous measure each. Easing himself onto the edge of the desk, Abasi set one glass down in front of Rishi, and picked up the other, the swirling liquid throwing patterns of light across the walls.

"Don't you have a ship to tend to?" Rishi muttered.

"She'll wait," Abasi said, and sipped his drink.

Rachael drifted in and out of sleep. She was never awake for more than a few hours before Milima arrived with something to eat and drink, followed by another dose of nightroot. Sleep would help her heal she was told each time she protested.

She couldn't really say how much time had passed. A few days, perhaps. She was lying in her narrow bed, staring at the ceiling, barely even sure how long she had been awake. The view through the porthole was pitch black. She supposed it must have been early in the morning.

Her shoulder ached, but the pain was duller now. She could feel a restless tingling running through her body. She couldn't remember the last time she had gone so long without moving. She sat up slowly, muscles stiffly protesting. She was in her underclothes, skin prickling against the cool air. Her left arm had been bound up in a cloth. A strange feeling of frustration flared inside of her as she looked at it. Fumbling with her other hand, she got the wrappings loose, revealing the hard iron, rust still flaking off of the edges. Then she got to her feet and pulled a dressing gown from the closet. With her shoulder stiff and aching, and her other hand fumbling within the confines of the thick gauntlet, simply trying to pull the gown on became almost impossible. She twisted and contorted herself, pain flaring in her shoulder, until she finally had the gown over her shoulders. Even then it took three tries to tie the cord about her waist. Her shoulder burned with fresh pain after her exertion. With a resigned sigh she picked up the sling that had been hung across the back of a chair and slipped it around her arm. Only then did she notice that the sleeve of the dressing had split around the iron gauntlet, torn by a edge as she'd pulled it on. She muttered a curse under her breath.

Hinges whispered to her as she opened the cabin door. Padding down the carpeted hall, she emerged into the darkened expanse of the hold. Over the loft, a single light shone. The wooden steps creaked softly as she climbed. The ghostlamp swayed gently over the narrow space, casting flickering shadows as Rachael threw herself down into one of the battered armchairs.

"Hey." Arsha said. The girl was sat in the chair across from her, feet tucked up on the old chesterfield. Her wings were pulled back, arcing up over the armrest of the chair. A bundle of cloth was resting in her lap. She appeared to be sewing something.

"What you got there?" Rachael said.

"It's just something I started working on. I couldn't sleep, so..."

Arsha held up what appeared to be a jacket, only most of the back was missing. "I figured if I can make the straps come down around the waist..."

It took Rachael a moment to see what she meant. The back of the jacket had been cut open, turned into a panel that could be secured by a pair of long straps. When fastened, they would leave two long slits running parallel down the back. Openings for her wings.

"Oh. That's clever, that is."

Arsha shrugged.

"I'm rubbish at sewing though. The seams are coming out all wonky."

Arsha held up the jacket for her to see. Rachael made a show of examining the girl's work, really not sure what she was supposed to be looking for. Glancing past the unfinished jacket, she noticed that even the shirt Arsha wore was really little more than a sheet with a hole cut for her head, tied about her chest and stomach with thin strips of cloth.

"Looks alright to me." She said. "'Sides, you'll get better, right?"

"You mean because I'll be doing this for the rest of my life?"

"Yeah, I guess. I hadn't really thought it like that." Rachael glanced down at her torn sleeve. Suddenly she laughed. "You'll be an old lady with wings and a walker. Flapping off down to the shops for a pint of milk and moaning how the wind keeps blowing your shawl all over."

Arsha smiled, and then all of a sudden the girl was laughing too.

"Do you think we'll get old together?" Arsha said. "Two little old ladies, sitting in a café somewhere, playing cards all day?"

Rachael's throat felt dry.

"Maybe?" She swallowed. "I've never really thought about... Stuff like that. Getting old."

As she paused again, Arsha set her sewing to one side.

"Rachael..."

"Did you talk to your dad?" Rachael said, cutting the girl off. "About your mum, I mean. About all that other stuff."

Arsha turned to look out of the porthole. The sky was still pitch black.

"Not really. He's had fifteen years to tell me. I guess if that wasn't enough..." She paused, and shook her head. "Honestly, I haven't really talked to anyone. The way they all look at me now... They don't mean to, but I can see it. All of them. They're waiting for something, but I don't know what I'm supposed to do, or say, or... I just don't know. It used to be easy. I thought of calling Shani but... I couldn't take it. Trying to explain, seeing her face... And then she tried to call me, and I couldn't even pick up my stone. I just let it chime out. She left all these messages and I haven't even listened to any of them. I feel so horrible. I know she's only... She's only trying to look out for me. Like she always does. She always tried to be like a big sister for me."

Arsha's hands twisted together in her lap, as the girl bit her lip.

"I'm such a coward. I wish I was strong like you," she said.

"Don't say that," Rachael said. "Don't act like I'm..."

"Like what?"

Rachael closed her eyes for a moment, letting out a heavy breath.

"Like I'm someone you should look up to. You keep thinking that I'm tough and all, that I know how to look after myself, that I'm all this stuff you want to be like, but I'm just a scared little girl, running away all the time. God, I run from everything. It's all I know how to do."

"You think I could ever believe that? Rachael, I've seen what you went through. Fates, I can barely even think about it, and you live with it every day. You're the strongest person I've ever met."

Rachael shook her head.

"Living with a hole in your chest isn't strong, Arsh. It's just a slow way of dying," she said, looking down at her hands.

There was a soft scraping sound, as Arsha lifted herself out of the chair. It took Rachael a moment to realise that it was the sound of

Arsha's wingtips brushing against the wall behind her.

Two steps covered the distance between their seats. Arsha's eyes narrowed in concentration for a moment, as she tucked her wings in close, and settled herself on the arm of Rachael's chair, their knees brushing together. Arms gently encircled her shoulders. With no strength to fight, Rachael let her head fall against Arsha's side. She closed her eyes and felt the gentle rise and fall of her sister's chest.

"I'm sorry," Rachael whispered.

"Me too," Arsha said.

"I just... I don't know how this is supposed to work."

"How what's supposed to work?"

For a moment Rachael's mouth felt too dry to even speak.

"Family," she said, at last.

The sun was long past set and two full moons could be seen, one high in a sparsely clouded sky, the other a perfect reflection in the still mirror of the ocean.

They had pulled in at Westfall a few hours past sun-down on their seventh day of travelling. They had not even taken on supplies yet. Abasi had paid the docking fees and handled the paperwork whilst everyone else slouched off to their beds.

The remainder of the journey had been a quiet one. The crew all carried a weariness with them, emotionally and physically exhausted. Nobody spoke much, and people kept to themselves. Rachael and Arsha had been glad of the quiet, staying shut up in their rooms mostly, sometimes together, sometimes apart. It didn't seem to matter. They were uncomfortable together, and just as uncomfortable alone.

After so many days of sleeping, she had found that she could barely close her eyes anymore. She began wishing for more nightroot as she lay on the covers each night, her aching muscles too warm in the still air, staring up at the ceiling.

So she had sat, and she had paced, and she had slipped out into the silence of the ship to wander its hallways and conceal herself in its quiet spaces, all the while feeling the thoughts tumbling over and over in her head. Trying to find the shape of the feelings that gnawed at her. She couldn't even give voice to the question that seemed to lurk at the back of head, like a buzzing sound just on the edge of your hearing. Each night it had been the same, endless hours of pacing, waiting for a decision to come. When it did, finally, she found that she felt no lighter for it.

She stood on the deck, feeling the breeze in her hair. The ship swayed gently on its mooring ropes, bumping against the wooden dock that reached out precariously from the cliff. Timbers creaked with each impact, like ribs moving to exhale.

She had learned to love this ship. She was amazed at how it could seem so ancient, and yet so new. Everything about it was like something clumsily crafted from pieces of the past, but the way it moved was just incredible. This lumbering beast that took to the air with such improbable grace. She was enchanted by the crackle of the lightning around the float-stones, and the way the iron outrunners caught the dawn light. She loved the sound of her feet against the wooden deck, and the wind running through the rigging.

It almost felt like it could be home. But it was not home. Then again, neither was anywhere else.

The bag over her shoulder was all she had left of her own. London was a world away and impossibly changed. She had nothing to go back to, and she could not let herself stay here.

She looked again at the lights of the town below them. Merchants and travellers came here from all over. Boats and caravans that she could stow away on. She'd muddle through somehow, find a way to live life on her own again. She had to. Some part of her even imagined that Justin might find her again. No matter how much she wanted to hate him, part of her still longed for that. She had to remind herself that it was Arsha he had wanted all along. Arsha, not her. He could not possibly come back to her now, when he had never truly been looking for her at all.

Arsha. Her new-found sister. She felt a tugging regret at the thought of leaving her. She pushed it away, stamping down the bitter sadness that roiled inside of her. It was better this way. Better for both of them. Shouldering her pack, she walked slowly down towards the gang-plank. At the edge of the deck she paused one last time, but did not dare to look back. She didn't think she could bear to.

She heard footsteps approaching. The soft steps could only be Arsha's.

"How's the arm?" Arsha said.

Rachael swallowed, her throat dry.

"Better," she said.

"Did you plan on telling me you were leaving?"

"Sorry," she said, eyes still fixed ahead. "It's not you. It's him. Your dad. What he did... I just can't be near him. I don't know how to deal with that."

"I know," Arsha said.

"But you want me to forgive him, don't you? You want me to stay," Rachael said, staring out at the lights of the town.

"Of course I do. But I don't even think I can forgive him. So how am I supposed to ask you to?"

Hearing the catch in Arsha's voice, Rachael turned to look at her. She was surprised by the determination in Arsha's face. There was a bag slung across her shoulder.

"You're coming with me?"

Arsha nodded, not meeting Rachael's eyes for a moment. For all the girl's determination, she still looked as if she might burst into tears at any moment.

"What else am I supposed to do?" Arsha said, wretchedly.

Without a word, Rachael touched a hand to her sister's shoulder.

"You don't have to do this, Arsh'. You don't owe me anything."

"Yes, I do. I do have to do this. Because you're right, and Daddy was wrong, and I love him so much that I can't... I can't be around him. Loving him and hating him and not knowing what way to feel, so my stomach just ends up spinning. I can't..."

Arsha tailed off. The girl seemed scarcely able to breathe.

"You... You got everything?" Rachael said, trying to give her a reassuring smile.

Relieved, Arsha drew a shuddering breath.

"Yeah. You?" the girl said, gesturing at Rachael's bag.

Rachael nodded.

"So, what happens now? I mean, Manindra and all that lot will still be after us. Me, I guess." Arsha said, a little nervously. "Or maybe you. I don't know. It's all so confused."

Rachael shrugged.

"We keep running. We look after each other. We see what happens next. It's... It's not all that bad a way to live."

"I guess."

"What about your dad?" Rachael said, nodding at the windows of the ship's bridge. "He's not going to try to come after us?"

"Maybe. I don't know," Arsha said. "I almost think he's expecting it. Fates, it just makes it worse. I want him to be angry or something. But he just... he looks at me like he's afraid. Like I'm going to punish him. Fates, I feel like I am punishing him."

Rachael shook her head.

"No, it's not about him, it's... It's about you. However much you love him, it doesn't mean you have to live with the things he's done, right? And it doesn't have to be forever. Maybe things'll get better. Maybe we'll come back, some day."

"Yeah. I think I'd like that," Arsha said.

"Come on," Rachael said. "It'll be an adventure. Or something."

A nervous smile passed between them as Rachael reached out to take her sister's hand, and they set off towards the lights of the town.

End of Book 1

www.ingramcontent.com/pod-product-compliance
Lightning Source LLC
Chambersburg PA
CBHW020928020726
47495CB00002B/388